PRAISE FOR *TO THE EDGE OF THE WORLD*

One of the *Washington Post*'s "Best Novels of 2006"

"Perhaps the best historical novel I have read...A stunning achievement of imagination and story-telling. In this novel Harry Thompson shows how the modern world was born, not in a laboratory, but on a storm-beset ship and out of a welter of ignorance, heroism and tragedy. A masterpiece."
—Bernard Cornwell, author of *The Last Kingdom*, *The Pale Horseman*, and the Richard Sharpe series

"...fascinating...Like O'Brian, Thompson gives us an entertaining grab bag of minor characters...this is good stuff indeed." —*Washington Post*

"[Thompson] used the artistic skills of a budding O'Brian and an astounding amount of research to tell the complicated story of the 1831 journey and its aftermath...[it] will delight O'Brian loyalists."
—*Chicago Tribune*

"Thompson's masterful storytelling brings all the shades of darkness and uncertainty of fate together with the flame of enlightenment and exploration. Recommended."
—*Library Journal*

"This is a fine, interesting and educational book, which I strongly recommend. It is nearly 800 pages long, but it maintains interest throughout the entire length."
—*The Roanoke Times*

"If you like seafaring adventure, then you'll want to travel the world in the almost 800 pages of *To the Edge of the World*...will fit well on the shelves of anyone who owns books by Patrick O'Brian...a thinking person's adventure."
—*Record-Courier*

"A master storyteller, Thompson tells the tale of two inquisitive men with irreconcilable world views." —*Pages Magazine*

MORE PRAISE FOR *TO THE EDGE OF THE WORLD*

"Deservedly Booker-longlisted, *To the Edge of the World* is by far the best historical novel I've read all year—an engrossing, thought-provoking page-turner that entertained me for hours on end and showed me many wonders."
—*Historical Novels Review* ("Editor's Pick")

"[Thompson] tracks the two men's paths with aplomb."
—*Publishers Weekly*

"A bestseller is born…an easy and picturesque yarn made muscular by historical fact and philosophical ideas." —*The Observer*

"A brilliant historical novel. An impressive book; something big that deserves attention." —*Mail on Sunday*

"Harry Thompson catches the atmosphere, and the language, of Victorian Britain with much skill and paints a vivid picture of the grim existence aboard … it's an excellent read, in the traditions of Patrick O'Brian."
—*Daily Telegraph*

"… a page turning action-adventure, combined with subtle intellectual arguments…[a] fascinating tale." —*Sunday Telegraph*

"Brilliant…terrifying, hilarious and uplifting…" —*Daily Mail*

"Thompson proves a master story-teller, whose vigorous command of character, period detail, weather conditions and fleeting emotions lifts the reader straight from his chair into the middle of a sudden storm."
—*Sunday Times*

"A ripping yarn…beautiful managed set-pieces, pacy, gripping and vividly chaotic."
—*Independent On Sunday*

"A fascinating read." —*The Times*

To the Edge of the World
—Book Two—

HARRY THOMPSON

MacAdam/Cage
155 Sansome Street, Suite 550
San Francisco, CA 94104
www.macadamcage.com

Library of Congress Cataloging-in-Publication Data

Thomspson, Harry, 1960—
[This thing of darkness]
To the edge of the world / Harry Thompson.
p.cm
Previously published as: This thing of darkness.
ISBN 1-59692-190-0 (alk. paper)
1. Fitzroy, Robert, 1805-1865—Fiction. 2. Darwin, Charles, 1809-1882—Fiction. 3. Beagle Expedition (1831-1836)—Fiction. 4. Ship captains—Fiction. 5. Naturalists—Fiction 6. Patagonia (Argentina and Chile)—Fiction. I. Title.

PR6120.H664T48 2006
823'.92—dc22

2006044978

Book Two paperback edition, May 2007
ISBN 978-1-59692-226-6

TO MY FATHER

without whose help this

book could never have been written

‘This thing of darkness I acknowledge mine’

The Tempest,

Act V, Scene 1

This novel is closely based upon real events that took place between 1828 and 1865.

South America: Patagonia & Tierra del Fuego
BRAZIL
A N D E S
Antofagasta
Pilcomayo
Paraguay
Paraná
Curitiba
Uruguay
Porto Alegre
URUGUAY
Coquimbo
Mt Aconcagua
Mendoza
Valparayso
Buenos Ayres
River Plate
Lobos Island
Maldonado
Montevideo
Talcahuano
Concepción
Rio Bio-Bio
Rio Leubu
ARAUCANIA
Fort Argentina
Colorado
Punta Alta
Bahia Blanca
Negro
Patagones
Atlantic Ocean
N
PATAGONIA
Chubut
Chico
Deseado
Port Desire
El Chaltén
FALKLAND ISLANDS
Dungeness Point
Tierra del Fuego
Cape Horn
0 100 200 300 miles
0 100 200 300 400 500 kilometres
SOUTH AMERICA
PATAGONIA

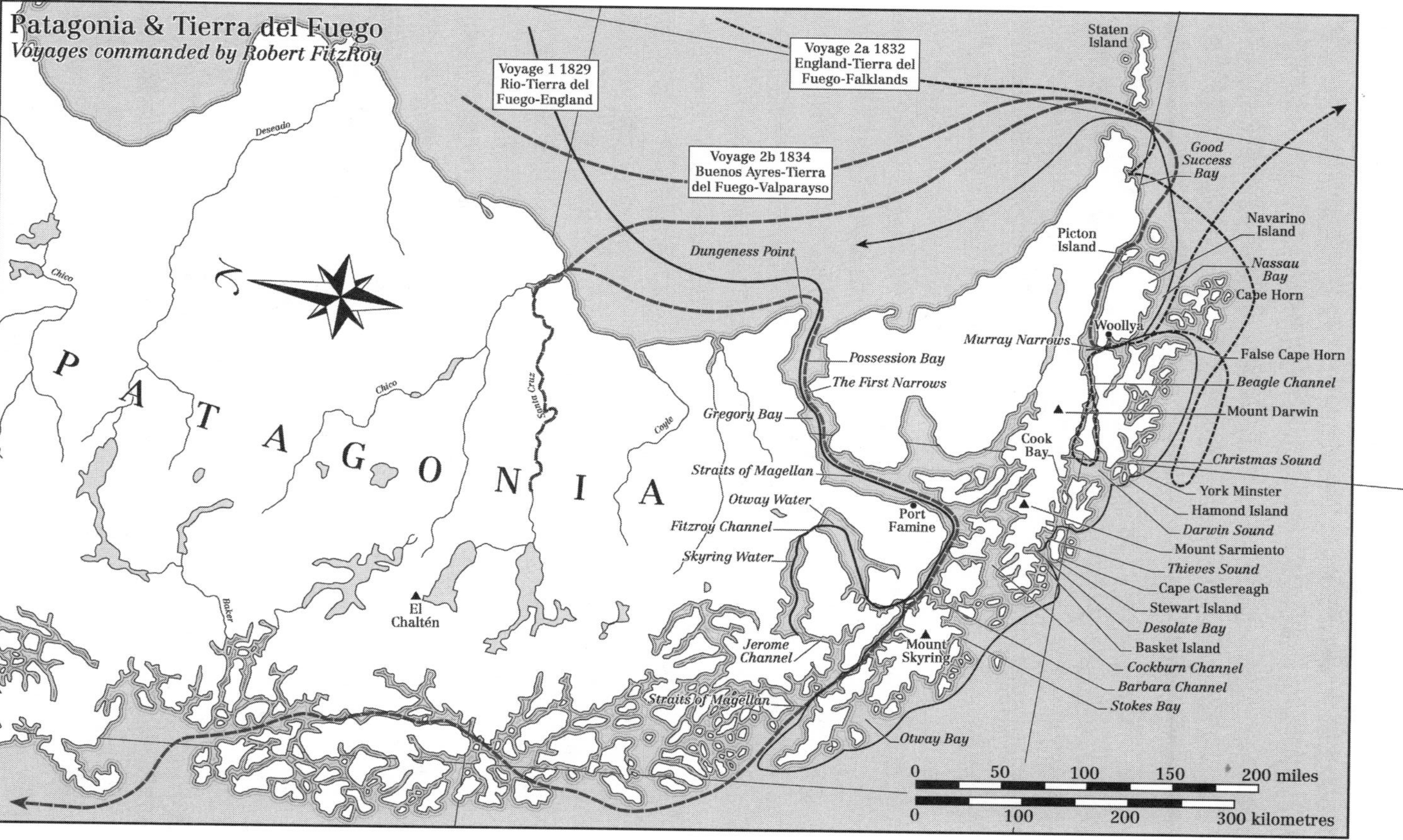

Patagonia & Tierra del Fuego
Voyages commanded by Robert FitzRoy
Voyage 1 1829
Rio-Tierra del
Fuego-England
Voyage 2a 1832
England-Tierra del
Fuego-Falklands
Voyage 2b 1834
Buenos Ayres-Tierra
del Fuego-Valparayso
Staten
Island
Good
Success
Bay
Navarino
Island
Nassau
Bay
Cape Horn
Picton
Island
Woollya
Murray Narrows
False Cape Horn
Beagle Channel
Mount Darwin
Cook
Bay
Christmas Sound
York Minster
Hamond Island
Darwin Sound
Mount Sarmiento
Thieves Sound
Cape Castlereagh
Stewart Island
Desolate Bay
Basket Island
Cockburn Channel
Barbara Channel
Stokes Bay
Otway Bay
Mount
Skyring
Port
Famine
Dungeness Point
Possession Bay
The First Narrows
Gregory Bay
Straits of Magellan
Otway Water
Fitzroy Channel
Skyring Water
Jerome
Channel
Straits of Magellan
PATAGONIA
Deseado
Chico
Chico
Santa Cruz
Coyle
Baker
El
Chaltén
0
50
100
150
200 miles
0
100
200
300 kilometres

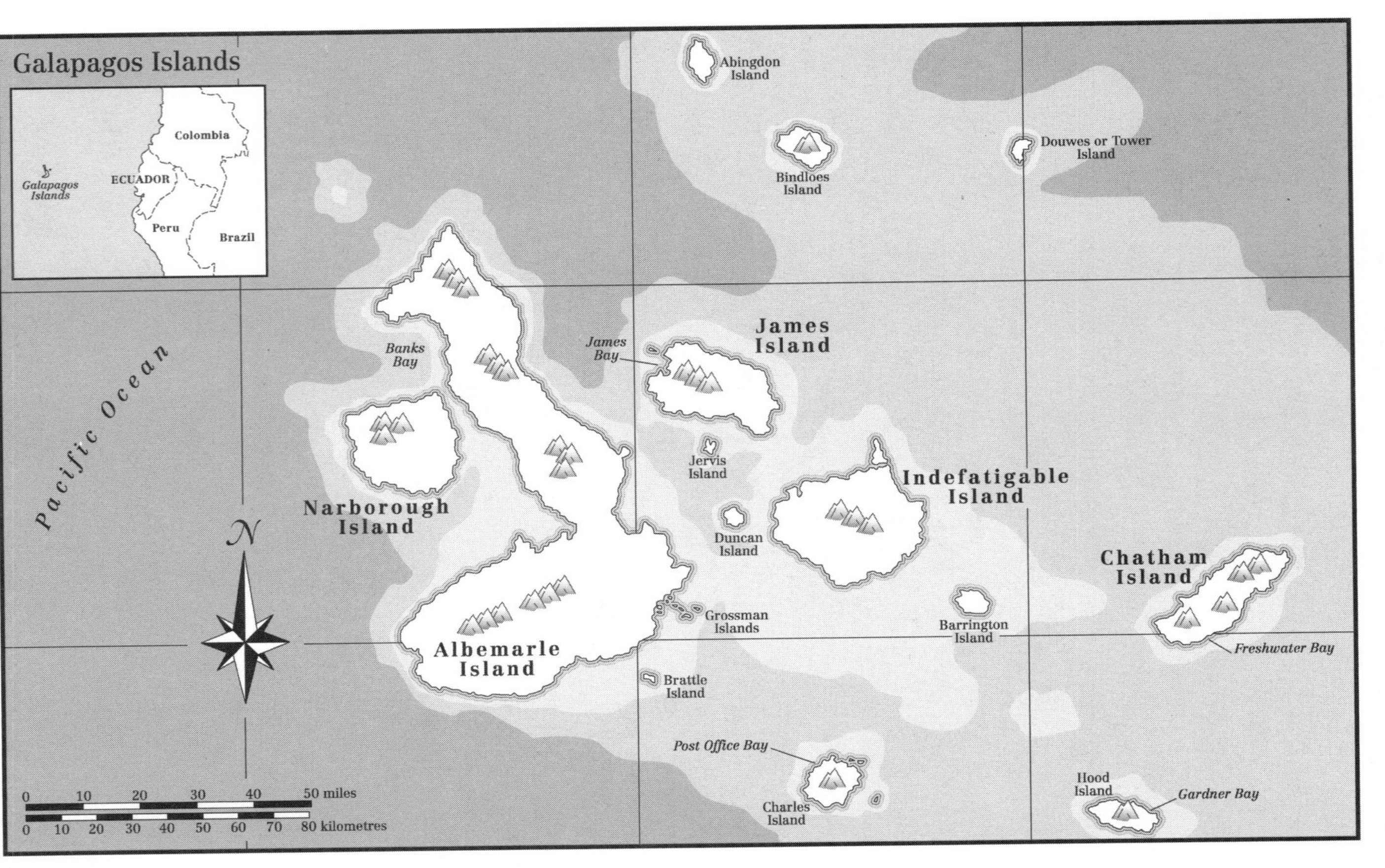
Galapagos Islands
Colombia
ECUADOR
Galapagos Islands
Peru
Brazil
Abingdon Island
Bindloes Island
Douwes or Tower Island
Pacific Ocean
Banks Bay
James Bay
James Island
Jervis Island
Narborough Island
Indefatigable Island
Duncan Island
N
Chatham Island
Grossman Islands
Barrington Island
Albemarle Island
Freshwater Bay
Brattle Island
Post Office Bay
Charles Island
Hood Island
Gardner Bay
0 10 20 30 40 50 miles
0 10 20 30 40 50 60 70 80 kilometres

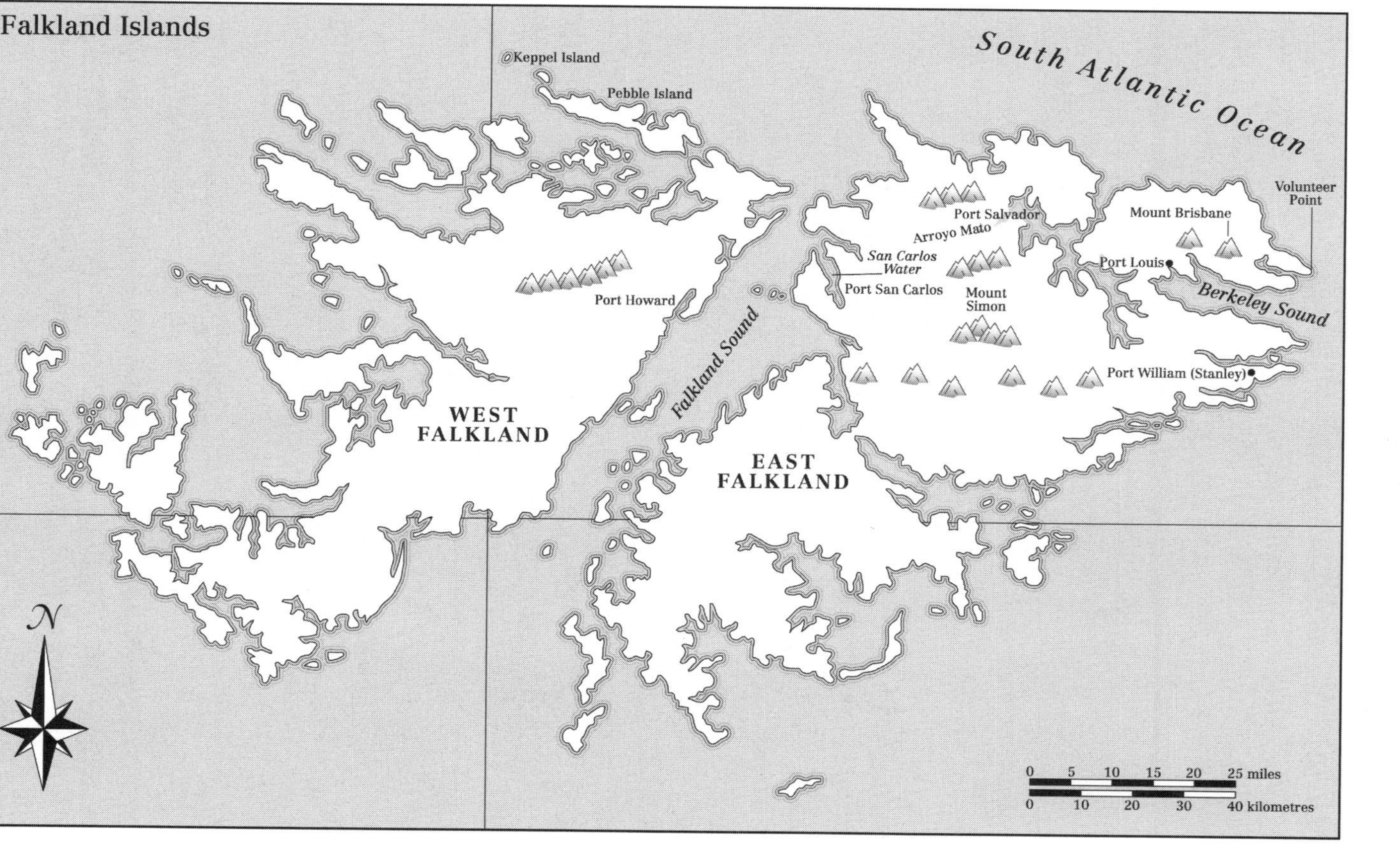
Falkland Islands
South Atlantic Ocean
Keppel Island
Pebble Island
Port Howard
Falkland Sound
WEST
FALKLAND
EAST
FALKLAND
San Carlos
Water
Port San Carlos
Arroyo Mato
Port Salvador
Mount
Simon
Mount Brisbane
Volunteer
Point
Port Louis
Berkeley Sound
Port William (Stanley)
N
0 5 10 15 20 25 miles
0 10 20 30 40 kilometres

PART ONE

CHAPTER ONE

Rio de Janeiro, 3 April 1832

They had come for Darwin at dawn. A hand clamped roughly over his mouth had wakened him from sleep, others had pinioned his arms, and a blindfold had been wound round his eyes. He had been led, stumbling and shaking with nerves, up the companionway and out on to the main-deck; there, he was roped roughly to a chair, which was lifted on to a plank and swung out over empty air. Wind blew against his cheek. He could feel the sway of the plank and hear the ripple of water below.

'Is that you, Darwin?' It was FitzRoy's voice.

'Yes.'

'Are you all right?'

'I – I think so. Will they kill us?'

'Will they kill us? What in heaven do you mean?'

A drumbeat commenced off to Darwin's right. His blindfold was whipped off, and a hideous apparition leaped into view: a crewman, semi-naked, daubed entirely in green, brandishing a rough-hewn spear. Other demoniacal beings swarmed about him, stripped to the waist, rings of red and yellow paint radiating out from their bulging eyeballs as they danced high and low.

'Welcome to the Kingdom of the Deep,' intoned the green crewman. 'I am King Neptune!'

'It is a sort of ritual they like to perform whenever we cross the equator,' explained FitzRoy, wearily. 'It is called "Crossing the Line". It affords them the greatest satisfaction.'

Darwin looked down, and saw that the rippling water below was contained in a huge sail held taut by several sailors.

'Shave them!' shouted King Neptune.

An evil-smelling mixture of paint and pitch was brushed about their faces, then scraped off again with a rusty iron hoop.

'Rinse them!'

Two grinning urchins appeared, extravagantly warpainted, who were revealed on closer inspection to be Musters and Hellyer. Gleefully, they emptied buckets of cold salt water over FitzRoy's and Darwin's heads.

'You see?' said Musters to Hellyer. 'I told you they would let us do it. What larks!'

'I assure you, Darwin, it would be a deal worse were you not my travelling companion,' insisted FitzRoy, in his most placatory tone.

'I do believe, FitzRoy, that this "ceremony" is in some way parodic of the sacrament of baptism. I am not sure that I entirely approve.'

'The effects of these mummeries are entirely positive on those who prepare them. They speak of them for a long time afterwards.'

Any further conversation was rendered out of the question as the two planks were dipped forward, and FitzRoy and Darwin tumbled head over heels, still tied to their chairs, into cold salty water.

'What fools these sailors make of themselves,' grumbled Darwin, as they towelled themselves off in FitzRoy's cabin shortly afterwards.

'It is an absurd piece of folly,' said FitzRoy.

'Most disagreeable,' said Darwin.

The rituals of the equator aside, it had been a largely uneventful crossing, punctuated only by the disappointment of not being allowed to put in at Tenerife, where news of London's cholera outbreak had preceded them. They had picked up the north-east trades at the Cape Verde Islands and had made rapid passage thereafter. Darwin had filled his time trawling for jellyfish and microscopic sea-creatures, using a home-made net constructed from bunting and an iron hoop. Lieutenant Wickham had cursed the 'Flycatcher Philosopher' for the specimens that oozed and glistened across his pristine deck, but always with his tongue in his cheek.

'If I were skipper, all your damned mess would be chucked overboard, and you after it!' he had bellowed.

FitzRoy's day was always the same: breakfast at eight, a morning inspection of the ship, a midday check on the chronometers, a one o'clock dinner of rice, peas and bread with Darwin, then the afternoon spent with Hellyer seeing to the ship's logbook and papers. He still found time, however, to teach Darwin how to dry, preserve and log his sea creatures; how to make drawings, notes and measurements; how to attach matching labels to the specimens and their containers, and how to catalogue when and where they had been caught. Darwin, for his part, was mildly surprised that FitzRoy did not spend his days striding about the deck in full dress uniform, like Nelson in the heat of battle.

When the day was over, after their antiscorbutic supper of meat, pickles, dried apple and lemon juice, Darwin would join Wickham or Sulivan for a little conversation at the wheel; unless it was a Sunday, of course, when Sulivan would be excused duty on religious grounds. On windless evenings in the tropics, Darwin sat out on a boom with Midshipman King, watching the waves furl past the prow. These were the evenings he liked best: when the air was still and deliciously warm, the heavens shone clear and high, and the white sails filled with soft air and flapped gently against the masts.

When the wind got up, however, and the *Beagle* bowled along, the old seasickness returned, and he took to his cabin at the 'lively' end of the ship. If Stokes was working at the chart table, he could not put up his hammock, so the assistant surveyor would allow him to lie curled on the tabletop instead, and would work around the philosopher's recumbent body. 'Old fellow, I must take the horizontal for it,' Darwin would gasp, before prostrating himself across unrolled charts of the Brazilian coast.

Jemmy Button would come by to sympathize. 'Poor, poor fellow,' he would exclaim, but then he would turn away, trying not to smile, for he could not understand how the mere motion of the sea could make anybody ill.

Sometimes, when FitzRoy was immersed in his paperwork, and Usborne or Sulivan was officer of the watch, they would discreetly reduce sail to lessen the philosopher's woes. There never was such a fine body of men, thought Darwin through his queasiness. He even forgave Sulivan for rousing him from sleep one morning, with the excited shout that a grampus bear had been seen swimming off the port bow. Haring up to the maindeck in his nightshirt, he had been greeted by the massed laughter of the morning watch. It was, of course, the first of April.

Two days later they had made Rio harbour, entering proudly under full sail, scattering flocks of yellow-billed boobies left and right. There they had careened to an extravagant stop alongside the *Ganges*, and FitzRoy had ordered every inch of canvas taken in and immediately reset. Every ship in harbour was watching, he knew, but he asked God to forgive him such little acts of vanity. The display was immaculate: no man-of-war of any nation would dare to take on this little sounding ship in a sail-setting competition again. Every skipper in Rio knew of the *Samarang*'s humiliation. Even Darwin volunteered to help with the sail display, so Wickham gave him a main royal sheet to hold in each hand and a topmast studding sail tack to bite between his teeth, and told him to let go the instant he heard the order to 'shorten sail'. Standing there in his top-coat and tails, his double-breasted waistcoat, his stock and his cravat, a rope in each hand and one clamped in his mouth, he made a remarkable sight. It was perhaps a little mischievous of Wickham to have positioned him like that some five minutes earlier than was necessary, but the philosopher was too excited to be part of South America's number one crew to notice his shipmates' amusement.

At midday FitzRoy and Stebbing rated the chronometers, double-checking the position of Rio de Janeiro on the charts, and were able to confirm what they had begun to suspect during the *Beagle*'s approach to the city: something was seriously wrong with the existing map.

'It is unmistakable.' FitzRoy outlined the problem to Darwin over dinner. 'There is a four-mile discrepancy between the positions of Rio and Bahia. Which means that one of them has always been located in quite the wrong place.'

'Who made the charts?'

'They are French, drawn up by Baron Roussin. The Admiralty has never seen the necessity of duplicating his work.'

'McCormick will be pleased.'

'The inconvenience is terrible.'

'Why? How long will it take Stokes to draw a new chart?'

'As long as it takes us to sail back to Bahia.'

'Back to Bahia? But that is eight hundred miles up the coast! Can you spare the time?'

'No. But I have no choice. I cannot complete a chain of meridian distances around the world if there is a flaw at the very commencement of the calculation.'

'How long will it set us back?'

'Two months. But I suggest that you would be best served by passing the time on shore, my dear fellow. You might profitably explore the tropical forest and collect specimens. I shall give Earle shore leave also, to make drawings, and Mr King.'

'Mr King?'

'To be quite frank with you, Mr Stokes will need the chart cabin all to himself. I do not wish the Admiralty's new map of the Brazils to have to incorporate our ship's philosopher's left knee.'

'Just think yourself lucky, my dear FitzRoy, that you do not have to journey back over the equator twice more.'

'Here's to that.'

They clinked their water-glasses.

Darwin removed his Panama hat – he had exchanged his top hat for a Panama as his one concession to informality – and mopped his brow. The thermometer read ninety-six degrees. He looked enviously across at Patrick Lennon, who appeared altogether cooler in an unbuttoned shirt and cotton breeches; but as the natural philosopher of the *Beagle,* Darwin did have certain standards to uphold. Lennon was a young, charming and energetic Irish coffee planter whom he had encountered at a formal dinner aboard HMS *Warspite*, who had offered to escort Darwin upcountry to see his *fazenda*. Their party was seven-strong in all: four Portuguese and a thirteen-year-old mulatto guide made up the numbers. They had started early, mounted on glossy black horses, and had ridden into the hills behind Praia Grande, through rounded plantations of coffee-bushes and rustling sugar cane. As the sun rose, the blue dawn light had faded away to be replaced by all the intense colours of the forest: slender green palms swaying like ship's masts, brilliant turquoise butterflies making random sallies, immense copper-coloured anthills inching methodically skyward, and all of it bedded in a warm, rich, red earth that accumulated stickily upon the fetlocks of the horses. Darwin was enraptured: no engraving, he thought, could ever capture the ruddy glow of this scene. The forest was at its most beautiful at midday, he felt, when the upper branches shone bright emerald, and shafts of sunlight filtered down as if through a transept window. Writhing beneath was a wild, untidy, luxuriant hothouse, criss-crossed by a hundred shady pathways.

They breakfasted on black *feijão* beans and *farinha* flour at Ithacaia, a poor African village twelve miles north of Rio. It was the Brazilian custom to breakfast many hours into a journey, and to rely on thick black coffee to wake the sleeper. Thereafter they pushed on, through veils of mimosa and mazy skeins of hanging tendrils, in the direction of Ingetado. The silence of the forest was astonishing: while the *Beagle*'s passage along the Brazilian coast had been greeted by a shore battery of insect-calls audible a hundred yards out above the surf, here in the vaulted forest no sound could be heard. The only exception was the determined chatter of an ebony battalion of shiny-headed leaf-cutter ants, which stretched as far as the eye could see in either direction. Darwin stopped to place a rock in their path. The ants would not head round it, but instead launched sally after furious sally against their immutable attacker. Was this the species discovered by Linnaeus in 1758? he wondered. Lennon and his companions could provide no help. Every time Darwin asked the given name of a flower, the same answer invariably came back: '*Flores*.' Whenever he enquired the identity of an animal, he was told: '*Bixos*.' Taxonomy, it appeared, was not a local speciality.

They slept in a thicket under the dim moonlight, and beneath the stars the forest came alive. A concert of rhythmic frogs began, lit by winking fireflies, the plaintive cries of snipes providing a contralto melody. Breakfast of *feijão* beans and *farinha* flour was taken at Madre de Dios village amid sheets of rain, birds fluttering madly between the passion flowers. After the deluge had abated, steaming columns of dense white vapour poured upwards from the surrounding woods as the moisture returned to the sky.

At the Rio Macaé, where they had to swim alongside the horses to ford the torrent, they came across a gigantic rock rising from a plain of rhododendrons.

'That is where a gang of runaway slaves hid out, not a year or two back,' related Lennon. 'They were all recaptured, except one old woman, who, sooner than be taken again, dashed herself to pieces from the summit.'

Darwin shuddered. The forest was a cruel environment, there was no doubt of that. Everywhere one looked, strangulating creepers twisted about each other like tresses of braided hair, each fighting to squeeze the breath from its adversary. Luxuriant parasitical orchids drank the fluid of their victims with dainty care. Lianas crawled over the rotting corpses of fallen trees, the trunks split and gaping open in the fixed attitudes of death. He felt torn between a sublime devotion to the God who could create such marvellous beauty, and awe at the cruelty of Him who would devise such a world, founded as it was upon a pitiless struggle for survival.

They slept the second night at Ingetado, following a hearty meal of *feijão* beans and *farinha* flour. In the morning they rode past a lagoon, many miles from the sea, its shores a mass of broken shells. Was this the proof of the Biblical flood that FitzRoy was so keen to establish? Darwin collected specimens, delving under logs and stones, chasing pale fat worms through clammy leaf litter, and peering into the rainwater traps of bromeliads in search of gaudy spiders. In a pile of decaying wood he found a wriggling heap of gorgeous orange-and-black flatworms, like striped and dandified slugs. But these were sea creatures! What were aquatic *planariae* doing here, so far from the sea? He had discovered a species new to science, he realized, but what was the connection between these land flatworms, their marine cousins and the flood? His brain whirled with possibilities.

They spent the third night in the *venda* at Campos Novos, where the innkeeper had learned a smattering of English and was keen to practise his skills.

'What have you for supper?' Darwin enquired hungrily.

'Anything you choose, sir,' the man replied grandly, his fingers spread upon his belly.

'Thank goodness for that! So, is there any fish you can do us the favour of giving?'

'Oh! No, sir.'

'Any soup?'

'Oh! No, sir.'

'Any bread?'

'Oh! No, sir.'

'Any dried meat? *Carne secca?*'

'Oh! No, sir.'

Lennon laughed like a drain. 'Welcome to the Brazils, Mr Darwin.'

After an interval, it was established by one of the Portuguese members of the party that the innkeeper could offer either *feijão* beans or *farinha* flour, or both.

On the fourth day the forest thickened and the showers closed in, and the little mulatto guide had to hack at the fronds with a sword to clear the path up into the high hills. Finally, towards the end of the morning, they reached Lennon's *fazenda*. A large bell clanged out and a cannon was fired to announce the arrival of the *senhor*, and a crowd of black slaves rushed forth to be blessed by the white men. A neat slave-line formed up in starched white smocks, to sing a Catholic morning hymn of the most sublime harmonic sweetness. Lennon lived like a little god here, Darwin realized, his wealth untold, his power absolute. The Irishman smiled and invited him on up to the house.

The *fazenda* proved to be a white-painted two-storey mansion with rustic blue shutters, a thick reed roof and a wrought-iron balcony, which sat on a gentle rise under a permanent blanket of low, sticky clouds. Even here, nature's myrmidons kept up their ceaseless assault: tree roots slithered across the courtyard, blotchy green mould insinuated itself beneath mirror-glass, while the opposing forces of mildew and whitewash grappled for possession of the walls. Dogs, baby chickens and little black children ran left and right through the ground floor of the house. Piles of banknotes lay aimlessly about the heavy gilded furniture, comprehensively chewed through by grubs.

'Nothing I can do with it,' remarked Lennon, indicating the money. 'Nothing I can do to stop it,' he added, with reference to its gradual consumption. 'I have everything I want here, without recourse to money. Take some, if you like.' Darwin declined as politely as he could.

A servant showed him to his room on the first floor. There were rifles mounted on the walls, a cast-iron cot in the corner, and no glass in the windows. In the dark, gloomy wardrobe were two jars of yellow fluid, the pickled grey snakes inside coiled lifelessly against the glass. He changed, laid out his sweat-stained clothes to be washed, and descended the stairs once more. Lennon had been joined by a short, spherical, olive-skinned Portuguese, and his younger, heavily made-up female equivalent, who had squeezed herself into a liberally frilled dress.

'Mr Darwin, I have the honour to present Dom Manuel Joaquem da Figuireda, my partner in business, and his daughter Donna Maria. Donna Maria is married to Mr Lumb, a Scotchman.'

Lumb, who had the lugubrious air of a half-asleep walrus, moved from the shadows to shake Darwin's fingers, but said nothing. Darwin sensed that Lumb had seen in Donna Maria a match to improve his financial situation.

'Do you ride to hounds, Mr Darwin?' asked Dom Manuel, unable to conceal a grin.

'Of course, Senhor. What well-born Englishman does not?'

'Excellent. Then tomorrow we shall have a hunt.'

'You have hounds, here?'

'We have five hounds,' said Donna Maria, in the clipped accent of one who has carefully studied a foreign language. 'Trumpeta, Mimosa, Clar-iena, Dorena and Champaigna.'

'But what do you hunt? Surely there are no foxes!'

'Monkeys, Mr Darwin. We hunt bearded monkeys!' Dom Manuel cackled and clapped Darwin on the back.

'You see, Mr Darwin, even here in the Mata Atlantica there is no aspect of civilized society that we cannot replicate,' smiled Lennon. 'Would you care for coffee?'

Coffee was kept bubbling continuously in a big black skillet on the iron kitchen range. Presently, a small greasy-fingered black boy appeared with a full jug and several cups, and handed one to Darwin.

'Pray excuse me,' said Darwin, with a trace of embarrassment. 'Would you mind if I exchanged my cup? There is a fingermark.'

Immediately, Lennon picked up a riding-crop and lashed it across the little boy's head, not once but three times. The child screamed in pain and terror. A red rivulet streamed from his nose, and across his upper lip, before dividing into smaller streams between his teeth; he fled sobbing from the house, a further coffee-cup tumbling with a smash as he ran. Darwin sat frozen with horror. Dom Manuel and his daughter continued to smile as if nothing had happened. Lennon, as charming now as he had been before the attack, offered his apologies: 'I'm sorry for the slave boy. Those people know no better. There are too many damned kids about the place. I think I shall sell some of them at the public auction in Rio.'

'The children will be sent to market...separately from their mothers and fathers?' Darwin was still stunned, so his words came out slowly.

'Oh, they are well used to it, Mr Darwin. Savages do not enjoy the same emotional closeness as we civilized people.'

They rode out the next morning, past the long, low sheds housing the hundreds of plantation slaves and the little stone chapel adjoining. Black huntsmen in maroon jackets rode ahead, to encircle the forest wildlife and drive it back towards the guns. Then an old Portuguese priest in a wide-brimmed hat blew upon a hunting-horn, and the main party moved forward. Before long they ran into the squawking, whooping mass of monkeys, parrots, toucans and other creatures that had been corralled towards them, all of which were unceremoniously blasted out of the sky. The monkey's prehensile tails tightened as they died, so their corpses hung farcically from the branches while the huntsmen rode around in circles beneath, trying to bring them down. Darwin did not enjoy his sport. The episode with the slave boy had affected him badly, and he was keen to return to the coast.

The next day, he seized the opportunity of accompanying the mulatto guide back to Rio de Janeiro; they took a different route, heading for the only ferry crossing on the Rio Macaé, riding in silence on account of the language barrier, which Darwin felt was the least of the divides separating them. He collected an insect that was disguised as a stick, a moth that was disguised as a scorpion, and a beetle that was disguised as a poisonous fruit, but his heart was no longer in his work.

When they arrived at the riverbank, a powerful black ferryman stood to attention alongside a rudimentary raft, a punt-pole held aloft by his side in the style of a medieval pikeman.

'*Onde você gostaria de ir, Senhor?*' asked the ferryman.

'I should like to cross the river,' explained Darwin.

Both guide and ferryman looked at him, their faces full of incomprehension.

'*Eu não entendo. Onde você gostaria de ir, Senhor?*' the ferryman repeated.

'I should like to cross the river,' explained Darwin for the second time, waving his arms in the direction he wished to take. But as he gesticulated, the big ferryman cowered, his pupils widening in fright; the man dropped his hands, shut his eyes, and dipped his head in supplication. He fell to his knees and began to beg for mercy in Portuguese, pleading with the white man not to strike him. Darwin immediately understood what had happened; and he felt only shame and disgust.

FitzRoy dined alone, his plate of rice and peas strangely devoid of flavour in the absence of his friend. A knock briefly and foolishly raised his spirits, but they fell once again when the door opened to reveal McCormick. Despite his ever-rigid bearing, the surgeon's moustache showed him to be in a state of some agitation. In his left hand, he carried a large wire birdcage, which housed a bright green parrot.

'Excuse me, sir, but I must speak with you.'

'I am at dinner, Mr McCormick. This is most incommoding – can it not wait until we are under way?'

'I am afraid not, sir. It is uncommon urgent.'

'So urgent that you have to bring your parrot with you.'

'I have purchased the parrot this very morning, sir – at a most Jewish price, as it happens – for reasons of scientific investigation. It belonged formerly to an English merchant seaman, from whom it has gleaned a rudimentary grasp of our language. I intend to make a study of animal intelligence, sir, and to investigate the extent to which such creatures appreciate the import of their words, and the extent to which they merely mimic what has been expressed in their presence.'

'I am glad to see that you are taking your responsibilities seriously, Mr McCormick. Pray tell me what English words your parrot has yet grasped.'

'As yet it has but two English expressions, sir. One of them is "Great heavens" –'

'Great heavens!' interjected the parrot.

'– and the other expression, common decency forbids me from repeating, sir.'

'Go to the devil!' shouted the parrot.

'That is the other expression, sir.'

McCormick's face remained blank, but the ends of his moustache twitched violently.

'But I must inform you, sir, that it is not regarding the matter of this parrot that I have come to see you.'

'Indeed.' FitzRoy transferred a forkful of peas elegantly in the direction of his mouth.

'No sir. I have come to see you regarding Mr Darwin, sir.'

'Indeed?' The peas paused in mid-air. 'What about Mr Darwin?'

'I have heard tell, sir, that Mr Darwin's specimens have been sent to England carriage free, aboard His Majesty's packet *Emulous*. Is this true, sir?'

'It is.'

'Great heavens!' observed the parrot.

'Then I must protest, sir.'

'About what, Mr McCormick?'

'Mr Darwin is not responsible for bringing together a natural history collection for the Crown, so it is not proper for the Service to see to the freight of his private specimens. Nor is it proper, sir, for his specimens to litter the deck, or for the ship's carpenters to make packing cases for their transportation.'

'What is proper, Mr McCormick, and what is not proper, are matters for me to decide.'

'I find myself in a false position, sir. Mr Darwin sits at your table, discussing books and whatnot, whereas naval practice dictates that any philosophical debate on board should fall strictly under my jurisdiction as ship's surgeon. Furthermore, sir, I hear that Mr Darwin intends to retain the right to ownership of his specimens upon their reaching England.'

'That is so,' confirmed FitzRoy.

'Great heavens!' added the parrot.

'Have you considered, sir, that Mr Darwin might intend to sell such items of natural history for his own personal profit?'

'Your suggestion is absurd, Mr McCormick.' FitzRoy's voice hardened. 'I suggest that you withdraw your allegation forthwith.'

'It is vulgar, sir, to receive money for one's researches.'

'I will say it once more, Mr McCormick. I suggest that you withdraw your allegation forthwith.'

'Great heavens!'

'I demand, sir, that Mr Darwin be dismissed from the *Beagle* immediately.'

'What?'

'I demand, sir, that Mr Darwin be dismissed from the *Beagle* immediately.'

'Go to the devil!'

'Otherwise, sir, I shall tender my own resignation as ship's surgeon immediately.'

'I accept your resignation, Mr McCormick.'

'What?'

'Great heavens!'

'I said, I accept your resignation as ship's surgeon, Mr McCormick.'

'Great heavens!'

'I think I have your gauge, sir,' said McCormick grimly, through hardened lips, 'and I shall make it known throughout Whitehall when I return. Rest assured of that!'

'You do not frighten me, Mr McCormick. Pack your bags and leave the ship immediately. You shall have ten minutes' warning.'

His face a mask of suppressed fury, McCormick picked up the bird-cage and headed for the door.

'Go to the devil! Go to the devil!' shouted the parrot merrily at FitzRoy, as its cage disappeared from view.

With a gentle downward pressure, Darwin sliced the head off the firefly. Its lifeless body continued to glow brightly against the gloom of the verandah steps.

'Yeurch,' said King.

'Look! Look at this!' said Darwin, eager with the excitement of discovery. Augustus Earle put down his fiddle – which in truth was a blessing, as his technique was rudimentary at best – and did as bidden.

'The glow is continuous in death,' explained Darwin, 'which means it is involuntary. So when the firefly winks his light, he is turning it off, not turning it on.'

'I see,' said Earle, returning to his fiddle.

The three had taken a cottage four miles south of the city, between Corcovado and the *lagoa*, on the road out to the botanical gardens. It was, to Darwin's mind, a veritable Elysium, free from seasickness and slavery. There were graceful coconut palms in front, with heavy clusters of fruit and long, plume-like drooping flowers. Passion vines climbed all over the house, dark crimson flowers concealed seductively between the leaves. He had spent a month making an exhaustive study of the insect life of the neighbourhood, with a pruriently thrilled Midshipman King as his sole audience. Together they had documented the gruesome habits of the hymenop wasp, which paralysed its victim before injecting eggs into the living tissue, there to hatch and feed and grow into fat, wriggling larvae. He found it hard to reconcile such suffering with the love of a merciful God, but then had not Job suffered horribly at the hands of the Lord? He did not, of course, share his theological confusions with his collecting partner.

King, in return, told him tales of the south, of icebergs and crimson seas and giant whales that leaped clean out of the water, tales that sounded too tall to be true. 'Come, King,' he would gibe informally, 'do not come your traveller's yarns on me,' and the boy would aver, hotly, that every word was true. He had discovered that he preferred King's company to that of Earle, whom he found rather intimidating. The artist was old now – he was nearly forty – and troubled by the rheumatism that comes with age, so he would sit barefoot on the verandah, painting or screeching away at his fiddle, while Darwin and King gleefully roamed the neighbourhood with their insect-nets. It felt as if they were on holiday from school.

Their supper guests arrived just before eight, brought by a covered cart with big solid chariot wheels, two spherical slabs of wood like Saxon war-shields. A pair of statuesque mulatto women alighted, attired in layer upon layer of brightly coloured shawls, their hair piled high and twisting into extravagant headdresses. Their lips and cheeks were rouged, their eyes rendered dark and mysterious by lashings of makeup. Darwin had no idea where Earle had procured them, but they resembled – he realized uncomfortably – two ladies of the Haymarket.

'Mr Darwin, Mr King, may I introduce to your acquaintance Rita and Rosa?'

This is all wrong, thought Darwin. He has introduced us the wrong way round. The man has no sense of propriety.

The introductions over, they went through to the supper-table. The ladies had no English, but seemed content to giggle among themselves. The only communication between the two halves of the supper-party was via Earle's pidgin Portuguese, a dialect in which the artist proved himself singularly adept at flirting.

The servant brought out bottles of red wine, and plates piled high with *feijão* beans, *carne secca*, bread and a strange, sausage-shaped, creamy-coloured fruit.

'Pray what is this?' asked Darwin.

'Banana,' replied Earle.

'Oh! I have never eaten a banana before.'

'*Ele nunca havia visto bananas antes*,' remarked Earle to the two women, who giggled voluptuously.

'May I know the source of the amusement?' enquired Darwin, reddening.

'I simply informed them of your virginity *vis-à-vis* the banana.'

The two women continued to giggle, one concealing her merriment behind a Chinese fan, and Darwin thought that perhaps there was something attractive about them after all. With a glass of wine under his belt, he was prepared to admit to himself that they did not share the normally disagreeable expression of the mulatto. They were not *ladies*, in the sense that Fanny Owen was a *lady*, but they definitely possessed a certain charm. He glanced across the table at King as if in search of endorsement, but the normally talkative lad had become utterly tongue-tied since their guests' arrival. In fact, he had spent most of the evening trying to steal furtive glances at the women's cleavage, between long periods spent staring fixedly at his plate.

'*Você gosta de bananas?*'

'Rita wishes to know how you like your banana.'

'I find it rather mawkish and sweet, without too much flavour, I am afraid,' replied Darwin stiffly; for some unaccountable reason he had begun to feel embarrassed.

'That is beyond my meagre Portuguese, I fear,' smiled Earle. 'I shall tell her yes.'

'*Você gosta do Brasil?*'

'How do you like the Brazils? Rosa wishes to know.'

'Tell her that hers is a most gloriously attractive nation, but that I most heartily wish it were not disfigured by the curse of slavery.'

Earle attempted a translation, and it was clear from the women's response that they were in agreement. They crossed themselves and spoke in low tones of something called a *matican*.

'The *matican*,' explained Earle, 'is a slave-hunter. He is paid to hunt down slaves who escape and to kill them, be they man, woman or child. And when he has run down his quarry, he slices off the ear as proof of death.'

'I used to do that with rats for my father, when I was a boy,' offered King, pleased at last to be able to contribute something to the conversation.

'Perhaps I will not translate that into Portuguese, Mr King.'

'Will you excuse me for a moment?' said Darwin suddenly, rising from his seat as he spoke, his gaze fixed unwaveringly on the window opposite.

'Is everything all right, Mr Darwin?' asked Earle.

Darwin did not answer, but shot through the doorway and out on to the verandah, reappearing a moment later on the outside of the window, his nose pressed to the glass. There, in front of his face, a tiny copper-coloured frog clung to the smooth surface, its eyes wide and unmoving, its throat palpitating silently to its own inner rhythm. Darwin reappeared in the doorway. 'That frog. It has suckers on its feet, so that it may climb a vertical sheet of glass!'

'Gosh!' said King, excited.

'Many of them do,' said Earle, who had to explain to the confused women that the gentleman was a *filosofia da natureza*.

Darwin resumed his seat, and the supper-party continued as before, Earle complimenting his guests extravagantly in Portuguese, Darwin offering the occasional politeness, and King unsure where to look. Eventually it grew late, but there was no sign of the two women preparing to leave or of their cart returning. As another burst of merriment erupted from their end of the table, Darwin was seized by an uncomfortable thought.

'I say, Earle,' he whispered awkwardly.

'Yes, Darwin?' Earle leaned back, his collar undone, his face flushed with drink.

'I hope it is not your intention that I...*entertain* one of these ladies after supper has finished.'

'Certainly not.'

'Of course not, of course not,' said Darwin hurriedly, his voice suffused with relief. 'I just thought for one moment that...' He tailed off.

Earle fixed him with a pointed look. 'Both these two are for me. You want company, Darwin, you go fetch your own.'

*

The *Beagle* sailed into Rio harbour – now correctly located on the Admiralty chart – in mid-May, ahead of time but low on fresh food and water. They had tried fishing for groupers, but fearless sharks would invariably seize the fish from the lines before they could be reeled in, so seamen Morgan, Jones and Henderson were detailed to take the dinghy (as FitzRoy had decided to rename the jolly-boat) on a snipe-shooting expedition around the islets of the bay. The voyage had left FitzRoy disturbed: they had passed two frigates anchored off Cabo Frio, which had been identified by challenge-and-response as the *Lightning* and the *Algerine*, engaged in salvaging bullion from the wreck of the *Thetis*. How many of his old shipmates had been taken by the sharks, he wondered. Or was such an end preferable to death by drowning, and that terrifying, lung-bursting moment when the victim knows he can hold his breath no longer and must accept his agonizing fate?

A knock at the door interrupted his morbid reverie. It was Seaman Morgan, who had built the coracle, and Volunteer Musters.

'Permission to speak, sir!' Musters stood ramrod straight.

'Yes, what is it, Mr Musters?'

'Able Seaman Henderson has cut his leg, sir, and will be unable to take part in the snipe-shooting detail. As the best snipe-shooter in the ship, sir, I would like to take his place. Furthermore, sir, as the expedition has no officer in charge, I feel it is only right that I should command the expedition, sir.' Musters had managed to cram his entire request into a single breath, and now exhaled with relief.

'Is this true, Morgan?'

'Henderson has cut his leg, sir, and the lad, I mean Mr Musters, well, he's a fine shot for his age, sir.'

FitzRoy smiled. 'Very well, Mr Musters, you may command the snipe-shooting expedition. As long as you remember that you are to do exactly what Seaman Morgan tells you at all times.'

'Yes sir!'

A beaming Musters retreated, Morgan clutching his cap behind.

The cutter collected Darwin, King and Earle late the next morning, together with a score of boxes, crates and specimen jars.

'My dear Philos! I see that you have been busy!' was FitzRoy's warm greeting to his friend.

'Indeed I have, my dear FitzRoy. Professor Grant always stressed the importance of the analytic method, by which one derives one's conclusions from as many observations as possible. I fear it will not please Mr Wickham, nor our Mr McCormick, who prefers to start with a hypothesis and illustrate it with observations; but then, he is a philosopher of rather an ancient type.'

'Mr McCormick is gone. Bynoe has taken his place.'

'Gone? Gone where?'

'He is "invalided home" once more, on HMS *Tyne*.'

'Well, my dear fellow, he is no loss. I must confess that he put me in mind of Mrs Campbell's performance as Lady Macbeth.'

Both men laughed.

'Mr McCormick was an empty-headed coxcomb, but I fear the consequences of his departure. I can ill afford the Admiralty's displeasure on this matter.'

'My dear FitzRoy, we shall not return to England these next two years, by which time I am sure that all will be forgotten. Now, let us to dinner, for I could eat a horse – or a plate of rice and peas, at any rate.'

'Rice and peas be hanged. Today, in honour of the philosopher's return, we shall have fresh snipe!'

The pair squeezed themselves into FitzRoy's cabin and ate royally, while Darwin told of his discoveries, of Earle's disgraceful licentiousness and of the idyllic cottage by the *lagoa*, upon which he had laid out no less than twenty-two shillings a week.

'I fear I shall have to write to my father for a further fifty pounds. In the meantime, you couldn't make it convenient…?'

'Of course. Seek out the purser Mr Rowlett after dinner, and tell him that I have authorized a loan. I fear that by the end of our voyage your poor father will have become a slave to his son's *divertissements*.'

'My dear FitzRoy, slavery is a term I would prefer not to hear used in jest. If you had only seen what I have seen!' And he proceeded to relate the story of his journey to the *fazenda*, the cruelties he had witnessed there, and his conclusions as to the social repercussions of the trade in human beings. 'I fear that slavery has already entailed some of its lamentable consequences upon the Brazilian nation, in demoralizing them by extreme indolence, and its accompaniment, gross sensuality.' As he fulminated, his thoughts strayed momentarily to Earle's two supper companions, hurrying quickly past the ambivalent feelings he himself had entertained that night. 'Slavery is an affront to every civilized nation!' he concluded hotly.

'Indeed it is. We must thank the Lord that ours *is* the only civilized nation. The only nation of any consequence to have abolished slavery, to have made it a capital offence, and to have taken action against the slavers.'

'Abolished slavery? But it is still legal in British dominions overseas!'

'It is only a matter of time before such vested interests are overcome. Already the free people of colour in South Africa have legal equality with the whites.'

'You say that we have taken action against the slavers – but here we are, sitting in a naval gunboat, in a harbour belonging to one of the world's biggest slaving nations. I am unconscious of you taking any "action".'

'I? My dear Darwin, I am the commander of a surveying-brig! Are you suggesting that I unilaterally declare war against a nation that our government considers to be its principal ally in South America?'

'Of course not. But I fail to see the logic of a policy that would see the captain of a Brazilian slaveship hanged were we to intercept him in international waters – yet should we meet him here in Rio, we should doubtless take high tea with him! Surely at the very least we should be blockading the coast against this inhuman cargo?'

'Darwin, do you have any idea for how many miles the coast of the Brazils extends? You would have a ninety-foot brig blockade a nation the size of Europe? My orders are to survey the bays and inlets of Patagonia and Tierra del Fuego. And my remit as commander of this vessel is to follow those orders, not to take issue with the policies of His Majesty's government.'

'You would follow any order you were given, however immoral, however illogical?'

'Now you are being absurd. My orders are not immoral or illogical. But in answer to your question, yes, I would follow any order given to me. Not to do so would constitute an act of mutiny.'

'But FitzRoy, picture to yourself the threat ever hanging over *you*, of *your* wife and *your* little children – those objects that nature urges even the slave to call his own – being torn from you and sold like beasts to the first bidder! And these deeds are done and palliated by men who profess to love their neighbours as themselves, who believe in God and pray that His will be done on earth! It makes one's blood boil to think that we Englishmen and our American descendants, with their boastful cry of liberty, have been and are so guilty.'

'Are you not forgetting the African who sells his brother man to the slavers, the Arab who first turned Africa into a slaving-ground, and every other nation on earth that partakes of this vile trade?'

'Do not try to abjure our national guilt over this matter, FitzRoy. The fact is, you Tories have always had cold hearts about slavery.'

'What gammon. I abhor slavery as much as you do.'

'But consider those innocent children, FitzRoy, plucked from the very bosom of their family! Brought up in a world where freedom is for ever to be denied them!'

'Mr Darwin, you will allow me to observe that I was enterd for the Service when I was twelve years old. Mr Musters is eleven. Mr Hellyer is twelve. Mr King has been on this vessel since he was ten. Almost every soul aboard has been afloat since they were young children. Some of the oldsters were once pressed men, torn from their families. It is the lot of each and every one of us to do exactly as we are told. If a sailor disobeys an order, he is flogged. If he disobeys again, he is hanged. If he escapes and is recaptured, he is hanged. If I did as you suggest, my fate would be no different. Do not speak of slavery as if it were somehow unique.'

'If an equivalent misery is caused by the will of our institutions, then great is our sin – but how this bears on slavery, I cannot see.'

'It appears that you cannot see very much. All is relative. Compare the lot of the starving farm-worker in southern England with the well-fed slave whose master is merciful.'

'At least the farm-worker suffers by his own hearth. Even the best-trained slaves wish to return to their countries.'

'Repatriation would be impossible. Nobody can hope to know which slave came from where. They do not even speak each other's language. I repeat, I am no advocate for slavery, but I have met slaves who knew enough of the world to realize that they were better off where they were.'

'And was their master present when they asserted so?'

'I cannot possibly recall.'

'Even if he was not, the slave must indeed be dull who does not calculate on the chance of his answer reaching his master's ears. It is you who are naïve, not I. I know what I speak of. My family has stood steadfastly against slavery for three generations. Both my grandfathers, Erasmus Darwin and the first Josiah Wedgwood, pledged to fight this scandalous trade. It was Josiah who produced the famous cameo depicting a Negro in chains with the slogan "Am I not a man and a brother?" – a brooch that he sold in the thousands, if not the hundreds of thousands, to concerned gentlefolk across Great Britain.'

'And where did the profits of that most popular trade find their resting-place? Were they donated to the fight against slavery? I very much doubt it.'

'I beg your pardon?'

'I believe that you heard me.'

'My grandfather lived right among his labourers, all fifteen thousand of them, at the Etruria works in Stoke-on-Trent.'

'And your uncle Jos? Does he live at the works? I think not. I think that the proceeds of the cameo to which you refer purchased him a handsome manor house, while his workers continue to live at the mercy of the factory system, a form of penury more iniquitous than which it would be difficult to imagine.'

'My uncle's workforce is free to come and go as they so please. How dare you make a comparison with the slave trade?'

'Free to come and go as they so please? So your uncle's workers are not tied to his cottages, his insurance societies, his penny-halfpenny wages?'

'Each and every one of the lower orders in my uncle's employ has the potential for advancement.'

'The potential for advancement? Fifteen thousand people are confined to your uncle's slums, amid disease, poverty, grime and filth, and you claim that any one of them has the potential for advancement when their families are daily broken up? When mothers and children are forced to labour twelve hours or more per day because their husbands and fathers earn insufficient for their keep? When babies are brought up by their sisters and fed on laudanum tonic to keep their silence? And a further consequence of the factory system, as we both know, is an entire absence of all regard for moral obligations relating to sex – you know well the manner in which many young women brought up in the shadow of our factories are forced to supplement their income!'

'How dare you, sir? How dare you?' Darwin's voice rose to a shout. 'Do you think that the lower classes of the Tory shires are happier? At least my uncle's workers do not starve, sir.'

'At least the farm-workers of England know what it is to see daylight, sir.'

'I thank my better fortune that living in proximity to you has not made me a renegade to my Whig principles. The devil take you, sir!'

His face drained of blood by fury, FitzRoy called for his steward. 'Tell Lieutenant Wickham to present himself to my quarters immediately.'

'Aye aye sir.'

The two fumed in silence in the few brief seconds before Wickham made himself known.

'Mr Wickham.'

'Sir.'

'Mr Darwin has made himself presumptuously impertinent to me. He will not be taking his meals in this cabin henceforth. Please escort him from my quarters at once.'

Cold with rage, Darwin rose to his feet, his neck bent as ever to avoid a collision with the ceiling, and stalked out. Wickham followed in silence and shut the door. As Darwin placed his first furious tread on the companionway, Wickham lightly touched his arm.

'Philos? It sounded as if you and the skipper had fallen to loggerheads back there.'

'You heard?'

'It could be heard throughout the ship.'

'Pray forgive me the disturbance.'

'Philos? If you would care to mess with us in the gunroom henceforth, I am sure it could be arranged.'

'Thank you most kindly, Mr Wickham. I appreciate your consideration.'

With that, Darwin climbed up to the maindeck and went into his cabin to begin packing. He was perhaps halfway through the task when a knock at the door announced the presence of Lieutenant Sulivan.

'Philos?'

'Yes?'

'Compliments of Captain FitzRoy. The captain extends his humblest apologies – he wishes to say sorry for his unreasonable behaviour – and begs you to continue to live with him.'

'Is this your doing, Sulivan?'

'No, Philos, it is not.'

Darwin considered. 'Please tell Captain FitzRoy that, on the contrary, the fault was entirely mine, and that I should be delighted to continue to live with him.'

Sulivan smiled with relief. 'Thank goodness for that. The skipper has need of you. You must forgive him, Philos. He is a remarkable man, and a brilliant officer. All of us reverence him. But the pressure placed upon one man's shoulders is immense.'

'I will tell you, Sulivan, he is altogether the strongest marked character that I ever fell in with. I never before came across a man whom I could fancy being a Napoleon or a Nelson. If he does not kill himself, he will achieve wonderful things.'

'Let us hope it is the latter, shall we?' replied Sulivan brightly, and headed back in the direction of FitzRoy's cabin.

*

Two cannon salutes, one each from the *Warspite* and the *Samarang*, rolled across Rio de Janeiro Bay as the wind rippled the *Beagle*'s sails and she made for the harbour entrance. She was a popular little vessel, who had impressed everybody with her smartness and efficiency, and the mighty stalwarts of the South American station were sorry to see her go. They knew, especially, that she was headed – unaccompanied – into unknown and uncharted waters, where a hidden spear of rock could send a little surveying-brig to the bottom at any instant, and they wished her well. The *Beagle*'s crew revelled in their moment of fame, and proudly put their backs into all the heaving and pulling of departure.

'Close-hauled, Mr Chaffers, we should be able to lay south-east comfortably,' FitzRoy remarked to the master.

'Come on, Mr Musters!' barked Midshipman King, at his young charge. 'Tail on to that rope and put some effort in! Damned kid, thinks he's a lieutenant already.'

Musters plunged on to the end of the rope and heaved with all his might. FitzRoy, pacing the deck, saw him totter with the effort.

'Is everything all right, Mr Musters?'

'I don't feel very well, sir,' replied Musters feebly. 'I feel hot and sweaty.'

'It is probably a little fever from your snipe-shooting trip. I am sure it is nothing. Come with me to Mr Bynoe – I have no doubt he will make much of you.'

FitzRoy led Musters below decks to the sickbay. The *Beagle*'s was a fully equipped modern pharmaceutic facility, with ventilation, hanging cots and a full range of medicinal drugs, quite unlike the dark, windowless, unhygienic sickbays of the past. It was with every confidence that FitzRoy flung open Bynoe's door; a feeling of assurance that evaporated immediately when he saw the expression of Seaman Morgan, who was seated on a stool within. Fear was etched around Morgan's eyes, his face a pale, sweaty mask.

'Hello, young 'un,' he breathed. 'You here too?'

No one was in the mood to correct the informality.

'Yes,' said Musters, biting his lip uncertainly, sensing that something was wrong.

'It's just a fever, lad. We'll be set all squares on the morrow,' Morgan reassured him, and all the adults in the room knew him to be lying.

'May I speak with you a moment, sir?' asked Bynoe.

He and FitzRoy stepped outside. Concern tinged the young surgeon's every word. 'I am afraid, sir, there is every certainty that these men have contracted malaria.'

FitzRoy was stunned. 'How? In the islets of the harbour?'

'They followed the snipe flocks into the estuary of the Macacu river.'

FitzRoy clenched his fist into a ball of frustration. 'I categorically ordered them to stay away from dry land.'

'They did, sir. They stayed out in the waters of the estuary at all times.'

'Then how…?'

'Pestilential malaria is caused by a miasma or vapour arising from marshland when it is affected by the heat of the sun. Dr Ferguson has shown that the poison is generated by the drying process, which is why hot climates are the most unhealthy. There were outbreaks in the marshes at Westminster, if you remember, during the hot summer a few years back. But the vapour can be carried out to sea by the winds. Many is the instance, sir, of native populations being decimated by European diseases brought by white explorers, the reason being that the vapours containing the disease are blown along on the same winds as their ships. The miasma is at its most concentrated in the darkness, so by sleeping in the estuary overnight, all three men will have undoubtedly exposed themselves to the windblown vapours.'

'Is there any physic that you can give them?'

'Quinine is known to alleviate the symptoms. The only cure lies with the Lord. Our best recourse is to pray, sir.'

'Thank you, Mr Bynoe.'

The surgeon returned to the sickbay while FitzRoy reeled back against the wall of the passageway in despair. He thought of the promises he had made to Musters's mother, of how he would take all care of little Charles. He struggled to make sense of the medical diagnosis. *If the miasma evaporates from the marshes during the heat of the day, why then is it at its most dangerous in the cool of the night? Is it because of a check to perspiration caused by sheets or blankets? If so, then why is a sleeper outside a tent more vulnerable than one inside?* Something was wrong with the orthodox medical explanation, he could tell – but what?

Overcome with his own intellectual impotence, he felt tears well in his eyes. They were tears of frustration, he knew, as much as tears of sadness.

Five days out of Rio, Bos'n Sorrell and his mates wrapped Mr Musters, Seaman Morgan and Seaman Jones in their hammocks, weighted them with roundshot, and sewed them in. Each was covered with a flag and placed in turn on a hinged plank, the same one that had been used when 'Crossing the Line', from which vantage-point they slid silently into the waters of the Atlantic. FitzRoy read the funeral service. No other sound was heard on deck.

'Poor kid,' whispered Jemmy, when he had finished.

'Poor kid,' echoed Fuegia, and then the deck fell quiet again.

The silence followed FitzRoy into his cabin afterwards, where he sat motionless before a blank page of the ship's logbook for the better part of an hour. Eventually Edward Hellyer, his budget of papers similarly ignored, ventured to speak.

'Sir?'

'Yes, Mr Hellyer?'

'Sir, why did God take Mr Musters? Had he done something bad?'

'No, Mr Hellyer, he had not done anything bad.'

'Then why did God take him, sir?'

I do not know how to answer that question.

'Maybe God loved Mr Musters so much that He wanted him at His right hand. I can think of no other explanation.'

There can be no other explanation. Dear Lord, how can there be any other explanation?

CHAPTER TWO

Punta Alta, Bahia Blanca, 22 September 1832

'By God, it's enormous.'

'What the deuce is it?'

'That will probably suffice with the pickaxe, Mr Sulivan. Here comes Philos to the rescue with his box of tools.'

'Thank heaven for that.'

Sulivan stepped back from the earth bank, perspiring. Embedded in the indigo clay before them, surrounded by a starburst of broken shells as if propelled violently through from the other side, a vast head, half exposed, grinned out at them. It measured a good four feet from side to side, each lifeless black eye-socket a whole foot in diameter.

Darwin picked his way up the beach, shivering. A chill breeze blew insistently from the south-east, and snow was visible on the distant Sierra de Ventana. Behind him, the descending tide had exposed a muddy lattice of shallow, silt-choked channels, a treacherous labyrinth into which FitzRoy had not dared steer the *Beagle*. Up and down the coast, as far as the eye could see, low sand hillocks lay in endless serpentine humps, forming a drab backdrop to an equally lifeless shore. One or two of the nearer humps had been garrisoned by mangy vultures, no doubt hoping that the unusual activity portended a much longed-for meal.

'This looks exactly like Barmouth,' he remarked, to nobody in particular. 'Except for the vultures.' Then he observed FitzRoy and his officers, some fifteen feet or so above the high-water mark, clustered about a section of clay bank that had collapsed, exposing its innards. Then he saw what held their attention.

'My God,' he said, arriving. 'What is it?'

'We were hoping you would be able to tell us,' admitted Bynoe, glad to hand over the baton of geological expertise.

'We thought it was a rhinoceros at first,' said FitzRoy, 'but it is far too large. These teeth are many times greater than those of any land animal living today.'

'What's the stratigraphic diagnosis, Philos?' said Sulivan good-humouredly. 'Tell us all.'

Darwin stared, transfixed, into the monstrous eye-sockets.

'I do believe it is a Megatherium,' he offered finally. 'If so, it would be only the second to be discovered. The first was found at Buenos Ayres in 1798, and resides in the King's Collection at Madrid – where, for all purposes of science, it is as much hidden as if still in its primeval rock. This is an incredible discovery!'

'How long has it been buried here, Philos?'

'Well, this earth is a conglomerate of quartz and jasper pebbles, which means it is comparatively new in geological terms. And these broken shells must also be of recent origin – all these creatures are extant today. This creature cannot be more than a few thousand years old.'

He indicated a small section of shoulder-plate that had been exposed by Sulivan's pickaxe, below the jaw-bone.

'Do you see how its bones have been buried in alignment? That suggests its remains were fresh and still united by their ligaments when they were deposited in the silt. This creature appears to have drowned.'

'Yet it is fifteen feet above the high-water mark,' FitzRoy pointed out, his heart thumping at the implication.

'Bless me, Philos,' said Sulivan excitedly, 'these could be the remains of an animal wiped out in the great flood itself. An animal too large to fit into the ark.'

FitzRoy observed that Darwin chose not to reply. Instead, the philosopher began to scratch at the exposed bank, where a number of jet-black plates, septagonal in shape and osseous in nature, protruded like bad teeth between the jumble of white shells.

'What are they, Philos? Are they part of its carapace?'

'I would say these were typical of the plates on an armadillo's back.

Except they are enormous. To sport such a coat, an armadillo would have to be the size of a carriage – perhaps eight feet high and ten feet long.'

'A giant armadillo!' Midshipman King conjured up a thrilling mental image of the creature rampaging down Piccadilly.

'"*The end of all flesh is come before me,*"' murmured Sulivan.

'Let us not waste any more time in chatter,' said FitzRoy. 'It will take all afternoon to dig this fellow from his grave.'

So they set to the cliff with a will, the soft conglomerate rock crumbling before their onslaught, and gradually the head of the Megatherium emerged. Each took a turn at making bolder progress with the pickaxe, while Darwin took charge of the more delicate excavations and made notes with his bramah pen. Their task was almost complete when a shout from below alerted them to the presence of two schooners running into the bay. At least, FitzRoy could not find a better description than 'schooner': the two vessels were tiny, no bigger than the *Beagle*'s whaleboats, but each was possessed of twin masts and a covered deck. The lead schooner appeared to be crewed by a single sailor of quite enormous bulk, who clung to the mast shouting and waving, the little craft lurching from side to side so violently beneath him that it seemed he must upset her. The overall effect was that of a hugely overloaded bobbin, its spindle swaying fit to break.

'He's calling to us,' said Sulivan.

Despite its ungainliness, the little schooner and its fellow-craft were being expertly piloted, sidestepping the muddy shoals and darting through the watery channels towards the beach at great speed.

'The Bill is passed!' bawled the man.

'What's that?'

'Are you Englishmen, sir? I said, the Bill is passed!'

A shudder of excitement ran through the little group. The Reform Bill had passed through Parliament at last!

'Mr James Harris, sir, and this is Mr Roberts.' Florid with exertion, the fat sailor squelched into the shallows, crushing a dozen small crabs in the process. His face wore a just-boiled look.

'Commander Robert FitzRoy, captain of His Majesty's surveying-brig

Beagle,' responded FitzRoy, stepping forward. He threw manners out of the window. 'Does His Majesty still reign or is there a republic?'

'I know not, sir. We spoke to a mail packet bound for San Francisco. All I know, sir, is that every man of property shall have the vote. The Bill is passed!'

Every man stood thrilled, transfixed, but fearful, too, that there might no longer be an England to go back to.

'You are sealers?' FitzRoy's practised eye took in the two vessels at a glance, both of them smeared with a filthy black cocktail of rancid seal and sea-elephant-oil. Harris and Roberts themselves were no less well greased.

'That we are, sir. I constructed them myself.' Harris gestured towards the boats, perspiring proudly. 'The *Paz* displaces fifteen tons, and the *Liebre* nine. I converted her from a frigate's barge.' Roberts's craft was little bigger than a coffin. 'As you will have seen, sir, the channels hereabouts are too shallow to risk a brig at low tide, or a barque. But at high tide an open boat like your own runs the risk of being swamped. The tide races are strong and the seas are uncommon heavy. These vessels present the ideal solution. The decks keep out the waves. If they go aground, one simply steps overboard and heaves them afloat. And one's own bodyweight answers admirably in trimming such craft.'

Yours especially, thought FitzRoy uncharitably. 'There are many such bays further down the coast?' he enquired.

'A hundred miles of them, sir, and each a maze of muddy creeks. But I am tolerably acquainted with them all.'

FitzRoy's mind raced, and a plan began to formulate therein.

The two sealers had come ashore to visit the fort at Argentina, the last permanent military encampment on the coast, in search of supplies. In view of Harris's advice regarding the incoming tide, FitzRoy instructed the shore party to pull the boats on to the shore and bivouac for the night, and went ahead with Harris and Darwin to the lonely outpost. A few miles' brisk walk across a level greensward, cropped short by semi-wild horses and cattle, brought them to La Fortaleza Protectora Argentina, a squat polygonal fortress some three hundred yards across, boasting thick mud walls and a defensive ditch. The walls were pitted and scarred, their wounds a vivid testimony to the number and intensity of recent Indian attacks.

An assemblage of creaking pulleys raised the main gate at their approach, and a reception party issued forth to greet them. At their head was an immensely tall half-caste mounted on a lean horse; dark of visage, his combination of army uniform and Indian dress was as confused as his lineage. Behind him rode several gauchos, wild, unshaven and desperate-looking, each man liberally adorned with knife-cuts; yet they were as gaily dressed as if in the service of an Eastern potentate. Gleaming white leather boots with shiny spurs jutted up from hand-carved wooden stirrups; voluminous scarlet drawers billowed over their boot-tops; and above those, the whole was enveloped by the swirl of their brightly striped ponchos. Bringing up the rear was a far less impressive straggle of uniformed foot-soldiers, sad-eyed white boys taken against their will from the suburbs of Buenos Ayres. The leader of this curious platoon spoke, in slow, deliberate Spanish. '*¿Viernes de Buenos Ayres con provisiones?*' Do you come from Buenos Ayres with supplies?

'I am a seal-man,' replied Harris in fluent Spanish. 'I have come to Argentina to purchase supplies.'

'There are no supplies here. Buenos Ayres has forgotten us.' The tall horseman spat derisively upon the ground.

'There must be beef,' objected Harris.

'There is always beef. But who are these men? They are not seal-men.' He indicated FitzRoy and Darwin.

'They have come by ship from England.'

'I am Commander FitzRoy of His Majesty's Ship *Beagle*.' FitzRoy spoke for himself, equally fluently, while Darwin, who was still learning the language, struggled to keep up. 'I represent King William of Great Britain.'

'I do not know of such a place. You must report to the commandant.'

The three allowed themselves to be led through the fortress gate to the far side of an outer courtyard where raucous children played. A group of naked and frightened Indian prisoners crouched shackled together, gnawing at the carcass of a roasted horse.

'What will happen to those men?' enquired Darwin of Harris.

'They will be sent north to be interrogated. Then they will be shot.'

'They will be shot? In cold blood?'

'You should see what the Indians do to white prisoners. Shooting is a mercy by comparison.'

The party was escorted to a simple room where pieces of rough wooden furniture stood upon a floor of beaten earth, and squares cut into the walls served as windows. There they were instructed to wait for the commandant. Two enormous pewter plates of beef were brought, one roasted, the other boiled, and an earthenware jug was filled from a water-butt in the corner. No cutlery or drinking-vessels were provided. Presently the tall horseman returned, fetched back by his curiosity.

'Your country,' he enquired. 'It is to the north?'

FitzRoy assented.

'Is it warmer or colder than here?'

'Great Britain is colder than here in the summer, but warmer in the winter.'

'I have heard of Mendoza, and the United Provinces, and of Roma where the Holy Father lives. But I have never heard of this country you speak of.'

'*I* have heard tell of Great Britain.'

The voice came from behind them: although weary in tone, its rich texture evoked the wisdom of years. All turned to see the *comandante* framed in the doorway. He was a lean, erect, narrow-shouldered man, somewhat lost in a bleached and frayed major's uniform, his sun-gnarled face divided by a sagging grey moustache. In any other army, in any other part of the world, he would surely have been pensioned off many years previously. Clearly normal rules did not apply out here at the frontier, here in his personal domain.

'Great Britain is a city in the country of London, which is connected by land to the United States of America. Am I right?' The major sat down stiffly opposite FitzRoy, Darwin and Harris.

'That is approximately correct,' answered FitzRoy, diplomatically.

'Please. Eat.' He gestured to the two vast mounds of beef.

'Will you excuse me?' Darwin, whose fingers were still caked with the blue clay of the Punta Alta shore, poured water from the jug on to his hands and rubbed them vigorously. For good measure he splashed some on his cheeks, still flecked with mud from his geological exertions.

'You are a Mahometan?' asked the major.

'No.' Darwin looked puzzled.

'Then why do you wash? I have heard that only Mahometans wash themselves.'

'I am a Christian. In our country it is common for Christians to wash.'

'You are a follower of the one true Catholic faith? You have confessed your sins?'

'No...I am not a Catholic, but I am a Christian.'

'If you are not a Catholic, you cannot be a Christian. You must be a Mahometan. It matters not. If you have a God, then you will be safe under my roof. You are sailors?'

'I am a sailor,' clarified FitzRoy. 'My friend Mr Darwin is a naturalist.'

The *comandante* looked puzzled. The term *naturalista* evidently fell outside the scope of his knowledge.

'A naturalist is a man who knows everything,' explained Harris helpfully through a mouthful of beef.

'You know *everything*?' The major raised an eyebrow.

'No, no. I should say I *wish* to learn everything about your country.'

'You are not a spy?' The old man's eyes narrowed.

'I wish only to learn of the animals and birds and plants and rocks. Today we have made a most wonderful discovery – a great head. The head of a mammal – a dead animal – many thousands of years old. It is as wide as a man is tall. On the beach at Punta Alta. It is a great rarity.'

'A big dragon-head.' Realization dawned upon the old major. 'The children like to play games with them. They knock out the teeth with stones. It is a good game.'

Darwin was momentarily nonplussed. The *comandante* gestured to the side door of the room. Darwin half rose from his stool, and craned his neck to see into the courtyard outside. There, grinning toothlessly back at him, was a Megatherium head identical – other than dentally – to the one they had spent all day excavating at the beach.

'I will sell you three for a paper dollar, if you wish,' said the major.

When the constraints of time eventually forced FitzRoy and his officers to abandon excavations at Punta Alta, the exposed cliff had yielded two further Megatherii, a Megalonyx measuring seventy-two feet from snout to tail, an icthyosaurus longer than the *Beagle* herself, an ant-eater the size of a rhinoceros, a twenty-foot armadillo, an extinct variety of horse and an aquatic rodent the size of an elephant. The ship's once-pristine deck was thick with giant bones caked in blue clay.

'Damned seal and whalebones!' Mr Wickham shouted in exasperation. 'Philos, you bring more dirt on board than any ten men!'

FitzRoy decided to run the *Beagle* back to Buenos Ayres to see if the specimens could be dispatched home by an English merchant there. Over a supper of water-hog shot by Bynoe, he and Darwin debated the implications of their haul.

'The approach of a general calamity – the rising waters – would have affected the animals' instinct for self-preservation,' hazarded FitzRoy. 'They would have been *drawn* to the ark. Then, as the creatures approached, might it not have been easy to admit some, perhaps the young and the small, while the old and the large were excluded?'

'I don't know,' said Darwin unhappily. 'The stated dimensions of the ark are but three hundred cubits by fifty cubits. How could all creation be herded into one vessel? Would the beasts not simply have destroyed one another? The story has always vexed me.'

'Master Charles,' admonished FitzRoy gently, 'does not the exclusion of these monstrous creatures answer your question? Where are they now? Drowned, of course, in the deluge.'

'Where, then, are the human fossils? If all humanity was wiped out at the same time, should not there be human bones entombed with those of the Megatherium, or the other great beasts that have been found across the globe? Perhaps these vast creatures walked the earth at a different date, an earlier date.'

'A different date? My dear fellow, I need hardly tell you of all people that the scriptures allow no room for debate on the issue. Genesis two, nineteen: "And out of the ground the Lord God formed every beast of the field, and every fowl of the air, and brought them unto Adam to see what he would call them." '

'Come, come, my dear FitzRoy, you know as well as I that the scriptures are contradictory. In Genesis one, twenty-four, the Lord brings forth all living creatures *before* He maketh man on the sixth day, having already created fish and fowl on the fifth day. What if, as de Luc contends, these "days" were not days as we know them but great ages, epochs lasting many thousands of years? What if man never encountered these monstrous beasts?'

'But, my dear Philos, you heard the *comandante.* A "dragon-head", he called it. What, pray, are dragons, wyverns, griffins and so forth, if not the memory of huge mammals and reptiles handed down by tradition? What were the leviathan and the behemoth if not the megalosaurus and the iguanodon? Human folk-history contains innumerable mentions of such beasts. As to the human fossils, de Luc also contends that, in many places, earth and sea have changed places over the centuries. Perhaps human fossils await discovery at the bottom of our great oceans.'

'But what if early man derived their dragon-tales from the discovery of great skeletons such as we have found? What if, far from actually encountering such beasts, they merely wove them into their myths and stories? Answer me this: if there was indeed an ark, why are the animals of the New World entirely separate from those of the Old? Why are the armadillo and the ant-eater confined entirely to South America, and the elephant and the rhinoceros restricted to the rest of the globe? If all creatures issued from the one ark, would they not follow each other to all corners? But no! All creation is divided into geographical groups. And what fossils do we find in South America? *Giant* armadillos. *Giant* anteaters. The monstrous relatives of the modern animal population. Just as fossil elephants and rhinoceros are only to be found in Africa and Asia.'

'Great heavens, Philos, one would hardly believe you a parson-in-waiting. Let me bring you over. Did not Noah's sons Shem, Ham and

Japheth go forth separately and beget the different races in the different parts of the world? Would it be beyond the good Lord to spread the animals of the ark over the lands newly laid dry *according to their origin*? Would He not logically return the armadillo to the lands whence it came, and the same for the rhinoceros? Besides, your argument is disproved by our friend the horse. The Spaniards introduced the horse to the New World. When they arrived, the horse was unknown to the native population. It has since thrived. Yet what did we discover at Punta Alta? A fossil horse. This is perfect horse-country, yet every horse that once inhabited these lands was wiped out at some point in history. Only a mighty deluge could have done such a thing. Which is why, perhaps' – FitzRoy smiled – 'the good Lord brought the Spanish here, to restock the horse population.'

'Please. My dear FitzRoy, I do not doubt the majesty of God's creation for one instant. But a wooden vessel, stocked with pairs of animals by a six-hundred-year-old man? Noah is said to have been fetched an olive-leaf by a dove when the waters receded. Yet how did a deluge that would flatten and submerge the very mountains themselves fail to uproot or flatten a simple olive tree? It is a most unbelievable tale!'

Irritation began to temper FitzRoy's affection for his friend. 'You doubt the Noachian deluge? Have you not seen the diluvial evidence for yourself? There are water-smoothed stones and shell beds on mountainsides, drowned creatures above the high-water mark, unsorted deposits of clay and gravel and huge boulders scattered across the high hills and valleys – why, the very shape of the hills and valleys themselves shouts out to us of the deluge. And what of the evidence of the heathen peoples? Mesopotamian texts speak of the earth being destroyed by a mighty flood. Even the Hindoos know of the deluge. They speak of one man alone, Manu, being spared by God from the destruction of all humankind. Clearly, it is a garbled account of the Biblical flood. With such compelling evidence before you, can you doubt that the creatures at Punta Alta were wiped out by a massive catastrophe – the very catastrophe described in such detail in the Book of Genesis?'

'I do not seek to undermine the Book of Genesis, FitzRoy, or the word of God. What do you take me for? But there are contradictions therein, anomalies, passages that could be interpreted figuratively. For instance, the lower one geologizes into the rock, the earlier the strata, the simpler the life-forms one finds: not human beings, but great reptiles, giant armadillos, even. Does this not suggest to you an older earth than one which was created in seven days?'

'You presume that the rock is older because the life-forms are simpler. You presume that the life-forms are simpler because the rock is older. You are dating one by the other. Perhaps the strata are not as simple or as progressively layered as you seem to think. What of the modern-day shells preserved in the clay *below* the Megatherium head? Besides, who is to say that a giant armadillo or ant-eater is any simpler than a small one? One might argue the very opposite. Your arguments begin to sound dangerously like those of your grandfather, or of Lamarck.'

'Perhaps the smaller versions of these creatures were better suited to the sparse vegetation of these parts. Perhaps their bigger cousins did not have enough to eat – who is to say? I am only speculating. Such enormous herbivores would have required a colossal supply of vegetation. Perhaps they were forced to compete for it, and lost that competition.'

'The vegetation of Africa is no less sparse than the vegetation of these parts, and yet it supports vast numbers of elephant and rhinoceros. In the Brazils, however, where the vegetation is lush and abundant, there are no large herbivores. What you suggest does not follow. Besides, we know nothing of the state of the earth before the flood – or the atmosphere surrounding it; we do not know if it moved in the same orbit; or if it turned on its axis in the same manner; or whether it had huge masses of ice near the poles. Have not fossil rhinoceros bones been found near the Arctic?'

'Cuvier believes that there may have been a series of floods.'

FitzRoy seized a book from the shelf behind his head and riffled through it. 'Allow me to quote Buckland, a geological authority without peer, I think you will agree. "The grand fact of a *universal deluge* at no very remote period is proved on grounds *so* decisive and incontrovertible that, had we never heard of such an event from scripture, or any other authority, geology *of itself* must have called in the assistance of some such catastrophe to explain the phenomena of diluvian action *which are universally presented to us*."' He slammed the book down on the table.

'"Great men are not always wise" – Job thirty-two, nine,' Darwin responded stubbornly.

On the point of raising his voice in frustration, FitzRoy thought better of it. 'Tell me, my dear friend, is it the case that you are no longer inwardly moved by the Holy Spirit?'

'Of course I am,' said Darwin, 'but...' He tailed off.

'Do you wish to talk to me about it?'

Spruced up with red ochre, coal-tar and whitewash, and scrubbed free of the fatty coating of a thousand boiled seals, the *Paz* and the *Liebre* had metamorphosed into smart little cock-boats. The crew gathered around admiringly as they bobbed jauntily beside the *Beagle*, while inside his cabin FitzRoy put the final touches to the contract: to Mr James Harris of the Rio Negro, for one year's hire of both boats, plus the services of himself and Mr Roberts as pilots, the sum of £1680.

'And I thought the headroom on the old *Beagle* was barely sufficient,' said Stokes ruefully, lowering himself into the main cabin of the *Paz*, which – although a spacious seven foot square – was an ungenerous thirty inches in height. He would be sharing this cramped space for the next twelve months with Roberts, the sealer, and Midshipman Mellersh.

'Pretty boats!' said Fuegia Basket, and clapped her hands with delight.

'Think yourself lucky you will not be sharing with Harris,' laughed Wickham, who was to have the privilege of wedging himself into an even smaller cabin in the *Liebre*, alongside the boat's owner and Midshipman King.

The prospect of being second-in-command of his very own vessel, on a year's expedition to survey the bays and channels south of Bahia Blanca, had seemed to King the very idea of heaven on earth; until, that is, he too had inspected the principal cabin. Then the reality – that he would be spending the whole of the following year squeezed into a corner by Harris's sweating bulk – had sunk in. He and Darwin stood forlornly at the starboard rail. The philosopher's initial guilty pleasure at getting their whole cabin to himself had dissipated somewhat, as he had come to realize how much he would miss the dependable Stokes, the egregious Wickham and his best pal, the young midshipman by his side. Sulivan, who would become acting first lieutenant of the *Beagle*, looked on with misgivings of his own, for he did not wish to accede to Wickham's position in such a manner. He steeled himself to beard FitzRoy in private.

'Let me go in Wickham's place, sir. It will be a rotten uncomfortable year for them, and Mr Wickham takes such a pride in the *Beagle*.'

'Your suggestion is generous to a fault, Mr Sulivan. However – naval etiquette bids me do otherwise. If the expedition is to divide in two, then my second-in-command must take charge of the second part.'

'Then how about Stokes? He has been with you from the start, sir – he has surely earned his place on the *Beagle*.'

'Mr Stokes is my best surveyor. I doubt that anyone else in the ship could map such a maze. Besides, were you to replace him, then I should find myself *sans* lieutenants.'

'If only the Admiralty had sanctioned the hire of two more luxurious vessels – they are but cockleshells.'

'Only cockleshells, I fear, possess a sufficiently shallow draught for the task. Besides, the Admiralty has not sanctioned the hire of any vessels.'

'But then how—?'

'They are requisitioned on my own responsibility.'

'You are not authorized?' Sulivan's face wore a faintly appalled look.

'I have memorialized Whitehall seeking authorization. I hope to obtain it retrospectively.'

'But if you do not?'

'Then I shall be sixteen hundred and eighty pounds the poorer.'

Sulivan gasped. It was an astonishing sum for one man to bear, even a wealthy man like FitzRoy.

'I believe that their lordships will approve of what I have done. But if I am wrong no inconvenience will result to the public service, since I am alone responsible, and am willing to pay the stipulated sum.'

'No inconvenience to the public service, perhaps, but to yourself? It would be more than mere inconvenience...' Sulivan's expression clouded over with worry.

I can ill spare the sum, it is true, but he cannot know that.

'I am willing to run the risk. Without it our task cannot – simply cannot – be completed. If the results of these arrangements should turn out well, then I trust I will stand excused for having presumed to act so freely. Besides, I have given my word to Jemmy, to York and to Fuegia that they will be home before the summer. I have given my word, Mr Sulivan, as one gentleman to another.'

The point, Sulivan had to concede, was unanswerable.

The little city of Buenos Ayres lay in flat green meadows along the river Plate's southern shore, hugging the ground, its domes and towers rising cautiously from rough, muddy streets and squares. The brown river washing thickly at its banks appeared richer and creamier than ever, as if it would curdle against the docks and jetties. As the *Beagle* made sticky progress upstream, the river seemed to adhere to her flanks and clog her passage.

The cannon-shot rang out unmistakably across the lapping water. Most of those on deck turned in time to see a white puff of smoke drift languidly up through the rigging of the city guardship. The three Fuegians, poised, alert, froze midway through a reluctant passage of Bible study with Mr Matthews. FitzRoy, on the poop deck, and Mr Sulivan and the master at the wheel, were held in a split second's limbo of indecision before their training took over. Darwin, confused, spun like a top, attempting to locate the source of the sound. Only the few oldsters on board who had seen action as nippers and powder monkeys in the Great War flung themselves instinctively to the deck. A second later, a faint whistle overhead, accompanied by the ripping of parting ropes, announced that the cannonball had passed harmlessly through the rigging. Only then did the realization dawn, fully, that the *Beagle* was under attack.

'How dare they?' exclaimed FitzRoy. 'How *dare* they? Bring her round, Mr Chaffers, and beat to quarters!'

She was already sailing as close-hauled as she could, some six points off the breeze, which was gusting from the northern shore. It was an easy matter for her to reach across the wind, her sails bellying, and swing into a course that would bring her bearing down alongside the guardship. The drums sounded their intent, and there was a scene of furious activity on deck as the guns were made ready.

'Damn them,' cursed FitzRoy. 'A shot into the works of a steam engine would not do so much damage as a shot too close to our chronometers.'

'But why did they fire at us?' asked a panic-stricken Darwin, who had located a safe place to hide, crouched behind the huge Megatherium head.

'Another revolution, I shouldn't wonder. Revolutions are the fashion in these parts. When they are not fighting the Indians, they fight each other. Whoever controls Buenos Ayres controls the silver route from Upper Peru. So it is just one *caudillo*, one strong man, after another – except that none is strong enough to hold on to power. They say General Rosas is the strongest, but he will not enter the fray until he is sure of victory.'

The *Beagle* was closing rapidly on the guardship now, and Darwin could see the gunners scurrying to their positions on the enemy vessel. The disparity in bulk between the two ships was becoming increasingly apparent as they drew nearer, the *Beagle* giving away a good few hundred tons to her rival. Surely, thought Darwin, we shall not dare to take on a ship twice our size, broadside to broadside? He buried his head as deeply as he could in the Megatherium's eye-socket.

'Mr Sorrell, back the fore-topsail!' ordered FitzRoy. Drilled to perfection a hundred times, the men jumped to their tasks, hauling the fore-topsail yard round in opposition to its fellows, to bring the *Beagle* juddering to a near-stop. The gleaming brass snouts of her new guns bristled aggressively along her starboard side: two six-pounders before the chesstree, a six-pound boat-carronade on the forecastle, and four lone, wicked-looking nine-pounders abaft the mainmast. As they drew alongside the guardship, FitzRoy leaped up on to the rail and, balancing there, shouted across the intervening channel of chocolate-cream water: 'If you dare fire another shot, we shall send our whole broadside into your rotten uncivilized hulk! Is that understood?' And then, for good measure, he repeated the statement in Spanish.

There was silence, and then, across the water, a brief flurry of activity as the Buenos Ayres gunners stood down from their posts. The *Beagle* drifted on past her, into open water, and Darwin drew his head cautiously out from the black depths of the eye-socket.

'You did not fire,' he ventured redundantly.

'I had no intention of doing so. The damage to the chronometers from our own recoil would have been catastrophic. Besides, such a firefight would have been sheer folly. We would have been blown out of the water. He was twice our size, did you not see?'

'But – but how did you know that their captain would not fire?'

'Did you see the state of that ship? The sails were mildewed, the paintwork filthy, and you can smell their bilges from here. You can tell a lot about a man from the state of his ship. My dear Philos, I knew he would not fire.'

By sundown they had swirled down with the current to Monte Video on the river's north-eastern shore, where His Majesty's frigate *Druid* was moored on permanent station. FitzRoy went across in the cutter to pay his respects to Captain Hamilton, and to make his formal report of the insult to the British flag – an incident that would not, of course, go unpunished. As he clambered aboard, he was stopped in his tracks by an apparition: a pale but welcome face he had never expected to see again.

'My God – Hamond!'

'FitzRoy!'

'I thought you drowned – lost with the *Thetis*.'

'N-no, sir,' replied Hamond, who had not outgrown his stammer. 'I was b-back in England, taking my lieutenant's examination – I'm a p-passed mid now. Everybody else d-drowned, sir.'

'But, my God, you're alive!'

And the two men threw their arms around each other in a most unnaval fashion.

By the time the *Druid* had hauled her anchor at sunrise, and had set sail for Buenos Ayres to demand the arrest of the guardship captain, FitzRoy had obtained not just restitution but a new mate: Robert Hamond would chum with Charles Darwin in the library of the *Beagle*.

The celebratory mood was not to last, however. A stack of mail had been waiting for Darwin in the *Druid* – he had excitedly unwrapped the latest volume of Lyell, sent by Professor Henslow – but then, lurking malevolently in wait at the bottom of the pile, he had spotted the black seal. Feverishly, he had torn open the letter, almost ripping it in two in his haste to get at the contents. His cousin, his sweet, mischievous cousin Fanny Wedgwood, was dead of cholera at the age of twenty-six. His thoughts flashed back to that perfect afternoon the previous summer when he had sat out on the porch with Fanny and Emma and Hen and Uncle Jos and Aunt Bessie, Fanny teasing him, inciting him to go on the voyage, urging him to take care of himself, Emma's arm curled about her sister's waist. Fan had worried for her cousin's safety, *his* safety, and now it was *her* fragile existence that had been crushed by a heartless or careless or loveless deity. He felt simultaneously lucky, and frightened, and angry at the senselessness of it. This was not some meaningless native whose life had been taken, but a beautiful, intelligent young *lady* in the prime of her life. He knew what FitzRoy would say, that it was God's wish, that one should not challenge His will, that there were reasons for everything that could not always be revealed to us. FitzRoy would probably be right, but that did not mean he wished to hear him express the sentiments. Damn it, he would follow the man anywhere – what magnificent pluck he had shown in facing up to the Buenos Ayres guardship – but he was always so *certain* of everything.

Darwin's reverie was interrupted by the crackle of gunfire. At first he thought it must be the *Druid*, laying waste to Buenos Ayres city centre in an orgy of retribution; then he remembered that the river Plate was so ludicrously wide at its mouth that a good hundred miles lay between the two cities on their opposing banks. No, the firing came from the centre of Monte Video itself. Presently a small boat appeared, rowed somewhat inexpertly by four gentlemen in top hats and tail-coats, one of whom stood up and began to wave and gesticulate frantically at the *Beagle*. FitzRoy came to the rail to try to discern what was being shouted, no easy matter as the man's relinquishing of his oar was causing the little boat to go round in circles.

'Where is the *Druid*, sir?' bellowed the slowly revolving figure.

'Gone to Buenos Ayres,' shouted back FitzRoy.

'Then you are our only hope, sir!'

Eventually the little craft was secured alongside, and the portly gentleman and his comrades were helped up into the *Beagle*.

'Richard Bathurst at your service, sir,' gasped the man. 'British consul-general in Monte Video. Allow me the honour of grasping your hand. May I introduce to your acquaintance Señor Dumas, the police chief of Monte Video.'

Señor Dumas made the position clear. 'There is mutiny in the city. President Lavalleja is away in Colonia, and the commander of troops here in Monte Video has seized power in his absence. He has opened the gaol and armed all the prisoners. They have occupied the citadel – the seat of government. It is a military *coup d'état*.'

'What do these soldiers desire to bring about with their *coup d'état*?' asked FitzRoy.

'Some wish for the reinstatement of President Rivera, who was overthrown by President Lavalleja. The Brazilian soldiers want the city returned to Brazil. The soldiers from the United Provinces want the city to become part of the United Provinces. The Uruguayan soldiers want it to remain part of Uruguay, although some of them want the country to revert to its old name of "Banda Oriental". The black soldiers want the slaves to be freed. They want many things. Please, Captain, you must help us. Only you can help us.'

'I feel for your predicament, Señor Dumas, but you must realize that I simply cannot interfere in South American politics. As captain of one of His Majesty's ships, I must maintain a strict neutrality at all times.'

'I don't think you understand, sir,' said Bathurst, who was still panting for breath. 'There are British families in the city whose lives and property are at risk. British women and children, sir, whose honour is at the mercy of these villains.'

'That changes the position. Then, sir, my forces are entirely at your disposal. How many are the mutineers?'

'Approximately six hundred, including the freed prisoners.'

'I can muster some seventy men all told.'

'We are four, sir, plus perhaps the same number in the city.'

'All stout men, sir, all stout men,' volunteered the third member of the party, a brisk elderly gentleman with a fierce military moustache, who had armed himself with a broom handle.

'I say – Colonel Vernon?' Darwin came forward, recognizing the voice.

'Good Lord – it's young Darwin, isn't it?'

'You know each other?'

'Know each other?' barked the colonel. 'More than that, sir! We have ridden to hounds together!'

'Colonel Vernon is the brother-in-law of Miss Gooch,' explained Darwin hurriedly, as if that clarified matters. 'But what are you doing here, sir?'

'I am making a tour of South America. I intend travelling by land to Lima, and so by Mexico back to Europe. May I introduce Mr Martens, who is the son of the Austrian consul to London? He is an artist travelling independently.'

'Delighted to make your acquaintance, gentlemen,' said Martens, a short, fine-boned character with coppery sideburns and a pugnacious expression.

'Gentlemen, please, time is pressing,' said FitzRoy, with a trace of exasperation. 'Where are the British families now?'

'They have taken refuge in the customs house on the mole.'

'Then our first task will be to stow them safely in the *Beagle*. They shall have the officers' cabins. Mr Bennet, prepare the ship's boats for their passage. Mr Chaffers, you will take charge of the *Beagle*. Trice up the boarding netting, load the guns and aim them at the shore. Should anyone approach who is not of our party, you have my permission to blow them to kingdom come. Mr Sulivan, you will organize a platoon of fifty men to be armed with muskets, pistols and cutlasses. Mr Bos'n, open the armoury, if you please. We shall make the best of our way to the fort, and attempt to secure it. I think it constitutes the key to the city. If we can but hold the fort and the harbour, then we shall be impossible to dislodge, and we shall control the approaches to Monte Video by land

and sea. The mutineers will have met no resistance as yet, so they will in all probability have relaxed their guard. They may even, if we are fortunate, have begun to celebrate their success somewhat prematurely. At any rate, we shall give them a substantial argument to convince them that they must not plunder British property.'

Darwin's admiration for the man redoubled. There are times when certainty *is* of paramount importance, he concluded, and this is one of them. British women were at risk, British women like Fanny Wedgwood, whose lives he could help FitzRoy to save. He would rather follow FitzRoy with fifty men, he realized, than anybody else with five hundred. And follow him he would, with a musket in one hand, a pistol in the other and a cutlass between his teeth.

'The very best of luck, sir! Give them hell, sir!' said Jemmy Button, warmly, appearing at the edge of the group in his morning-coat and kid gloves.

'I say,' murmured Colonel Vernon, 'is that an *Indian*?'

'A Fuegian Indian, yes,' confirmed Darwin.

'Extraordinary.'

The men of the *Beagle* formed up on the mole between a rickety line of dockside cranes and a collapsing row of wooden sheds opposite. There they began their march into the city, through the long narrow avenues that followed the line of the peninsula. The river was a constant presence, a deeper brown here than at Buenos Ayres, but catching the sun, a dark rectangle glittering to left and right at every intersection. Legions of rats scattered at their progress, darting from their hiding-places in the mounds of vegetables, offal and stale fruit that lay strewn across the cobbles. Although the occasional crack of gunfire could be heard echoing down side-streets, there was no sign of the mutineers, who remained barricaded in the citadel. The city appeared empty, save for the occasional carrion, human and bovine, and the rodents busily gorging themselves upon it. The citizens, who were well used to such episodes, had wisely disappeared into their houses. The sailors could hear the eerie percussion of their own marching footsteps reverberating back from the walls, an intrusion that sounded almost impolite in the quiet, narrow lanes.

Beyond the moated, muddy walls of the city, the bay curved round to the west, where it swept up into the towering headland that gave Monte Video its name. There, atop the peak, sat the Fortaleza del Cerro, a white, elegant beacon risen above the chaos. The rough track to the fort was deserted. It took them a full two hours to march its length, FitzRoy striding grimly at their head. Darwin, who had matched him stride for stride with manly enthusiasm at the outset, began to sweat uncomfortably in his top-coat and thick woollen waistcoat, but he was determined at all costs to keep up. Bathurst, the consul-general, panted by his side, his little legs working like pistons.

Really, if its defenders had been determined, the fort would have been impervious to any sort of attacking force, unless supported by several men-of-war with heavy cannon. Certainly their approach – in fact, their entire progress around the bay – could have been spotted from the battlements without much trouble. But FitzRoy had been correct in his surmise: when they reached the edge of musket range he sent scouts forward, who reported that the fort's gates were flung wide open. The building was guarded by just two men, both of them insensibly drunk by the looks of it and fast asleep. Six stealthy matlows were dispatched, who overwhelmed the guards and placed them under arrest. Within the quarter-hour, the *Beagle* party had taken possession of the fort.

FitzRoy and Sulivan strode out on to the high, flat roof and sized up the situation. A magnificent panorama presented itself. A distant church bell struck three at that moment, and the little white city set on its jutting finger of rock in the sunshine looked for all the world as if it were at peace with itself.

'What do you say, Mr Sulivan? Two miles and a half as the crow flies? Well within the range of these sixty-four pounders?'

'Absolutely, sir,' grinned Sulivan. 'They're sitting ducks.'

The fort's big guns, trained west and south to deter invasion by land and sea, were hauled round to the eastern side to face the citadel. Now the picturesque vista was gated off by the stark black silhouettes of the gun barrels, arrayed in parallel lines along the battlements. Geometric pyramids of cannonballs were hastily assembled at their base, proclaiming a veritable abundance of ammunition.

'Señor Dumas?'

'*¿Capitan?*'

'I should be very much obliged if you would lead a deputation to the mutineers. Kindly inform them that the Royal Navy has taken possession of the fort and the harbour, and that HMS *Druid* shall return from Buenos Ayres on the morrow. Their position is hopeless. They have until nightfall to return to their barracks, after which no more will be said about the incident. If, however, they fail to comply, I will begin shelling the citadel at first light. And when HMS *Druid* appears, I shall signal to her to do likewise.'

Dumas scurried off to carry out his appointed task. There was nothing left to do but to blockade the main gate, post sentries and wait. A store of juicy beefsteaks was located in the kitchens, which were cooked up in the little courtyard, and washed down with flagons of beer from the cellar.

Munching hungrily on a fat steak, Darwin was swept by a sense of exhilaration at their easy victory, coupled with a faint, muddled tinge of disappointment that FitzRoy had avoided bloodshed once again. Oh, to have *really* tested himself as a sportsman, to have potted a swarthy mutineer or two!

Colonel Vernon strolled over, a massive slab of grilled beef in one hand.

'A very good afternoon to you, Colonel,' said Darwin politely. 'And how are you enjoying your tour?'

'Well, to be quite frank, my dear chap, I hadn't thought Uruguay up to much before today. But now I realize that the place is capital – simply *capital*!'

The next day passed as if the revolt had never occurred. The mutineers had accepted FitzRoy's offer, sobered up, and returned to barracks. For the citizens of Monte Video, life returned to normal, if indeed there had been anything abnormal about the previous day's events. President Lavalleja returned from Colonia, and announced that FitzRoy would be fêted at a grand restoration ball, to be held at the Teatro Solis. The streets were mysteriously cleared of debris, the shops were opened, and the ladies of Monte Video recommenced their elegant daily promenade through the streets, in their close-fitting gowns and black silk veils. Veils that concealed not just their heads and shoulders but one eye as well, leaving the other to flutter its dark, enticing invitation; or so it seemed to Darwin and Hamond, who sat in the Plaza Independencia with Augustus Earle, admiring the spectacle.

'They are veritable angels,' groaned Darwin, as one lady sashayed by, her skirts clinging to the outline of her hips as she passed. 'And most demure – the veil is a most demure touch. They are gentlewomen, there is no question of that.'

'They d-do not walk, they g-glide,' moaned Hamond.

'It makes one realize how foolish many Englishwomen are, who know neither how to walk nor to dress.'

'How ugly the word "m-miss" sounds after "s-senorita".'

'It would do the whole tribe of Englishwomen a great deal of good to come to South America. The grace of these Spanish ladies is almost…well, *spiritual*.'

Augustus Earle said nothing, but did not take his eyes off the view.

Darwin and Hamond had occasion to continue their conversation the following Saturday night at the Teatro Solis, where they sat in a gilded box observing the whirling dance-floor below. The ladies of Monte Video had exchanged their silken veils and slinky gowns for ostentatious hair-combs and the most extravagant peacock gowns, which – from above – unfurled as swirling rosettes with every swing of the wearers' hips. The music was slower than at an English ball, and the dancing more formal, but it was one-on-one: there were no linked arms, no set-tos, no bow-and-curtsies. The dancers seemed to stare into each other's eyes with a studied ardour. There was something unsettling about the cool, intense formality of it all, and Darwin began to feel hot under the collar. He noticed Augustus Earle, who had somehow managed to secure himself a dancing partner, advancing boldly through the fray. It was hard to say which was the more irritating: that Earle knew the steps, that he had bothered to shave and spruce himself up (the first time he had done so in many months), or that he had found a partner with such apparent ease.

'That man,' observed Darwin, who after several months' abstinence had drunk rather too well, 'is unduly forward.'

'He has m-missed his step?' said the equally inebriated Hamond, misunderstanding.

'I mean, I fear that his intentions towards that good lady might not be as...respectful of her honour as she might wish.'

Earle's dancing partner chose that moment to throw back her head and let out a lascivious laugh, soundless above the blare of the orchestra.

'The way her hair is b-brushed back into a b-bow...reminds me of a p-painting of the Virgin I once saw. She has the s-same innocence.'

'And yet anybody here might ask her to dance. Anybody! There is no master of the ceremonies. The arrangements of the house are quite unsatisfactory.' Darwin warmed to his theme. 'The event is entirely open – *entirely* open – to the lowest classes of society, and yet nobody seems to have imagined the possibility of disorderly conduct on their parts. How different are the habits of Englishmen, on such jubilee nights!'

'Quite d-different.'

Augustus Earle had succeeded in snaking one arm round his uncomplaining partner's waist.

'One might fear for public decorum at such an event!' Darwin grumbled.

'Perhaps they are happy b-because they are not d-dead. All my friends are d-dead,' said Hamond, balefully, taking another gulp of lemon shrub.

'That's true. They could have been killed in the revolution. *We* could have been killed in the revolution.'

'We could all d-drown in the south.'

'We could indeed.'

This particular thought crystallized, hard, in the mist of Darwin's drunken reasoning. He could have died in the mutiny. Thank heaven FitzRoy had avoided a firefight. He might, as Hamond had so graphically put it, drown in the south. But he wasn't ready for heaven yet.

'If we d-drown, do you think we shall g-go to heaven?' Hamond had read his thoughts.

'Of course we shall.'

But would he? Had he not doubted the scriptures? Had he not questioned the Biblical account of the flood? Would the Lord not damn him in the hereafter on account of his presumption? Should he not atone, now, before it became too late?

'Hamond?'

'Yes?'

'Do you think there must be an English chaplain here, in Monte Video?'

'Of c-course. There is an English chaplain in every m-major city.'

'Do you feel it would be wise to have the sacrament of the Lord's Supper administered to us previous to journeying south?'

'What – right now?'

'When else? We set sail on the morrow. It is an ordinance that many see as a vow to lead a better life – a vow that might stand one in good order with the Lord.'

'I s-see what you mean.'

And so it was, after a few discreet enquiries, that two somewhat confused gentlemen – fortified still further, following their earlier conversation – could be seen hammering on the door of a house in the Avenida Bolivar, in the small hours of Sunday.

'He's taking an unconsciably long time. An unconsciousonably long time.'

'Perhaps he's s-sleeping.'

'It *is* a Sunday morning.'

Finally, they heard the sound of bolts being scraped back, and the door creaked open. A bushy-eyebrowed gentleman in a nightcap and gown stood before them, peering irascibly through the yellow glow of an oil lamp.

'*¿Qué diablos quieres decir con, golpeando mi puerta a esta hora?*'

'Reverendo Mr Maynard? We are British.'

'I said what the devil do you mean, hammering on my door at this hour?'

'We were h-hoping you might administer the Holy S-Sacrament. In case we d-drown.'

'It wants twenty to two in the morning!'

'We appreciate the lateness of the hour, sir, but it is most – *most* important that you administer the Holy Sacrarament, so that we do not go to hell.'

'To hell? That is precisely where you deserve to go, waking decent gentlemen at all hours of the night! Get out of here at once, before I call the watch, do you hear? Go to hell indeed, sir! Good night, gentlemen – if I may call you that!'

Maynard withdrew and slammed the door loudly in their faces, leaving the pair alone in the darkened street.

'Hamond?'

'Y-yes?'

'I don't think that went particularlarly well.'

The Patagonian shore lay low on the horizon, no more than an ill-defined smudge of blue on the starboard beam. The *Beagle* plunged through the swell, holding her course loosely, sacrificing navigational precision for speed, lest any rudder adjustments slow her progress. FitzRoy was keen to get south, to carry out the task in hand. They had been delayed quite enough by indiscriminate gunfire, by army mutinies and by grand celebrations. The fossils had been successfully dispatched to England and the decks were pristine once more – how Wickham would have approved, had he been present. A repentant Darwin lay curled on the chart table in the throes of sickness, as so often before, except that this time the sea had little to do with his condition. Hamond, who was in a similar state, could enjoy no such luxury, but instead suffered in silence at his station, a pale, dull-headed presence on the maindeck. His only consolation, perhaps, was that his condition did not stand out, for it was the first morning of official winter beard growth. With the breeze getting up, and drizzle flecking their faces, all the crew sported rough coats, greased boots, southwesters and a day's stubble.

There were exceptions to this grimy parade, of course: Jemmy Button could be seen promenading around the deck in a dress-coat of well-brushed scarlet broadcloth, a cravat, a fob watch and his favourite white kid gloves. He had manfully sweated his way through the tropics in this and similar outfits, and now that the weather had cooled down was reaping the reward for his persistence. All knew, however, that the smallest blemish on his boots, the faintest smear of tar or grease, would send him scurrying below, to where Messrs Day and Martin kept the officers' shoe-cleaning materials. Jemmy was also clean-shaven, and York likewise, for the Fuegians concurred with the better elements of British society in regarding facial hair as rather primitive, more a matter for beasts than for men; although these days, of course, the two Fuegians used a razor, rather than plucking out each hair with a sharpened mussel-shell. As for their mentor, the Reverend Mr Matthews, he, too, wore no beard for the simple reason that he had tried and failed to grow one.

The only member of the crew who would naturally have sported any facial growth, Augustus Earle, had suddenly left the ship in Monte Video. Officially, the artist had cited advancing rheumatism, a condition that would not have benefited from the bleak chill of a southern summer, but many suspected that a certain competing attraction in the Uruguayan capital had also influenced his decision. His last-minute replacement, the little Anglo-Austrian Conrad Martens, now sat in the lee of the poop deck, wrapped in a tight Petersham coat, completing a topographical sketch of the coastline. Fuegia Basket, still religiously attired in her increasingly shabby royal bonnet, peered over his shoulder for a moment, then skipped up the companionway to hold York Minster's hand. As she did so, Mr Matthews stepped diplomatically to the other side of the burly Indian. For all his attempts to ingratiate himself with the Fuegians, he had learned the hard way that it was not a good idea to cross the invisible line separating York from his beloved.

'What are you doing?' Fuegia asked Sulivan, who was standing at the rail with a spyglass, jotting down notes with a metallic pencil.

'I'm keeping a geological record of the coastline. I'm writing down all the stones. For the philosopher, who is too sick to do it himself.'

He showed her his pad, upon which he had scribbled: '*Thick white layer. Chalk? Pumiceous? Layer of porphyry pebbles above.*'

'Poor, poor Philos,' said Jemmy. 'He does not like when the boat goes up and down.'

'Absolutely,' said Sulivan, sparing Darwin's blushes as to the real cause of his sickness.

'My confidential friend Mr Bynoe will make him better. He has many good medicines.' Jemmy had taken to calling Bynoe his 'confidential friend' after trying out various of his remedies for stomach upsets and minor ailments. In fact, so impressed had Jemmy been with Bynoe's assortment of jars and bottles that the incidence of his supposed illnesses had escalated dramatically. It was a rare day indeed when he could not be seen marching proudly from the sickbay with a phial of Gregory's powder, calomel or some other such purgative.

Suddenly York seized Sulivan by the arm, his normally implacable features lit up by surprise. 'Look, Mr Sulivan, look! A bird, all same as a horse!'

'Where?' Sulivan spun round.

'There! Running on beach! A bird, all same as a horse!'

'On the beach?' Even Sulivan, with his astonishingly keen vision, could barely make out the beach, let alone any details thereon. 'Do you see anything, Jemmy?'

'Oh yes Mr Sulivan, a big bird. It is running fast. It is a tip-top goer!'

'Bird all same as a horse!' parroted Fuegia Basket.

'Blessed if I know what they're talking about,' said a peevish Matthews, squinting at the horizon.

Sulivan raised his spyglass to one eye and scanned the distant shore from left to right. Then, as he scanned back again – there! He saw it. A large male rhea, scampering into the shallows, its powerful thigh-muscles flexing and unflexing with every stride.

'It's a rhea, York, an American ostrich. But that you could see it from here! Captain FitzRoy – an incredible thing, sir.'

FitzRoy came over, and was apprised of the astonishing discovery – made a full two and a half years after they had first come aboard – that the Fuegians' powers of eyesight were well beyond those of normal men.

'I have heard tell of such birds, sir,' said Jemmy dismissively. 'In the land of the Oens-men they are common-or-garden.'

York glared at Jemmy, who took a nervous step behind the tall figure of Sulivan.

There is so much that we do not know about them, thought FitzRoy. *I have been so determined to bring them forward into our world that I have neglected to study what makes their own world so different, so special.*

'Does everybody in your country have such powerful eyesight, Jemmy?'

'Of course, Capp'en Fitz'oy. My tribe is a good tribe, see very far. My country is a good country. Plenty of trees. Plenty of seals. When you see Woollya, you will say, "This is a beautiful country, as beautiful as Great Britain."'

Jemmy favoured FitzRoy with a warm, proud smile. FitzRoy smiled back.

He has not seen his country for nigh on three years, he thought. *By the Lord's grace, I hope he shall not be in for a rude shock.*

CHAPTER THREE

Good Success Bay, Tierra del Fuego, 17 December 1832

The *Beagle* nosed cautiously into a thick bank of alabaster fog. Even here, in the safest anchorage on the east coast of Tierra del Fuego, it was as well to be careful. Since its discovery by Captain Cook in the previous century, the bay had yet to be surveyed properly, so the little brig felt her way forward, her decks cool and damp in the waxy air of the early morning, her sails hanging limp. Momentary eddies in the mist revealed only the dark, featureless forest: scores of fallen beech trees lay uncleared amid the ranks of their silent fellows, like a battalion of foot-soldiers cut down by musket fire, frozen for ever at the moment of impact. The vegetation was as thick as in any tropical jungle, yet here it was drained of all colour and movement. In these solitudes death, not life, seemed the predominant spirit.

Their voyage south had taken them through a series of startling natural phenomena, as if nature wished to signal that the boundaries of human civilization had been crossed, that they were entering her domain. Each spectacle had been more extraordinary than the last. Not far south of the river Plate, they had woken one morning to find the *Beagle* turned red. The entire ship was covered from topmast to keel by miniature crimson spiders, millions upon millions of them, each furiously competing to trace out its gossamer web in the calm morning air. The first breath of wind had blown them all out to sea in an agitated red cloud, never to be seen again. Then, off the Bay of San Blas, it had snowed butterflies. A vast white cloud of fluttering wings two hundred yards high, a mile wide and several miles deep had enveloped the ship. Fuegia Basket had stood in the heart of the blizzard, twirling and flapping her arms with delight. They were, calculated Darwin, a variety of *Colias edusa*. But what had caused these huge migrations? The animals were hurtling to their destruction, but to what end? It was hard to see a purpose, divine or otherwise, in this almighty extermination.

Near the entrance to the Straits of Magellan the sea itself had turned crimson: the cause, they soon determined, a monstrous shoal of tiny crustaceans. But more impressive still were the humpback whales that twisted and churned at the centre of the maelstrom, gorging themselves on their infinitesimal prey by the ton. One great beast flung himself almost completely out of the water, landing with a magnificent crash that sent a shudder through the hull of the *Beagle*; and Darwin remembered Midshipman King, and his earnest claims made out on the verandah of the little house at Corcovado, and he wished then that he had not seen fit to doubt his young chum.

This clammy morning in Good Success Bay found a quiet, solitary figure up at the cathead, half enveloped in mist. Bynoe, taking his morning constitutional around the deck – as surgeon he was spared the discomfort of night watches – spotted Jemmy Button there, and sensed at once from the Fuegian's defeated posture that something was wrong.

'Jemmy? Are you all right?'

'My confidential friend.'

The greeting was not delivered in Jemmy's usual effusive style; rather, it came out in a husky croak, and Bynoe could see that his eyes were rimmed with wet.

'Jemmy? Have you been crying? What is the matter?'

'My father is dead.'

'Your father…? What makes you think that?'

'A man came beside my hammock in the night. He told me.'

'What man? York Minster?' Jemmy and York messed together, forward with the crew. Fuegia, for obvious reasons, slept aft at the officers' end of the ship.

'No, not York Minster. A man.'

'A crewman?'

'Not man from this world, Mr Bynoe. A man from this other world.'

'That's a dream, Jemmy, just a dream.'

Jemmy shook his head. 'No, my confidential friend. Not a dream. A man from this other world. My father is dead. It is very bad.' He reached up and wiped the corner of his eye with his sleeve.

'Jemmy...I am sure that when we get back to Woollya you will see that your father is alive and well. Mark my words.'

Jemmy smiled, with pity and affection combined, at Bynoe's lack of understanding; and the surgeon could not think of anything else to say.

Further along the rail, FitzRoy scanned the curtain of white and called for another depth sounding. Forty fathoms, came back the reply, and clean sand as before. Still, the billowing fog would reveal nothing. Darwin came to join him, glad of the chance to be up and about at last.

'My dear FitzRoy, whatever do you look like in that beard? It has become quite patriarchal!'

'Much like yourself, I should imagine.'

'I? I resemble nothing so much as a half-washed chimney-sweeper!' Darwin grasped his own enormous beard, leaving a gingery tuft protruding from his clenched fist. 'What a pair we must make. Tell me, my dear friend, shall I have a chance to explore the beech forest?'

'Of course, when the fog lifts. But be careful. Stick to the guanaco paths. When Cook was here, Mr Banks and Dr Solander mounted an expedition into the forest and became lost. Then night fell, and two of the men died of cold. Solander himself was lucky to escape with his life. I should not wish the same fate to befall our own dear Philosopher.'

'Rest assured, I—'

Darwin's next words were cut off by a blood-curdling cry from the forest. It was a human cry – at least, he thought it was a human cry – but it seemed to him an utterly primeval sound, a harsh, rudimentary cry left over from the dawn of creation. Then, as if on cue, the milky curtain parted to reveal the source of the noise. There, not eighty yards distant, on a wild crag overhanging the sea, perched a small group of naked Fuegians. As they became visible to the *Beagle*'s crew, so they became aware of the ship and sprang up, gesticulating and yelling, their long hair streaming, each of them waving their tattered guanaco-skin cloaks. In answer to their calls, other ragged, yelling creatures emerged from the entangled forest, until the little crag was clustered with frantic, energized figures. One young Fuegian, his face daubed black with a single white band, began to hurl stones, as if to drive the *Beagle* away, but of course the projectiles fell well short of their intended target.

'My God,' breathed Darwin. 'They are naked. Absolutely naked, in this inclement country. I had never, ever imagined anything like this. It is incredible.'

Those who had not journeyed south on the first voyage were transfixed. Hamond stood open-mouthed at the rail. Matthews, although he kept his feelings in check, could not disguise his fascination. Those like FitzRoy, who knew the Fuegians well, watched the watchers, riveted to see again their own initial reactions.

'Look – look at that one on the right!' Darwin pointed out an older man, with circles of white paint round his eyes, his upper lip daubed with red ochre, his tangled hair gathered in a fillet of white feathers. 'He is like a stage devil from *Der Freischutz*! My God, FitzRoy, they are demoniacs! They are like – like the troubled spirits of another world!'

'They are no worse than I supposed them to be,' said Matthews piously.

Hamond shook his head sadly. 'What a p-pity such fine fellows should be left in such a b-barbarous state.'

'Fine fellows?' Darwin raised his eyebrows. 'I would hardly dignify them with the description "fine fellows". They are hideous! Their growth is stunted, their features are literally beastly, their skin is red and filthy, their hair is greasy and tangled, their voices are discordant and their gestures are violent! To think Rousseau believed that savages in a state of nature would lead idyllic lives! Why, if the world was searched, no lower grade of men could be found. They are barbarians, my dear Hamond, utter barbarians!'

'They are ignorant and savage, perhaps,' said FitzRoy softly, 'but not contemptible. Does not the example of our friend Jemmy here indicate what may be done to improve their lot?'

For the first time, the officers at the rail turned to look at Jemmy. His face, they realized, was burning with shame and humiliation.

'Philos is right,' he said, jabbing out each word. 'These men are not men. They are beasts. Fools. My land is quite different. My tribe is quite different. You will see. My friends will be happy to see Capp'en Fitz'oy. My friends will honour Capp'en Fitz'oy, will honour all *Beagle*. These men are *beasts*.'

Four days later, Darwin arrived at dinner clutching a copy of Commodore Byron's *Narrative*; it was an uncannily calm and sunny day off Cape Horn, and Bynoe's skill as a marksman had provided their table with a fat roast steamer duck each.

'So much for the famous Horn,' remarked Darwin breezily. 'A gale of wind is not so bad in a good sea-boat. Have you read this?'

'I suggest you wait until we ship a sea or two before you write off the famous Horn,' replied FitzRoy drily. 'And yes, I have.'

'Not only are these Fuegians of yours cannibals, it would seem they practise incest and bigamy as well. After the shipwreck Byron lived with a native who had two wives, one of whom was his daughter! And he beat them both regularly! Poor Byron was treated as a dog – quite literally. They fed him on scraps.'

'Disagreeable as it is to contemplate a savage, Philos, and unwilling as we may be to consider ourselves even remotely descended from human beings in such a state, remember that Caesar found the Ancient Britons painted and clothed in skins exactly like the Fuegians.'

'Worst of all,' said Darwin, ignoring him, 'is this passage here:

> "A little boy of about three years old, watching for his father and mother's return, ran into the surf to meet them; the father handed a basket of sea-eggs to the child, which being too heavy for him to carry, he let it fall; upon which the father jumped out of the canoe, and catching the boy up in his arms, dashed him with the utmost violence against the stones. The poor little creature lay motionless and bleeding, and died soon after. The brute his father shewed little concern about it."

Was a more horrid deed ever perpetrated? They are the most grotesque race. I feel quite a disgust at the very sound of the voices of these miserable savages!'

'Forgive me, Philos, but I think you are wrong to distinguish them as a race. I think there is more variance between any two individuals than between the different races. Could three more distinct individuals exist than Jemmy, York and Fuegia? Yet are any of them so very different from Englishmen you have met?'

'Well, it is true that I could scarcely have believed how wide was the difference between a savage and a civilized man. It is more strikingly marked than between a wild animal and a domesticated pet! But is that not what you have done with your three savages – tamed them, like dogs? They do not yet appear to boast of human reason or of the arts consequent to that reason. Take these very ducks, here. What was it York Minster said, when Bynoe shot them? "Oh, Mr Bynoe, now much rain, much snow, blow much." It appears the steamer duck is some sort of sacred animal to him! He considers the elements themselves to be avenging angels! Only in a race so little advanced could the elements become personified so. It is absurd.'

'If you will suffer me to object, Philos, you say they are backward, and do not share all our qualities, but what of their own qualities? What of their astonishing gift for mimicry? They can instantly memorize and repeat several lines of an alien tongue!'

'Come now, that is merely a consequence of the more practised habits of perception, and the keener senses, common to all men in a savage state.'

'What of their unique powers of eyesight?'

'They live upon the sea! It is well known that sailors, from long practice, can make out a distant object better than a landsman.'

'What of their powers of intuition?'

'Such powers are more strongly marked in women, as well as being characteristic of the lower races. They are powers characteristic of a past and lower state of civilization. Does not man achieve a higher eminence, in whatever he takes up, than a woman can attain? There is your proof.'

'You continue to speak of the "lower races". There are no such things. Genesis one, twenty-six: "And God said let us make man in our image." There is nothing in the scriptures about lower men. Genesis nine, nineteen: By the three sons of Noah "was the whole earth overspread". Esau begat the copper-coloured race, with the daughter of Ishmael. No doubt the climate, and their diet, and their habit of living have all helped to adapt them, but they are men, Philos, just as you and I.' *Please, my friend, it feels as if I am losing you. Please turn back before it is too late, for this way blasphemy lies.*

'My dear FitzRoy, the races may have been *conceived* in equality, but who would deny that they are now utterly distinct and utterly unequal? The emotional and intellectual faculties of the Fuegian Indian have been diminished. Their language scarcely deserves to be called articulate – it sounds like a man clearing his throat. Even their gestures are unintelligible! If, as you say, they have been rendered hideous by cold, want of food and lack of civilization, then have they not *become* a lower race? What skills they have may now be compared to the instinct of animals, for they do not seem to be improved by experience. Their canoes, for instance, have not changed at all since Byron wrote his book a hundred years ago.'

'The fact that their society has degenerated does not make them a lesser race. They are innocent, that is all – innocent of so much. What of the English, when the Romans left our shores? Were we then a "lesser race"? Progress is a social ideal, not a measure of physical development. History is not by definition a process of improvement.'

'You think not? I tell you, FitzRoy, at some future period, not very distant I imagine, the civilized races of man will almost certainly exterminate and replace the savage races throughout the world. It is already happening. Wherever the European has trod, death pursues the Aboriginal. Varieties of man act upon each other as do species of animal. The strong extirpate the weak. There is nothing we can do about it.'

'Yes, there is. I have tried in my small way to do something about it. I do not compete with the Fuegians. I support and encourage them because I am a Christian and such is God's command.'

'But not all men are as upright, as dedicated to God's truth as you are, my dear friend. Already the Europeans are reaching further south, beyond Punta Alta. The Fuegians cannot survive, just as the Aborigines of Australia cannot survive, or any other of the degraded races of blacks. And when the higher apes, the anthropomorphous apes, are exterminated in turn, then the divide between man and the animal kingdom will be even greater, and civilized man will reign supreme.'

'What do you mean, "the divide between man and the animal kingdom will be even greater"? How can it become greater, or lesser?'

'I mean the gap between the Caucasian and the lower apes – such as the baboon – is greater than the gap between, say, the Negro and the gorilla.'

'What are you saying? I cannot believe you are saying this!'

'Come, FitzRoy. Look at the orang-utan – its affection, its passion, its rage, its sulkiness, its despair. Then look at the savage – naked, artless, roasting its parent. Your Fuegians remind me of nothing so much as an orang-utan taking tea at the zoological gardens. Compare the Fuegian and the orang-utan and *dare* to say that the difference is so great.'

FitzRoy was angry now.

'Oh, I *dare* to say that, Philos, I *dare* indeed. We humans – notice how I use the word *we* – walk on two legs; the apes – be they "higher" or "lower" – walk on four. We humans feel love and affection, and reason, and shame, and embarrassment, and pride. The apes have only a breeding season, a cycle of sexual receptiveness. We have a complex vocal language. They do not. We are, in the main, hairless. They are covered from head to toe in fur. They are *animals*. You can civilize a human, *as I have proved*. You cannot take an orang-utan to enjoy a civilized conversation with His Majesty the King of England.'

'My dear FitzRoy, I can see that I have angered you. I do not set up for one second to deny that man is created by God to reign over the animals, that the two are utterly separate, that there can be no transmutation between one and the other. As I told you, I have no truck with Lamarck. I meant only that the Fuegians have fallen so far as to *adopt* some of the ways of the animal kingdom. They seem to exist, for instance, in a state of equality like a herd of cattle; a way of living that can only retard civilization and prevent improvement. And man here is in a lower state of improvement than in any other part of the world.'

FitzRoy did not know whether to make concessions to Darwin's conciliatory tone or go on the attack; but he was saved from the need to decide by a knock at the door.

It was Sulivan. 'I'm afraid it begins to look pretty filthy to westward, sir. The barometer is falling. I think you had better come on deck.'

FitzRoy rose. 'Well, Philos. It seems you spoke too soon about the famous Horn.'

What had begun as an ominous line of inky clouds on the western horizon was to become a twenty-four-day nightmare for the crew of the *Beagle*, as gale after gale pinned them just to the west of Cape Horn. Pummelling winds and relentless seas battered them day and night, until everyone and everything in the ship was drenched. At the end of each watch the exhausted men, with no dry clothes to change into, turned in 'full standing': bones aching, they retreated to their soaking hammocks still wrapped in their sopping oilskins, and fell asleep in an instant.

The temperature plummeted. Even though it was supposedly the middle of summer, the watch on deck were whipped by sharp snowflakes and stung by driving hail. It was impossible to stand upright below decks, and almost as difficult on deck, where the planking had become a slippery sheet of ice. Masts, spars, rigging, everything was sheathed in a thick icy coat, which had to be continually chipped off at severe risk to life and limb. Even the officers of the watch froze into ghastly attitudes, their oilskins masked with ice, lashed to the wheel under a crazily swinging oil lamp. Great green rollers powered ceaselessly aboard, a good foot of water coursing freely through the gunports, but the momentary relief such waves afforded, being warmer than the air, was soon lost as further layers of ice crusted quickly on the men's clothes.

In the poop cabin behind the wheel, Darwin lay in a permanent pool of vomit, his specimens ruined, his dried-flower collection a sodden mess. Christmas came and went, and New Year too, but nobody noticed. There was no sign of a let-up in the mountainous breaking seas. Finally, on 13 January, through sheets of spray that obscured the horizon, they caught sight of the stark black tower of York Minster, their destination, looming amid driving clouds. They had come just a hundred miles in three and a half weeks.

'There she is, sir – jolly old York Minster!' yelled Bennet cheerily over the howling wind.

'Excellent!' FitzRoy was in a good mood. He had just been to inspect the chronometers with Stebbing. Oilskin thrown off, his head wrapped in a towel to prevent dripping, he had dried the glass top of each machine and scattered flour upon it. Then, through a magnifying glass, he had checked the grains for signs of vibration or slippage from the horizontal. Nothing. Every chronometer and every gimbal was in perfect working order.

'Biblical weather, ain't it, sir?' roared Sulivan.

'Now we know how Noah felt,' added Bennet. 'Do you think we shall have the full forty days and forty nights?'

'"In the morning thou shalt say, would God it were even. And at even thou shalt say, would God it were morning!"' Sulivan laughed out loud. FitzRoy gave silent thanks that the men of the *Beagle* were so indefatigable, so good-natured, whatever the obstacles placed in their way.

An albatross wheeled about the ship, gliding effortlessly against the buffeting wind. On each pass it would sweep gracefully down into the wave-troughs, breaking the occasional crest with an exploratory wingtip, before soaring up the face of the next rising arch, never once needing to flap its wings.

'That bird. How long has it been following us?' FitzRoy asked, disappearing up to his thighs in a surge of green seawater.

'As long as we've been on watch, sir.'

'And has it been flying clockwise about the ship throughout?'

'Yes sir. Leastways, I think they always do fly clockwise, sir.'

'I wonder – is that because of the magnetism of the earth? If one were to release an albatross in the northern hemisphere, would it fly anti-clockwise?'

'Shall we try to catch it, sir?'

'No, no. I do not wish to lose an officer to the cause of natural philosophy, however noble the enquiry. But it leads one to ponder the incredible migrations of birds, their astonishing sense of direction – might it be magnetic, do you think?'

Another peak furled across the deck, water blasting violently through the gunports. FitzRoy yelled into Sulivan's ear, 'Mr Sulivan, would you ask Mr May to have the gunports secured? Let us try to reduce the amount of water on deck. It is like trying to stand in a sluice.'

'Pardon me, sir, but do you think that is a good idea? The weather is worsening. If any really big waves get up, and the deck becomes flooded, fixed gunports could trap the water in the ship, sir.'

He indicated the line of cliffs off to the north-east, all of two hundred feet in height, where a vast battering surf was sending spray scattering over the cliff-tops.

'Let us put our faith in the old girl – she is more buoyant than she used to be,' insisted FitzRoy.

'Very well, sir.' And Sulivan rushed off in the gap between waves to locate the carpenter. He found May in the galley, desperately trying to warm himself against the scalding iron of Mr Frazer's patent closed stove.

'Mr May? Captain says you're to secure all the gunports.'

May sighed. Although hardly dry, he had at least steamed a little water out of his saturated clothing over the preceding two hours. Now he was to go back on deck, and give himself another soaking. 'Aye aye sir.'

'And Mr May?'

'Sir?'

Sulivan hesitated. He would never countenance disobeying any superior officer, but this was not exactly disobedience.

'Keep your handspike about you in case they need to be opened in a hurry.'

'Sir.'

On the way back up to the maindeck, Sulivan put his head round the door of FitzRoy's cabin to check on Edward Hellyer. It was the young clerk's first real storm.

'You all right, young man?'

'Yes sir, thank you, sir.' Hellyer, pale and scared, did not look at all convinced.

Sulivan glanced over the boy's shoulder at the ship's log. 'Hard at hand, I see,' he said approvingly, and scanned the boy's work. 'Well done, Mr Hellyer. That's first-rate. When we look back and argue about this here blow, your log is the place we'll come for all our answers. You're doing a splendid job.' He clapped Hellyer on the back and the lad seemed to brighten up, for the moment at least.

By the time half an hour had elapsed, it was clear that an already desperate situation was getting worse. FitzRoy's concern was for the masts, which for all their girth were straining like saplings. 'We must take the topgallant sails off her. She is careening to her bearings.'

Bos'n Sorrell resorted to the speaking-trumpet: 'Very well, my lads, very well indeed! Topgallants clewed up and furled!' In an instant the icy rigging was alive with dark shapes, carrying out the order with well-drilled precision.

'I fear, sir, we cannot carry the topsails much longer,' said Sulivan. He knew that FitzRoy liked to keep a main topsail and five reefs as a minimum, even in the worst weather, to ensure steerage way. But such a rig would be impossible to maintain any further: the wind was screaming through the rigging now, and increasingly mountainous seas were rising ominously beneath the ship. The boundary between sky and sea was becoming blurred: seething white froth filled the air, and breakers were hurling themselves continuously across the deck. FitzRoy gave orders to take her down to storm trysails, close-reefed. He was now barely in charge of the *Beagle*: the storm had all but wrested control of her.

The men were still in the rigging when they saw coming towards them, head-on, a vast, implacable cliff of grey water advancing at speed. *Dear God*, thought FitzRoy, *that wave is almost as tall as the boat is long. A monster*. The equation was simple. Any taller, and they would go down. Any less, and they might ride it. With mounting horror, he saw Nicholas White, the seaman clinging to the jib-boom end, disappear into the face of the wave a good fathom under, as the little brig tried desperately to climb its featureless slope. All on deck stood frozen with fear. The two men clinging to the staysail netting were next to disappear, as the wave swallowed the *Beagle*'s entire bow. But she was still rising, her deck sloping further and further back, until it seemed she must be catapulted vertically into the raging sky. Then, at last, she breasted the wave, and FitzRoy felt his stomach plummet with the ship as she surfed crazily down the other side. There was White, still alive, gasping on the jib-boom; there were the sailors on the staysail netting, spluttering and choking but indubitably alive.

Any relief FitzRoy might have felt was short-lived. Another towering, monstrous wave was racing in on the heels of the first, only this time the *Beagle*'s momentum had been checked, her way deadened. She sat motionless in the water, waiting for the impact. There was nothing anybody could do but pray, and hold on tight.

The wave crashed front-on into the bow with a sickening shudder. The ship trembled from end to end at the shock. A pulverizing mass of green smashed across the deck, driving the air from the sailors' gasping lungs. Darwin, who had been shivering in his hammock, too sick to sense the danger outside, suddenly found himself submerged, as a wall of freezing seawater blasted the library door from its hinges and engulfed him. Again the *Beagle* tried to rise up the face of the wave, but this time she was only partially successful. She slewed wildly to port before tipping crazily over the crest and careening sideways down the backslope. Not only was her momentum checked now, but she was sitting beam-on, dead at the helm and thrown off the wind. If a third wave came, she was a sitting duck.

All eyes squinted fearfully into the driving sleet, trying to separate the scudding black clouds from the maddened, frothing water. Then they saw it: a third wave, taller than a townhouse, towering over the *Beagle*, bearing down upon them. The ship lolled, helplessly, like a beaten drunk trying to stand up and throw a last punch. *We're going to drown. What is it like to drown?* was all that anybody aboard the *Beagle* could think.

Like a broadside of cannon from a mighty frigate, the wave smacked hard into the ship's side, its whole immense crushing weight pounding on to her deck. The world simply turned black. Men floundered and struggled and fought, not to keep their balance or their bearings but to live, just to live. Then the world cleared, but it had been turned on its side. The *Beagle* was on her beam-ends, her lee bulwark three feet under, and she was struggling unsuccessfully to rise again. The lee-quarter boat, a brand-new reinforced whaleboat constructed by Messrs William Johns of Plymouth on the diagonal principle, and mounted several feet higher than the whaleboats of the previous voyage, had filled with water and disintegrated as surely as if it had been made from pasteboard; but its new improved davits clung stubbornly to the *Beagle*, refusing to let go, the wreckage of the whaleboat threatening to drag its mother ship down into the lightless depths.

The port side of the deck was trapped several feet under, labouring under a colossal weight of water that could not escape, Sulivan realized, because of the sealed gunports. Through a faceful of blinding spray he saw FitzRoy, Bennet and a terrified Hamond at the lee quarter, helped by three ratings, hacking at the tangled whaleboat davits with hatchets; but at the bulwark there was only Carpenter May, up to his waist in water, struggling vainly with his handspike to free one of the secured gunports beneath the surface. Sulivan splashed frantically across the deck to May, seized the handspike, plunged into the frozen darkness, located the gunport, and with one burly heave, burst it wide open. Immediately, water surged out through the newly opened escape route, and slowly, very slowly, the *Beagle* began to right herself.

A fourth wave now, all of them knew, and they were dead men. Now, with the gunport open and the wreckage of the whaleboat cut adrift, all eyes looked to windward, screwed up against the blinding sleet, searching for the fourth and final instalment, the wave that would bring about their end. But it did not come. For twenty, thirty, forty seconds they waited, as the *Beagle* rose agonizingly back towards an even keel, staring into the maelstrom. But the fourth wave did not come.

'What would Captain Beaufort have called that, then? A force fifteen?' Sulivan was breezy and light-headed with relief. Driven almost back to

Cape Horn by the storm, they had run in behind False Cape Horn and sought refuge in the Goree Roads. There they had dropped anchor in forty-seven fathoms, friendly sparks flashing from the windlass as the chain hurtled round it, to rest and lick their wounds.

'I made a terrible mistake. You saved all our lives. After all the modifications I made to the *Beagle*, I thought...Well, the simple fact is, I was too proud.'

'Hang it, sir, that's tosh and you know it. You cannot blame yourself every time we run through a bad blow. It was the modifications that saved us. The old *Beagle* would have been crushed to matchwood. Yet not a spar was lost, nor a single man for that matter.'

'I should never have ordered the gunports secured. You were right and I was wrong.'

'The man has not been born, sir, who never makes a mistake,' responded Sulivan. 'All of us make mistakes, all the time. It is how one reacts to one's mistakes that is the measure of a man.'

'Put like that, Mr Sulivan, I suppose it does sound better,' conceded FitzRoy.

'That's more like it, sir. Now, shouldn't you be sitting here with charts and diagrams, trying to discover the measure of that storm?'

'There is no need. I have its measure already. You forget, I have had twenty-four days to think upon it.'

'And?'

'And the globe spins eastward. So does water, at a greater velocity – although with many a back-eddy. The atmosphere, which is almost free of obstacles, spins yet faster still. It too has back-eddies of wind, which articulate storm-breeding counter-spirals near the poles – together with a steady-flowing undertow at the equator – that's the trade winds. All the elements are pluming forward to the east, all of them by-products of the pull that affects the earth. You see? The weather may appear unpredictable, Mr Sulivan, but it is not. Its effects are complicated, but its core principle, as laid down by God, is blindingly simple. And if we understand the mechanical principle behind it, there is no reason to doubt that, one day, we shall be able to foretell the weather.'

FitzRoy had become increasingly animated as he warmed to his pet enthusiasm, the cares of leadership slipping visibly from his shoulders; Sulivan regretted that Darwin chose that very moment to march in and interrupt the captain's monologue.

'Good morning, Philos. I trust this lovely calm morning finds you well?'

Darwin stood and stared at FitzRoy as if he were quite mad to ask such a question, after all that they had endured. But having held the pose for a moment he relaxed suddenly, and shook his head in bemused wonderment.

'It's my own fault, I suppose, for agreeing to spend several years cooped up in your little cock-boat. All my papers and specimens are ruined – *all* of them – and not a few of my books. Luckily volume two of Lyell is unscathed, for I have not yet commenced it, as is my copy of *Persuasion*, for all that it is worth.'

FitzRoy roared with laughter. 'All of those unique specimens lost, and the means to interpret them, but you still have your Jane Austen! Why, we will turn you into a gossiping fishwife yet! Pray tell, Philos, why on earth you have such frivolities in your possession.'

'My sister Caroline packed it for me. It seems my family think you to be quite the Captain Wentworth, for some reason. And I suppose, after yesterday, that they are right.'

'Oh, but we have Mr Sulivan to thank for yesterday's heroics.'

'Not a bit of it!' protested Sulivan. 'But see here, Philos – I have brought you a present.' He leaned down under the table and produced a carefully wrapped box. 'Something else that survived yesterday's tribulations.'

'What is it?'

'The start of your new collection.'

Darwin unwrapped the packing and levered off the lid to reveal a sweetly glowing nasturtium flower – except that it was twice the size of any nasturtium he had ever seen before.

'It is a *Tropaeolum*. I discovered it in the Brazils. A *Tropaeolum majus*, I suppose, if its Peruvian cousin were to become the *minus*.'

'But, Sulivan, this is your very own specimen – I cannot possibly accept it as a gift!'

'You can, Philos, and you will. Thy need is greater than mine.'

'It is remarkable – wonderful! My dear fellow!'

'Mind you keep the little chap warm, now. I wedge him behind the galley stove at night, and stand him beneath the skylight by day.'

'You are too kind. I am overwhelmed.'

There was a knock at the door.

'Bless me,' murmured FitzRoy. 'The place is become like Regent Circus this morning. Come!'

FitzRoy's steward opened the door, and the three men could see the burly figure of York Minster silhouetted behind him.

'Er…Mr Minster, sir,' said the steward, unsure exactly as to how one might introduce such a 'gentleman'.

'Do come in, York, if you can find room.'

The Fuegian moved forward, as impassive as ever, although FitzRoy thought he detected a shade of contempt at the sight of three grown men sitting round a flower.

'I am sorry that we have failed to reach your homeland, York,' FitzRoy went on. 'Perhaps it was a mistake to try the direct route. But rest assured, I will get you there, either via the Magellan Straits and the Cockburn Channel, or by following the Beagle Channel westward to the sea. Here, let me show you a map.'

'York wishes not to go home.'

'I beg your pardon?'

'York wishes not to go home. York and Fuegia will live at Woollya with Jemmy, and Mister Matthews.'

'But the Woollya people are not of your tribe, York. That might be extremely dangerous, both for you and for her.'

'York wishes not to go home. York and Fuegia will live at Woollya with Jemmy, and Mister Matthews.'

There was silence in the little cabin. FitzRoy stared at York. Was he afraid of any further sailing? Would Matthews's mission represent a link to the world he was leaving behind? Or did he have some deeper plan? The Fuegian's face gave nothing away.

'Very well, York,' he said. 'So be it.'

*

They found the eastern entrance to the Beagle Channel easily enough, to the north of the Goree Roads, concealed behind Picton Island. There were thirty-three in the party, divided between the remaining three whaleboats: FitzRoy, Darwin, Bennet, Hamond, Bynoe, the Reverend Mr Matthews, the three Fuegians, and twenty-four sailors and marines. Sulivan had been left in command of the *Beagle*. Towed behind them was the yawl, into which had been loaded all the tools and implements needed to build the mission, together with the fabulous assortment of goods donated by the Church Missionary Society.

The early reaches of the channel were not as arrow-straight as the central section where they had discovered Jemmy, nor were the forested sides as vertiginous. There were settlements along the shore, where the arrival of three boatloads of pale-skinned human beings caused nothing less than a seismic shock. As they tacked slowly up the channel into the prevailing westerlies – the yawl being so overloaded that only sailpower could drag it forward – they saw panic-stricken, gasping men running at speed along the shore to spread news of their arrival. The runners were naked, their hair matted with clay and their faces decorated with white spots, and they ran so fast that blood poured from their noses and foam gurgled from their panting mouths. Canoes began to follow their progress at a distance, each marked by its distinctive plume of blue smoke.

'How incredible,' breathed Darwin, 'to go where man has never yet been.'

York sat back in the lead whaleboat, laughing immoderately. 'They are big monkeys. Fools! Ha ha ha!'

'These people are not my friends,' said Jemmy, his face a mask of shame. 'My friends are different. My friends are very good and clean.'

Fuegia, by contrast, was terrified, and after her first glimpse of the running men would not look again.

She has seen what she truly is, reflected Darwin.

The little girl buried her face in York's lap, her eyes screwed shut – which was a problem, as she had now become so fat that the sailors ideally wanted to shift her position to windward with each tack.

'Big monkeys! Fools!' shouted York, his taunts filling the echoing sound.

FitzRoy stared at Matthews, sitting vacantly in the stern, the breeze ruffling the down on his upper lip. *In many ways he is the fulcrum of all this activity. Yet he shows no emotion. There is no reluctance, no hesitation, but also no enthusiasm, no energy of character.*

Was Matthews steeling himself with quiet stoicism, sitting there in blank-faced silence, or was he just an unqualified teenage catechist, quaking on the inside? FitzRoy attempted the usually unrewarding task of making conversation with him.

'Mr Matthews, how are you looking forward to such a great challenge, which may very well become your life's work?'

'I fully intend that the natives shall receive all instruction in the principles of Christianity, sir, and in the simpler acts of civilised life.'

Another platitude. Surely the Church Missionary Society could have found someone more dynamic for their great enterprise? As they drew closer to their destination, FitzRoy's confidence in the chances of Matthews's success dwindled with every passing mile.

Darwin wiped a splash of seawater from his beard and stared at the youth. *He must be out of his mind*, he thought.

By the time the walls of the Beagle Channel narrowed, and it became recognizable as the ravine they had discovered almost three years previously, there were some thirty canoes in their wake, carrying at least three hundred Indians. Their pursuers stayed back, though – at night their fires were visible off to the east – preferring to shadow the little convoy at a distance. When the *Beagle*'s boats reached the turn-off to the Murray Narrows, the wind funnelling southward out of the channel suddenly filled their sails, and they surged ahead of their retinue. It meant, as they curved back round upon themselves into the bay at Woollya, that they would have a good few hours of peace in which to establish a camp.

For all apart from Jemmy, it was their first sight of Woollya, and the sun nudged aside the persistent grey clouds in celebration. There, in a sheltered cove, nestled an acre or so of rich, sloping pastureland, well watered by brooks and protected on three sides by low, wooded hills. The pretty little natural harbour was studded with islets, the water smooth and glassy, with low branches overhanging a rocky beach. It was so beautiful, so unexpected amid the wilds of Tierra del Fuego, that it possessed an almost dreamlike quality. It was the perfect place to build a mission.

'Jemmy, it's – it's idyllic,' said FitzRoy.

'I told you.' Jemmy beamed with pride. 'My land is good land.'

'The Lord is merciful,' said Matthews, with what sounded like relief.

FitzRoy gave the order to begin unloading the yawl. An area of pasture was staked out for the mission buildings, boundary markers were put up and sentries placed at each corner. There were wigwams over to the north side of the cove, but they were deserted. Darwin investigated a tall green cone on the shoreline, prodding it gingerly with a stick.

'It's a midden. An old shell-midden,' explained FitzRoy.

'Good grief,' said Darwin, withdrawing the stick. 'A nine-inch-thick coating of pure mould. Look – there are seasonal layers. One might be able to date this, like the rings of a tree.'

Something, some primitive instinct, told both men suddenly that they were being watched. They stood stock still, eyes fixed on the treeline. FitzRoy gestured the sailors to quieten their unloading. Each man held his position, tensed, motionless, silent. And then, at last, there was a rustling in the trees, and an extremely old man, painted white from head to toe, emerged into plain view.

'He's as white as a miller,' whispered Darwin.

The old man walked slowly and deliberately in a straight line towards Jemmy Button. The three Fuegians had been standing watching the unloading, Jemmy in his smart scarlet dress-coat and fashionably tight stockings. The white-painted man, ignoring York and Fuegia, took up a position a foot away from Jemmy and defiantly began to harangue him.

FitzRoy and Darwin came cautiously across. Presently the old man finished his tirade.

'What does he say, Jemmy?'

Jemmy stumbled, red-faced with confusion.

'I – I do not know. I do not understand him.'

'But that is your language, is it not?'

'English is my language now. I forget this language.'

'You have *forgotten* your own language?'

'I was young boy when I came with you. For many years I do not need it.' Jemmy turned to the old man. 'I do not understand you. *No sabe.* I do not understand you.' He seemed almost panic-stricken.

'I think he's telling the truth,' said Darwin.

There was another volley from the old man, who gestured angrily to FitzRoy and his companion, followed by an inadvertent guffaw from York Minster.

'Do you understand him, York?' asked FitzRoy sharply. 'Do *you* speak Yamana?'

'Yes.'

'You never told us you could speak Jemmy's language. Not once in three years.'

'You never ask me.'

FitzRoy could have strangled him, in theory at least. 'What does the old man say?'

'He says you are dirty men. You have hairs on your face. That is very dirty.'

'Capp'en Fitz'oy?' said Jemmy nervously.

'Yes, Jemmy?'

'I am afraid to stay here.'

With the Church Missionary Society's collection of soup tureens, tea-trays, beaver hats and fine linen forming another incongruous cone in the centre of the marked-off area, a party of sailors set to chopping the beech-logs, which, with the planking carried in the yawl, would go to construct the three mission cottages. Another group began turning over the topsoil for the vegetable garden, where they would sow carrots, turnips, beans, peas, leeks and cabbages. It was late in the year for planting – the various unforeseen delays on their journey south had seen to that – but many of the sailors had been farm-labourers in more prosperous times, and were sure that the tubers and seedlings would survive. The profusion of wildflowers in the Woollya meadows – none of them known to

European eyes – and the rich dark soil, which was softer and more fertile that the usual acidic peat of Tierra del Fuego, augured well.

By the end of the first day, the canoes of the pursuing Fuegians were arriving by the score. Tribesmen came by land too, sweating and exhausted, until eventually a crowd of several hundred had been disgorged on to the beach. What had been a pleasant, deserted Eden became a milling throng, a semi-permanent camp the size of a small town. The Indians sat in naked rows, staring intently at the strange pale men going about their mysterious business. Their principal fascination, however, was reserved for Jemmy Button, who was followed by a hundred pairs of eyes wherever he went: they could not take their eyes off his lurid tail-coats, his polished boots and his gleaming white gloves. Not without trepidation, he went among them handing out little presents, nails, buttons and the like, which were invariably received without a sound or any flicker of expression. The natives of Woollya were, of course, no different from those they had seen further east, and Jemmy felt as naked as they were in his shame.

'They are monkeys. Fools. Not men!' said York with derision. To the Yamana, York appeared as one of the white men, a foreigner by dint of his European clothes; but more than that, he carried an aura about him, a sense of innate power, and they gave him a wide berth.

By night, the Fuegians would steal. No matter how many sentries were posted, the sailors would wake up with items missing – knives, spades, hammers, even their clothes and shoes – for there was nothing the Indians would not take. Even by day, the bolder ones were capable of the most audacious thefts. One Fuegian almost succeeded in removing Hamond's axe from under his arm without his noticing. Just as the haft disappeared, Hamond felt the faintest disturbance and turned to challenge the thief.

'Hey! That's m-my axe!'

The man nodded in supplication and returned the implement gracefully.

FitzRoy tried to defend the Fuegians later that night, as the officers lay in their makeshift tents, mere sailcloths slung across crossed oars.

'Think what treasures such tools represent to these men! Imagine the

Beagle's crew, surrounded by untended piles of gold and jewels. What would be the result?'

'We're all going to d-die in our b-beds,' said Hamond gloomily.

On the third day, Jemmy became excited, and announced that his family were approaching. Asked how he knew such a thing, he said that he had heard his brother shouting from his canoe, about a mile and a half away. The Fuegians' powers of hearing, it seemed, was as astonishing as their powers of sight. Sure enough, a quarter-hour later, a canoe containing Jemmy's mother, brothers and sisters swung into the bay. They stared in wonder at his finery, and the little girls blushed and hid in the bottom of the boat. Jemmy's elder brother, who appeared to have been elected spokesman, circled Jemmy cautiously and addressed him at length.

'I do not understand. *No sabe. No sabe.* Why you no speak *English*? Why you *no sabe*?' hissed Jemmy, urgently, and all could see that he was humiliated by the state of his family.

'Fools! Beasts!' chortled York Minster.

Eventually, Jemmy recalled enough rudimentary Yamana to conduct a halting conversation with his brother, punctuated with bursts of English and the occasional Spanish or Portuguese word. He was most concerned to clothe his family as soon as possible, and managed to persuade his mother into a smock. His brother was induced to cover his nakedness with a Guernsey frock, breeches and a lady's tartan cap.

'What does your brother say, Jemmy?' asked FitzRoy, desperate to make sense of whatever he could.

'He says my father is dead. He is dead at the last moon.'

'I am sorry, Jemmy. I am very sorry.'

Incredible. It is just as Bynoe said.

'Me no help it. Me know this already. Also, he say my mother was very sad when I leave. She look for me many months, search every bay, search every island.'

Darwin, who did not believe this for a second, thought that two horses in a field could not have been less interested in each other than Jemmy and the members of his family. In fact, the sound they made when speaking to each other, he concluded, was exactly that made by a man trying to encourage a horse – a sort of clicking noise produced from the side of the mouth. For all this scepticism, however, Jemmy's family became familiar figures around the camp; the elder brother was nicknamed Tommy Button by the sailors, and the younger one Harry Button.

Bennet and Bynoe made earnest efforts to engage with the Fuegians: the coxswain cast embarrassment aside, and sang and danced for them, accompanied by the surgeon on a Jew's harp. The natives' ability to remember and mimic the words was extraordinary, but sadly their sense of rhythm was non-existent; so much so that when they attempted to join in, despite being word perfect, they would frequently start singing several seconds in arrears.

After two weeks' hard labour the mission was finished, and the crew could look proudly upon three log cabins with thatched roofs and a substantial vegetable garden, the whole enclosed by an elegant white-painted picket fence. The central cottage was given to Matthews, who assiduously furnished it with the best that the charitable ladies of Walthamstow had to offer – lacework, linen and framed samplers embroidered with improving texts – until it looked from the inside like a respectable parlour in rural Essex. The Fuegians were not the only ones capable of nocturnal stealth: all those implements most valuable to the new mission – spades, axes, knives and so forth – had been secreted by night in a false ceiling built into Matthews's cottage, and in a cellar under the floorboards. The cottage to Matthews's right was given to Jemmy Button, and the cottage to his left to York and Fuegia, who were married – Matthews officiating – in a short ceremony that bewildered most of the participants and nearly all of the onlookers. FitzRoy himself gave the bride away, unsure whether the ceremony represented an important bridge with civilization or a desperate attempt to prolong an unconvincing illusion. They sang a hymn together, and Bennet felt more self-conscious than he had done dancing a jig for the natives.

On the day after the wedding they were due to take their farewells. Darwin emerged bleary-eyed from their tent to a grey and pleasantly sticky morning, rubbed his eyes, and thought about heading down to the shore to begin the daily task of washing his pale flesh before a hundred pairs of bewildered eyes. FitzRoy, pushing the canvas flap aside, crawled out into the daylight and stood beside him.

'Not such a bad day,' ventured the Philosopher.

'I beg to differ,' said FitzRoy abruptly. 'The women and children are gone.'

'I beg your pardon?'

'I said, the women and children are gone. It must mean they are planning an attack. I can think of no other explanation.'

Darwin peered at the patient multitude drawn up in lines beyond the mission's boundary markers. FitzRoy was right. Every single woman and child had vanished, Jemmy's mother and sisters included. Innumerable ranks of seated men returned his gaze implacably. A cold shudder ran down his spine. 'Could we repel such an attack?'

'Repel it? We are outnumbered more than ten to one. Even with guns, I doubt we could repel it. No, my friend, I intend to forestall it.' And FitzRoy stalked off to the perimeter, to discover what, if anything, the sentries had noticed during the night.

Nobody, of course, had seen or heard a thing. But as FitzRoy made his rounds, the old white-painted man stood up and approached McCurdy, one of the foretopmen, who stood at the nearest sentry-post. Nervously, McCurdy planted his feet apart and indicated, as had been made clear many times to the Fuegians, that they should not pass the boundary fence. The old man stared at him.

'He's a regular quiz, this one, sir,' said the sentry edgily. Suddenly, the old man spat directly into his face.

'Do not retaliate!' called FitzRoy. 'Do you hear me, McCurdy? Do *not* retaliate.'

'Aye aye sir.'

'Continue to indicate with your body position that he must not cross the boundary fence.'

'Sir!'

The old man essayed an extremely realistic mime of how McCurdy would shortly be eaten, after he had been first killed and skinned.

'If you retaliate, there will be a massacre. Simply block his path, but try to smile.'

McCurdy managed a glassy grin. The old man produced an axe, one that had been stolen a few days earlier, and raised it threateningly above his head, as if daring the sentry to take it off him. FitzRoy strode across with a rifle and fired into the air. All the Fuegians recoiled at the report of the weapon, but afterwards simply looked confused; a few scratched the backs of their heads, inspecting themselves for damage.

'Obviously they have never encountered a firearm,' said FitzRoy. 'Wait here.'

He ducked into Matthews's cottage and reappeared, holding a cut-glass Walthamstow vase, tapping it to indicate its solidity. Then, with the missionary framed open-mouthed in silent protest between his doorposts, FitzRoy placed the vase at a distance and blew it to pieces with his rifle. The old man stood paralysed with amazement, the stolen axe frozen mid-whirl above his head. A ripple of consternation passed through the native ranks. FitzRoy put down the gun, walked back to the old man, and gently prised the weapon from his fingers, giving him a polite pat on the back as he did so, as if to apologize for the peremptory nature of his display.

'That's told 'em, sir,' muttered McCurdy, under his breath.

The rest of the day passed uneventfully, but there was no hiding the palpable air of tension that clung about both sides of the divide like a chill mist. FitzRoy doubled the guard on the camp that night but, as it turned out, there was no need. When dawn broke, it transpired that – without any of the sentries seeing anything – every single one of the Fuegians had simply melted away. The little cove was utterly deserted.

The sailors' departure was postponed for several days, but the great army of Fuegians did not come back. Were they merely biding their time, or had the display of firepower frightened them away for good? How FitzRoy fervently hoped that the latter was the case, that the little mission would be given a fair chance to take root.

One day in late January he gave the order for Bennet to head back to the *Beagle* with one of the whaleboats and the yawl, while he and the other officers explored and surveyed the western arm of the Beagle Channel. They would return to Woollya to check on the progress of the mission after a month. Lashing rain attended the day of their departure.

Before leaving, he went to see Matthews in his snug little parlour, where he found him buried deep in the scriptures.

'I feel obliged to make clear, Mr Matthews, that whatever your heart may feel, if your head tells you to return to England aboard the *Beagle*, then you must grasp the opportunity at once. No shame would attach to you, were you to take that decision. No honest man would blame you for such a course of action.'

'Captain FitzRoy, whether or not I should be blamed is neither here nor there,' replied Matthews blandly. 'The Lord God has given me a task, which I intend to fulfil to the best of my ability.'

He is either extraordinarily brave or he has no real understanding of what he is about to undergo.

'You are certain?'

'Absolutely.'

'Then I wish you the very best of British luck, and may God protect and preserve you.'

'Thank you.'

Down at the little jetty they had constructed, they said their farewells to Jemmy, York and Fuegia.

'You don't have to stay, Jemmy, if you don't want to,' FitzRoy offered. 'You may return to England with us, if you prefer.'

Jemmy shivered damply in his favourite pink suit, a bright slash of incongruous colour against the glowering sky. He stared at his shoes, where teeming raindrops were attempting unsuccessfully to garner a foothold on the glossy leather.

'No, Capp'en Fitz'oy. This is my country. These are my people. These are my friends and my family. I must stay here at Woollya. And – Capp'en Fitz'oy?'

'Yes Jemmy?'

'Thank you, Capp'en Fitz'oy.'

'Thank *you*, Jemmy.'

'Goodbye, Jemmy, old son,' said Bennet.

'Goodbye, Mr Bennet.'

'Now you'll be able to build that city you always dreamed about,' added

Bennet softly. 'That big white city, with wide avenues, and squares, and fountains, and coaches, and all the ladies and gentlemen parading about.'

'Maybe one day you will come back to see it, Mr Bennet?'

'Yes, Jemmy, yes, I will. I will come back to see it.' And Bennet felt himself crumple inside, and he hugged Jemmy tightly, as much to disguise the tears that were coursing down his cheeks as anything else.

'Goodbye, Jemmy,' said Bynoe.

'Goodbye, my *confidential* friend.'

A little round cannonball rushed at FitzRoy, almost knocking him over. 'Fuegia love Capp'en Fitz'oy. Fuegia *love* Capp'en Fitz'oy.'

'Captain FitzRoy loves Fuegia,' he whispered, and stroked her hair, and York did not object because he saw that the captain's eyes were wet with tears as well.

The four boats pulled away into the sound, until the waving figures on the jetty were enfolded by the gloom and lost in streaming rain. Eventually, the distant glow of the mission oil lamp was all that remained, a tiny spark in the great dark shadow of Tierra del Fuego.

CHAPTER FOUR

The Beagle Channel, Tierra del Fuego, 6 February 1833

'It is amazing!' remarked Darwin.

'What is? The glacier?'

The surveying party were setting up their instruments on a level stretch of beach opposite the face of a sheer, overhanging glacier, a frozen cascade of beryl not a mile distant across the channel. It was a gorgeous and unexpectedly sunny day, and the brilliant colours within the ice cliff seemed to oscillate as they watched, shifting from jade through to amethyst and back again.

'No! I mean – of course – that the glacier is beautiful, but I was referring to Lyell.' Darwin sat down on a rock, quite oblivious of its slimy coat of putrefying seaweed, so excited that the book shook in his hands. 'Lyell has rejected the Biblical flood!'

'What?' FitzRoy could not believe his ears. Lyell, the eminent geologist, who had personally asked FitzRoy to supply specimens from the voyage to provide proof of the Noachian deluge?

'Here – he rejects the idea of a sudden débâcle at any point in the earth's history. He claims that any changes have been "gradual, constant and unimaginably slow".'

FitzRoy felt the cold knife of betrayal slide between his ribs. 'Then how does he explain the disappearance of the great beasts that once roamed the earth?'

'He thinks they simply died out of their own accord. That all species have a natural lifespan.'

'But what of our Megatherium, with its modern-day shells above and below?'

'Ah – here – he has an answer to that very question. He believes that marine invertebrates, no, any cold-blooded species, have a longer lifespan than their warm-blooded equivalents.'

'Indeed? And how, pray, did a land animal drown fifteen feet above the sea?'

'Well...I suppose it would have to have fallen into a river, drowned, then the body would have to have floated out to sea, sunk, and then the land would have to have risen above sea level. Over many, many thousands of years.'

'Lyell has taken leave of his senses.'

Darwin thought that he had better divert the course of the conversation.

'By the bye – do you think that this channel will lead us to the sea?'

'I am certain of it.'

'Then the south side – the mountain range on either side of the Murray Narrows – is effectively broken into two huge islands.'

'Indeed.'

'The island to the east side of the narrows consisted of stratified alluvium, like the north side of the channel here. But the island to the west' – he indicated the glacier suspended implausibly over the opposite shore – 'is constructed from old crystalline rock. Look.'

'What of it?' said FitzRoy irritably.

'Well, Jemmy told me that the land on his side of the narrows teems with fox and guanaco. But the island across the narrows, just a few hundred yards away, has neither. It is why such animals are unknown in York's country. So the animals only exist on the newer, alluvial rock.'

'Go on.'

'Well, the conditions, the vegetation, the habitat of the western side are the same. But if the guanaco or the fox ever lived there, something wiped them out. Then, when the lands were repopulated, the animals were obviously unable to get back westward across the channel. If the species indeed has a "natural lifespan", it was not that which ended their existence on those shores opposite.'

'By Jove, Philos, I do believe you are right.' FitzRoy found himself immensely cheered all of a sudden. 'Hang Lyell – I think you have it!'

Darwin smiled, happy to bathe in the glow of his friend's approval. Inwardly, he remained unsure, his mind a whirl of questions and answers – Lyell's suggestion that the land could rise and fall posed many of them – but he was relieved at least to have restored FitzRoy's mood.

'Excuse me, sir.' It was Hamond. 'I thought you m-might like a m-mug of t-tea, sir.' Since the storm off Cape Horn, his stutter seemed to have got worse.

'Why, thank you, Mr Hamond. Another mug would certainly not go amiss.' Between them, the surveying party had worked their way through four gallons that day already.

'The theodolite is set up, sir, and the m-micrometer and b-board, and Mr B-Bynoe is waiting with the b-bearing book.'

'Excellent, Mr Hamond. I shall be there as soon as I have drained this tea.' FitzRoy bent down to pick up his sextant and chronometer.

'Sir!' Hamond almost shouted. 'L-l-l-l-'

'What is it, Mr Hamond?'

'L-l-l-l-*look*, sir!'

Their gaze followed the line of Hamond's jabbing finger. There, right before their very eyes, the glacier was in calf. A huge sliver of ice a thousand feet high had parted from the ice cliff, and was falling, silently and gracefully, away from the main body and into the sound, like a white lace handkerchief dropped from a marble balcony into a deep blue pool. A moment later, an earsplitting thunderclap reached their ears; the three men stood transfixed as sound and vision were reunited, rapturous at one of nature's most awesome sights. As they watched, the enormous ice-spear scythed into the depths of the channel, then re-emerged in glittering, shattered chunks. A creamy wash furled out from the impact, no more than a distant spreading line on the smooth surface of the water, and a moment later a reverberating crash echoed from one cliff to another.

'Incredible. Quite incredible.'

'M-m-magnificent.'

'Oh, my God,' said Darwin, horror-stricken. 'The boats!'

'What?'

But Darwin was already away, hurtling hell for leather, Mr Lyell's considered opinions scattered wildly across the pebbles, as he raced down the shore towards the two whaleboats. A second or two later, FitzRoy and Hamond realized what Darwin had been quick-witted enough to apprehend first: that the boats were drawn up untethered on the quiet shore, that the huge wave now racing across the channel would surely suck them out to sea in its undertow, and that they were many a mile from the relative safety of the Woollya mission. Some of the crew had realized the danger too, and were rushing pell-mell down the beach; but it was clear, as the surging barrier of foam arched into a curling ten-foot breaker, that Darwin was the only one with a chance of reaching the boats first. Indeed, as long as he did not stumble over his own bootlaces, he was their only chance. Gasping for breath, his lungs bursting with pain, his long legs devouring the shingle, he flung himself forward, hurling himself upon the adjacent boat-ropes just as the wave erupted in a convulsing maelstrom over his head.

It was, in fact, the second time in less than a month that the philosopher had suddenly found himself on the end of a battering-ram of icy seawater. This time, as he swirled upside-down in the churning spume, he suffered the added discomfiture of being pelted with a thousand stones by the frothing, maddened undertow. His feet jammed in the shingle and he straightened his knees, doggedly fighting to hold on to the boats as they shot past him on the accelerating backwash. The first crewman got to him in four feet of cerulean water and crushed ice, on the point of being dragged out into the middle of the channel. They formed a human chain to reel the two whaleboats and their protector back to the shore.

'I n-never knew how d-devilish p-painful cold could be,' stuttered Darwin, in a passable imitation of Mr Hamond, as they pulled him out half frozen to death.

He was their hero that night, and they fêted him as such around their campfire under the stars. They exchanged his sodden morning-dress for spare sailors' ducks and an old coat, so that – with his winter beard – he looked more like an inmate of the parish workhouse than a gentleman naturalist. 'I feel like a bear in an overcoat, grizzled and rough,' he complained, with a big grin plastered over his face.

Everybody roared with laughter, and ladled extra rations of salt pork, venison and ship's biscuit into his bowl.

That night, as Bynoe, Hamond and the men slumbered softly in the firelight, FitzRoy and Darwin sat up late, wreathed in blankets on the bare shore, tendrils of warm smoke entwining themselves round the swirls of their condensing breath.

'I say, FitzRoy.'

'Yes?'

'Do you ever think about…women?'

'Women?'

'Yes.'

FitzRoy's mind darted back to the recurring image of a pool of hot wax, congealing against Mary O'Brien's white skin.

'No. That is, I try not to. It is a distraction.'

'I have been thinking about women. All my sisters' letters ask me if I shall settle down upon my return – if I shall have a little wife for my little parsonage.'

'And what have you decided?'

'I have been considering the claims of my cousin, Emma Wedgwood. In many ways she is an eminently suitable candidate.'

'Do you love her?'

'Of course not.' Darwin laughed. 'She is my cousin. I love her as such, I suppose. But she is personable and charming and kind, qualities that augur well. What qualities would you look for in a potential wife?'

'I fear I have given it no thought. I do not really have time for such matters. I do not even write home.'

'You do not write *home*?'

'Oh, I cannot defend myself – certain people have been very kind in writing to me, and I have been shamefully remiss in failing to reply. But this Service is too important to allow myself to become distracted by correspondence. And I do not like to think of the men in the packet ships, risking their lives to deliver anything but the most vital consignments – your geological samples, for instance.'

Darwin wore a guilty look.

'My dear Darwin, forgive me. I do not mean to upbraid you. Mine is an idiosyncratic view, not shared by many. Letters from home are essential, of course, for maintaining the morale of those on board. In my case, it is also true that – as I have told you – I regard the *Beagle* as my home.'

'A home without women.'

'That is a sacrifice that all of us in the Service must make. But, pray, tell me where your thoughts lead you in this matter.'

'Well, I have made a list' – Darwin produced a crumpled piece of paper from his pocket – 'detailing the arguments in favour of and against marriage.'

'I am keen to hear them.'

'Well, marriage would of course bring with it the demons of fatness, idleness, anxiety, responsibility, perhaps even quarrels. I should lose the freedom to go where I like, and the conversation of clever men at clubs. I should be forced to visit relatives, to bend in every trifle, and to have the expense and anxiety of children. There would be less money for books. There would be a terrible loss of time – how should I manage my business if I were obliged to go walking with my wife every day? I never should know French, or see the Continent, or go to America, or go up in a balloon. I should be a poor slave, FitzRoy, worse than a negro.'

'It sounds as if your mind is made up. Bachelorhood beckons!'

'But wait! One cannot live a solitary life, friendless, childless and cold, with groggy old age staring back into one's wrinkly face from the looking-glass! There is many a happy slave, after all.' He gave FitzRoy a sidelong look, and both men smiled at the memory of their quarrel. 'A clever wife would be quite ghastly and tiresome. Romance, of course, palls after a while. No, I have decided upon a nice, soft, quiet wife who can play the piano in the evenings. Certainly, such a wife would be better than a dog.'

FitzRoy succeeded – just – in suppressing the desire to burst out laughing. He composed his features into their most solemn look. 'My dear Philos. If you indulge in such visions as nice little wives by the fireside of your country parsonage, then you shall certainly make a bolt from the *Beagle*. I fear you must remain contented with Megatheriums and icebergs, and not surrender yourself to these animal desires.'

Darwin looked searchingly at FitzRoy, wondering for a moment if he was being teased, but his friend remained convincingly po-faced. 'Well, I shall have plenty of opportunity to make my mind up, seeing that I am more than nine thousand miles from home.'

'Ah, my friend, then you have an advantage over me. For I am barely ninety miles from my home, which means I have precious little time to worry about who shall play the piano to me in the evenings.'

The smile that FitzRoy had been fighting to keep hidden finally crept out, and lit up his face.

The sun continued to shine, remarkably, for several days more, so it was with pink and blistered faces that they made their next discovery: that the Beagle Channel split into two arms, each ravine as deep as its fellow. In either direction, countless snowcapped peaks, four thousand feet in height, plunged directly into the water to continue their descent almost the same distance below the surface. Each arm was so straight that, in the far distance, the water disappeared over the horizon between its framing mountain walls. They sailed up the northern arm, where a pod of hourglass dolphins took it upon themselves to entertain them, leaping and gambolling before the whaleboats' bows.

To the north, the range of mountains soared to a single immense peak, rising sheer out of the water to almost seven thousand feet, which was studded with gigantic glaciers laced with tints of sky-blue and sea-green. At first they thought it must be Mount Sarmiento, but they were too far to the south-east. It was, they realized, an even bigger mountain, almost certainly the highest in Tierra del Fuego. FitzRoy named it Mount Darwin, foremost peak of the Darwin range, in honour of his friend. At the end of the northern arm they came to a large sound, bleak, desolate and deserted, which connected with the southern arm. They were, FitzRoy calculated, in the further reaches of Cook Bay, which opened out into the Pacific not far from York Minster. He gave the flat sheen of water the title of Darwin Sound, 'after my dear messmate, who so willingly encountered the discomfort and risk of a long cruise in a small loaded boat'.

They headed back by the southern arm, to the indignant fury of various kelp geese, steamer ducks and magellanic oyster-catchers. FitzRoy and Darwin even hauled one of the giant kelp strands out of the water on to a shingle strand, to see how far the plant's tendrils delved beneath the surface. The kelp was nearly four hundred feet long, and teemed with life: thickly encrusted corallines, molluscs, fish, cuttlefish, sea-eggs, starfish and, hiding in the monstrous entangled roots, a battalion of crabs of every size and variety. An excellent supper of kelp and baked crab followed.

As they approached the divide in the channel once more, they saw flashes of colour in the distance: a daub of pink here, a dash of scarlet there. FitzRoy reached for the spyglass. It was a small flotilla of native canoes. Even distorted by the spyglass lens, what he saw turned his stomach to ice. One man wore a beaver hat. Another had an earthenware chamber pot on his head. A laughing child brandished a soup ladle and a piece of tartan rug. The flashes of colour were strips of cloth, tied about wrists and foreheads, cloth which FitzRoy immediately recognized as having belonged to Jemmy's suits.

'Dear God,' he said, and passed across the spyglass.

'Savages,' growled Darwin. 'Damned *savages*.'

'Shall we apprehend them, sir?' asked Bynoe.

'There is no point. Let us make all speed to Woollya. We have no other recourse. Oars and sails. Row as if your lives depended on it!'

As they shot past the little flotilla, a Fuegian pulled a face at them, and mockingly waved an elephant's foot umbrella stand above his head.

As the two whaleboats determinedly rounded the headland into Woollya Cove, every gun bristling, upwards of a hundred Fuegian natives scattered simultaneously, like a shoal of fish surprised by approaching sharks. Two removed their feet from a round pink object as they fled, which revealed itself to be the foetal, naked person of Mr Matthews. Thus released, the missionary leaped to his feet and ran screaming towards the boats, all pretence at passivity gone, yelling the Lord's Prayer at the top of his voice. 'Our Father! Our Father who art in heaven! Hallowed be thy name, O Jesus Christ, oh hallowed be thy *name*!'

Matthews splashed frantically into the shallows, oblivious to the icy cold, and leaped into the burly red-coated arms of Marine Burgess, bringing him down in a tangled, soaking heap. So hysterical was the missionary that he refused to release his protector; Bynoe and Hamond had to disconnect his desperate bear-hug limb by paralysed limb before they could haul him into their boat. The other marines moved to secure the now empty beach.

'Matthews! Are you all right! What were they doing to you?'

'Yes! Yes! I think so! Our Father who art in heaven, hallowed, hallowed, *hallowed* be thy name!'

'Matthews!' FitzRoy grabbed a freezing ear in each hand. 'What were they doing to you?'

'They were shaving me.'

'*Shaving* you?'

'They put their feet on my head, and plucked the hairs from my upper lip one by one with mussel shells! The savages! By God, FitzRoy, it hurt like the devil!'

'Where are your clothes, man?'

'They took them! They took everything! They took them and tore them into strips and distributed them among the other savages!'

'Where is Jemmy? Is Jemmy all right?'

'I think so. They took everything of his, all his clothes too.'

'And York and Fuegia?'

'Oh, York is *fine*. York is just *fine*.'

There was no time to find out what this last remark meant. The sailors fanned out to search the property. They found Jemmy, crouched, naked and mud-stained, in the trampled remains of the vegetable garden, his hands covering his genitals in shame. His bare feet were sore and bleeding, unprotected by the hard calluses that soled the other Fuegians' feet. Anger, misery and embarrassment curdled as one on his features.

'Jemmy, are you all right?'

'My people,' he spat bitterly, 'are fools. Damned *fools*.'

'They took everything?'

'*Everything*. They are all bad men, they no *sabe* nothing, nothing at all.

They are all very great damned fools.'

'Did your family not try to help you? Your friends? Your brothers?'

'My brothers steal most things of all! What fashion do you call that? My *brothers*!'

'What about York? Did he not try to protect you?'

'You ask York,' said Jemmy savagely. 'You ask York why he no help me.'

As if on cue, York Minster opened the door of his cottage and strolled nonchalantly out. Unlike the homes of Matthews and Jemmy, which had been gutted of their contents, their doors left hanging limply from their hinges, a glimpse over York's shoulder revealed a picture of domestic contentment. A smiling Fuegia Basket – or was it Fuegia Minster now? – sat in a rocking chair by the hearth, swaying gently back and forth, her stockinged feet stretched out on a woollen rug, a rag doll cradled in her arms. Improving religious prints decorated the walls. A half-eaten pot of marmalade sat on an occasional table. Clearly, York and his belongings had survived the return of the natives utterly unscathed.

'York?' said FitzRoy, in disbelief. 'They took none of your property?'

The big Fuegian said nothing, but merely glanced back inside the hut, as if to say '*Is that not self-evident?*'

'Why did you not help Jemmy and Mr Matthews?'

York smiled one of his cruel, wolfish smiles. 'They are many men. York is only one man.' And he strolled back inside and took his place at the hearth alongside Fuegia.

'Jemmy is *rude*,' confided Fuegia to FitzRoy through the doorway. 'Jemmy has *no clothes*!' she giggled.

When Matthews had calmed down sufficiently, he was able to tell his story.

'For the first few days after you left, there was quiet. Then, on the third day, the savages came back. They sat there, like a pack of hounds waiting to be unleashed. The next morning at sunrise they all began to howl – a sort of lamentation. Then that old scoundrel made a great parade of threatening me with a rock. I had to give them presents – clothing, crockery and food. Then they made the most hideous faces at me, and held me down and tore off my clothes and pulled out some of my hair.

They did the same to Jemmy – Tommy Button burst out crying to see it, then they shouted at him and he joined in! They destroyed the garden – Jemmy tried to tell them what it was for, but they destroyed it anyway. Of course that filthy swine York did nothing to help. Didn't lift a finger. They didn't dare touch *him*, oh no. And everything they stole, they distributed equally between all the savages. Everyone got a share.'

'How primitive,' said Darwin.

'Ah, but they did not find the really valuable things they wanted! They did not find the secret cellar with the tools, or the compartment in the roof. The stupid, filthy, godless *savages*.'

'I presume,' said FitzRoy gently, 'that you would prefer to leave off this place, and take up your berth on the *Beagle* once more.'

'Captain FitzRoy,' gasped Matthews, 'wild horses could not persuade me to remain for one second further in these detestable latitudes. I cannot return home – the disgrace would be too great. My brother is a missionary in New Zealand. I shall make my way there.'

This was a very different Matthews, naked in his candour, from the young man who had been so ready to clothe himself with truisms and platitudes.

Once the excitement of the rescue had subsided, it was a subdued FitzRoy who took stock of the situation. The prospects for the little settlement, he realized, were bleak indeed. The seeds of civilization had been sown, but it was too late in the season for them to come to maturity. Jemmy, at least, was determined to continue, determined to make something of the Woollya mission. Like Matthews, the attack by the locals seemed to have wrought a change in him, but change of a more positive kind: a kernel of resistance had been exposed, once the soft outer layers had been peeled away. FitzRoy did all that he could to help: Jemmy was clothed once more, the whereabouts of the mission tools were revealed to all three Fuegians – each of whom was sworn to secrecy – and it was impressed upon York, in no uncertain terms, that the three must stick together through all their tribulations. That, said FitzRoy, was the civilized, Christian way. He would visit them again, he promised, in a year's time, when the surveying expedition left Tierra del Fuego for the last time, on its way home to England.

'I do hope,' said FitzRoy to Darwin, 'that our motives in taking them to England will become understood and appreciated among their fellow natives over the coming year so that our next visit might find them more favourably disposed towards us.' It was, he knew, a near-forlorn hope. 'After all, our three Fuegians possess the sense to see the vast superiority of civilized over uncivilized habits.'

'Indeed so,' said Darwin with a tinge of regret. 'Yet I am afraid that it is to the latter they must return.' *Their visit to our country has been of no use to them*, he thought. *No use whatsoever.*

Once more there were farewell hugs and tears, and once more sleeting rain attended their departure. Only this time there was no oil-lamp glow to act as a parting beacon, for it had been smashed and stolen, the meaningless pieces shared out as far-flung booty. As the whaleboats glided out into the sound, the three little cottages were soon lost to view, swallowed by the primitive dark.

CHAPTER FIVE

The Falkland Islands, 1 March 1833

As the *Beagle* weathered the northern opening of Falklands Sound, the lookout spied a sail nosing above the northern horizon. The pendant numbers were prepared for the call-and-response.

'From the cut of her topsails, she's British,' said FitzRoy, squinting into his spyglass, 'but in these waters it pays not to take chances.'

'Why? What chances are there to take in these waters?' enquired Darwin peevishly.

'Because our friends in Buenos Ayres are forever beating the drum about the islands belonging to them.'

'I would have thought that Buenos Ayres was welcome to them.' Darwin indicated the miles of low, dismal moorland and sodden peat bog rolling away to starboard. He pulled his benjamin tighter about him, as the raw wind sent another squall of hail clattering off his back.

'My eye, Philos!' objected Sulivan. 'Why, this is God's own country! There are fish in the sea and cattle on the land, and not a factory or coach road in sight. Here is nature in the raw! And where else, Philos, could you enjoy all four seasons in one day, except perhaps up a Welsh mountain?'

Darwin smiled. 'I think you make my point for me most admirably. But what business have we here anyway, grabbing an island hard by the back door of Buenos Ayres?'

'On the contrary, Philos,' said FitzRoy patiently, 'we did not "grab" the islands. John Davis discovered them in 1592, when they were quite empty. The French *thought* they had discovered them in the last century, and founded Port Louis, then sold the place to Spain. The British in Port Egmont only discovered the Spanish in Port Louis five years later. Not long after that the Spanish were kicked out. But they, and their heirs, the Buenos Ayreans, have been bleating about it ever since.'

'Well, I think it looks a squalid little place.'

Sulivan clapped Darwin on the back. 'That's as may be, Philos – Port Louis is also the only place to take in supplies within three hundred miles of jolly old Terra del, and we have no supply tender. So you had better learn to enjoy it!'

Hamond brought news of the other vessel. 'It's HMS *Challenger*, sir. One of our b-brigs. B-bound for Valparayso, Chili via P-Port Louis. C-Captain Seymour, sir.'

'Not Michael Seymour? He was a fellow pupil of mine at the Royal Naval College. So old Seymour has himself a brig! What splendid news.'

Within the quarter-hour, the *Challenger* had run the Union flag up her mizzen-mast, inviting the captain of the *Beagle* to come aboard. Side-ropes and a boat-rope were rigged to receive the visiting cutter, and FitzRoy soon found himself on the *Challenger*'s poop deck receiving an enthusiastic welcome from his old schoolfriend.

'FitzRoy, my dear chap. Thank God you are alive.'

'Should I not be?'

'We knew you to be surveying in the vicinity of Cape Horn – those terrible storms! At least five vessels are missing, presumed lost. You were able to find a safe anchorage?'

'A safe anchorage? Far from it! We were under way throughout, for twenty-four days. We were lucky not to be taken by Old Davy.'

'By the deuce, you must have the best of sea-boats to have come through such a blow in one piece.'

'She's a good old girl. But, my dear Seymour, you have your own fine brig – my congratulations to you, old friend. These are splendid news indeed. What business have you in Port Louis?'

''Tis but a flying visit. The Falklands are to have a permanent garrison, and we are merely their transport. Allow me to introduce to your acquaintance Lieutenant Smith.'

Smith stood drinking at the scuttle-butt with four of his marines. He was young and rosy-cheeked, and his curly blond locks gave him the air of a mother's boy, but his bearing and handshake told FitzRoy otherwise.

'I'm delighted to make your acquaintance, Lieutenant. How many are to be in your garrison?'

'Just myself and the four men you see here, sir.'

'You are to garrison the Falkland Islands with *five* men?' FitzRoy could not hide his disbelief.

The young man coloured. 'I gather, sir, that our presence is to be symbolic. As I understand it, the belief in Whitehall is that Buenos Ayres would not dare attempt to occupy a territory defended by British troops for that would constitute an act of war.'

Or they might just consider such a small garrison to be evidence of a lack of will on London's part, thought FitzRoy.

'Well, Captain Seymour, the *Beagle* is bound for Port Louis so I can save you a journey. I should be delighted to ferry Lieutenant Smith and his men the rest of the way.'

'FitzRoy, old man, that would be capital! You oblige me by your kindness, you really do. By the bye, do you have a Mr Darwin in the *Beagle*?'

'He is our natural philosopher.'

'Excellent. I have a letter for him, which I was to have left in the store at Port Louis. It is from a Professor Henslow at Cambridge University, marked "Most Urgent", so the port-admiral in Rio decided to forward it post-haste. Now you may pass it to him directly.'

Darwin stood clutching the letter in a lather of excitement.

'Well?'

'The Megatherium heads, FitzRoy, and the other fossils, have been displayed before the cream of the academic world, at the Cambridge meeting of the British Association for the Advancement of Science. They were announced by Buckland himself. *Buckland himself!* Listen to this: "The fossil Megatheriums were fabulously prized, revealing features never seen before. Darwin is the word on everybody's lips. Your name is likely to be immortalized." Did you hear that, FitzRoy? My name is likely to be immortalized!'

'Philos, this is the most wonderful intelligence! Let us hope that some of your escalating fame shall accrue also to those officers who have furnished you with specimens. Mr Sulivan, Mr Bynoe—'

'But, of course, my dear FitzRoy. You have my every assurance on that point.'

'I must say I am relieved that the packing-crates were consigned to England in one piece. I was not entirely convinced of Mr Lumb's reliability on that count.'

'Well, most of them were. Henslow says, "The majority of specimens arrived in good order, but what on earth was in packet 223? It looks like the remains of an electric explosion, a mere mass of soot!" Good Lord, I wonder what it can have been. I fear I do not have an adequate record, after our soaking off the Horn.'

'Excuse me sir,' piped up Edward Hellyer, from the corner, 'but I have a record of the contents of every packing-crate consigned by the *Beagle*, sir. I maintained my paperwork in waterproof bags, sir.'

'You did? Well *done*, young man! Capital news!' Darwin was so delighted he looked as if he might burst.

'Well done indeed, Mr Hellyer,' said FitzRoy with quiet pride.

'The future has become a brilliant prospect, FitzRoy. I must collect as many specimens here in the Falklands as I possibly can.'

'Indeed you must. A Falklands kelp goose is the thing, I am told. It is different from the Fuegian variety, and no specimen has yet been captured. Let us see who can bag one first, shall we? Although I fear my skills with a rifle are as naught compared to yours.'

'Nonsense, my dear FitzRoy. I am sure you are my absolute equal in that respect. But let us have ourselves a sporting contest: the Captain's Cabin versus the Library. The first to boast a Falklands kelp goose is the winner!'

They shook hands on the wager.

They were still sixty miles short of the mouth of Berkeley Sound, the long inlet that sheltered Port Louis, when a reception committee appeared to shepherd them into land: swarms of tiny prion birds fussed about the rigging, black-and-white Commerson's dolphins formed a guard of honour before them, and tiny penguins with extravagant orange eyebrows splashed perplexedly in their wake. There was even a new kind of dolphin that nobody had seen before, which Darwin insisted be logged for posterity as *Delphinus FitzRoyi*.

As they rounded Volunteer Point, they overtook another sail: the sealing-schooner *Unicorn*, labouring eastward, which vessel signalled the *Beagle* to heave to. She was low in the water and clearly overloaded, but not with seals; rather, she was full to the gunwales with people. The *Beagle* pulled alongside, and this time it was FitzRoy's turn to receive a visitor. The *Unicorn*'s master, a short bustling sealer with side-whiskers and the broken remnants of a Scottish accent, panted up the man-ropes and made himself known.

'William Low sir, sealer, of Port Louis. Thank goodness you're here, sir, thank goodness you're here.'

As FitzRoy identified himself, he realized that the name was familiar. Then he remembered why – three Patagonian Indians and a stuffed horse on the windswept beach at Dungeness Point, back in April of '29.

'Forgive me, Mr Low, but I believe I was once passed a missive of yours by some Horse Indians.'

'Ah yes sir, the letter, the letter. Always does to keep in wi' the natives in my line of business.' Low spoke quickly and restlessly, and described impatient circles as he talked. 'I say "my line of business", sir, but my business is as good as shot. I am nearly ruined, sir – confined at anchor for sixty-seven days by the gales around the Horn, like a pea on a drum we were, and nary a fur seal to be had. Then on top of all that, sir, I needs carry the survivors of two other sealers. The *Magellan*, she's a Frenchy, and the *Transport*, she's a big Yankee boat. Both of them shivered to smithereens off the Horn, see, but they limped as far as West Falkland before running aground in the shallows. I needs ye to take some of them off my hands, sir.'

'Your humanitarian instincts do you credit, Mr Low. I should be delighted to help. May I introduce you to our ship's philosopher, Mr Darwin?'

'You say you are a resident of Port Louis, Mr Low?'

'Aye, that's right, sir, since eight years.'

'I don't suppose you could tell me if there is a bank in Port Louis where it might be convenient for me to cash a banker's draft on my father's account? I appear to find myself somewhat short of ready currency.' Darwin concealed his embarrassment beneath a cloak of insouciance.

'A bank, sir? There are but five buildings in Port Louis. The population's but twenty-three, just now. There's a general store...The storekeeper Mr Dickson, he's a Pat – from Dublin, sir – he looks to the Union Jack and flies it on a Sunday, or when a ship's in port. He might give ye a few bob up front if ye make it worth his while, sir, that's if ye can get a word in edgewise. Then there's Mr Brisbane, the local agent, who stands me in accommodation for the winter. Then there's a Frenchy, a soldier, the Capitaz we call him, and a German gent—'

'Pray excuse me, sir,' Bos'n Sorrell bobbed up and interrupted, 'but would that be Mr Matthew Brisbane, formerly master of the *Saxe-Cobourg*?'

'Aye, it's Mr Matthew Brisbane right enough.'

'That's my former ship, sir! Mr Brisbane and I were rescued from the wreck of the *Saxe-Cobourg* by the *Beagle*, back when Captain Stokes was in charge. He's a gentleman, sir, is Mr Brisbane.'

'Aye, that he is, sir, that he is. He's sailed more sea miles than I've had pusser's peas, has Mr Brisbane. Reckon he'll be mighty cheered to see you, will Mr Brisbane.'

'Extraordinary,' murmured FitzRoy. 'There must be fewer than a hundred Britons in the whole of South America, yet we continue to exercise a happy knack of finding one another. Tell me, Mr Low, as Berkeley Sound is new to me, would you be kind enough to act as our pilot on the approach? I take it you know the bay well?'

'I ken these islands like the back of my hand, sir. No need to flurry yourself – Berkeley Sound's no more difficult than a shilling trip round the harbour. But if you needs help I'm your man.'

'Well, Mr Low, your expertise is preferable to navigation by guess and by God. Which is in part why we shall be here for the next few months: we are to survey the islands for a new Admiralty chart.'

'A few months?' Low scratched the wiry stubble which stuck out haphazardly from his chin like scythed cornstalks. 'D'ye ken there's over four hundred islands? And as many bays and inlets. Just now I'd say you're looking at a good year, at the very least.'

'Four hundred islands?' FitzRoy's heart sank. They were fifteen months into their voyage, and their task was beginning to look nothing short of impossible. To map the Falklands, the whole of the South American coast from Punta Alta downwards, and to complete the survey of Tierra del Fuego, not to mention the constellation of tiny islands that lay to the south of Chili, in such a limited time? Had the Admiralty simply given him enough rope with which to hang himself?

'Mr Low,' he ventured, 'I apprehend from your earlier remarks that the sealing season is now at an end.'

'That's if it ever began, Captain FitzRoy.'

'Tell me, Mr Low. What might your answer be, were I to suggest that I should like to buy your boat?'

With Low piloting, the *Beagle* taking the lead and the *Unicorn* falling into line behind, the two vessels ran confidently into Berkeley Sound the following morning. A straggle of hollow-eyed, exhausted French and American sealers slumped lifelessly on the decks of both ships, shivering in their tattered clothes. Gruel-coloured clouds scudded across the sound, sweeping down from broad, peat-thick valleys, before buffeting away across low ridges littered with grey quartz boulders. Not a single tree or shrub broke the monotonous, sombre moorland; brackish pools of yellow-brown water, gleaming dully here and there, furnished the only relief from the drab uniformity. Monstrous wild bulls bellowed at them as they passed, like Cretan sculptures made flesh, their horns jabbing accusingly from the scurrying mists at those who would trespass upon their domain.

'Look 'ee, sir – see them? They're descended from escaped cattle, left behind by the Spanish sixty years ago,' related Low. 'We shoots the cows for food, so there's a good many more bulls just now.'

'They are so grotesquely large,' observed Darwin. 'Why did the Europeans stock the islands with such an enormous breed?'

'Och, but they was quite normal-sized to begin with. They've grown bigger since. They've separated out too. See these here brown bulls? South of Choiseul Sound they're white with black heads and feet. And over west they're smaller, and lead-coloured, and the cows calve a month earlier.'

'They have changed size and split into three varieties in sixty years? Mr Low, that's quite impossible.'

'I'm telling you straight, sir. The wild horses now, they've shrunk. They're two-thirds the size of a normal horse – and there was no horses, mind, before the Frenchies and the Spanish came.'

'I find this impossible to credit.'

'Even the foxes are different, sir. See, they're smaller and redder in West Falkland than in the east. And the Fuegian fox is smaller still. But they're all of them twice the size of a British fox.'

Darwin's imagination performed somersaults. Self-selecting breeds? Inter-island mutability? But Lyell's latest volume had been quite explicit on this point. Variations within species were separately created by God at localized 'centres of creation'. Creatures could not simply adapt themselves in this radical manner. This strange, mad, half-Scottish sealer must be wrong.

Low was staring at him, reading every nuance of his scepticism.

'Here's Port Louis now, sir. Ye can ask the old 'uns there about it.'

Five little white crofters' cottages had materialized at the head of the rain-soaked sound. The capital of the Falkland Islands looked no more substantial than a large moorland farm.

'Dickson'll have the flag up for ye, sir, just you wait and see,' Low informed FitzRoy.

But as they waited and watched, heaving to before Port Louis, the Irish storekeeper did not make his expected appearance. The little settlement sat silent in the early-morning drizzle.

'It's very q-quiet,' said Hamond.

'Where the devil is Dickson?' said Low. 'That feller needs told to stay off the hard stuff.'

'Never mind Dickson – where the devil are the rest of them?' demanded Darwin.

'Should there not be boats?' FitzRoy asked. 'I see no boats.'

Low nodded. 'There should be a jolly-boat before the store. There should be people. Bairns.'

'Well, if they will not come to us, then we must go to them.'

FitzRoy gave orders for the cutter to be put into the water. Sulivan, Hamond, Darwin, Bynoe, Mr Low and Lieutenant Smith accompanied him on the short pull across to the settlement. As they stepped on to the pebbly beach, the silence was tangible.

They found Dickson in his store, face down, his throat cut, his blood soaked dry into the bare boards. The place had been looted and wrecked.

'Murderers,' breathed Sulivan. 'Rotten filthy murderers.'

FitzRoy turned Dickson's body over. 'Mr Bynoe?' he asked calmly.

'The blood is still sticky in one or two places. Given the damp conditions, sir, I'd say this was done yesterday.'

'So the assailants cannot have gone far. Mr Sulivan, take Mr Low and Mr Hamond and see if you can find Mr Brisbane. Here – take this.' He offered one of his pistols to Low, who accepted it gingerly, looking almost as nervous as Hamond beside him.

Sulivan's party found the next-door house, where Low lodged with Mr Brisbane, quite empty. There was no sign of the agent, but his half-eaten breakfast lay abandoned on the table. Whatever had occurred, Brisbane had obviously been taken unawares. FitzRoy, Bynoe and Lieutenant Smith, meanwhile, pushed carefully at the door of Jean Simon, the Frenchman: creaking, it swung carelessly open to the touch. They discovered the 'Capitaz' in his front parlour. He had obviously put up a terrific struggle. There were knife-slashes to his jacket and forearms, and blood was spattered on the walls. He had been dispatched by a gunshot, and lay against the far wall, his arms raised in useless protest, a look of astonishment fixed for ever on his face. A similar scene of horror presented itself in the adjoining houses. The entire population of Port Louis had either been done to death, had fled or had been led away.

'It would seem, Mr Smith, that your posting is to be anything but symbolic,' remarked FitzRoy grimly.

The young lieutenant breathed hard and tightened his grip on his rifle.

Reinforcements were hurried across from the *Beagle*, and the surrounding area was searched. FitzRoy discovered Mr Brisbane himself, or rather Mr Brisbane's feet, protruding from a hastily piled mound of rocks. The agent had been executed by a shot to the back of his head, presumably while kneeling, some two hundred yards behind his house. The corpse had subsequently been disturbed and chewed by dogs. The discovery brought a tear to the corner of the boatswain's eye. 'The filthy swine! Who would do such a thing to a gentleman like Mr Brisbane? He was a gent and a plain man, was Mr Brisbane.'

'I promise you, Mr Sorrell, we shall apprehend the villains who perpetrated this horror. You have my word on it.'

Finally, in the murky interior of a distant outhouse, they found the remaining inhabitants of Port Louis: two children, three women and a handful of older men, quaking with fear but alive and unharmed.

'Mr Channon! This is Mr Channon, sir!' Low identified the individual nearest to the door, who was blinking back the daylight that had suddenly flooded the little shed.

'Dear God! Have they gone? Please God, have they gone?'

'My name is Captain FitzRoy. You are quite safe. But who are "they"?'

'The Buenos Ayreans. They said they would take the islands back for Buenos Ayres. They took us prisoner!'

'How many Buenos Ayreans?'

'Ten. I think it was ten. Under a Captain Rivero. They have murdered Mr Brisbane in cold blood – and Mr Dickson. Lord preserve us!'

'We know. We have found them both. Do you know where these Buenos Ayreans have gone?'

'They planned to wait for the *Unicorn*, to murder Mr Low and steal his boat. But when they saw the naval vessel flying the Union flag make its way up the sound, they took fright and fled. They headed west, by the path to Port Salvador. They told us to stay here or they would come back and kill us. But they have taken all the horses.'

'This is Lieutenant Smith, of His Majesty's Royal Marines. You have my word – and his – that we will catch these murderers and bring them to justice. Now, let us get you all out from this damp shed, and before a warm fire.'

'The whole matter is so sordid,' Darwin concluded angrily. 'Our country, dog-in-a-manger fashion, seizes an island and leaves to protect it a Union Jack. The possessor has, of course, been murdered, and now they send a lieutenant, with four sailors, without any instructions, to deal with any eventuality! It is a paltry little police action unworthy of the Crown. And here are we, supposed to be going about the business of surveying and specimen-collecting, and instead we find ourselves embroiled in a contemptible little colonial war, in which an army of ten has attacked a town of twenty-three inhabitants!'

'We really have no choice in the matter,' said FitzRoy wearily.

'You know as well as I do, FitzRoy, that Buenos Ayres will paint this across South America as a just revolt, of their poor subjects groaning under the tyranny of England.'

'And you know as well as I do that what occurred was cold-blooded murder.'

'I fail to see why we cannot just give back the islands.'

'Back to whom? The penguins?'

'If necessary, yes. This is a miserable little seat of discord. The only thing these islands are worthy of is the contemptible scene that has been acted upon them.'

'You seem to forget that one of my duties as captain of one of His Majesty's vessels is to protect British subjects under any circumstances. That is a duty I do not intend to neglect – under any circumstances.'

'Without horses, it will be damn-near impossible to run them to ground,' said Lieutenant Smith. 'Any assault would be visible a mile off across these moors.'

'How about a night attack?' suggested Sulivan.

'It would only work if we could completely surround them in pitch darkness,' FitzRoy pointed out. 'They will not sleep far from their mounts, and will not be so foolish as to give away their position by camping around an unextinguished fire.'

'Have we the men to surround them?'

'We are nine marines on the *Beagle*, sir,' said Serjeant Baxter, 'plus however many matlows the captain can spare.'

'It is not enough,' said FitzRoy. 'Even if we could take up position in the dark, they are as likely to escape during the confusion of a night attack as during the day. No, gentlemen. We have two advantages. First, these are adventurers, not regular troops. Mr Channon tells us they wear no uniforms. So they will be cold and damp and tired, and will have to warm their bones by day. So they should assist us by giving their position away. Any column of smoke will be visible for miles. Second, the mobility they are relying upon will make them over-confident. They will be expecting an attack by sea from the east, and will be prepared at any time to flee further west. If we can anticipate their flight, indeed if we can precipitate it, our men could be lying in wait for them as they flee. Let them ride to us on their horses.'

Sulivan scanned the sparsely detailed Spanish chart they had come to improve.

'To be lying in wait to the west, sir…well, that would entail our men marching fifty miles across open country from San Carlos Water, through soaking peat bogs and knee-deep swamps, with heavy packs.'

'Exactly. Not only will they not expect anyone to arrive from that quarter, they will certainly not be expecting it in three days' time.'

'Three *days*?'

'The *Beagle* can reach San Carlos Water betimes in the morning. After that, it is up to the Royal Marines. Lieutenant Smith? Serjeant Baxter? Can you and your men manage twenty-five miles a day across such terrain?'

'No question, sir,' said Smith confidently.

Serjeant Baxter's jaw hardened. 'We'll do it sir.'

'Observe,' said FitzRoy. 'To the west of Port Salvador there is only high ground – but it is split in two by a single valley here: the Arroyo Mato. If we can induce our quarry to head into that valley, they will fall into our trap. Mr Smith?'

'It sounds good, sir.'

'I think that on this occasion you had best dispense with your scarlet jackets, gentlemen. You will need to blend in with your surrounds rather better than you are accustomed to. And you and I, Mr Sulivan, shall also dispense with our uniforms. We shall approach from the east at first light in the *Unicorn*, disguised as sealers.'

'As sealers?'

'It is an obvious subterfuge to mask our approach. When this Captain Rivero sees us coming, he will see through it at once, and think it the best shot in our locker. With any luck he and his men will canter off up the valley, too busy mocking our efforts at concealment to be on their guard.'

'Will Mr Low consent to your using his boat in such a manner?'

'As of tomorrow, Mr Sulivan, the *Unicorn* will not be Mr Low's boat. It will be my boat.'

'*Your* boat?'

'My boat.' FitzRoy stood up to indicate that the discussion was over. 'Good luck, gentlemen. It's neck or nothing.'

'Good luck, sir.'

As Smith and Baxter made their exits, Sulivan hung behind, his face taut with concern.

'Yes, Mr Sulivan?'

'Sir, the *Unicorn*, I…'

'Mr May has looked her over. She is oak-built in a British yard, copper-fastened throughout, a hundred and seventy tons burthen, a first-rate sea-boat in very good keep, wanting only one or two sheets of copper and an outfit of canvas and rope. She will be ideal for our purpose.'

'But the cost, sir—'

'Six thousand paper dollars, that's about thirteen hundred pounds, for immediate possession, plus the services of Mr Low as pilot for a year. We can salvage the extra canvas and rope from the two wrecked sealers. She shall be renamed the *Adventure*, in order to keep up old associations, and we shall hire the American sealers to crew her. Mr Chaffers shall be her skipper, assisted by Mr Bennet and Midshipman Mellersh, until such time as Mr Wickham can pass over from Punta Alta. I shall send Mr Usborne to take his place.'

'American sealers? But—'

'I have memorialized the Admiralty requesting twenty supernumerary sailors for the longer term, and for the cost of her purchase to be defrayed. You do realize, Mr Sulivan, that the *Beagle* is the only survey vessel in operation today with no support tender? On our last voyage we were three ships, surveying only Tierra del Fuego. Now we are but one vessel, given a much wider area. The only way for us to complete our allotted task is if the *Adventure* surveys the Falklands for us, and is then adapted to carry our forward provisions. We shall get on faster, and much more securely, with a consort.'

'You know what I am saying to you!' burst out Sulivan. 'What if the Admiralty will not defray the cost? You have yet to hear about the *Paz* and the *Liebre*!'

'What if they will not?' asked FitzRoy lightly. *What if they will not indeed?* He thought of the letter he had just penned to Beaufort. '*I beg you, sir, pray fight my battle*,' he had written.

'What is most clearly expected of a gentleman,' he told Sulivan, 'is public service. Given voluntarily, and if necessary at his own expense. My conscience, Mr Sulivan, goads me to do all I can for the sake of what is *right*, without seeking for credit, or being cast down if everyone does not see things in the same light. I do not think there will be any more surveys of this area. Anything left undone by ourselves will remain neglected, to the detriment – very possibly the fatal detriment – of mariners to come. Further, the credit of the British as surveyors will be injured. I am not prepared for either of those eventualities to happen.'

'I know, sir, but *thirteen hundred pounds*?'

'Come, Mr Sulivan.' FitzRoy placed a hand upon his lieutenant's shoulder. 'What if our forthcoming action is a disaster? What if, by some mischance, the *Unicorn* is lost or taken? I have no other recourse – without you would prefer me to risk Mr Low's boat at no cost to myself?'

'No sir, but—'

'I may not proceed very quickly at my work, being only a beagle. But, at the end, a beagle is an animal with other worthwhile characteristics, I believe. Now, I think we have more important business at hand, do we not?'

'Yes sir, but…'

Sulivan gave up. Overwhelmed with concern as he was, he knew that nothing would divert FitzRoy from his course, once his mind was set. He could only pray that his friend had not just brought about his own financial ruin. The *Beagle*'s contingent of officers had now been reduced to a mere skeleton – the two of them apart, there were only the bos'n, the purser, Mr Bynoe, Mr Hamond and little Mr Hellyer remaining. Somehow, they would just have to make do.

Dense forests of entangled foliage writhed and coiled about each other, the swaying verdure teeming with life. Broad streams rolled and tumbled down side valleys before rushing to join the main torrent that parted the sodden moorland of the valley floor. But these teeming forests lay below the surface, on the kelp-choked coast of the islands, and the rivers and streams did not move, for they were rivers of barren, lifeless rock: great boulders and tiny pebbles of quartz, seemingly frozen in the act of flowing down the shallow valleys. How typical of this wretched place, thought Darwin, that everything should be so topsy-turvy. But from what peak had these numberless rocks been torn? There were no mountaintops here. Had they been brought from somewhere else by the deluge? How had Lyell's 'gradual change' turned parts of these drab, flat islands into what resembled the aftermath of a huge explosion?

The *Unicorn* slipped cautiously into Port Salvador, rain lashing her decks, the grey dawn slanting its uncertain light between the lowering clouds and rolling moors. It rained persistently in the Falklands, of course, but this was relentless. *Let us hope the marines have managed to keep their powder dry*, thought FitzRoy. Scouts had located Rivero's band the previous evening, exactly where he wanted them, grilling beef on the shore in the eastern reaches of the inlet, at the base of the Arroyo Mato. *Let us hope they have not had the wit to move position by night. Let us hope they are sufficiently unimaginative to head straight up the valley when they are disturbed. Let us hope that Smith and his men have located them too, and are in position.* What had seemed such a simple plan three days previously now seemed riddled with imponderables.

As FitzRoy intended, the *Unicorn*'s masts came into plain view long before the vessel itself, so that by the time they caught sight of Rivero's camp, it had become a scene of frenetic activity. Men were unravelling themselves from saddlecloth blankets and fumbling for guns and knives; others were on their feet already, untethering the horses. There were hasty confabulations on the shore.

Come on, come on, thought FitzRoy. *Make a run for it.*

He became aware of a set of white knuckles, gripping the rail to his right. It was Hamond. 'W-will we engage them, sir?'

'No, Mr Hamond, not if everything goes according to the plan. That side of things is up to Lieutenant Smith.'

'I h-hope everything goes according to the p-plan, sir.'

FitzRoy took pity on his old shipmate. 'If we find that we must engage them on shore, Mr Hamond, I should like you to stay aboard, and take charge of the *Unicorn*. Is that understood?'

'Y-yes sir. Th-thank you sir.'

But there was to be no shore engagement. The Buenos Ayreans were mounting their horses and trotting west up the valley, following the course of a muddy stream that tilted up between the boulders. It was all going according to plan. So far. FitzRoy raised his spyglass.

'They are putting the horses along.'

Come on, Smith. Where are you?

Rivero and his men had ridden a hundred yards up the valley now, their riderless mounts roped obediently behind, but there was still no sign of the marines. Perhaps the forced march had proved an impossible task? Perhaps they were trapped in a bog somewhere, up to their knees in stinking, cloying mud?

Suddenly a shot rang out, and the lead rider tumbled from his horse. A volley of firing followed, as Smith's marines stepped out from their concealing boulders on either side of the valley. Four or five more horsemen toppled from their saddles. The riderless horses, panicking, careered off in all directions. One Buenos Ayrean was dragged away by his terrified mount, his foot caught by the stirrup, his arms desperately shielding his head from the rocks that threatened to batter him to pieces. Another horse and rider could be seen galloping away at full speed up the valley. Two or three men had their arms up in attitudes of surrender.

'One of them at least has made his escape,' said FitzRoy, 'but I think we have the majority.'

'Bravo!' said Sulivan.

'Yes! B-bravo!' echoed Hamond.

The survey party worked with a renewed will thereafter. With Captain Rivero held in irons in the *Beagle*'s hold, awaiting trial in Rio de Janeiro, and all but one of his men killed or captured – Lieutenant Smith and his men had ridden off in pursuit of the escapee – the sailors' spirits were high on victory. By day they sprayed their names, and those of their friends and family, about the islands: Port FitzRoy, Darwin Harbour, Mount Usborne, Mount Sulivan, Port King, the Wickham Heights, and – in honour of FitzRoy's sister – the Fanny Isles. By night they sat around wreckwood fires telling stories and singing comic songs, and the devil take the hail-showers. They were, as Sulivan put it, 'in high feather'. They had two months to fill while the newly fitted-out *Adventure* was born from the remains of the old *Unicorn*, and they used them to cover huge swathes of territory.

A blustery morning found them setting up their lead- and transect-lines in a nearly closed bay to the south of Berkeley Sound – which, being naturally sheltered against the worst gales, seemed a better site for a harbour than Port Louis. The sudden bustle of unusual activity had not gone unnoticed, however. As the officers began to take their initial measurements of time, latitude and true bearing, an interested pair of eyes kept watch from the tussock grass above the beach. Yet although he could not be seen from the shore, the watcher was himself vulnerable to being observed from the higher ground behind; and so it came about that Darwin, returning from collecting geological specimens, caught sight of the watcher without being spotted in return. As stealthily as he could, heart pumping with excitement, he withdrew his geological hammer from his bag, and crept forward. So intent was his victim upon the inexplicable activities of the surveyors, that he seemed oblivious of what was about to befall him. Darwin raised the hammer high above his head, and brought it down with all his might. His victim collapsed with a howl of agony. It was the last sound he would ever make, his skull smashed in two as if it had been a boiled egg. On the beach, every man in the surveying party stood rooted to the spot, chilled by the sudden cry of mortal pain.

'Mr D-Darwin!' said Hamond. 'G-Good God, what was that *sound*?'

Darwin stood there looking sheepish. 'I've just killed the most *enormous* fox,' he said.

'It's fascinating. Either its senses have been quite dulled by the absence of predators, or it was so tame that it did not care.'

Darwin wriggled closer to the embers of the fire in his sleeping-sack. At the invitation of Mr Low, four officers were spending the night in the comparative warmth of the late Mr Brisbane's front parlour. Mr Hamond lay curled on the table-top, Mr Sulivan across three aligned chairs, the captain in a sagging flock sofa a good foot shorter than he was, while Darwin had bagged the warmest spot: he lay in the fireplace, staring at the orange glimmer of the peat as it ebbed in the darkness.

'I got the notion to use my hammer from Pernety,' he went on. 'I read that when he came here in 1764, the birds were so tame they would sit on his finger and allow themselves to be killed with a blow to the head. Since then they have been shot for food, and are more wary. I do believe that some of the birds here are migratory, and in Europe their nestlings are afraid from birth. There are rooks in Britain that will flee at the mere sight of a raised gun. What I should like to know is, has this acquired knowledge become hereditary? Has learning transmuted, if you will forgive the expression, into instinct?'

'It is a fascinating argument,' said FitzRoy. 'There is no question that mutability takes place *within* species, in consequence of altered climate, or food, or habits. Look at the Falklands cattle. But by what mechanism could *knowledge* be passed on through heredity?'

'I r-remember three hairy sheep being b-brought to England from S-sierra Leone as a c-curiosity, sir,' chipped in Hamond. 'Within a year they b-became woolly!'

'Exactly,' said FitzRoy. 'They were changed by *external* factors. It would not surprise me, for instance, to discover that the Falklands fox and the Fuegian fox are one and the same. That the animal has migrated eastward on the Falklands current, perhaps carried on floating ice or driftwood, and has increased in size here. All those penguins are obviously highly nutritious.'

'I'm afraid that point of view puts you in direct opposition to Lyell, my friend,' said Darwin. 'His latest volume rules out that very thing. He would ascribe every variation of that kind to its own "centre of creation", and therefore to its own species.'

'I am beginning to be less impressed by Mr Lyell with every passing day. He extols the virtues of gradual geological change, yet rules it out in animal variation.'

'Is that the johnny who denied the Biblical flood?' asked Sulivan.

'Yes.'

'He should take an excursion to the South Atlantic by surveying-boat. The evidence would be right before his jolly old eyes.'

'Mr Lyell is a genius,' said Darwin sniffily. 'He believes that the differences between two species of the same animal in two different regions cannot be superinduced during a length of time on account of the immutability of species.'

'It all depends on how one defines a species,' suggested FitzRoy. 'Every animal varies more or less, in outward form and appearance, from its fellows that habit different surroundings. But to fancy that every kind of mouse which differs externally from the mouse of another country is a distinct species is to me as difficult to believe as that every variety of the human race is a distinct species. A mouse is a mouse. A human is a human, be he an Englishman or a Fuegian. A fox is a fox, whether it be a Falklands fox or one of the type that Philos spends his days hunting to extinction in Shropshire. But a mouse cannot transmute into a cat. A fox cannot transmute into a penguin. A monkey cannot transmute into a human.'

'Philos is making a damned good job of extinguishing the race of Falklands foxes too, if you ask me,' said Sulivan. 'Expect to see it classified with the dodo soon.'

A chuckle ran round the room, and the hot breath of Darwin's laughter momentarily flared the glowing peat in the grate. 'I intend to make a special study of the tameness of the animal population before we leave,' he said. 'To ascertain by experimentation how fast each species learns from danger – then, perhaps, to take specimens on board, and see if their offspring really can receive their parents' newly acquired knowledge at birth. That way, I hope to prove whether or not Mr Lyell – Eeeegh!' He let out a piercing yell of disgust.

'W-what is it?' said Hamond, quaking.

'A rat! A huge rat!' shouted Darwin. 'Two huge rats! Oh, my God, they are attempting to share my sleeping-sack! Aaaah!' He wriggled frantically in the hearth.

'Sounds like they have heard about your special study, Philos, and are putting themselves forward!'

A roar of laughter rolled about the room at table-top level, punctuated by the anguished squeals of the philosopher, twisting and squirming below.

The next morning after breakfast they retreated to the *Beagle* – the rats having become something of a handful during the night – still debating the issue of animal variation. It was with regret that FitzRoy told himself he must break off to catch up with the ship's log, and requested his steward to locate Mr Hellyer. But a few moments later the steward returned with the news that Mr Hellyer was not to be found.

FitzRoy strode out on deck. 'Mr Bos'n, have you seen Mr Hellyer this morning?'

Sorrell fidgeted uncomfortably. 'Mr Hellyer, sir? I ain't seen him since yesterday, sir. I thought he was with you, sir.'

Further searches revealed that Hellyer was not on the ship.

'I thought I gave express orders that no one was to go out of sight of the vessel by himself except in civilized parts,' fumed FitzRoy. 'It is a standing order that every man who goes ashore must be accompanied by at least two others.'

'I'm sorry, sir,' stumbled Sorrell. 'I can't say I saw him leave the ship, sir.'

Eventually, it was discovered that one of the Frenchmen had spotted Mr Hellyer the previous afternoon, heading east along the shoreline, away from the *Beagle*. The whaleboats were launched, but it seemed to take an age to lower them into the water. FitzRoy and Bynoe and Sulivan ran along the beach instead, fanning out as they did so, calling Hellyer's name, panic inflecting their voices, fear energizing their efforts.

In a little creek, a mile from the ship, Bynoe found Hellyer's clothes, together with his watch, in a neat pile. Beside them lay his gun, which had been discharged. Hellyer himself looked almost angelic, calm-featured, eyes closed, mouth open, floating palely just below the surface; his ankles still entwined by the kelp fronds that had held him in their sinuous embrace as the tide rose over his head. Not a foot from his outstretched hand, its neck broken by the bullet's impact, floated the wave-tossed body of a Falklands kelp goose.

FitzRoy came in response to Bynoe's shouts; he said nothing, but drew his sword. Without removing his coat, he plunged into the water up to his chest, cutting back the kelp fronds. He raised Edward Hellyer's white, lifeless body up high, and lifted it out of the creek and on to the shore. There, he fell to his knees, wrapped the boy's pale form tightly in his arms, and he began to heave, uncontrollably, with great, shaking sobs. Tears coursed down his cheeks, running unchecked, until they mingled with the seawater that streamed from his uniform into the cold Atlantic.

CHAPTER SIX

Patagones, Patagonia, 6 August 1833

The tiny settlement of Patagones, defended by nothing but a wooden palisade, huddled against the crumbling bank of the Rio Negro. Only the fortified stone church stood out and beyond the defences, atop the bank, as if daring the godless Indians to do their worst. Just a few years back, there had been no white settlement this far south, but the fort at Argentina had held, and now more and more settlers were pouring across the Rio Colorado, fired by greed and bravado, ready to risk all they possessed to join the great land grab. But Patagones felt alone and exposed. Every whisper, every waving grass-stalk in the plains to the north, west or south occasioned a twitch of fear from its inhabitants. The east, where the blue Atlantic formed an implacable bulwark, was the only direction upon which they could safely turn their backs. The Horse Indians never attacked across water. They did not care for water. So the arrival of the *Paz* on this August morning was an unremarked event. The little village lay hushed in its inconspicuous hollow as James Harris, Charles Darwin and his new servant Syms Covington rode the tide in through the estuary.

In truth, Darwin was glad to be off the *Beagle*. Since Hellyer's death, a vexation of the spirit had seemed to settle upon her company. FitzRoy's agony had been almost unbearable to watch. Unable to deal with his own helplessness in the matter, he had surrendered to the foulest of tempers instead. The officers had a code for it: 'How hot is the coffee this morning?' they would ask each other. The crew had learned to be more unstinting in their efforts than before, more exact in their work, to avoid their master's terrible displeasure. FitzRoy had wrestled with his faith, trying to come to terms with the act of God that had robbed an innocent, well-meaning boy of his life. The more he tried to convince himself that the tragedy had been part of some greater plan, the more uneasy Darwin had become. The moral certainty of Christianity was starting to exasperate him. He was a Christian, of course, but he was not *certain* of anything.

The only joy of the preceding few months had been the universal hilarity with which the crew had acclaimed the return of Lieutenant Wickham. Wreathed in a huge beard, every part of his face so bronzed and blistered by sun and salt that he could barely speak, Wickham had stepped aboard with the air of a crazed Byzantine hermit rescued from his pillar. He had been too bemused to see the joke at first, for his fellow officers on the two small boats looked little different, but Sulivan had clapped him on the back and made a fuss of him, and soon Wickham had found himself laughing with the rest. Despite conditions that had caused even the most experienced of them to feel continuously seasick, he and his men had completed their task ahead of schedule, even discovering a new river – the Chubut, the Indians called it – in the process. They would now transfer to the *Adventure*. That vessel was currently floating alongside the *Beagle*, before being warped to her, heaved 'keel out' and coppered below, to protect her from the shipworms of the Pacific. It promised to be a dull, claustrophobic August. For Darwin, the wildlife and geology of the pampas loomed large as an interesting, exciting alternative.

Harris, who was still contracted to the *Beagle* for another six weeks, had offered to accompany Darwin on an overland expedition from the Rio Negro all the way up to Buenos Ayres, a distance of more than five hundred miles. As for the servant, well – why not? FitzRoy had a steward. The officers had a steward. Why shouldn't he, Darwin, have a servant too, to do the messy tasks like skinning animals, carrying heavy fossils or retrieving shot ducks from wet kelp? The only slight difficulties had been in actually locating a servant and paying for him. FitzRoy had relented and donated Covington, the ship's fiddler, on the basis that he was by far the most promising student in his Sunday reading and writing classes, and that, as a horse-butcher's son, he knew something of animal anatomy. Darwin could not say he cared unduly for his new helper: although reasonably handsome of face, he was big-boned, mulish and ginger, and had nothing to say for himself. There was an odd, almost accusing look in the boy's eye. He was expensive too: as to the six-hundred-pounds-a-year cost, Darwin had decided that his father – in due course – would undoubtedly see the wisdom of his decision, and would forward him the money. In the meantime, he had secured another loan from Mr Rowlett, the purser. He was aware that his increasing requests for funds were causing him to resemble the midshipman in *Persuasion*, but there was no doubting that the addition to his status served him well. Covington had even packed his master's equipment for the trip: clasp knife, preserving spirit, specimen jars and corks, pencils and notebooks, guns and ammunition, compass and geological hammer, a spare pair of stockings and – a little touch of civilization – his cotton nightcap and a selection of silk handkerchiefs.

Harris, who was evidently a familiar face in Patagones, had managed to hire an armed escort in the shape of five gauchos. They were tall, leathery, swaggering men, with luxuriant moustaches and long black hair that snaked down their backs. They were reverentially, grinningly polite from the start to Don Carlos, their *naturalista*, although their extravagant manners were clearly no more than a patina with which to coat a life lived at the edge of extreme violence. Each was badly disfigured by knife-cuts, a testament to the gaucho habit of settling even the pettiest disagreements with slashes to the nose or eyes. They looked, thought Darwin, as if they would cut your throat and make a bow at the same time. They wore white-striped ponchos and white boots, they rode white horses, they even smoked strange little cigars wrapped in white paper, which they called *cigaretos*. Before they knew that Darwin had learned Spanish, he listened to them conversing with a sixth gaucho, newly arrived in Patagones: was Don Carlos a *gallego*, the man wanted to know – was he worth robbing and murdering? No, they replied. This one is rich. This one is worth protecting. The rewards will be better.

The intelligence brought by the new arrival was encouraging for their prospects of a safe passage. General Rosas had been appointed by the government in Buenos Ayres to launch a war of extermination against the Indians, and to cleanse the countryside between the Rio de la Plata and the Rio Negro of their presence. To this end he was encamped eighty miles to the north, on the Rio Colorado, and had established a line of *postas*, or sentry-posts, between there and the capital. This would be the safest trail for Don Carlos to follow. Without further ado, that very afternoon, the party set out for the Rio Colorado, the gauchos in line ahead, their robes flowing, their spurs and swords clanking. They did not need supplies: they would eat on the hoof.

The countryside beyond Patagones was baked, lifeless, as bare and bristly as pigskin. What few grass-stalks eked out an existence here were brown and withered, the solitary bushes stunted and spiny. Bright splashes of colour, though, were provided by flamingos, poking about for worms in the *salinas*, great beds of salt five inches thick and many a league long. The gravel around these salt-flats was scattered with marine shells. The sea had been here, all right. But a single flood, of forty days and forty nights? Could it have left such thick salt deposits? Darwin knew in his heart that Lyell was correct on this point at least, that the ground hereabouts had been uplifted from the seabed.

Some twenty-five miles into the journey a lone tree appeared on the horizon, the solitary, neighbourless inhabitant of the arid plain.

'*Walleechu*,' said Esteban, the gaucho leader.

'I beg your pardon?' said Darwin.

'*Walleechu* – the god of the Indians.'

'The local Indians worship this tree,' explained Harris. 'It is the only one they have ever seen.'

As they drew closer, Darwin could see that, although bare of leaves on account of the season, the tree was festooned with offerings: cigars, bread, meat, strips of cloth, flasks of precious water and other offerings hung from its branches by lengths of coloured thread. About its base were strewn bleached horse-bones, the remnants of religious sacrifices.

'The Indians call it god. We call it dinner.' Esteban grinned as he unhooked the food and drink from the tree and placed it in his saddlebag for later consumption.

'Um...should we really be doing that?' asked Darwin guiltily.

'It makes them happy.' Esteban shrugged his shoulders. 'They think

God has paid them a visit.'

The gauchos spurred their horses northwards once more, their robes rippling. The Englishmen headed off in pursuit, Darwin with a degree of *élan* gleaned from years of experience, Harris's horse straining under the immense weight of its rider, Covington bringing up the rear, mute and ungainly on his long-suffering mount, saddlesore but uncomplaining.

That night they lay out under the stars in the boundless stillness of the plain, the Milky Way wheeling gloriously above them, its myriad uncountable pinpricks blurring into a soft arch of light that Darwin wished he could reach out and touch.

'It is the most beautiful thing I have ever seen,' he thought, then realized he had spoken aloud.

Harris, who had guzzled most of the food from the tree and was labouring at his night's rest, adjusted his bulk for a better look.

'The Indians believe that the stars are old warriors. That the sky is the field where they hunt ostriches. All those milky clouds of stars are the feathers of the ostriches they kill.'

How blissful, Darwin reflected, to be able to believe such a thing.

'Don Carlos?'

'Yes, Esteban?'

'May I ask you a question?'

'Of course.'

'Is it true that if you made a hole in the ground, if you dug far enough, you would come to a country where there was six months of day, and six months of night, and where the people walk upside-down?'

'One question with about twenty answers,' murmured Harris.

So Darwin discoursed at length about the rotation of the earth's axis in relation to the sun's light, about the earth's gravitational field, and about the broad make-up of the planet's various peoples. Harris came to his rescue whenever his Spanish faltered, until finally Esteban seemed satisfied.

'Don Carlos?'

'Yes?'

'May I ask you another question?'

'Of course.' Darwin wondered what great scientific or theological principle he would have to translate into pidgin Spanish next.

'You have travelled to many lands. Is it not true that the ladies of Buenos Ayres are the handsomest in the world?'

'Charmingly so,' Darwin reassured him, as solemnly as he could.

'Do ladies in any other part of the world wear such large combs?'

'No, they do not.'

'Look there!' said Esteban to his fellows. 'A man who has seen half the world says it is the case. We always thought it so, but now we know it!'

'Now may I ask *you* a question, Esteban?'

'Of course, Don Carlos.'

'Do you and your friends believe in God?'

Esteban laughed.

'In God, Don Carlos? There is no God. As you saw yourself – if you give your most precious thing to God, you might as well throw it away.'

The next day they passed the ruins of *estancias* – once-substantial farms, built by courageous but foolhardy settlers who had pushed just a few miles too far into unsecured territory. The buildings were blackened ruins, their corrals smashed down, the remains of their vegetable gardens parched and lifeless.

'The Indians always fire the farms,' explained Esteban, 'so that they cannot be reoccupied.'

'What happened to the farmers?' asked Darwin.

'What always happens to farmers. The young girls are taken as slaves. The rest – the men, old women and children – are tortured to death. They have their faces cut off and their throats slit.'

Darwin shivered. 'Are there any Indians here now?'

'Do you see any?'

Darwin scanned the empty horizon. 'No.'

Esteban laughed. 'Don Carlos, even if there were Indians here, you would not see them. They are too clever. But do not worry – we are not farmers, waiting like stupid fat ostriches to be put to the slaughter. We have fast horses, and guns, and knives, and we know how to use them.

And you will see, Don Carlos, before the year is out, General Rosas will have destroyed every single Indian between the Plata and the Negro.'

'Have you and your men ever been attacked by Indians?'

'Of course. One time at Punta Alta there were four of us. We were surprised by Araucanians – raiders from across the mountains, to the south of Chili. They are the most dangerous. They use *chuzos* – long lances. I was the only survivor. I had the fastest horse.'

Darwin scanned the horizon once more, his stomach fluttering.

'Tell me, Don Carlos, do you like beef?'

'Do I like beef? Yes. Why?'

Esteban indicated a solitary Friesian cow, wandering the umber plains against a sky of the palest blue. 'Dinner for tonight,' he replied, and gave one of his fellow gauchos the nod to run it down. The man pulled his *bolas* out of his belt and set off after the animal, the three stone balls blurring into a perfect circle above his head as he thundered in pursuit. The cow gave a great moo and turned to flee, but the *bolas* whizzed with deadly accuracy from its assailant's hand: the speeding arc of the stones intersected with the graceful, rhythmic parabola of the animal's gallop, each bringing the other to an abrupt, chaotic stop. The cow lay pinned in the dust by the thongs, thrashing helplessly. Its distress cries were cut short in an instant, as the hunter dismounted in one swift move, drew his knife from his belt and slit the animal's throat. Then, before its death throes were even complete, the dust around it a red slick, its bulging white eyeballs staring up in terror, the gaucho sliced into its rump, cut out a block of steak sufficient for eight men, and wrapped it in his saddlecloth.

'Sharp work,' murmured Covington admiringly, opening his mouth at last. The *Beagle*'s voyage was the first time he had journeyed beyond the confines of rural Bedfordshire; it drew him closer to home to witness some skill or accomplishment that would have garnered a reassuring nod back in Ampthill.

'Are we going to just…*leave* the rest of it?' Darwin indicated the body of the cow, which had finally given up its struggle for life.

'There are many cows. You will see. They once belonged to the *estancias*. The Estancia del Rey had a hundred thousand head of cattle. There are still many left, running wild.' He indicated another cow on the northern horizon. 'Tell me, Don Carlos, do you use the *bolas* to catch cattle in your country?'

'Er, no, no, we don't.'

'Ah, so you use the *lazo* instead. Would any of you like to try the *bolas*?'

Harris declined, perhaps wisely in view of the fact that he appeared to weigh almost as much as his horse. Covington shook his head politely, out of deference to his master. Darwin, however, was enthusiastic: he took the *bolas* that had been unwound from the dead cow and whirred them above his head. It seemed easy enough.

He set off at a gallop, the others in pursuit. This time the cow, an Ayrshire, had considerable advance warning of his intentions, and began its flight at once, but Darwin's big white stallion soon overhauled it. Before long the two beasts were galloping alongside each other across the level ground. The philosopher unhooked the *bolas* from his saddle and rotated them at high speed about his upraised wrist; he took aim; and then he let fly. The *bolas* flashed from his arm and wrapped themselves neatly about the animal's fetlocks, bringing it crashing to the ground.

Unfortunately, it was the wrong animal. Darwin's horse, which had been *bola*'d many times as part of its training, knew exactly what to do: let the legs go limp, go into a roll, being careful not to crush one's mount. As horse and rider went flying, it even managed to deposit Darwin with some precision into a passing thornbush.

The gauchos arrived, almost sick with laughter. 'We have seen every sort of animal caught, Don Carlos, but we have never before seen a man caught by himself!'

Darwin's morning-coat was ripped almost beyond repair, but he did not care. Let them laugh – he would soon be in the way of it. He felt free, and wild, as if he was living the life of his dreams. If there was danger, then it gave the trip a relish, like salt to meat. That night, as they lay out under the stars, when he was absolutely sure that nobody was looking, he surreptitiously pulled off his nightcap and threw it away.

General Rosas' camp lay on the far bank of the Rio Colorado, a square of covered waggons a quarter-mile across that fenced in an entire army division and all its artillery pieces. After two and a half days without encountering a living soul, all of a sudden the empty landscape swarmed with soldiers: soldiers marching, soldiers riding, soldiers cleaning their weapons, soldiers lazing about, soldiers eating, drinking, gambling or picking fights with each other. The river itself, thick and muddy and bordered by reed-beds, cut and twisted through the baking plain; an immense troop of mares was being driven across it, on their way to provide food for the divisions fighting in the interior. Hundreds upon hundreds of horses' heads all pointing the same way protruded from the turbid current, ears alert and nostrils distended with effort, turning this way and that like a flotilla of fish, as if guided by a single collective intelligence.

'The gauchos love Rosas,' Harris explained to Darwin in English. 'They think he is one of them. He even dresses like them when he is among them. Anything they can do – horse-breaking, bareback-riding, whatever you care to name – he can do just as well. And he is a mortal strict disciplinarian. When he makes rules, he sticks by them. At his *estancia* once, he banned the carrying of knives on a Sunday. Then his steward pointed out that the general himself was carrying one. So he had himself put into the stocks for the day. When the steward took pity and released him, he had the man put in there instead, for violating the law. If he is not in charge of this country within a year or two, I'll eat my hat.'

'I should very much like to meet this General Rosas.' Darwin turned to Esteban. 'How do we get across?'

'How do we get across, Don Carlos? We do what the horses do. We swim.'

So saying, the gaucho stripped naked, rolled his clothes and belongings into a bundle, and strapped them to the top of the bewildered horse's head with his belt. Then he drove the animal down the riverbank with a hefty smack, plunged into the water after it, and held on to its tail while it pulled him across. Whenever the horse tried to turn, or dislodge him, or alter its course, he splashed water in its face to keep it on track. Pulling powerfully against the flow, it was not long before the animal had breasted the current, and horse and rider stood dripping on the opposite bank.

Darwin was next to go, and made the crossing with surprising ease.

He was able to enjoy the luxury of donning his battered morning-coat once more, while simultaneously enjoying Harris and Covington's floundering progress through the Rio Colorado's glutinous brown soup. How preposterous Covington looked – he even swam gracelessly – while Harris resembled a vast pink sea creature, his glistening flesh porpoising unpleasantly through the turgid waters.

Once dressed and reconstituted on the far side, the party reported to Rosas' sentries. They were escorting the famous English *naturalista* Don Carlos, Esteban explained, who had travelled many thousands of leagues in the hope of an audience with the mighty General Rosas. After an hour or so's delay, they were informed that the general had indeed granted an audience to his distinguished visitor, but that he would not be at liberty to meet him until the following day. So, for the next twenty-four hours, they had no option but to kick their heels around Rosas' camp. There were a good many gauchos in Rosas' ranks, men exactly like those of Darwin's escort, but the vast majority of the uniformed foot-soldiers milling about were either black – former slaves, presumably – or of mixed race. Darwin thought he could detect some Indian blood present as well. 'I know not the reason,' he remarked to Harris, 'but men of such origin seldom have a good expression of countenance.'

'They are a bunch of cut-throats, if you wish my opinion,' said Harris. 'We should stay close to the cut-throats we have hired.'

After an uneasy night spent huddled within the perimeter of the campfire glow, Rosas' sentries came for Darwin at first light. It was time to meet the general.

'I am indeed honoured that the famous English *naturalista* Don Carlos has come all this way to my humble camp. Please, I beg you to suffer my tardiness.'

In truth, Darwin had only been waiting five minutes in Rosas' tent, but from the gravity of the general's apology one would think it had been an hour.

'Please, say no more of it. And I am – I am not really very famous in my own country.'

'Don Carlos, I am not a man of science. But His Majesty's Navy would not appoint a *naturalista* for a voyage of such importance were he not of some standing. Is it not so?' Rosas smiled, displaying a set of perfect teeth. His was a dazzling, expensive smile, almost bereft of humour but awash with charm. His English was near-perfect, the language of an educated man, with only the faintest trace of an accent.

'I suppose so,' conceded Darwin immodestly.

'I knew it to be the case.'

Darwin could not believe how youthful the general seemed: he was forty years old, perhaps, but he possessed the athleticism and energy of a much younger man. Rosas' manner was warm and charismatic. His face was handsome and open, with a proud jawline and a strong, aquiline nose, the whole framed by neatly clipped sideburns. Only the defiant gleam of his dark, hooded eyes did not match the conventional picture of the romantic hero. He was not attired in his gaucho's costume today, but was immaculately kitted out in full dress uniform, with a red sash, a high, stiff collar and lashings of gold braid.

'You must excuse the formality,' said Rosas, catching Darwin's gaze island-hopping down his brightly polished brass buttons. 'Even in the midst of a war, one must conduct formal parades. But between you and me, Don Carlos, I am at my happiest out of uniform, dressed informally, out riding with my cattle, or playing with my children. I have an *estancia* – did you know that? – with three hundred thousand head of cattle. I am a simple man at heart, a family man. I loathe and despise war. But when our children are threatened, when our farms are threatened, when Christianity itself is threatened, what can we do but take up arms?'

'What indeed?' said Darwin, eager to agree with his charming host. 'Is the war going well?'

'As the gauchos always say, Don Carlos, "*¿Quien sabe?*" – but I am optimistic. You see, my friend, we are facing a new kind of war here today – not a conventional war but a war of sudden terror. We have all been reared on battles between great warriors, between great nations, between powerful forces and political ideologies that dominated entire continents. And these were struggles for conquest, for land, or money, and the wars were fought by massed armies. But a new and deadly disease has arisen – that is the only word for it – a desire among our enemies to inflict destruction unconstrained by human feeling on our women, on our children, on our civilian population. Our new world rests on order. The danger is disorder, and it is spreading like contagion.'

'I have seen the burnt-out *estancias*.'

'Then you will know exactly what I mean. We are so much more powerful in all conventional ways than those who would spread terror in our midst. The Indians do not have large armies or precision weapons. They do not need them. Their weapon is chaos. Even in all our might, we are taught humility. But in the end, Don Carlos, it is not our power alone that will defeat this evil. Our ultimate weapon is not our guns but our beliefs. Ours are not European values – they are the universal values of the human spirit. The spread of freedom is the best security for the free. It is our last line of defence and our first line of attack. Just as our enemy seeks to divide in hate, so we have to unify around an idea. That idea is liberty.'

'I suppose...the Indians would say it is their land to do what they wish thereupon.'

'Of course, Don Carlos, of course. When I speak of liberty, I speak of liberty for all. But they must accept liberty before they can enjoy its benefits. And what benefits, Don Carlos! At present, the land is unused, unexploited. What potential there is for farming, for mining, for shipping. What potential there is for jobs for all Indians, on the farms, on the mines, at the ports! Instead their chiefs and their priests insist upon preserving a medieval way of life. They deny progress. They deny civilization. They deny liberty itself. Their leaders are self-appointed – they even deny the will of their own people. Many of the followers of these leaders are fanatics, willing to die for their cause. My troops have just returned from an engagement in the *cordillera*. They killed a hundred and thirteen of these extremists, including forty-eight men, and recovered many stolen horses. My troops tell me that one dying Indian seized with his teeth the thumb of his adversary, and allowed his own eye to be forced out sooner than relinquish his hold. Another, who was wounded, feigned death, keeping a knife ready to strike one more fatal blow. I tell you, they are quite fanatical.'

'Forty-eight men dead!' Darwin did a little high-speed mental arithmetic. 'So…sixty-five of the dead were not men?'

'Sadly, Don Carlos, however surgical one attempts to be when one strikes at the heart of terror, there are always civilian casualties. These are to be regretted. Besides, the Indians do breed so. But my men are always careful to spare the lives of children caught in these encounters – they are given the chance to build new lives as servants in the great houses of our most powerful families. Don Carlos, I would be the first to admit that troops in this war, or any war, can occasionally let their enthusiasm run away with them. But to rein our troops in, to force them to fight with one hand tied behind their backs, could be fatally damaging to our cause. If we do not act strongly now, we will be guilty of hesitating in the face of this menace, when we should have given leadership. That is something history will not forgive. But before those history books are written, we will hunt down our adversaries, and we will continue to do so for as long as it takes to bring them to the justice that they deserve. This is not the time to falter – I will not be party to such a course. We must show that we have the courage to do the right thing.'

It was a powerful speech, and Darwin felt fairly blown away by the sheer persuasiveness of it. Rosas appeared to him as a Christian knight, standing defiant, boldly protecting the vulnerable and the innocent.

'They tell me, General, that this is a war with no prisoners taken.'

'On the Indian side, perhaps. They murder, they torture and they mutilate. We, of course, take our enemies prisoner in the conventional way. But I must stress that this is not a conventional war. So they are not *prisoners of war*. They are criminals, and liable to the due process of Christian justice as would any criminal be. And, as I am sure you aware, the penalty for murder, or for helping to plan or carry out murder, is death.'

'Of course.'

'Tell me, Don Carlos, are you disturbed by the sight of blood?'

'Not at all. I am a keen sportsman. Why, only yesterday, one of my gauchos slit the throat of a cow! I assure you, such things do not bother me.'

'Good. Then what you are about to witness will not seem very different.

Come with me.'

He led Darwin out of the tent and across the makeshift parade ground, through a blizzard of salutes. They arrived at a large, fenced-off compound, where Indian prisoners knelt in chains, their eyes blindfolded and their mouths tightly gagged. Rosas spoke to the adjutant, who had three prisoners separated from the others and brought into an adjoining tent. Three loaded pistols were placed on the table opposite.

'These men,' Rosas explained to Darwin, 'were captured at the recent battle in the *cordillera*. We know from our spies that they were on their way to a general council of the Indians to plan a new wave of atrocities. They have already been condemned to death by due process of law. I am now prepared to offer them an amnesty – to show mercy – if they will only tell me where the council is taking place.'

Darwin looked at the three, who stood blinking and panting, their gags and blindfolds having been removed. They were superb physical specimens, in their mid-twenties perhaps, tall and muscular, each between six and seven feet tall, with long, wild, jet-black hair and coppery skin. Rosas nodded to the adjutant, who picked up the first pistol and placed it between the eyes of the first Indian.

'*¿Donde sera la reunion?*' demanded Rosas. Where will the council take place?

'*No sé,*' replied the Indian blankly. Rosas gave another nod, and the adjutant shot the prisoner through the head. Darwin almost jumped out of his skin. His ears rang from the deafening report of the gun. Blood pooled at the far wall of the tent, where the impact of the ball had flung the Indian's body. Darwin found himself gagging for breath.

The adjutant placed the second gun against the forehead of the second Indian. A cloud of blue smoke hung in the air from the first shot, making the general's point as eloquently as ever he could have done himself.

'*¿Donde sera la reunion?*' demanded Rosas, more forcefully this time.

'*No sé,*' replied the second Indian, bluntly, defiantly.

Again, Rosas nodded. Again, the adjutant shot the man clean through the head. This time Darwin was prepared, but that did nothing to lessen the shock. He had seen public hangings outside the Old Bailey, of course, but this was a different sort of execution. Somehow the baying crowds, the food stalls, the ribald remarks, the sheer distance involved when the unfortunates of Newgate met their fate, all combined to lend the proceedings an air of bleak levity. This was altogether starker, more brutal. The second Indian jack-knifed backwards and slumped to the ground, his chains clanking once before falling silent. The adjutant placed the gun at the third Indian's temple, smiling this time. Rosas spoke once more. '*¿Donde sera la reunion?*'

'*Adelante. Dispara. Yo soy un hombre. Sé como morir.*' Go ahead. Fire. I am a man. I know how to die.

Rosas looked at him. '*Tu deseo ha sido concedido.*' Your wish has been granted.

Darwin stared hard at his feet. The noise of the third gunshot assaulted his eardrums. When he looked up, the third Indian was dead.

'Do you see what I mean?' asked Rosas. 'They are fanatics.'

'I can tell that what you have witnessed has disturbed you.'

Rosas' voice was full of concern. They sat in his quarters once more, a plate of fresh meat interposed between them on the table, but Darwin did not feel like eating.

'Allow me to apologize for your distress. But when you have seen what I have seen, Don Carlos – dead children, mutilated women – I must take the tough decisions that are necessary to modernize our society. Patagonia and the pampas must be opened up to free and fair settlement, and these criminals must be wiped out as part of our programme of national consolidation. Ours is a passion allied to reason, Don Carlos, an alliance of strength and justice for the many, and not the few, for the future, and not the past. We must develop a strong, united society, which gives each citizen the chance to develop their potential to the full.'

Sincerity shone from Rosas' every pore; Darwin felt the warmth of the general's conviction, and his doubts began to recede once more.

'I have heard tell, General,' he ventured, 'that you are the only man capable of bringing together Buenos Ayres, and Mendoza, and the United Provinces, and all the countries of this region.'

'Please, Don Carlos, I do not seek power for myself. I only want what is best for Buenos Ayres. But I tell you that if the countries that depend upon the silver trade were to form a federation – the federation of *Argentina*, let us say – with a single currency, a single defence policy, a single economic policy and a single law, then the benefits of such co-operation would be immeasurable. I do not speak of amalgamation into a single, huge nation, of course – nothing could be further from my mind – but to be left out of such a union would be a catastrophe, whether or not I were to lead it. It is better, is it not, to be a leading partner, helping to shape such a federation from the inside, than to be isolated on the outside?'

'Absolutely,' agreed Darwin. Rosas' logic was unanswerable.

The general indicated the plate between them. 'Please. Have something to eat. You must recruit yourself, and settle your stomach.'

Darwin took a reluctant bite. 'What is it? Veal?'

'Puma. Our puma-extermination programme has been a tremendous success. Already we have killed over a hundred pumas in three months. The benefits to agriculture are incalculable. I tell you, Don Carlos, the power of progress, allied to our essential values and beliefs, will prove unstoppable.'

Every syllable the general uttered seemed to be filled with integrity and scrupulous candour. Whatever the atrocities committed by either side in this nasty little Latin American war, here, Darwin felt, was a man with at least the potential to lead his people to some sort of salvation.

'Don Carlos, I am afraid that my time is running short. But before you return to your own country, let me make you two presents. First' – the general drew a piece of paper from the table drawer, scribbled a few lines thereon and sealed it with red wax melted in the candle flame – 'let me give you a passport. If ever you should meet any problems with officialdom, this paper should see you safely through. It is valid for all the territories under army control. Woe betide the man who dares harm any traveller carrying such a passport!

'Second, Don Carlos, I hope you will forgive my presumption, but I notice that your morning coat has become ripped. While I cannot hope to replace the costume of an English gentleman here on the Rio Colorado, I am told that you like to ride with the gauchos' – Rosas snapped his fingers, and a servant appeared at the tent flap – 'and that you are fast becoming an expert with the *bolas*.'

The servant marched across and presented Darwin with a complete gaucho costume – spurs, boots, striped white poncho, voluminous scarlet drawers – and his very own set of *bolas*.

'General Rosas! What a wonderful present! I couldn't possibly—'

'We will make of you *un gran galopeador* yet, Don Carlos!'

'I am indebted. Thank you so very, very much.'

'And remember.' Rosas reached across and clasped Darwin by the wrist. 'When you return to England, tell them that we are fighting the most just of all wars, because it is a war against barbarians.'

He is man of quite extraordinary character, thought Darwin. *I know that he will use his influence to the prosperity and advancement of his country.*

He walked from Rosas' tent in a daze.

'How was it?' asked Harris.

'Amazing,' replied Darwin. 'Quite amazing. He is an incredible man.'

Alongside a row of tents, a figure in bright clown's makeup was performing a slapstick act before a row of cross-legged troops.

'Who in God's name is *that*?' asked Darwin.

'Oh…the general likes to surround himself with the latest comedians and entertainers.'

'He did not strike me as a humorous individual.'

'Indeed not. But I dare say it makes him popular among the troops.'

Harris had woken that morning with a stomach complaint, having eaten none too wisely the previous evening, and announced to Darwin that he would travel with the next convoy of soldiers instead, in the hope of catching him up at some point. So it was that a column of six gauchos took the road north out of camp that day, a proud Don Carlos among their number, the solitary, lumbering figure of Syms Covington bringing up the rear in his naval ducks.

I really must get him a servant's uniform, thought Darwin. *He's making me look absurd.*

*

There were seventeen *postas* strung between the Rio Colorado and Buenos Ayres, a total of seventeen days' ride across the stark emptiness of the pampas. Throughout their journey, the evidence stacked up against FitzRoy and his Biblical flood. On the first day they crossed an eight-mile-wide belt of sand dunes, almost certainly the former estuary of the Rio Colorado at the point where it had entered the sea. On the second day, they came upon gigantic heaps of half-buried animal bones – the result, Esteban told him, of the *gran seco* drought of 1827–30, when a million cattle had perished for want of water.

What would be the opinion of a future geologist viewing such an enormous collection of bones? wondered Darwin. *The bones of all kinds of animals, embedded in one thick earthy mass? Would he not attribute it to a flood having swept over the surface of the land, rather than to the common order of things?*

He learned to catch partridge in a different way, by riding round them in ever-decreasing circles until the birds were sufficiently confused to submit uncomplainingly to their fate. He tried to catch armadillo, but they buried themselves in the sandy soil so quickly that he could not grab them fast enough. Esteban showed him how to fall from his horse directly on to one before it could disappear. The beast curled into an armoured ball in the gaucho's arms, like a giant woodlouse.

'It seems almost a pity to kill such nice little animals – they are so quiet,' said Esteban with a jaunty grin, sharpening his knife on the armadillo's hide before sliding it ruthlessly between two of its armoured plates. 'Dinner for this evening, my friends,' he announced.

At the *posta* that night, little more than an open shed with stabling for the horses and a fire of thistle-stalks, Darwin sat playing cards with the gauchos, drinking *maté* tea and smoking their little paper *cigaretos*. He lost money, of course, but that was as nothing to the joy of his companionship with these wild men. Covington, like Banquo's ghost, was a pale, sullen presence somewhere behind him, but he did his best to forget about Covington during the evenings. He had spent much of the day teaching the boy how to shoot birds with a rifle, using mustard-shot and dust-shot so as not to damage the all-important skins; by evening, Covington's principal duty was to melt into the background. Somehow, the servant's relentless indifference impinged upon the masculine solidarity that bonded him to these marvellous warriors, who were so fearless, so alert, so attuned to their surroundings. A faint cry in the distance, a call from the pampas so slight that Darwin had barely noticed it, froze the card-game in an instant. Every head inclined. One of the gauchos went to the door, knife drawn, and placed his ear to the ground. Then he stood up and laughed. 'Only a pteru-pteru, boys,' he said. 'Only a pteru-pteru.'

On the fourth day, Darwin galloped after a rhea, a South American ostrich, which scooted along the brow of a hill and opened its wings to catch the wind, like a ship-of-the-line making all sail. Proudly, he brought it down with his *bolas*, and the gauchos cut its throat. Covington skinned it, which left the boy crimson to the elbows; they kept the meat for dinner and the skin to be packed up and sent back to Henslow. Then they found its nest, packed with some twenty huge eggs, and rifled that too.

'If you are a *naturalista*, Don Carlos, then you should seek the *Avestruz Petise*,' said Esteban, as they loaded armfuls of eggs into their saddlebags.

'An *Avestruz Petise* – what's that?'

'It is a *ñandu* – an ostrich. But it is smaller, and more beautiful, with feathers down to its claws. Its white feathers are tipped with black, and its black feathers likewise are tipped with white. It is very rare indeed. I have only seen one in my whole life.'

'Esteban, I should very much like to capture an *Avestruz Petise*.'

They roasted Darwin's rhea at the *posta* that night, the best-kept sentry-post they had yet visited. The *posta*-keeper, an old black lieutenant, had been a slave in the West Indies and spoke English. Clearly, he took pride in his command and had worked painstakingly to improve the rudimentary little lodge. He had built a special room for visitors, decorated with crucifixes and engravings cut from the scriptures; there was a small corral for the horses, beautifully constructed from sticks and reeds; there were even little flower-beds planted around the building, which the lieutenant watered assiduously. It might have been a pretty freeman's cottage on Jamaica, but for the defensive ditch, and the line of straggly, beady-eyed vultures waiting hungrily for the next Indian attack.

'By your leave, sir,' said the lieutenant respectfully, 'but I believe you are the famous *naturalista* from England? I am very proud, sir, to have you as guest at my *posta*, sir, very proud indeed.'

'Thank you,' said Darwin graciously. 'Pray tell me, what is your name?'

'My name is Michael, sir. I have no other name. I have the honour five years ago to be released from my servitude to Mr Henry Morgan, sir, of Kingston, and to be made a free man. But there are not many opportunity for a free man in Kingston, sir, so I coming south, sir, to Buenos Ayres, where I am conscripted to the army, sir.'

'Conscripted? That cannot have pleased you, after all those years as a slave.'

'Oh, sir, I tell you, General Rosas is a great man, sir. He has give me this *posta*, sir, to command all by myself. Now the general, sir, he has make my dream come true, sir. He is an uncommon great man, sir.'

'Will you not join us, Michael? Will you not come and play at cards with us?'

'Oh no sir. Michael is a black man, sir. I cannot sit at cards with white men, sir, that would not be right, it would be disrespectful, sir.'

Embarrassment and confusion mingled in Darwin's expression. 'Really. I should be quite honoured.'

'No sir. You are most kind to Michael, sir, but that would not be the right thing, sir, not the right thing at all.'

He headed off to fuss over the night's bedding. The gauchos cackled quietly among themselves.

'I don't know why he bothers with his flowers and crucifixes so,' said Esteban, 'when all he has to look forward to is a knife in his back.'

'What do you mean?' asked Darwin sharply.

'*Posta*-keeper is the shortest job in the world, Don Carlos. The Indians will come. Maybe not tonight or tomorrow night. Maybe next month. But they will come one night, when he is alone. And they will kill him and burn his *posta*. To be a *posta*-keeper, my friend, is a one-way ticket to hell!'

'I thought you did not believe in God.'

'I do not believe in God. But I never said I do not believe in hell. We are all of us going to hell, Don Carlos!' Esteban laughed, cheerfully and throatily.

Michael reappeared with a fresh pot of *maté* and a solicitous look. 'I bring you some fresh hot tea, sir. I think maybe your old tea was gotten a little cold, sir.'

'Michael...?'

'Yes sir?'

'Do you not worry that perhaps, one night, the Indians will come?'

'Oh, they will come right enough, sir, they will come, I know that for sure. And when they come, Michael will sell his life dearly, sir, I know that for sure as well.'

'But aren't you...aren't you *scared*?'

'Michael has live a long time, sir, long enough for any man. And the general, sir, he has give me my dream, a little house of my own, sir, and make me a happy man. So when the Indians come to take it back sir, well, then Michael won't have nothing to live for no more, sir. So Michael will sell his life dearly, sir, when they come.'

He smiled at the simplicity of the equation, and moved away once more.

After the fifth *posta*, a black peaty plain opened out before them, with meadows of long grass and silvery patches of surface water. Ducks and cranes congregated on the mirror-smooth pools, and flocks of ibis flapped overhead. It was, Darwin told a phlegmatically unimpressed Covington, exactly like Cottenham Fen. They saw herds of wild deer, and clusters of ostrich, cattle and wild horses cropping the increasingly lush grass. That night giant hailstones as big as apples fell upon the *posta*, leaving the ground all about strewn with dead animals, and badly cutting the face of a gaucho who put his head outside to take a look.

'One more cut won't make a difference to *that* face,' remarked one of his fellows.

When the meat from the animals pounded to death by the hailstones ran out, one of the gauchos killed a deer, by the simple expedient of walking up to it and slitting its throat.

'They are afraid of men on horseback. Not of men on foot,' he explained.

The complete opposite of the reactions of a British deer, thought Darwin. *Yet the responses of a British deer are established from birth. Proof – absolute proof – that knowledge can transmute from generation to generation.*

Late on the eleventh day, as they trotted across a gently undulating plain of emerald grass, the breeze gusting in their faces, the gauchos stopped dead as one, as if someone had flicked an invisible switch. A deer stood silhouetted on the crest of a rise ahead, itself stock still, ears pricked. Esteban motioned urgently for silence.

'What is the matter?' hissed Darwin.

'That deer. Something has alarmed it. Something upwind. Something out of sight.'

He gave the order to dismount, and to keep as low as possible. One of the gauchos darted forward, his knife clamped between his teeth, and as he approached the brow of the rise, slithered forward on his belly. Peering over the ridge, he made hand signals back to the rest of the party.

'Three horsemen. They don't ride like Christians,' said Esteban.

'Are they Indians?' hissed Darwin, shocked.

'*¿Quien sabe?* If they are no more than three, it does not signify.'

'What if there are more than three? Maybe there are hundreds of them nearby!'

'*¿Quien sabe?* But load your pistol, and be ready to ride.'

Darwin's heart pounded in his chest. Indians, here, so close to Buenos Ayres!

A few minutes ticked by, excruciatingly slowly, but nobody moved an inch. Darwin's stomach felt impossibly heavy, like a pound of lead. The watcher on the hill lay stock still on his stomach, staring intently ahead. Then, finally, he moved. He stood up with a hearty belly laugh, and began to wave his arms manically back at them.

'*¡Mujeres!*' the man shouted across the meadow.

'They are women!' said Esteban with relief. 'That is why they don't ride like Christians – they are women!'

'*Women?*' said Darwin, incredulously. 'Women from *where*?'

The mystery was solved a mere league further on: a new *estancia* spread itself confidently before them, clean white lines at right-angles to the shining turf. The added presence of an entire troop of cavalry, heading south from Buenos Ayres, had obviously emboldened the womenfolk sufficiently for them to go out exploring for ostrich eggs.

Darwin's party approached the *estancia*'s main gate in scrupulous observation of the correct etiquette. There they waited, without dismounting, until the proprietor Don Juan Fuentes was fetched.

'*Ave Maria*,' said Esteban, saluting him.

'*Sin pecado concebida*,' replied Don Juan. Conceived without sin.

After that they were permitted to dismount, and their horses were taken away to be stabled. Following a passage of stiltedly formal conversation concerning conditions on the trail, a request was made – and granted as a matter of course – for overnight accommodation within the *estancia* walls. Furthermore, the celebrated *naturalista* Don Carlos was invited, as Don Juan's guest of honour that night, to a grand supper in the main house.

The sun blessed the *estancia* with its last few precious rays, then withdrew for the night. Safe inside the compound, Darwin decided to go for a stroll around this isolated outpost of civilization. The troops had lit their campfires, and were busy slaughtering a mare for their evening's feast. The hideous squeals of the victim gave the flickering firelight a primitive aspect: a bucket had been fetched to collect the animal's blood for drinking, and the thick crimson liquid pooled in the rusty vessel as if some Aztec ritual were being prosecuted. Liquor bottles were busily uncorked, and many a *cigareto* was ignited in the fire. The troops were at ease, confident. They knew that they were on the winning side, that Rosas would lead them to victory. Darwin retreated inside before the knife quarrels began.

Don Juan Fuentes' guests assembled in their finery for supper at ten, far later than they would have done in Europe: there were cavalry officers in full dress uniform, and ladies of the house in figure-hugging gowns that flared from the hip. There were knives and forks and bowls too, the first cutlery Darwin had seen for some weeks, but the bowls held nothing but vast mounds of mare's flesh, exactly like those the troops were busy wolfing outside. The rough-hewn tables and chairs, the jugs of water and the beaten-earth floor put him in mind of a monastic refectory. There was no glass in any of the windows, and mosquitoes clouded the wavering candlelight like motes of soot. The talk was of General Rosas, and war, and the inevitability of final victory; such was the cultural and technological superiority of the white Christian race. Only when Darwin lit a *cigareto* with a Promethean – the new kind, which could be struck dry against any surface – did the talk of war cease. All talk, in fact, ceased. The table was paralysed, spellbound. Darwin struck another Promethean against his teeth. A rich landowner from Cordoba offered him a whole dollar for one of these magic sticks. The ladies' interest in the English *naturalista* suddenly blossomed. Then Darwin went one better: he produced his pocket compass. Unbounded astonishment followed, as the stranger proved himself capable of pointing out the approximate direction of Buenos Ayres, Cordoba and Mendoza, all by reference to a tiny machine kept in his pocket.

The lady to Darwin's left, a slender beauty with raven hair piled up in a jewelled comb, levelled her deep, dark eyes with his and told him that she had not been feeling well all evening: would he care to come to her room later that night, to effect a cure for any lingering traces of her ailment, using his little magic device? How on earth to react to such a brazen request? Thank heaven that Covington was elsewhere, making a fool of himself with the gauchos, no doubt, and not here to drink in his master's rich embarrassment. What perverse, sullen pleasures would he have taken from such an exchange? Darwin dithered. Really, he did not know how to behave in such circumstances. Was this *señorita* really a *lady*? Were there any real *ladies* in this part of the world? The question hung, pregnantly unanswered, between them. Then, the *señorita* settled the issue: she leaned forward, elegantly, seductively, and offered Darwin a morsel of roasted mare's flesh from the end of her own fork. He recoiled in astonishment. What manner of etiquette was this? Really, he had chanced among barbarians.

Making his excuses as hastily as possible, he drew back his chair, stumbled to his feet and took his *cigaretos* and Prometheans out into the night air. The cooling breezes of August took the edge off his anxiety, and soothed the sweat from his brow. He felt his pulse rate diminish. A silhouette staggered towards him out of the firelight, losing itself momentarily in the intervening blackness, before lurching finally into the oil-lamp glow at the door: a grinning soldier, quite profoundly drunk.

'Good evening,' said Darwin, politely, in Spanish.

The man bared all his teeth in a wolfish smile. Then he vomited, suddenly and violently, and a stream of regurgitated mare's blood splashed red across Darwin's new white boots.

They stayed three more days at the *estancia*, and towards the evening of the second day Harris caught them up. He was attached to a small troop of horsemen heading swiftly northwards, and was sweating profusely. To Darwin, the sight of a half-educated Englishman, even one with large damp patches spreading south from each armpit, was an improvement on the local sophistication level that could hardly have been bettered had King William himself shown up.

'Terrible business at *posta* four,' said Harris matter-of-factly.

A sinking feeling settled upon Darwin's gut.

'The place was burnt to the ground when we got there. Indian attack. Of course the *posta*-keeper had been murdered, poor devil. Elderly negro fellow. He had eighteen *chuzo* wounds. They cut him to pieces.'

'Did he sell his life dearly?' asked Darwin, his voice barely audible.

'I beg your pardon?'

'Nothing…it is nothing.'

'Did he sell himself dearly, did you say? I've really no idea.'

Darwin was keen to be away after that, to get back on the trail with his gauchos, to recapture the heady sense of freedom that had characterized the earlier part of the trip. They left the weary Harris behind again, a little miffed perhaps, but the sealer's spirits were soon raised once more by the enticing prospect of a feast of roasted mare's flesh. The party travelled north, across rich green plains thick with milling herds of cattle, horses and sheep, interspersed with beds of giant thistles that towered high above their heads. Finally, on the twentieth day, they came to the outskirts of Buenos Ayres. But all did not seem well. Plumes of smoke drifted upwards from the city centre. There was precious little traffic on the road.

'This is not good,' said Esteban, checking and rechecking the smoothness of his dagger's slide into and out of its scabbard. 'Don Carlos, you must push on to the city?'

'Yes...I mean, I have to rendezvous with the *Beagle*.'

'Very well. Then we shall proceed. But slowly.'

They pressed on watchfully, the outlying barns and cowsheds of the city gradually falling behind. Presently, they came to a roadblock, manned by a heavily armed gang of cut-throats. Rifles jutted at them from both sides of the road. The dangers of putting a foot wrong were emphasized by the swaying corpses of three or four fellow travellers, which dangled unpleasantly from the surrounding branches.

'What is happening in the city, my friends?' asked Esteban, loudly and confidently.

'What is happening, *friend*, is that we have taken control of the city for Rosas,' said the leader of the cut-throats, clearly enjoying his newfound status. 'No more will government officials plunder the state. No more will judges be bribed. No more will the head of the post office sell forged government notes. Either you are for Rosas or you are with our friends here.' He motioned to the corpses swinging waxen in the trees.

'We come from General Rosas' camp on the Rio Colorado,' avowed Esteban. 'We are his men.'

'What about *them*?' The cut-throat gestured to Darwin and Covington.

'This is the famous British *naturalista* Don Carlos and his servant. They are guests of General Rosas.'

'What is in these bags?'

'Specimens. Don Carlos is a *naturalista*.'

'What is a *naturalista*?'

'One who collects specimens.'

'The revolutionary government cannot permit foreign agents to enter Buenos Ayres. The British have seized the Islas Malvinas, our sovereign territory as determined by God.'

'These are not foreign agents. These are the guests of the general.'

The cut-throat leader jammed his rifle under Darwin's chin and motioned for him and Covington to dismount. Darwin, shaking, climbed down from his horse. Covington did likewise, mutely obedient. *We might be about to face our deaths, and he steps down like a misbehaved dog*, thought Darwin disgustedly.

'All foreigners have the potential to act as foreign agents. You gauchos may proceed. These two we will have to execute.'

'No! Wait! Wait one minute! Please!' Darwin, his words tumbling over one another in agitation, fumbled in his saddlebag, and finally – after a prolonged agony of searching that could not have lasted more than a second or two – produced General Rosas' 'passport'. The sentinels unfolded it with exaggerated gravity, and scanned it for several long minutes.

They cannot read, realized Darwin eventually. *They cannot damned well read.*

'This is General Rosas' seal. You may proceed. We are sorry to have held you up, sir.'

Relief sluiced through Darwin's mind, the lock-gates thrown open. His breathing came in short, deep gasps. *Thank you, Lord, oh, thank you, Lord.*

He touched his horse's flanks lightly with his big, burnished spurs and the beast began to walk slowly forward towards safety.

'Wait.'

What now? What now?

'This one.' The leader of the roadblock indicated Covington. 'Does he have a document?'

'No,' answered Darwin on Covington's behalf. 'He is my servant.' Thankfully, Covington did not understand Spanish.

'Then he must remain in custody until his credentials have been established. He must wait here with us.'

'Covington? They say you must wait here. With them. Until your… credentials have been established.'

'Sir.'

He doesn't even seem put out. The boy isn't even bothered. Does he not realize the danger he is in?

'I am sure you will be fine, Covington.'

'Sir.'

Grabbing his reins, Darwin urged his horse towards Buenos Ayres as quickly as dignity would permit, Esteban and his gauchos hard behind.

'"Until his credentials have been established"?' asked Darwin disbelievingly of Esteban, when they had rounded a bend in the road. 'How on earth can we "establish his credentials"?'

'How much money have you got?' asked Esteban.

'Philos! You are here, you are alive and well, and what is more you are become a gaucho!'

'I may thank kind Providence I am here with an entire throat.'

The lean, bronzed, powerful-looking stranger in gaucho rig who had thrown open the door of the captain's cabin of the *Beagle* bore only a passing resemblance to the pink, soft-cheeked young man dropped off at the Rio Negro six weeks previously. FitzRoy was extraordinarily glad to see him: as the ship had inched its way back up the coast, he had found himself frustratingly reminded at every turn of how solitary was the life of a naval captain. The slightest attempt to initiate a serious conversation with any of his officers, be it about geology, theology or zoology, had foundered on their continued respectful deference. He could have propounded any view, however nonsensical, and it would have met with polite acquiescence. He wanted to be *challenged*. He wanted to use his *mind*. Darwin, meanwhile, was solicitous.

'My dear FitzRoy, what news of the *Paz*, and the *Liebre*, and the *Adventure*? Will their lordships pay?'

'There is no decision yet. In truth, Philos, I am upon thorns to know the result. I must wait until Chili, it seems. But, my dear friend, tell me of your hair's breadth escapes and accidents! How many times did you flee from the Indians? How many precipices did you fall over? How many bogs did you fall into? How often were you carried away by floods? I am vexed to think how much sea practice you have lost, but I am *so* envious and jealous of all your peregrinations.'

'I'm sorry about the sea practice but, my dear FitzRoy, it is such a fine, healthful life on horseback all day – eating nothing but meat and sleeping in a bracing air! One awakes as fresh as a lark. Harris hired five gauchos. They were so spirited and bold, so modest respecting themselves and their country, so invariably obliging, so polite and so hospitable. I am sad to say, though, that they laugh at all religion.'

'So you have not passed your time among gentlemen?'

Darwin laughed. 'The complete and utter absence of gentlemen did strike me as something of a novelty.' He proceeded to describe his journey in detail, right up to and including the Buenos Ayres revolution that even now was making itself heard: occasional distant gunshots ricocheted within the walls of the city, before reverberating out into the harbour. He did not, of course, mention that he had very nearly returned to the *Beagle* minus one of her crew. Amazingly, as luck would have it, he had found a bank open and functioning amid all the looting and carnage, and had managed to draw a bill for fifty pounds against his father's account with Robarts, Curtis & Co. of Lombard Street. The entire sum had been used to purchase Covington's freedom, and not, he had sensed, before time: the servant's trigger-happy jailers had quite clearly grown bored with their supine hostage.

FitzRoy's eyes narrowed when he heard of the roadblock and its cohort of armed thugs. 'This city is an absolute mess. It is all the fault of that butcher Rosas.'

'Come, come, my dear chap, the general cannot have known that this revolt was to take place in his name. This, doubtless, was the act of the general's party, and not of the general himself.'

'Philos, I doubt that anything very much happens in this country without the general has intended it, or sanctioned it at the least.'

'Personally, I found him to be a most charming and charismatic man. He is a strong commander, perhaps even a ruthless one, but are not all the most successful military men so?'

'Charming and charismatic he may be, but he is engaged upon the most barbaric war of extermination against the Indians.'

'I think you will find it is the Indians who are responsible for the most barbaric of atrocities. Why, one of the *posta*-keepers I met was brutally murdered not a few days afterwards.'

'He was not by any chance black, was he, this *posta*-keeper?'

'How did you know?'

'Were not the majority of the *posta*-keepers black?'

'Yes, but I fail to see…?'

'Rosas makes officers of the blacks and he makes the *posta* a command. But the price of their promotion is death. It is the same with his armies. The front ranks, those who must take the most risks, are always black troops. Or they are "friendly" Indians, like the Tehuelches, to whom he has given the ultimatum, join the extermination or be exterminated.'

'I find your cynicism hard to credit. I tell you I have met the man – he is not some cold-eyed, calculating Tory minister. He is young, he is enthusiastic, and sincerity radiates from his every pore. As he told me himself, he is a liberal man.'

'A man should be judged by his actions, not by his own assessments of those actions.'

'Of course there are atrocities committed by both sides, FitzRoy. It is a brutal war against a godless enemy who is prepared to torture and kill without limit. Rosas has to meet fire with fire. But he does, at least, have the grace to spare the children of his enemies.'

'Spare them? He sells them as slaves!'

'They are sold as servants. There is a distinction. I believe that in their treatment there is little to complain of.'

'Well, the slavers' days are numbered. The news from London is that slavery has been banned throughout the empire. There are to be police ships hunting down the slavers. I am hopeful of a command myself in future.'

'This is excellent news. But we must not confuse the inhuman trade in human flesh with what is happening here in Latin America. What we are witnessing is the process of history. The inevitable eclipse of a weaker, primitive, heathen race by a stronger, more civilized Christian race. Be those races black or white is neither here nor there.'

'Is not one of the essential tenets of Christian civilization the *protection* of the weak, rather than their extirpation?'

'You are talking of mercy, of charity and of compassion – qualities that determine *how* a Christian should go about his business. But such qualities alone cannot prevent the victory of the strong over the weak. It is an unstoppable process. It is what happens throughout the animal kingdom every day, and humans are no different.'

'Perhaps they should strive to be so.'

'Perhaps, but Rosas is the stronger so he will win. It is clear to me that ultimately, he must be the absolute dictator of his country. It is the only way forward.'

'That is certainly the general's intention. Although whether the medieval dictatorship that will result constitutes progress, or will merely be a measure of how far man has fallen from his original state of innocence is open to debate.'

'You must forgive me, FitzRoy, but my appetite is getting the better of me – food supplies in the city were somewhat limited. I will take my supper in the gunroom, if they will have me – I believe that gunroom tea is at six – that is, if you don't mind?'

'No...of course not. As you will.'

Darwin swept out, his white gaucho robes rustling behind him. Suddenly, FitzRoy felt crestfallen. *Six weeks I have waited for someone to talk to*, he thought. *And now he is gone to gunroom tea, because I will not allow him his opinions without contradicting every single one.*

'Shall I be footman? Or, as in the household of a *Yorkshire* gentleman such as Mr Stokes, maid-of-all-work?'

A chuckle ran round the table. Gunroom tea that night was indeed a jolly affair, for Wickham, Stokes and the other officers had come across from the *Adventure* for a final meal together before heading south once more. It was Wickham who was ribbing Stokes now, passing around big hunks of roasted ostrich, the gunroom table being far too crowded for the steward to squeeze in and attend to his duties as he should.

'I'll have a leg, please,' replied Stokes, raising another laugh, for each of the bird's legs was bigger than his own brawny arm.

Darwin felt in his element. Here, embraced by the collective warmth of the gunroom, he felt able to recapture some of the camaraderie of the pampas, where he had enjoyed so many marvellous roast-meat suppers. And this evening there was snuff to follow. He proceeded to regale the company with tales of his *bolas*-lessons, the bringing down of his own horse and, finally, his successful capture of a rhea in full flight.

'Sounds a whole lot easier than shooting the blighters,' remarked Sulivan. 'This little fellow ran like the wind, scooting in and out of the bushes on his little furry feet. It took Martens three shots to bring him down.'

The little artist blushed in acknowledgement of his marksmanship.

Something jarred in Darwin's memory, but he could not work out what.

'How prime, though,' said Stokes through a mouthful of meat. 'Tastier than usual. It had odd feathers, didn't it?'

Sudden, hideous realization flooded through Darwin's mind.

'Oh, my God. Put that down!' he shouted, grabbing the bone from Stokes's hand just as the mate was about to take a bite, his teeth clamping shut on empty air.

'Philos? What's the flurry?'

'Stop eating! Stop eating! Give me the bones!' Darwin was positively frantic. He could quite clearly make out traces of feathers just above the claws of Stokes's ostrich leg.

'What is it?'

'It is the *Avestruz Petise*!'

'The have-a-what?'

'The *Avestruz Petise*! Where is the skin of this bird? The beak, the feathers?'

'In the galley, I suppose, but—'

'Nobody is to touch a morsel of this bird until I get back, do you hear?

Not a morsel!'

Darwin tore out of the room, his striped poncho flapping behind him, leaving behind a bewildered silence.

'Whatever has got into old Philos?' wondered Sulivan at last.

'It's all those wide open spaces. One tends to lose one's sense of perspective, out on the plains,' suggested Conrad Martens, taking a discreet bite of *Avestruz Petise.*

CHAPTER SEVEN

Woollya Cove, Tierra del Fuego, 5 March 1834

The weather had deteriorated on their final approach to Woollya, and with it a blanket of apprehension had been cast across the spirits of the crew. All were afraid of what they might find. It had been more than a year since their previous visit: only the Reverend Richard Matthews, perhaps, secretly wished ill on the fortunes of the settlement – if not those of its inhabitants – for fear that he be cajoled into taking up his place at the head of the mission once more.

'Terra del has recollected her old winning ways, I see,' said Darwin bitterly. The deck heaved beneath his feet, as the ship beat against a blue swell that was obstinately forcing its way up the Beagle Channel. 'How I have missed her gentle breath. What a charming country.'

Nobody spoke. Nobody felt like replying.

'If anyone catches me here again, I will give him leave to hang me up as a scarecrow for future naturalists,' he continued, addressing his remarks to no one in particular. As the old, familiar waves of nausea wallowed up from his gut, he stomped off below to 'take the horizontal for it' before it became too late.

The weather, in truth, had been unusually kind of late. They had enjoyed a fine Christmas at Port Desire in southern Patagonia: FitzRoy had determined that the crew of the *Beagle* should take on the crew of the *Adventure* in an athletic contest similar to the ancient Olympic Games. There had been running, leaping and wrestling matches, although the brutal favourite was undoubtedly the old sailor's game of Slinging the Monkey, in which some poor unfortunate was slung by his heels from a wooden tripod and swung from side to side, being beaten by all and sundry. The moment he managed to land a blow in return, he was permitted to swap places with the recipient. Darwin, as a landsman, had found it all rather barbaric, and had gone off shooting instead, procuring a two-hundred-pound guanaco for the Christmas roast. But he had to admit that FitzRoy's methods worked. All the officers and men were in a state of cheery perspiration when he returned, just as the captain (with the aid of a few dubious statistical calculations) declared the Olympic Games an honourable draw, and handed out prizes all round.

Just how well FitzRoy handled his crew was thrown into sharp relief at their next port of call, the Bay of St Julian. Both Drake and Magellan had been forced to execute mutineers here, variously beheading or hanging, drawing and quartering their victims. The surrounding place names – Execution Island, the Isle of True Justice, Tomb Point – bore witness to a very different era of seafaring. Darwin explored a few miles inland, coming across the fossil remains of a huge unknown mammal and, atop a hill, a desiccated wooden cross left by Magellan's expedition, shrivelled but intact after three centuries in the parched Patagonian air.

Thereafter the *Adventure* had turned east, Wickham and Co. gliding away to complete the Falklands survey under the expert tutelage of Low, the sealer; it was with considerable pride that FitzRoy had watched her go, her expensive transformation into lissom white swan now complete. By his side at the rail, breathing in his admiration of her sweeping, mellifluous passage, stood Coxswain Bennet. He had been earmarked as one of the *Adventure*'s contingent, but had begged his superior's permission to remain aboard the *Beagle*. The potential fate of Jemmy Button and his fellows gnawed away in a dark corner of his imagination just as furiously as it did in FitzRoy's own thoughts.

They had surveyed Wollaston Island and Cape Santa Inez on the way south, and the skipper had brought the suggestion of a tear to Hamond's eye by naming an inlet 'Thetis Bay'. They had scraped a submerged rock while working out of one uncharted harbour – a hair-raising moment, but fortunately the offending obstacle had not pierced the two inches of reinforced fir sheathing installed by FitzRoy at such enormous personal cost; the copper had been ripped from her false keel, but that was all.

Thereafter she had become the first full-sized ship to enter the Beagle

Channel, squeezing in through the northern end of the Goree Roads behind Picton Island. The appearance of a brig in full sail had generated the same levels of native excitement as had their previous expedition in whaleboats: there were signal fires, frantic running men and a small flotilla of canoes trailing in their wake, smoke pluming behind them like so many tiny steamships. Some of the Indians waved their spears aggressively, but gestures that had felt threatening in an open boat seemed little more than pitiful when viewed from the heights of the *Beagle*'s heavily armed deck. Other natives sallied forth boldly to trade fresh fish and crabs in return for scraps of cloth.

'Where are you going?' was one shouted question that FitzRoy was able to decipher amid the chatter, from his rudimentary grasp of the Yamana language.

'Woollya,' he replied, pointing up the narrow channel between the cream-topped peaks.

'Much fighting at Woollya – many deaths – many bad things happen,' was the substance of the man's ominous reply.

'Tell me more,' he entreated this messenger, but to no avail. Either his request was unintelligible, or there was no more to tell. The canoes peeled away before the *Beagle* got near Woollya, as if they could not bear to be present when she reached journey's end; as if they were ashamed to share the decisive moment when FitzRoy and his crew finally learned the truth.

The breeze shooed them through the Murray Narrows – familiar territory now – and then died away, leaving them in a calm, hushed world beyond. A demure veil of mist rose up from the water, through which small dark islets loomed one by one, counting down the yards to their goal. Even though they could see little, it was safe to take the ship through, for Woollya Cove and the whole of Ponsonby Sound had been surveyed during their last visit; so FitzRoy let the *Beagle* drift in as far as she could, her canvas gently flapping. There, as they hove to off Woollya, the mists finally parted, reluctantly, guiltily, to reveal the three mission cottages.

Each was a blackened, burnt-out ruin. The little white picket fence was thrown down. The neat lawn was weed-strewn and overgrown. This was not the mission but its skeleton, soundless, lifeless, picked clean of every scrap of re-useable material. Not a single teacup, not even a fragment of a teacup, remained. The place was utterly deserted. Not a living soul stirred. Only their own heartbeats could be heard.

In silence, they put the boats down, FitzRoy steeling himself as best he could. Nobody said a word. The splash of the oars, as they beat against the protesting waters, sounded a deafening tattoo within the misty confines of the bay. The scrunch of gravel as they ran into the beach was positively ear-splitting. As they stepped ashore it began to rain, great freezing dollops of it, lashing at their backs and spattering contemptuously against the splintered, carbonized planking of the three huts. There were, at least, no dead bodies. There was nothing. The secret cellar of Matthews's old cottage was thrown open, the black pit below an empty hole denuded of its former treasures. Silently, discreetly, the missionary mouthed a prayer of thanks for his own deliverance.

FitzRoy knelt in the vegetable garden, which had obviously been left entirely to its own devices since the previous year's trampling-down. There, nestling amid the disordered wet grass, lay a clutch of entirely healthy turnips and potatoes, which had pushed their way optimistically to the surface.

'You see?' he said, staring bleakly up at Sulivan and Bennet, the rain streaming off his face. 'It could have worked. It *would* have worked.'

Grief and defiance were mingled on his face. Bennet did not dare reply.

'You did everything you could. There was nothing more you could have done,' Sulivan reassured him.

'That's utter rubbish and you know it,' replied FitzRoy savagely. He looked back at the pathetically hopeful row of vegetables. 'Have these dug up and fed to the men. We might as well try to salvage something from this whole sorry mess.'

In the gloom of the afternoon, when the rain had washed away the mists, only to replace them with a wake of haggard, sorrowful clouds, FitzRoy sat alone in his cabin, running the events of the previous four years back and forth in his mind. What could he have done differently? What *should* he have done differently? Was there any point in crucifying himself? He looked across at the seat where Edward Hellyer had once sat, gazing up at him in awe and admiration. Yes, there was every point in doing so.

An urgent knock at the door interrupted his reverie. It was Bennet.

'Sir – a canoe. I'm sorry to interrupt, sir, but – there's a canoe.'

'Thank you, Mr Bennet. I shall be up presently.'

He tried not to let his heart thump. It was probably nothing – probably just a passing native family. *Compose yourself. You are in command, remember. It is time that you justified the Admiralty's faith in you, and that of your officers and men.* He smoothed down his uniform and stepped on to the deck.

To the naked eye, the canoe was just a dark, approaching blot far out in the sound, distinguishable from the surrounding islets only by its gently rocking motion. He took the spyglass proffered by Sulivan. It was an unusual vessel, smaller than the average native canoe, remarkable both for the ragged flag flying from its prow, and for the absence of any sacred fire amidships. There were only two souls aboard. The first was a slender young woman paddling the craft, who – FitzRoy thought – conformed more to the Western ideal of beauty than to the burly, well-fed look that appealed to most Fuegian men. The other occupant was a man, naked and wretchedly thin, with long, disordered hair. FitzRoy felt that he did not recognize either individual, but it was hard to be sure, for as he raised the spyglass to his eye the man hurriedly concealed his face behind his hand in shame. For a moment he thought these two gestures unconnected, but then he remembered the Fuegians' extraordinary powers of eyesight. Even with the naked eye, the man could probably see the ship better than he could discern anything in the canoe through the blurry-edged lens of the 'bring-'em-near', as Jemmy had liked to refer to his spyglass. As FitzRoy continued to squint into the eyepiece, the Fuegian turned his back, apparently to avoid being recognized, and dipped his free hand over the side, before bringing it up to his face. *He's washing himself*, realized FitzRoy. *He's cleaning his face.* Finally, having completed his ablutions, the passenger brought his gaunt face slowly into view. He lifted one hand to his forehead, looked directly at FitzRoy, and touched the peak of an imaginary cap in naval salute. It was Jemmy Button.

Or, rather, it was Jemmy Button's shadow: a pale wisp of the sleek, well-fed, well-groomed boy they had left behind. As the canoe drew closer, FitzRoy finally had a proper view of the Fuegian's squalid condition. His hair was unkempt, greasy and matted, his eyes red-rimmed from the effects of woodsmoke, his modesty covered by a wretched scrap of Walthamstow blanket slung about his hips. His skin was stretched taut across the concentric rungs of his ribs. So complete and grievous was the change that FitzRoy feared he might weep.

'My dear FitzRoy, you are crying,' said Darwin, who had materialized at his side, and he realized that in fact he had already let his emotions show. The philosopher put a consoling hand on his shoulder.

'Forgive me, Darwin…it seems I am disposed to play the woman's part today.'

'My dear man,' murmured his friend, 'poor Jemmy's appearance would be enough to move hardier souls than sailors.'

FitzRoy pulled himself together with an effort, and called for his steward. 'Fuller.'

'Sir.'

'Would you set the table for six, please? Mr Button is returned to the ship, and I should like to invite him and his companion to take supper with me. Would you also extend the invitation to Mr Bennet, Mr Bynoe, and to Mr Darwin, of course.'

'Aye aye sir.'

Jemmy's canoe was made fast alongside, and a peculiar little pantomime was enacted between the two Fuegians. Jemmy politely motioned for his companion to go ahead and scale the battens, saying to her in English, with a little bow, 'After you, Mrs Button.'

A scared look passed fleetingly across the woman's face as she responded, 'No, after *you*, Mr Button.'

'Please, Mrs Button, after *you*. Ladies first is proper.'

'Please, after *you*, Mr Button.' And then, after a frightened pause, 'Mrs Button no want go on ship.'

Jemmy put his arms tenderly about his wife and stroked her hair. 'Jemmy not be long. You wait here, Mrs Button.' Clutching a bundle wrapped with the remaining portion of blanket in the crook of one arm, he clambered aboard more nimbly than any of the crew had ever seen him move before.

'Jemmy, thank God you're alive.'

'Capp'en Fitz'oy. I knew you will come back. I say to Mrs Button, Capp'en Fitz'oy will not forget Jemmy, he will come back. She no believe you will come, Capp'en Fitz'oy, but I say to her, Capp'en Fitz'oy is English gen'leman, his word is his bond. He will come back for Jemmy Button.'

'You are married, Jemmy. My hearty congratulations.'

'Congratulations, Jemmy old son,' added a husky-voiced Bennet.

'Well done, Jemmy,' from Bynoe. 'She's a fine catch.'

'Thank you, my confidential friend. Jemmy is not proper married, like in church, but Jemmy remember words, say them again, so to be married in sight of God.'

'Your wife…she speaks English.'

'English Jemmy's language, not Yamana. English *good* language. Jemmy teach Mrs Button English. Capp'en Fitz'oy always say Jemmy is English gen'leman.'

As he uttered these last words, Jemmy's voice tailed off, and he looked down at his naked, emaciated frame. The others instinctively followed his gaze.

'Mr Bennet?' asked FitzRoy. 'Perhaps you would take Jemmy below and find him a suit of clothes. The best we have to offer.'

'It would be a pleasure, sir.'

Half an hour later, a fully clothed, scrubbed and shod Jemmy Button sat down to supper with FitzRoy, Darwin, Bennet and Bynoe, while Sulivan took command of the watch on deck. Despite being wooed with presents of handkerchiefs, blankets and a gold-laced cap that one kind crew member had purchased in Rio for his own wife, nothing would induce Mrs Button to leave her station in the bobbing canoe alongside. She sat alone and frightened as darkness fell; hers was an empty place at dinner. Fuller fetched plates of fish and crabmeat, followed by fresh-boiled turnips and potatoes. Jemmy held up his outer knife and fork and grinned at

Bennet. 'With each course, you move in to the next two pieces of cutlery.' He repeated Bennet's own words back to him, even the inflections exact after four years.

'You remembered,' said Bennet. 'Sharp as a tack.'

Jemmy grinned again, this time with pride and pleasure at his accomplishment.

'So, Jemmy.' FitzRoy broached the obvious subject as gently as he could. 'If it's not too…painful, perhaps you could tell us what became of the mission.'

'The Oens-men came, Capp'en Fitz'oy, when the leafs turned red. Always when the leafs turn red there is no food, the Oens-men are hungry. So they come to my land. Yamana people always leave tents, run away. But Jemmy cannot leave mission. Have to stay with mission. Many Yamana people at mission, bad people, try to steal Jemmy's tools, Jemmy's clothes. Look for Jemmy's things, not look for Oens-men. God sends Oens-men to punish them. Oens-men come from the mountains behind Woollya, surprise Yamana people. Much fighting, many dead.'

'And York? Fuegia? Did they survive?'

Jemmy's face clouded with anger.

'York go to secret place under Mister Matthews's floor, take big spade. Says he will kill anyone who comes near. Pick up big stones. Oens-men afraid – not come near him. After Oens-men are gone, York says to Jemmy, it is not safe at Woollya. We must take tools, knives, axes, all precious things, go to York's land with Fuegia. Jemmy says yes, I will go with you. York makes big canoe. Before we leave, York sets fire to mission. Says bad people must not live there. We leave at dawn, travel west towards sunset. Sleep on island where channel goes two different ways. Jemmy wakes in night – hears noise. York is above him. York have moved quietly, like big cat. Jemmy tries to get free, but York have put his knife *here*, at Jemmy's throat. Makes Jemmy take off clothes. York takes *everything*, Capp'en Fitz'oy, *everything*. All Jemmy's clothes. Take shirt, breeches, gloves, nice shiny boots. All tools, *everything*. Leaves Jemmy to die on island. He say Jemmy foolish, he say white man foolish, he say Capp'en Fitz'oy foolish, all believe York lies. He say if Mister Matthews stayed he will kill him too.

York say he too clever for white men, have clever plan from beginning. I say Capp'en Fitz'oy not foolish, I say Capp'en Fitz'oy English *gen'leman*. Keep his word. York laugh at Jemmy. Not see him again.'

Oh, but he was right, Jemmy – I have been so very, very foolish. York has outwitted us all. He meditated taking the best opportunity of possessing himself of everything right from the start. That is why he would not be left in his own country – for he would not have known where to look for poor Jemmy to plunder him. Such a betrayal – such a tragic course of events – and all for a box of tools. Everything undone for a box of tools.

'Then what happened, Jemmy? How did you get away from there?'

'I swim home, Capp'en Fitz'oy! York think is too far for Jemmy – many miles – thinks Jemmy will die. York say Jemmy go soft in Wal'amstow. But Jemmy good swimmer, like seal. Jemmy not soft. Jemmy swim all way back here. So York is big fool, not Jemmy.'

'And how are you now, Jemmy? Are you well, in yourself?'

'I am hearty, sir, never better. Jemmy eat plenty fruits, plenty birdies, ten guanaco in snow time. And too much fish,' he avowed, patting his stomach exaggeratedly. All present knew that he was lying.

'I am glad to hear it, Jemmy,' said FitzRoy limply, unable to think of any other response.

Jemmy put down his fork. 'Jemmy bring presents. Look.' He dragged his bundle from under the table and unwrapped the blanket. 'No money. No shops. Jemmy cannot buy presents. So he make them himself.'

With a flourish, he produced a handmade bow and arrows, and a quiver painstakingly sewn from guanaco-leather.

'For my old friend Schoolmaster Jenkins, of St Mary's Infants' School. Please to give to him.'

'I'll make sure he gets it, Jemmy, I promise,' said FitzRoy.

'These are for you, Mr Philosopher.' He handed to Darwin two immaculately carved spear-heads.

'Why, thank you, Jemmy. That's…that's most extraordinarily generous of you.'

'And for you too, my confidential friend.' There were two further spear-heads for Bynoe.

'Jemmy, I – I'm speechless.'

'For you, my great friend Mr Bennet, and for you, Capp'en Fitz'oy, I give you this.' Reverentially, he unrolled two otterskins, carefully cleaned and preserved. 'Better than guanaco-skin. Better than sealskin. Very difficult to find. I catch them myself for my friends. My friends from Englan', who will never let me down as long as I shall live.' Jemmy's voice cracked as he reached the end of his speech.

'Thanks, Jemmy,' said Bennet, his voice so hoarse with emotion it could hardly be heard in the little cabin. A big fat tear rolled off the end of Jemmy's nose and fell with a splat on to the linen tablecloth.

'Jemmy, I...' FitzRoy tailed off in desperation. A low ululation of distress could be heard floating up from the canoe outside.

'Mister Button! Mister Button!' came Mrs Button's plaintive call.

'Jemmy,' said FitzRoy, taking the Fuegian's hands urgently in his own, 'do you want to come home with us? Home to England in the *Beagle*?'

'Mister Button! Mister Button!' came another moan from outside.

'Capp'en Fitz'oy, I...'

Jemmy's eyes were wet with misery. 'Jemmy must stay here with Mrs Button. She not want to come on the *Beagle*. Much scared of white people. Mrs Button is with child.'

'Congratulations, Jemmy...I – I didn't realize.'

'Jemmy's home is here. I am English gen'leman, Capp'en Fitz'oy, but Jemmy's home is here. Do you understand?'

'I understand. I understand, Jemmy, my dear, dear friend.' He clasped the Fuegian's hands so tightly that his knuckles blanched.

'But Capp'en Fitz'oy will come back? Will come back in the *Beagle* again to see Jemmy Button?'

'I...I'll do my best, Jemmy. It depends where the Admiralty sends me. But I promise I will do my level best to visit you in the future.'

'Thank you, my friend. I say to Mrs Button, Capp'en Fitz'oy will not forget Jemmy Button. He will come back. Capp'en Fitz'oy is English gen'leman.'

'Mister Button! Mister Button!' The call from outside was shot through with distress. FitzRoy relaxed his grip.

'You had better go, Jemmy. I should like to keep you with us, I should like that so very much, but I fear that you must leave.'

'Goodbye, my dearest friends. Jemmy will always remember you.'

'And we will remember you, Jemmy, I give you my word.'

'As an English gen'leman, Capp'en Fitz'oy.'

'As an English gentleman, Jemmy.'

The *Beagle* slipped her moorings at first light, and drifted serenely away from the shore on the morning tide. As she stood out of Ponsonby Sound, Jemmy and his wife crept wearily out from the clump of rushes where they had hidden for the night, their bodies curled protectively around a full blanket-load of presents. The Fuegian lit a signal fire to herald the ship's departure. FitzRoy and Darwin stood on the poop and watched the insubstantial column of smoke make its connection between the lonely meadows of Woollya and the passing clouds above. A gust of wind caught it and bent it like a reed, but it refused to break.

'Perhaps…perhaps some shipwrecked seaman will one day hereafter receive help and kind treatment from Jemmy Button's children. Perhaps they will be prompted by the traditions they will have heard, of men from other lands. Perhaps they will have an idea, however faint, of their duty to God as well as to their neighbour.'

Or perhaps, more likely, it has all been in vain. Literally, a vain scheme, conceived on too small a scale, with disastrous consequences for those poor souls involved against their will.

'My dear FitzRoy, I do not doubt for one second that he will be just as happy as if he had never left his country.'

'Do you really believe so?'

'I do.'

You are wrong, my friend, for I have given him a taste of a better life, then snatched it away. I have taken away his innocence, something I had no right to do. I wanted to bring him closer to God, but at the end it was I who played God, with the lives of other men.

The tiny figure by the signal fire was waving now, his hand describing wide, metronomic arcs as if he were copying the gesture from a handbook. Discreetly, Darwin left FitzRoy to his private agonies and wandered along the deck. He found Bennet grasping the rail with a hopeless ferocity, peering into the dawn light as if terrified of the moment when he might no longer be able to distinguish Jemmy from his surroundings.

'What really hurts, Philos,' said the coxswain, without averting his gaze even for a second, 'is that I know I'll never see him again.'

'I do not think any of us ever will.'

'It could all have been so different. If only we'd...if we'd...I don't know.'

'May I ask you a question, Mr Bennet?'

'By all means.'

'Do you believe in God?'

'Do I believe in God? Of course I believe in God, Philos. That is...on days like today...sometimes it's hard, Philos, sometimes it's hard. But do I believe in God? Yes. Yes I do. Leastways, I'm sure I do.'

PART TWO

CHAPTER EIGHT

Valparayso, Chili, 2 November 1834

'Raise tacks, sheets an' mains'l haul
We're bound for Vallaparayser round the Horn!
Me boots an' clothes are all in pawn
An' it's bleedin' draughty round the Horn!'

So sang the crew, with a surge of relief, as the *Beagle* and the *Adventure* finally drew a line under the year's surveying and headed for the sanctuary of Chili's warm, fruit-laden valleys – except that, of course, there was no longer any need to proceed via the Horn.

They had repaired the damage to the *Beagle*'s keel by running her up to the Rio Santa Cruz in Patagonia and beaching her in the estuary, where a forty-foot tide swept in and out. Laid up on the sands amid a crowd of disgruntled sealions, the little ship had assumed the proportions of a leviathan, her fat, glistening, slimy belly towering above the crew, as if she might subside and suffocate them were she to breathe out. While Carpenter May and his team set to work, FitzRoy had mounted an expedition upriver to try to reach the Andes from the east. Amid swarms of persistent horseflies, they had man-hauled the whaleboats against the icy current for three back-breaking weeks, using track ropes fastened to lanyards made from broad canvas strips. For two hundred and fifty miles they had pulled, up a lonely, twisting glen lined by black basalt cliffs. The countryside around, if one could call it that, was a featureless plain of volcanic lava, punishingly hot by day and freezing by night, its ebony sheen flat to the horizon. But the river had cut deep into the lava: the ravine up which they slogged was three hundred feet in depth and more than a mile across. Beady-eyed condors stood sentry on their basaltic battlements, but otherwise there were precious few living creatures to be seen. There were Indian tracks about their camp in the mornings, though, evidence that they had been thoroughly investigated during the night. Here, well south of the front line against General Rosas, it appeared that the white man constituted a mere curiosity and not an adversary to be feared. There were puma tracks, too, for the Indians were not the only lords desirous to know who had intruded into their land. As with the Indians, the men on watch had seen and heard nothing, not even a rustle in the reeds.

In silence the party trudged upriver, each man feeling the curious self-consciousness that comes from the knowledge of being watched. The Andes came in sight, and the river assumed the milky blue colour characteristic of glacial melt, but thereafter the mountains seemed to maintain a constant distance, refusing to come any closer. The men stood in their echoing glen and gazed at the distant snowy peaks, knowing that they had become the first Europeans to behold this view, but knowing also that they could go no further. It was, thought FitzRoy, a wild and lonely prospect, entirely fit for the breeding-place of lions.

Whether it was the isolation of their surroundings, or a sense of compromise brought on by the failure of the Woollya mission, FitzRoy and Darwin felt instinctively drawn to one another, not just emotionally but in their scientific analysis of the surroundings. Climbing the valley was like walking through a cutaway diagram of the different geological layers: with the precision of a well-set-out textbook, the scenery invited the two men to reconsider their arguments. Two weeks upriver they encountered a vast layer of marine detritus a hundred feet thick, containing smooth-rolled stones and the shattered remnants of delicate shallow-water sea-shells embedded in viscous mud. The shells, Darwin had to admit, had been smashed, crushed and mixed together as if by a great catastrophe. Whatever it was that had brought so many stones to one place must have been an event of terrifying force. Perhaps they had, after all, been torn down by the great tides of a flooded world. FitzRoy, too, felt in a mood to compromise. It had been so much easier to imagine the Biblical flood in the midst of Tierra del Fuego's lashing storms, but here in the desiccated plain his sense of certainty began to evaporate. Could such a vast layer of sea-detritus really have been effected by a forty-day flood? Surely it would have required an inundation of immense duration to roll these shingle-stones so smooth? How many millennia would the river have taken to cut a ravine through three hundred feet of solid lava? A sense of anxiety assailed him: the new science of geology promised to order God's universe, but here it also seemed to open the prospect that man might be more insignificant than he had ever realized. Was the world really aeons old, as Lyell was now suggesting? Was man really lost in time as well as in space?

'"The wilderness has a mysterious tongue, which teaches awful doubt,"' said Darwin, quietly, feeling Shelley's lines appropriate to the moment. FitzRoy felt bound to agree with him.

Conrad Martens sat down to paint the scene; then, with their food almost exhausted, FitzRoy gave the order to turn back. It took them just two days to shoot back downriver, to the rejuvenating sight of the *Beagle* standing at anchor, fresh-painted and jaunty as a frigate, and a cheerful, welcoming, 'Hello hello hello!' from Sulivan.

The *Beagle* had gone on to complete the survey of Tierra del Fuego, while the *Adventure* had committed the last bays and headlands of the Falklands to paper. Finally, in late June, the two ships had battled through the western end of the Magellan Strait and stood out into the long swell of the Pacific, every inch of canvas straining. Here was a rugged granite coast pounded by angry seas and howling gales, splintered by the elements into a constellation of islands, the larger peaks stabbing out from the surf like the spires of inundated churches, the smaller shoals a clutter of headstones at their base. A Herculean surveying job lay before the two crews, far greater in scope than anything ever dreamed of in Whitehall. Safe anchorages were hard to come by: if there was space for only one vessel, then FitzRoy made sure, like a hen fussing over its chick, that the *Adventure* won the berth. One inky night the *Beagle* had nearly come to grief: peering into the blackness through driving rain, the lookout man had discerned a wall of rock looming off the starboard beam. Sulivan – who had charge of the middle watch – yelled an order, whereupon the watch scrambled to run the main-tack on board and haul off the main-sheet. The ship sprang forward like an arrow from a bow, the lee-clew of the mainsail scraping hideously along the black cliff face as it did so. A moment's indecision from any quarter would have been fatal, and once again all on board had reason to bless the rigour of FitzRoy's training.

Eight hundred miles of broken coastline were mapped and named: Mellersh, Forsyth, Stokes, FitzRoy and Rowlett lent their names to islands, as did the sadly departed *Paz* and *Liebre*. King and Chaffers gave title to a lonely channel each, while Bynoe was awarded a whole cape. Time and again the elements threatened to batter them to destruction. Even though the *Beagle* and the *Adventure* were working no further south than France lies to the north, giant icebergs barged each other aside in their efforts to get at the little ships and crush them to matchwood. Ceaseless rain and relentless waves saw to it that, month in, month out, nothing on the ships was allowed to dry out. The men's clothes literally rotted on their bodies. Endless applications of salt rubbed their skin red raw. Their lips split and bled. The lack of fresh food in the southern winter took its toll: the purser, Mr Rowlett, lay in the sickbay of the *Beagle* doubled in agony with some unknown stomach complaint; even Stokes, the indefatigable Stokes, lay prostrate in the grip of a chronic chest infection, coughing up blood.

Finally, FitzRoy decided that his crew could stand it no longer, and ran north for Valparayso, praying all the way that the pair would pull through. At Cape Tres Montes, where a jutting peninsula forces the jostling battalion of islands to an abrupt halt, they beat out through relentless gales into the Golfo de Peñas – the aptly named Gulf of Pains – pursued by a derisive, shrieking pack of fulmars, shearwaters and diving petrels. Here they buried Rowlett at sea, sewn with due formality into his hammock, the final stitch through his nostrils, two roundshot at his feet to weigh him down. For Darwin, who had persuaded the amiable purser to advance him so much money during the voyage, the awful and solemn moment when the unforgiving waters covered his friend's body brought a vague, inexplicable thrill of guilt. FitzRoy's black despair was more focused, more ferocious in its intensity. He retreated into silent, furious thought. Rowlett, at thirty-eight, had been the oldest man aboard: he had, quite simply, not been strong enough to cope with the demands of the south. Stokes was younger, tougher, fitter, a teeth-gritted fighter. He would make it to Valparayso.

At last, after several hundred miles of impenetrable rain-soaked forest, the heavens cleared – as they always did at these latitudes – and Valparayso Bay opened out before them in the sunshine. The sky was clean and blue, the air was electric-dry, the sun was warm and forgiving: all nature here sparkled with life. The little town lay pillowed against rounded hills of warm red earth. Low, whitewashed houses with terracotta-tiled roofs curved around a crowded harbour embroidered with dainty sails. Higgledy-piggledy cottages, piled one on top of another, tumbled flower-strewn down the gentle slopes. Heady, aromatic vapours raced each other from the shore to be the first to greet the ships. And there, standing in an attitude of stern, avuncular protection behind the harbour's fringing hills, its sides a shifting palette of soft lilacs and violets in the delicate afternoon haze, was the snow-capped peak of Volcan Aconcagua, the highest point in the Americas.

There were rich English merchants aplenty in Valparayso – one of them, Richard Corfield, an old classmate of Darwin's from Shrewsbury. There would be parties here, and dinners, and good food, and female company too. The officers could shave their beards. They could dress decently. After the wintry beating they had taken, it felt as if they had suddenly fetched up in Paris or London on a perpetual summer's day. All, of course, were hungry for news from home. Was Lord Grey still the prime minister? No, he had resigned, but there was no word of a successor. Were the Whigs still in government? Yes, but they were calling themselves the Liberals now. Was the country now covered from end to end by railways? No, not yet, but it was only a matter of time. Darwin, who could not wait to get off the ship and sleep in a real bed once more, gathered his belongings and moved into Corfield's house. Most of the officers secured little cottages with flower-bedecked gardens where they could rest and recuperate, at least when they were not required to be on duty. FitzRoy, though, refused to leave the *Beagle*. He would neither abandon Stokes, who was best treated in the sanitized confines of the ship's sickbay, nor call a halt to the drafting of the Tierra del Fuego charts. Every evening he sat alone in his cabin, working late into the night, completing Stokes's task of converting their raw, soaking, hard-won observations into crisp, clean, dry maps. Wickham was deputized to attend the customary official functions and to carry out the normal shore duties of a visiting British naval captain. FitzRoy dared not be diverted, dared not slacken at his task, not even for second. His determination was intense, his concentration furious. The voyage of the *Beagle* must be flawless in every respect.

Rowlett's death is upon my hands, he thought. *He put his trust in me, as so many have, and I failed to deliver him safely to his destination. At the very least, these charts will become his memorial. It is incumbent upon me to ensure that they are worthy of his memory.*

Twelve bloodshot eyes stared in disdainful response, as Darwin waved the packet provocatively back and forth before the weary scarlet eyelids. One of the condors hunched its shoulders with boredom. Another tested a manacled talon against its fetters for the hundredth time that day.

'Another glass of wine, old man?' asked Corfield.

'If you please,' said Darwin eagerly, feeling light-headed with pleasure after so long without tasting a drop. 'It is extraordinary. Look! They have absolutely no sense of smell.'

Again he waved the little packet in the air, to the supreme indifference of the assembled condors. Then he unwrapped it, and tossed the meat at the feet of the nearest of the gruesome creatures. Instantly, the whole garden went crazy, as the cackling recipient ripped and tore at his feast with beak and claws, while the other five thrashed violently at their manacles in an effort to steal it from him.

'You are a marvel, Darwin,' said Corfield over the din. 'I shall never forget you standing by the gas-light in our sixth-form bedroom, trying to divert the flame on to some magnesium with that little brass pipe of yours. It is a wonder you didn't blow up the whole school.'

'Why do you have condors in your garden, anyway?'

'Do you have any idea how difficult it is to buy peacocks in these parts?'

joshed Corfield. 'I bought them for sixpence each from an Indian. Quite a number of landowners hereabouts have them. It is the fashion, I suppose. I wouldn't go too close – they are deucedly filthy creatures. That's why they are tethered.'

'I presumed it was to stop them flying away.'

'Oh, no, they cannot fly away very easily. They need a cliff and a prevailing wind to take off, especially after a feed. Rather like myself, old man. But they are absolutely riddled with lice. The one on the end is dying – look. All the lice crawl to the outside feathers when the bird is about to die.'

'Remarkable,' said Darwin, with genuine fascination.

'Remarkable, but disgusting. Actually, I think I shall get rid of them. The squawking gets on one's nerves after a while.'

Corfield's spacious garden, bisected by a clear rivulet of Andean water, stretched out languorously behind his attractive single-storey mansion in the wealthy suburb of Almendral. All the rooms opened directly on to a central quadrangle, and it was to this courtyard that he and Darwin repaired to escape the screeching and flapping of the merchant's pets. Corfield was short, balding, florid, dapper and confident.

'So – for what purpose may you have come to these parts?'

'My principal aim is to make an expedition into the high Andes. It is my dream to stand on an Andean pinnacle and look down on the plains of Patagonia below. I am a ship's naturalist now, you know.'

'You have come to admire the beauties of nature, eh? Well, I should be fain to have accompanied you, were you heading to St Jago. I myself enjoy admiring the beauties of nature, in the form of the rather fine *señoritas* there!'

'My intention is to prove Lyell correct,' Darwin pressed on, undaunted. 'Lyell is a geologist. He believes that geological change is an immensely slow process—'

Corfield cut him off: 'The cove who wrote *Principles of Geology*? I have all three volumes on my library shelves.'

'There is a third volume of Lyell?' Darwin could barely contain his excitement.

'Help yourself, old boy.'

'My God, Corfield. I cannot tell you how pleasant it is to meet with such a straightforward, thorough Englishman in these vile countries.'

Corfield laughed uproariously. 'Well, my dear man, I am a sufficiently thorough Englishman that I shall desist from accompanying you up the Andes! You are welcome to all those lice-ridden hovels in the mining districts. But if there is any material assistance I can offer in effecting your purpose, then I promise you of my service.'

'I say, Corfield, there is. Would you mind awfully cashing a bill for a hundred pounds for me? It is on my father's account. His money is as good as the bank.'

'I know. My father gets all his financial advice from yours. That would be no problem, old fellow.'

'This is most awfully generous of you.'

'Don't mention it. But I must say, Darwin, the last I heard you were bound for the parsonage! You're the last person I expected to see pitching up in Valparayso.'

'Oh, but I am a priest-in-waiting. The little wife and the little parsonage will follow in due course, have no doubt of that.'

But would they? Suddenly, Darwin was suffused with the certain knowledge that he had been putting off the parsonage because he no longer wanted it. He wanted to bestride the Andes. He wanted to uncover the mysteries of the scientific world. *He wanted to make a difference.* His father would be apoplectic with rage, of course. But then, his father was ten thousand miles away.

The supper party in Darwin's honour convened from nine o'clock in the long hall that spread itself along the southern side of the inner quadrangle. The *estrado*, a low, raised platform that ran the length of the inside wall, was scattered with carpets and velvet cushions for the women to sit upon, cross-legged like Moors. Leather armchairs were brought for the men. The first to arrive was Señora Campos, a tall, elderly, aristocratic Chilean lady with something of the condor in her demeanour. Her eye lit upon Corfield's atlas, which lay open on the piano, displaying a gaudy map of central Chili over which Darwin had pored enthusiastically that afternoon.

'*¡Ah! Esta es contradança!*' she announced. It is a country dance. '*¡Qué bonita!*'

Corfield whispered low in Darwin's ear: 'The standards of education in Chilean society may not be what you are used to, old man.'

Corfield's mulatto servants – or were they slaves? Darwin could not be sure – brought a huge gourd of *maté* on a silver salver, with sugar and orange juice mixed in, and a silver tube for sucking up the brew.

'It is considered rank bad manners to wipe the drinking tube after a lady has sucked it,' whispered Corfield, as Señora Campos lifted the tube to her parched lips.

Gradually, the other guests assembled: Major Sutcliffe, Mr Kennedy and Robert Alison, all merchants; Renous, a German trader; Señor Remedios, an elderly Chilean lawyer; and three young local *señoritas* who, it appeared to Darwin, had designs to become the *señora* of Corfield's household. Like the women of Buenos Ayres or Monte Video, they wore slender, figure-hugging garments, arranged nonchalantly to reveal their white silk stockings and pretty little feet. To his embarrassment, he could clearly see the embroidered garter visible beneath one girl's diaphanous petticoat. And, of course, the inevitable silk veils swirled up from their waists and over the backs of their extravagant hair-combs, before tumbling down over their faces, leaving one black, brilliant, inviting eye uncovered in each case. They took an unnecessarily long and lascivious time sucking at the drinking-tube. This was, he reflected, only an approximation to civilization.

'How wonderfully strange,' said Señora Campos over dinner, 'that I should have lived to dine in the same room with Englishmen. As a girl, I remember that at the mere cry of "*Los Ingleses*", every soul, carrying what valuables they could, took to the mountains.'

'Pirates,' explained Corfield helpfully. 'They used to loot the churches.'

'I assure you, madam, that most of my countrymen are the most devout Christians,' Darwin reassured her.

'But how is that so, Señor Darwin? Do not your padres, your very bishops marry? It is a strange idea of Christianity.'

'It is a different sort of Christianity, madam, but it is Christianity all the same.'

'What surprises me,' said Major Sutcliffe huffily through a mouthful of ragoût, 'is that here we are in the modern age, and I cannot walk down the street without being followed by a gaggle of wretched children shouting *pirata* at me.'

'My servant,' offered Señor Remedios from beneath a pair of extravagant white eyebrows, 'saw your ships arrive in harbour. He said there was talk that your captain might be a pirate, or a smuggler.'

Darwin snorted. 'The person who could possibly mistake Captain FitzRoy for a smuggler would never perceive any difference between Lord Chesterfield and his valet!'

Renous the German, whose hair bristled spikily like a hedgehog poised to defend itself, posed a direct question of the lawyer: 'Tell me, Señor Remedios, what do you think of the King of England sending out a collector to your country to pick up lizards and beetles, and to break stones?'

'*Hay un gato encerrado aqui*,' replied the old man. There is a cat shut up here.

'What does he mean?' hissed Darwin to Corfield.

'It is a local expression,' Corfield hissed back. 'It means all is not well.'

'No man is so rich as to send out people to pick up rubbish,' concluded the lawyer. 'I do not like it.'

Renous gave Darwin a sympathetic look. 'I am something of a collector myself, Señor Darwin. I once left some caterpillars with a serving girl, giving her orders to feed them leaves so that they might turn into butterflies. The news was rumoured through the town, and the padres were consulted. The governor had me arrested on charges of sorcery. I suffered an unpleasant few days in the town lock-up before the mix-up was corrected.'

'So much for your modern age, Major Sutcliffe!' said Mr Kennedy, laughing.

'But are you not curious, Señora, concerning the works of nature?'

persisted Darwin. 'Why a caterpillar turns into a butterfly? Why a volcano erupts? Why there are mountains here in Chili, but Patagonia to the east is as flat as a pancake?'

'All such enquiries are useless and impious,' replied Señora Campos with a sniff. 'It is quite sufficient that God has made the mountains thus.'

One of the sultry young women giggled.

There was a moment's awkward silence, before Corfield intervened, to steer the conversation discreetly on to other matters. Further dishes were brought, all of them of a fiery intensity, before the repast concluded with a very English jelly-pudding.

'Thought I'd make you feel at home, old man,' murmured Corfield, simultaneously managing a sly wink at the young lady to his right, as two scoops of jelly wobbled on to her plate.

Darwin waited for his own pudding to cease shimmying before he plunged in his spoon, but mysteriously, it refused to comply. Instead, the faintest of vibrations could be seen to agitate the translucent sheen of its surface. Inexplicably, the jelly seemed to tremble more, not less, the longer it sat on his plate.

One of the young women screamed. Señor Remedios hurled back his chair and jumped to his feet with an alacrity that belied his years. The servants were already running for the doorway, but it was a close contest between them and the guests. Even the English merchants had leaped up from their seats and were now hastening from the room. Darwin, dumbfounded, was left alone at the table. 'What is it?' he asked.

'An earthquake,' said Corfield, wiping his chin with his napkin and straightening his clothing as he, too, prepared to leave.

'Oh,' said Darwin stupidly.

'We have them every day or two in these parts. It is why we always leave the doors open, in case they jam shut. The vast majority amount to nothing – just a little rumbling sound. But then again, the entire town of Copiapó was flattened a few years back. Are you coming?'

Darwin rose to his feet with as much dignity as he could muster. 'That was rather a case of the devil take the hindmost,' he said disdainfully.

'There is a want of habit in governing their fear in these parts. Unlike your Englishman, it is not a feeling they are ashamed of.'

'So I saw.' Darwin gave Corfield a nod of mutual superiority, then made for the door with noticeably more haste than would otherwise have been necessary.

'Come along – press it on! Lend a hand there, Covington!'

Darwin had set out for the Andes at dawn, on one of Corfield's horses, sitting astride Corfield's horsecloths, wearing Corfield's boots, spurs, stirrups and hat. His father, he assured himself, would settle his account with Corfield in due course. He had also hired two *guasos*, Mariano and Gonzales by name, in an attempt to re-create the atmosphere of his Patagonian expedition; but these Chilean gauchos, who had formerly been in the service of Lord Cochrane, were far too deferential. They refused, for instance, to take their meals with him, preferring to eat with Covington instead. Their dress, excepting a pair of absurd six-inch spurs, had none of the extravagance of their Patagonian counterparts; they wore plain ponchos and worsted leggings of a muted green. They knew nothing of the *bolas*. They never ate meat. They were, decided Darwin, men of the serving classes rather than true men of action. He felt secretly glad that, at the last minute, he had decided not to don his own gaucho costume.

He had also recruited an *arriero* – a muleteer in a felt top hat – who brought with him ten mules, led by their *madrina* or godmother, an old steady mare with a bell around her neck that the other beasts would follow anywhere, even over a precipice if necessary. This was a handy arrangement, as it was only necessary to recapture the *madrina* after a night's grazing, and the others would come obediently to heel. Each mule could carry a staggering three-hundred-pound load up the narrowest of defiles, which was why he had felt no compunction in bringing with him an entire bed, borrowed from Corfield's house. True, the frame was an unwieldy shape, but Covington had been deputized to walk behind the animal, on watch for any awkward shifts of balance. The bed would certainly provide a solution to the lice problem that Corfield had warned him about.

The party trudged upwards for hours through delightful sunshine, the scenery becoming increasingly verdant the higher they climbed. They passed shepherds' cottages, their shiny lawns smoothed out beside crystal-clear streams, and emerald fields studded with dairy cattle, all standing motionless like china figurines. There were groves of oranges and figs, and fluttering orchards of peach-blossom alive with humming-birds. Finally, a breathtaking view of Valparayso – Paradise Valley indeed – opened out far below, amid patchwork fields. It was, thought Darwin, joyfully, exactly like the colour-plates of the Swiss Alps one saw in annuals. He was not so carried away with enthusiasm, however, as to allow his sense of scientific enquiry to remain dulled. Where, he wondered, were all the wild animals? He had seen the occasional fieldmouse, and indeed had succeeded in catching one. In the still of the evening, he had heard the faint cry of the *bizcacha*, a burrowing rodent, and the unpleasant call of the goatsucker bird, which was said to be able to milk tethered goats with its beak. But that was all. Paradise Valley seemed a strangely depopulated Eden, as if the world was indeed brand new.

Of marine life, however, there was evidence aplenty. There were thick shell-beds arrayed in terraces up the mountain slopes, so vast they had been hacked into by local farmers as a source of lime. What on earth had caused these terraces to bank up there, covered as they were in sand and sea-rolled shingle? Many of the shells were embedded in a reddish-black mould, which under Darwin's portable microscope revealed itself to be marine mud, the minute, decomposed particles of organic bodies. He dug deeper, to find fragments of ancient pottery and the imprint of some plaited rush, long since rotted away. This made no sense. If, as Lyell insisted, shell-beds on mountainsides had been lifted gradually from the sea over limitless, timeless aeons, how could there be evidence of human habitation buried within? Perhaps FitzRoy was right after all. Perhaps the Old Testament was right. Perhaps this was the drowned detritus of the great flood.

Remember what Professor Sedgwick impressed upon you, he told himself. *One piece of evidence proves nothing to the geologist. Only an overwhelming mass of evidence can prove anything. Hold your tongue until you know the truth.*

'What are you looking for, Don Carlos?'

Mariano, tugged by curiosity, had wandered across from lighting the campfire.

'I am trying to establish what these sea-shells are doing here, halfway up a mountainside.'

'They are not sea-shells, Don Carlos. They are mountain-shells.'

Clearly, the *guasos* knew even less of the natural world than their gaucho cousins.

Darwin sat in silence until Mariano had wandered away, watching the valleys blacken and the snowy peaks of the Andes turn ruby in the setting sun. In the half-light, he perused Corfield's copy of Lyell's *Principles of Geology Volume 3* once again. Lyell was utterly unequivocal. The sea had been uplifted to the mountainsides. The process had occurred gradually, over countless millennia: like the formation of sedentary rock, it could never be witnessed by the naked eye. It was a process that was now completed, and indeed had been completed long before man had ever walked the face of the earth.

He gazed once more at the inexplicable staircase of shell-terraces below, marching down the mountain slopes to the sea. The evidence simply did not fit. Perturbed, he crossed the field in which they had made camp, changed into his nightclothes, jammed on a new nightcap, pulled back the sheets and climbed into bed.

In the clammy light of dawn, the view had all but disappeared. A fog bank had rolled in far below, curling into ravines, turning solitary hillocks into islets, and washing in slow-moving waves against the implacable black rocks. Shivering with cold, a warming cup of *maté* clasped between his hands, Darwin entertained the thought that the caves and bays of Tierra del Fuego must look like this from the air. Even as he shared the observation with himself, a gentle, rippling sea breeze caused the fog to eddy and break upon a shell-terrace far below, like a wave furling upon a beach.

Suddenly, his blood seemed to stand still in his veins. His heart felt as if it had stopped. His hands fell limp, and the cup of *maté* tumbled soundlessly to the grass at his feet. The answer – the answer to everything – had come to him so suddenly he almost believed for a moment that he had been shot. The shell-terraces were *beaches*. Each terrace was a beach. Each one had been wrenched into the air by an earthquake – a big earthquake, not the constant, minuscule tremors that plagued the inhabitants of Valparayso. The mountains were indeed rising from the sea. But they weren't doing it gradually. They were doing it in a series of violent lurches. They hadn't stopped rising – they were still doing it. Much of the uplift had occurred within the lifetime of man. That was why he had found pottery. It was why so few animals lived here – it was new country. Lyell was wrong. FitzRoy was wrong. The Bible was wrong. He – Charles Darwin – had the answer. How he burned with excitement, with pride, and with an overwhelming sense of *ownership* of this amazing, incredible idea.

'Is everything all right, sir?' Covington had spotted the teacup at his master's feet.

'Yes – no…That is, everything's fine.'

Dare he try to share his discovery with the mule-headed Covington? How he wished that FitzRoy were here. How he wished he could send a semaphore telegraph, right this minute, all the way to Henslow in Cambridge. *Dare* he try?

'Do you see these shell-terraces on the mountain slopes?' he began.

'Shell-terraces, sir?'

'Yes. Shell-terraces. Do you see how they rise, in steps?'

'Steps, sir?'

'Yes. Steps. They…Oh, never mind.'

'I'm sorry sir, I don't—'

'Go and…go and pack up my linen. I shall be there directly.'

'Aye aye sir.'

Still bewildered as to where he had gone wrong, Covington stomped off to see to his master's bedding.

'As for London – what is London? We can do anything in my country.'

This man should meet Lieutenant Sulivan, thought Darwin. His chest pulled taut and his head feeling light from the altitude, he sat upon a wrought-iron chair at the centre of a sunlit lawn, drinking chardonnay with Mr Dawlish, a mine-owner from Cornwall.

'You have never been to London, I take it?'

'Of course not,' said Dawlish. 'Whatever for would I wish to visit London? What is London?'

'What indeed?' said Darwin, for the avoidance of argument.

At the edge of the lawn, where ugly mounds of scarred earth formed primitive ramparts about an ink-dark mineshaft, a wiry, sweat-bathed Chilean miner in a leather apron emerged blinking into the light. He stood shaking on the rim of the shaft, ribs protruding, nostrils distended, muscles quivering, knees trembling with exertion. On his bare back, a two-hundred-pound load of copper ore strained against his shoulder-straps. He stared at the seated pair boldly from beneath his tight-fitting scarlet skullcap. Unsure how to respond, Darwin waved back limply, a gesture he regretted the moment he had made it.

'The shaft is four hundred and fifty feet deep,' explained Mr Dawlish, to account for the miner's shaking knees.

'There is a ladder?'

'No. But there are notched tree trunks, zigzagging up the inside. And I allow them to stop once for a rest, on the way up. They are fed upon boiled beans and bread twice a day – which is better than agricultural workers. They are also given two days off every three weeks.'

'That is generous,' agreed Darwin, comparing the arrangement favourably with conditions in his uncle's factories.

'I like to be generous. I was a miner myself, you see, back in Polzeath.'

'Really?'

'I came out here to make my fortune. I had heard that the Chilean mine-owners threw their copper pyrites away, thinking it useless. It was true. They knew nothing of the roasting process, which removes the sulphur prior to smelting. So for a few dollars I bought one of the richest veins in the country. And look about you now!'

Darwin looked about him. Mr Dawlish's property certainly did not *feel* as if it were at the heart of a mining-district. There were no clanking wheels, no roaring furnaces, smoke or hissing steam-engines. Just a series of holes in the ground. The mine was so primitive, in fact, that it had to be drained by men hauling leather bags of water up the shaft. All the ore, it transpired, had to be shipped to Swansea to be smelted.

'This mine is worth eight thousand pounds. I paid three pounds and eight shillings for it,' said Mr Dawlish expansively. 'As for London,' he repeated, 'what is London? We can do anything in my country.'

Idly, he picked a louse from his scalp, and flicked it away. Darwin felt relieved that he had brought his own bed.

'London *is* where the King lives,' he retorted, suddenly keen to ascribe at least one virtue to the British capital.

'I heard that George Rex had died,' said Mr Dawlish.

'He did. But there is a new king now.'

'Indeed? And how many more in the Rex family are yet alive?'

Darwin found himself lost for words.

They pressed ever upwards, past thundering mud-coloured torrents, to regions where the rocks lay freshly split and scattered by a thousand earthquakes. They hurried on past overhanging boulders that teetered implausibly above their heads, and precipices that fell away sheer to either side. The lush greenery of the lower slopes gave way to a matt-purple rock dotted with tiny alpine flowers, a landscape that was stark and majestic but never quite beautiful. They crossed rickety suspension bridges, mere bundles of sticks knotted together with thongs of animal hide, which swung precariously above rushing gorges. Led by their *madrina*, the mules never put a foot wrong. Only when they reached the snowline was Darwin's confidence shaken: here the near-vertical strata had been eroded into wild, crumbling pinnacles interspersed with columns of weathered ice. Atop one of the ice-towers, the melting snow had revealed the perfectly preserved body of a pack-mule, entombed upside down, all four legs in the air, frozen stiff where it had tumbled to its death from the path above.

Finally, with pounding heads and panting chests, they breasted the Peuquenes Ridge, the continental divide, at a height of thirteen thousand feet. Here, amid frost-shattered stones bathed silver by the moonlight, they made camp. A million stiletto stars pricked the night sky. So dry and still was the air that sparks flew from the saddle straps, and static electricity lifted the wool of Darwin's waistcoat. The *guasos* lit a fire, using little white flints that they gathered locally: Darwin was overjoyed to discover that these 'flints' were actually slivers of tropical sea-coral, baked rock-hard by volcanic action. But there was to be no hot food: the potatoes refused to cook, even though they sat boiling on the fire all evening.

'This cursed pot does not choose to boil the potatoes,' said Mariano, who had never made camp so high before.

'I told you we should have brought the old pot,' said Gonzales. 'This pot is cursed.' He, too, had never camped at such heights.

'It is the altitude,' Darwin tried to explain. 'There is less oxygen up here, so the water boils at a lower temperature. That is also why it is so difficult to breathe – why we are suffering from *puna*.'

'*Puna*, Don Carlos? *Puna* is caused by snow. Wherever there is snow, there is *puna*. Everybody knows that.'

The two *guasos* shook their heads at the Englishman's ignorance. Covington, unsure who to believe, stared dumbly at the ground. Darwin did not care. He was in heaven. He was the first geologist in all history to pass between the summits of the Andes. His cold supper of dried beef and palm-treacle tasted like manna from heaven.

I am alone here, he thought. In the electric silence of the mountain-tops, he felt as if he could hear the chorus from Handel's *Messiah*, in full orchestra, trumpeting all its glory inside his head.

The next day they followed the path of an old watercourse, down into the dip that separates the Peuquenes Ridge from the higher Portillo Ridge to the east. To Darwin's astonishment and delight, the dry stream-bed levelled out, then began to wind its way uphill. This was incredible. Visible proof that the second ridge had uplifted since the first, that its rocks were younger. The Portillo Ridge appeared to be constructed of volcanic lava, which had solidified into porphyry, as if the lava had somehow been injected between the sandstone layers of the Andes. All along the *cordillera*, volcanic cones broke the jagged asymmetry of the mountain chain. What connection did these volcanoes have with the earthquakes that were jolting the Andes by stages into the air? Did the violence of the earth tremors release vents of lava that erupted at high pressure between the gasping rocks? Darwin's brain whirled, trying to encompass it all.

There were more frozen mules by the wayside now, and clusters of wooden crosses alongside the track. Condors wheeled in and out of the icy clouds above. They were forced to stop every fifty yards for the mules to catch their breath. The lack of air produced the same sensation, Darwin noted, that he used to feel after a school run on a frosty day. The footprints of the mules crushed the snow crimson – not blood, as he first thought, but the tiny spores or eggs of some primitive organism, measuring less than a thousandth of an inch in diameter beneath the all-seeing scrutiny of his microscope. Finally the party arrived between the enclosing walls of the Portillo Pass, the 'little door' in the mountains, and gazed in awe upon the flat, featureless plains of the pampas below: a vast, sleeping expanse broken only by the rivers that ran away like silver threads in the rising sun, before losing themselves in the immensity of the distance. He had achieved his ambition.

They began their descent towards the border-post of the Republic of Mendoza. At their second halt Darwin laid animal-traps, and succeeded in catching another mouse.

'This mouse is different from the mice on the Chilean side.'

'Of course,' said Mariano, taking a cursory look. 'Chilean mice are different from Mendocino mice.'

'All the animals on the Chilean side are different from all the animals on the Mendoza side,' explained Gonzales, as if he were addressing an idiot.

'*All* of them? Are you sure?' He had to be careful here. Mariano and Gonzales had already failed to distinguish themselves on the natural philosophy front.

'Everybody knows this, Don Carlos. The condors, well, they can fly across from one side to the other. But the animals – they will not cross the passes. It is too cold. So the Chilean animals and the Mendocino animals, they are all quite different.'

Darwin reeled. This meant that the animals had come into being *after* the Andes had risen – and the Andes were still rising. So they could not, in fact, have been created by God on the sixth day. The two sets of animals were either new creatures, or – the terrifying enormity of the possibility raised the hairs aloft all the way down his spine – they had somehow transmuted, or metamorphosed, from original, common ancestors. At once, he felt puny and insignificant before the vast and scarcely comprehensible scale of such changes; one man alone, in the vastness of the *cordillera.* But at the same time he knew that the whole edifice of Christianity must heave and shake before the remorselessness of his logic, like an Andean pinnacle crumbling before the simple power of an earth tremor. *If I am right*, he thought, *if I am right – then my findings will be crucial to the theory of the formation of the world.*

'If you please sir – would you like me to kill and skin the mouse, sir?' enquired Covington, politely and resentfully.

How Darwin burned for a FitzRoy or a Henslow to be present.

The Mendoza customs and border-post proved to be a grubby hovel, staffed by two unshaven soldiers and a pure-bred Indian tracker, who was retained as a kind of human bloodhound in case any smugglers should attempt to give the post a wide berth. The three men were jumpy, and utterly bewildered by the concept of a *naturalista.* In an attempt to ease the administrative deadlock, Darwin produced his passport signed by General Rosas. One of the soldiers, a lieutenant who could read, perused the document and shot Darwin a look of disgust.

'If you are protected by the general, then you may proceed. The man who would deny passage to a servant of the general is not long for this world, as you are most probably aware.'

Darwin decided to let the accusation that he was anyone's 'servant' pass. 'The general has influence in Mendoza?'

'No, the general has no influence in our country. But it is only a matter of time. He has seized Buenos Ayres. He has taken control of most of the United Provinces. Many people have died. He is cleansing the country of Indians as far south as the Rio Negro. Now his armies are massing on the Mendoza border. We Mendocinos shall not be able to stop him. It is only a matter of time before we all become part of your general's empire.'

The last few words dripped from the officer's tongue like bad wine. Darwin remembered FitzRoy's caustic assessment of the general's motives, and reflected uneasily that perhaps his friend had been right, after all. He adopted his most soothing tones.

'I am not a personal acquaintance of the general. This passport was given to me as a representative of His Majesty King William IV of Great Britain.'

At this the other soldier perked up.

'Heh – Great Britain. That is near England, right?'

'After a fashion,' Darwin replied.

'You are a *pirata*?'

'No…no, I am not a pirate. As I told you, I am a *naturalista*. The two are really quite different.'

'*Naturalista…pirata…*Why do you *Ingleses* not keep to normal occupations?' the soldier grumbled to himself.

By nightfall, relations had improved sufficiently for Darwin's party to join the soldiers for supper around the rudimentary table of the border-post. His bed, which they had accepted without demur as part of a *naturalista*'s travelling accoutrements, had been installed in the back room. The border guards ate in silence, chewing slowly on hunks of boiled beef, while Mariano and Gonzales finally induced the recalcitrant potatoes to succumb to their fate. Halfway through the meal, a large black wingless bug fell from the thatched roof with a plop on to the table, where it sat, paralysed with confusion.

'What is that?' asked Darwin.

'It is a *benchuca* bug,' said the lieutenant. 'A bloodsucker.'

Experimentally, Darwin extended a fingertip towards the bewildered beast. Instantly, it seemed to come to its senses, seizing the digit between its forelegs and sinking its sucker into his flesh. Over the next few minutes it grew slowly fatter as it gorged itself with blood, until eventually it resembled a huge distended purple grape clamped to the end of his finger. Finally sated, it fell off, whereupon Darwin whipped out a little jar of preserving-spirits and swept the creature into it.

'Ha! You may have brought your own bed to avoid the lice, Don Carlos,' guffawed Mariano, 'but the *benchucas* live in the ceiling!'

That night, he discovered exactly what Mariano meant. As Covington, the soldiers, the muleteer and the two *guasos* slept swathed in blankets under the stars, he lay besieged between his crisp linen sheets. There seemed to be a whole army of *benchucas*. It was the most disgusting feeling to wake in the night, and sense their huge, soft, wingless bodies crawling all over him, sucking at his flesh. He lit a candle and burned several from his skin, but the supply seemed limitless. *A plague of benchucas*, he thought to himself. *How Biblical. Perhaps the Lord has visited them upon me, on account of my presumption.*

The next day they set off for the city of Mendoza, a two-day ride across baking, deserted plains. At one point a huge swarm of locusts flew overhead, heading northward in the direction of the city, a seeming harbinger of the destruction due to be unleashed by General Rosas. The swarm began as a ragged cloud of a dark reddish-brown colour, like smoke from some great plains fire, billowing several thousand feet into the air. Then a curious rushing noise made itself heard, like a strong breeze swishing through the rigging of a mighty ship-of-the-line, and countless millions of the insects whirred overhead. Occasionally, confused outriders crashed blindly into the slower-moving mule train below: more than one dazed locust hurtled into the yielding softness of Darwin's feather pillows, then marched testily up and down the bedlinen in search of food.

Mendoza's spires rose listlessly from the open plain ahead. They found the city forlorn and bereft of spirit, its inhabitants dazed like cattle, stupidly awaiting their fate. Robbed of all energy, one or two gauchos lounged drunkenly in the streets. Mariano and Gonzales tipped their hats politely to a fat negress astride a donkey, her face disfigured by a huge goitre. Darwin bought an entire wheelbarrowload of peaches for threepence. They did not stay. Mendoza could await General Rosas without them.

They recrossed the Andes by a different route, taking the Uspallata Pass, a long, barren valley populated by innumerable wretched dwarf cacti. After a hard day's ascent through crumbled rocks, at a height of seven thousand feet, they came upon another marvel: an entire grove of petrified fir trees, jutting out from the mountainside at an acute angle. There were perhaps fifty marbled columns in this ghostly forest, as snow-white as Lot's wife, their trunks a stout five feet in circumference, their leaves and branches long since lost to history. They were perfectly crystallized: the tiniest details of the bark were visible, and the rings within the wood were as easy to count as those of a living tree. They projected from a sandstone escarpment, which meant that they must once have lain at the bottom of the sea. This eerie grove high in the freezing mountains, Darwin realized, had once waved to the breezes of the Atlantic shore. The trees must have become submerged and petrified *before* they were uplifted into the mountains. The land had sunk before it had risen. The surface of the earth must be in a state of continuous agitation, no more than a thin crust over a viscous layer, that heaved and buckled throughout countless millions of years. Once more his whole being thrilled to the enormity of his discoveries; once more he had to bite his lip in frustration that there was no one present to discuss them with, no one to sit back and whistle at the size of the fire he would light beneath orthodox opinion.

The pass itself was a chaos of huge mountains, criss-crossed haphazardly by profound ravines, a place so cold that the water froze solid in their bottles. The *guasos* called it Las Animas – the souls – in memory of all those who had slipped and plunged to their deaths. The mule train, piled high with bulging sacks of geological specimens, snaked the whole length of the treacherous pass and across the Bridge of the Incas, a flimsy arch dripping with icicles; a seemingly bottomless abyss yawned invitingly below. Darwin's bed sashayed at the back, its swinging motion caricaturing the gait of the animal that bore its weight; but the mule, like its companions, stayed surefooted throughout.

Shortly before they reached the top of the first ridge, they came upon low walls – the ancient ruins of a long-forgotten Indian village.

'Who lived here?' asked Darwin.

'Nobody lives here, Don Carlos,' explained Gonzales. 'Nobody can live here. It is too cold. There is *puna*. And there is no food, no water. Only snow, for the whole year.'

'I know that nobody lives here *now*, but obviously, somebody once did.'

'*¿Quien sabe*, Don Carlos?'

'How old are these ruins?'

'*¿Quien sabe*, Don Carlos?'

It was incredible. An entire mountain village, its walls thrown down by countless earthquakes no doubt, situated in a location where human life was completely unsustainable. There was only one possible conclusion: that the whole village had been jolted high above the snowline over thousands of years, by the monstrous, churning, grinding, heaving forces at work far below.

A golden dusk was settling on the lush green fields above Valparayso as Darwin marched down the valley, striding out in front of his mule train, bursting with energy, life and confidence for the future. The boughs hung heavy with glowing peaches, and the scent of drifting woodsmoke infused the air. A sweetly competing aroma of drying figs wafted down from the flat rooftops and out across the sunlit fields, where weary labourers could be seen walking home from their day's toil in the orchards. A church bell tolled lazily in the warm summer air. After the freezing, barren heights of the Andes and the stifling, deathly stillness of Mendoza, there was something welcoming, something...well, almost *English* about the scene. Perhaps a certain pensive English stillness was missing from the mood, but otherwise the similarities were unmistakable. As Darwin stood admiring the view, Covington, who was leading his master's horse, caught up.

'My water bottle, if you please, Covington.'

'Aye aye sir.'

I do wish he would leave off the nautical responses, thought Darwin irritably. *He's not on the ship now.*

Covington shuffled round to the horse's flank to retrieve the water bottle, placing his left hand clumsily on the animal's withers as he did so. Suddenly, with a strangled cry, he leaped back as if stung by a wasp.

'What *is* it?' snapped Darwin.

'There!' was Covington's garbled shout.

An indistinct black shape flapped unpleasantly between the animal's shoulder-blades.

'What on earth—?'

Mariano came up and shooed the creature away. It vanished into the dusk in a rustle of leathery wings, leaving two small bloody wounds where it had sat.

'Vampire bat, Don Carlos,' said the *guaso* matter-of-factly.

Darwin shuddered. No, this was not England. This was a very, very long way from England, a very long way indeed. And it was time, frankly, to be going home.

They attained the sanctuary of Corfield's mansion on the afternoon of the following day, to be greeted by the master of the house with his customary unflappable, immaculate style. White wine was brought, a great fuss was made of the explorer, and Darwin sat back in the garden to regale his host with tales of geological castles in the air: the beaches in the mountains, the river bed that flowed upward, the two sorts of mouse, the petrified forest, the deserted village in the clouds.

'Do you not see, Corfield?' he pressed home the point excitedly. 'There can be no reason for supposing that any great catastrophe has *ever* been visited upon the earth, in any former epoch! The Biblical flood is a myth!'

'I don't gainsay it, old man,' murmured Corfield soothingly.

As he spoke he blurred horizontally in the oddest fashion, before dividing into two Corfields, one on either side of Darwin's field of vision. All of a sudden, a huge wave of nausea welled up from below, far worse than anything Darwin had ever experienced on the *Beagle*.

'Corfield, old fellow?'

'Yes?'

'I think I'm going to be sick.'

A dark, fuzzy shape obscured the daylight that streamed in through the window. Somebody's silhouette. His sister Susan, perhaps, or Catty come to read to him from one of her Society for the Diffusion of Useful Knowledge publications. Except that this did not look like his bedroom at the Mount. Where the deuce was he? A noise burbled from the mouth of the silhouette – words, soothing words, like running water gurgling across pebbles. He tried to make sense of them. As his eyes adjusted to the light, the silhouette took on a familiar aspect. The features blurred into view. A nose, eyes, a mouth. He remembered that face from somewhere. The face was telling him that everything was going to be all right. The face was something to do with a sea voyage he had once been on. The *Beagle*. That was it. It was all coming back now. He was the ship's natural philosopher on HMS *Beagle*. He could hear waves – waves on the shore.

'Philos? Are you awake?'

Bynoe tried again, still softly, but with a little more urgency this time. Darwin was stirring. 'Philos? It's me, Bynoe.'

'Bynoe?'

'How are you feeling?'

'I…Where am I? How came I here?'

'You are at the house of Mr Alexander Caldcleugh.'

'Who?'

'Caldcleugh – he is a British mine-owner. You were taken ill at Mr Corfield's house, but he is from home. He had to visit St Jago on business last month. You were moved to Mr Caldcleugh's house because he resides closer to the shore – I estimated that the sea air might hasten your recovery.'

'Last month? How long have I been here?'

'Six weeks.'

'Six *weeks*? Then it is 1835! But what—?'

'You have had a high fever – possibly typhoid, I'm not sure. But you are much better now. Here, I have brought you some calomel. The Indian servants wanted to treat you using traditional herbs, all sorts of mumbo-jumbo, but I have been sure to keep you well supplied with modern medicine.'

'My dear Bynoe, how long have you attended upon me?'

Bynoe's vigil had stretched through every long day of the previous six weeks. 'Not long…just long enough to see you well again.'

'I had some wine – I think the wine was bad…'

'Perhaps it was the wine. *¿Quien sabe?* But you are on the mend now, Philos, and that is all that matters.'

A sudden stab of fear sliced through Darwin's brain, as the details of his Andean expedition came jolting back. 'My specimens! Where are my specimens?' He raised himself weakly on to one elbow.

'Do not trouble yourself, Philos. Your specimens are in good hands, you may be satisfied of it. Sulivan and I labelled them all up in your behalf, and had them packed into cases, with the help of your servant Covington. He is a most assiduous and intelligent fellow – I think you underestimate him.'

'But where are they?'

'Lieutenant Wickham said they were too many for the hold of the *Beagle*, especially as we are revictualling. But luckily for you the *Samarang* was in port, and Captain Paget agreed to take them on board. He will make sure they are delivered to your Professor Henslow, you can rely upon it.'

'Thank goodness for that.'

Darwin sank back into his pillow, relief washing over him. Then a further shaft of clarity pierced his delirium. 'Bynoe?'

'Yes?'

'Why is Lieutenant Wickham in the *Beagle*? He is the commander of the *Adventure*.'

A cloud passed across Bynoe's sunny countenance.

'Things have changed in the *Beagle*, Philos.' He sighed, turning his face to the window.

'What do you mean?'

'All is not well in our little vessel, my friend. I had hoped not to bring such matters to your attention, in your enfeebled state. But you have always been too sharp for me, Philos.'

'What has happened? What is the matter?'

'You will find out when you are recuperated. But I adjure you not to bother yourself now. You will be up and about soon, I am sure of it, but you need be in no hurry. The *Beagle* will wait for you. To be honest, Philos, there is not a great deal of activity aboard the *Beagle* at present. Everything has ground to a halt.'

CHAPTER NINE

Valparayso Harbour, 11 January 1835

FitzRoy sat in his darkened cabin, staring at the charts of Tierra del Fuego that lapped meaninglessly across his table. He had put aside his pen several hours ago. It lay idle beside his mapping instruments, its nib dry and tired. The steward had brought dinner many hours previously, but FitzRoy had not acknowledged the knock at the door. Not a morsel of food had passed his lips all day. He was no longer hungry. It was as if all visible life in the cabin had slowed to a stop: the only movement remaining between the four walls was his pulse, beating quietly and desperately in his wrist.

His mind, though, was too filled with thoughts to be stilled, rushing, tumbling thoughts, each individual idea shining with clarity, but when mixed together, a dazzling incoherent whirl of insight that came too fast to be unravelled, marshalled or properly evaluated. Concentrating hard, he grabbed a passing gem from the torrent, and tried his damnedest to isolate it and appreciate its import. *The survey of Tierra del Fuego is not good enough*, the thought commanded him. *It needs to be done again. There are unnamed islets, imperfect depth-soundings, uncharted rocks. All of it must be done again, and done properly this time.*

He knew deep down that this was the only course. Sitting motionless in his seat, he experienced the same rising and falling sensation in his stomach that one endures when passing rapidly over the brow of a hill – a combination, he realized, of exhilaration at the chance to put right his mistakes, and fear at the thought that it might yet prove an impossible task. The solution to this dichotomy came to him in another brilliant revelation. This time he would not plot a course through the labyrinth. That had been his mistake. He would let the path choose itself.

The pure light of heaven would shine forth in the darkness and illuminate their way.

As if on cue the door opened, flooding the little cabin with a dazzling light. The dust-motes went scurrying into the corners in a panic. Had the Lord sent a messenger? No. It was Darwin. He seemed excited. He was brandishing a piece of paper. Had he not been ill, been gone a long time?

'FitzRoy – my dear man – how are you? The most marvellous news! I have a letter from Henslow. The *Avestruz Petise* – the little ostrich, you remember? – it has arrived safely in Cambridge, and has been christened *Rhea darwinii*! And moreover – the specimen of that yellow tree fungus which the Fuegians eat has also been catalogued – it too is new to science and has been named *Cyttaria darwinii*! This is an auspicious day indeed!'

Darwin continued talking, but the words melded into an unbroken babble in FitzRoy's head. Something about a letter. How Darwin was a sensation in England. Then he remembered, grasping a hard concrete fact from the racing flow of his subconscious, that he, too, had received letters. Letters that Darwin ought to read. He pushed them across the table.

Stopped in his tracks, Darwin read the first missive with horror-stricken fascination. It was from the Admiralty.

> Regarding the commission of the auxiliary surveying vessels *Paz* and *Liebre*. Their lordships do not approve of hiring vessels for the Service and therefore desire that they be discharged as soon as possible.

The second letter commenced with a severe reprimand for the time taken in completing the survey of Tierra del Fuego and the Falklands, before going on to address the hiring of the *Unicorn* and its rebirth as the *Adventure*:

> Inform Captain FitzRoy that the lords highly disapprove of this proceeding, especially after the orders which he previously received on the subject.

'But this – this is a disgrace!' began Darwin indignantly. 'This is an entirely political manoeuvring. Much as it grieves me to say it, I fear that this has been effected by the Liberal administration solely because you are of a Tory family.'

'Headquarters have not thought it proper to give me any assistance. But assistance shall be provided from another quarter.'

Unsure what he meant, Darwin continued to vent his outrage: 'Whatever shall we do for room? I shall have trouble enough storing my collections! How shall I fit into the library with Stokes, King, Hamond *and* Martens?'

'Martens? Martens is gone.'

'Gone? Gone where?'

'There is no money for Martens. I sold the *Adventure* for seven thousand paper dollars – a loss of fifteen hundred dollars in all. Much of the money I received went to paying off her crew. It grieved me sadly to bring her to the hammer, but my friends here on board were seriously urgent on the matter. So the *Adventure* is gone.'

Suddenly, FitzRoy felt overwhelmed by a wave of sadness, at the loss of his beautiful white schooner, and also at the loss of an old comrade. 'The *Adventure* is gone. Skyring is gone.'

'Skyring? Who is Skyring?'

FitzRoy pushed another Admiralty missive across the table. Darwin read it aloud:

> Regret to inform you of the death of Lieutenant William Skyring of HMS *Dryad*, formerly of HMS *Beagle* and HMS *Adelaide*, murdered by natives on the coast of West Africa, May 1834.

'I took his command,' explained FitzRoy, mournfully. 'The *Beagle* was to have been his. Instead he has been murdered. At first I blamed myself. Then I realized that his death is part of God's plan. The good Lord has a task for all of us. My task is to return to Tierra del Fuego to begin the survey all over again.'

'What?' Darwin almost jumped out of his skin.

'My task,' FitzRoy reiterated patiently, 'is to return to Tierra del Fuego—'

'Have you taken leave of your senses?'

'The good Lord has commanded me—'

'Of this the good Lord deliver us!' Darwin protested. 'This is madness! You will have a mutiny on your hands! If you think for one minute that I would be prepared to risk my life by going back round the Horn – I signed on for this trip with the intention of visiting the coral islands of the Pacific, not to sit in a glorified skiff being battered by South Atlantic gales year in year out until her brittle perfectionist of a captain is finally satisfied with his labours!'

Of the competing emotions accelerating unchecked through FitzRoy's brain, anger came to the fore. He felt his gorge rising. 'My decision on the matter is final.'

Darwin could hardly believe his ears. He, too, began to flush angrily. His weeks at leisure in Chilean society had reminded him what it was to live an independent life, his every move no longer subject to the arbitrary whim of one man.

'Then I am afraid you must travel without a naturalist. I shall return to stay with Mr Corfield, or Mr Caldcleugh, at whose home I have been convalescing, and shall find a different passage.'

FitzRoy's eyes flashed. 'As always, you have taken so much, and have made no provision in return. I suppose we shall have to organize a party on board.'

'A party? What are you talking about?'

'A party to thank all those members of the British community here, whose favours you have so readily accepted.'

'There is no need for that! What ever do you mean by it?'

'I mean, sir, that you are the sort of man who would receive any favours and make no return!'

His face white with rage, Darwin stood up and stalked out of the cabin, slamming the door behind him. On the maindeck he ran into the shocked figure of Lieutenant Wickham, who tried to remonstrate with him: 'Confound it, Philosopher, I wish you would not quarrel with the skipper when he is overtired.'

'Overtired? His mind has become deranged! You may inform him of my resignation as natural philosopher of the *Beagle*. I shall not reside a moment longer in this ship of fools!'

Angrily, Darwin brushed Wickham aside and headed to his quarters to collect his belongings. Wickham, perturbed, knocked softly at the door of FitzRoy's cabin. There came no answer.

The landscape of the captain's cabin had turned cold, bleak and empty. In the grey, muddy light, the colours of the little room had receded to a flat, dull monotone, the few simple items of furniture assuming ghostly outlines and washed-out hues. The faint noises of the ship – the creaking of the rigging, the slap of water against the hull, the mutter of distant voices – had blended into a continuous note so muffled as to be unintelligible. None of this, however, mattered to Robert FitzRoy: he was no longer there, except physically. He was in another place.

That was the only way to describe his fear: another place. There was no logic to it, he knew that. He wanted to fight whatever it was that held him in the dark, that toyed with him, but there was no physical adversary present. There were not even any physical symptoms about his person. There was just a shapeless, nameless dread that had removed him to its lair, a place more terrifying than any nightmare he had ever endured. The harder he tried to escape, the more tightly he was confined there. Fright and hopelessness crowded his mind, his own personal prison guards in this other place.

His physical body lay curled in its cot, sobbing uncontrollably. How long had he been crying? Hours? Days? They were not tears of relief but tears that drowned him, tears with no beginning and no end, tears that welled up unchecked from somewhere deep inside. And when his tear ducts finally dried up, he continued to sob, heaving incoherently, his misery compounded by shame and self-loathing and lack of comprehension and anger at the pointlessness of it all. Sweat poured from his body. The letters from the Admiralty had prompted this change in his mental state, that much he knew. They had been the trigger, but no more. What had followed had been not just terrifying, but terrifyingly inexplicable. What in God's name was happening to him? He hugged his pillow for comfort, the only familiar point of reference in this alien environment. He wanted to turn over, but he could not remember how to do it – it seemed a colossal, unimaginable task, too frightening even to contemplate.

He had tried ordering himself out of his malaise. *Get up. Go over to the washstand. Call for water. Shave. Tasks you have completed easily, unthinkingly, a thousand and one times.* He had even got as far as putting his feet on the floor, but as soon as he had done so, a sudden wave of panic, an awful onrushing knowledge of impending doom, had broken over him, had driven the breath from his body. He had subsided back into the cot, palpitating, short of breath, every limb leaden with unaccountable fatigue.

He tried again. *Who are you?* Nobody. *What do you feel?* Nothing. *What can you do?* Nothing. *What do you know?* Nothing. *What do you understand?* Nothing. *I am nothing. There is nothing.* His entire being was reduced to a pure and simple manifestation of panic, an urgent physical discomfort with no prospect of relief, a sense of falling with no concluding impact to bring about merciful release.

Desperately, he fought to clear his mind. Even in the midst of the two great storms they had endured, at Maldonado and off Cape Horn, he had not been so overwhelmingly afraid. But he had to do something. *The more you manage to do, the less you will want to die.* Shaking, unable to stand, weak with lack of food, he succeeded with a supreme effort in surmounting the lip of the cot and collapsing to the floor. Slowly, very slowly, he pulled himself by his fingertips across the floorboards. At last, he reached up to the tabletop for pen and paper. *Please God, give me the strength to do what I have to do.*

He had the pen in his hand now, but he had forgotten how to write. There was no feeling in his arm, no feeling flowing through his hand, no feeling directing the nib.

Concentrate. You cannot escape this…creature. But you can free others from the consequences of its hold upon your spirit.

Laboriously, agonizingly, he began to write, each letter a station of the cross, until finally he was finished. There, on the floor between his enfeebled arms, wet and blotchy with his renewed tears, lay his written resignation as captain of the *Beagle.*

'Sir. I must ask you to reconsider. There is a universal and deeply felt grief on board at your decision.'

'Flattered as I am by the concern of the men, Lieutenant Wickham, I have no option but to resign my command. You saw for yourself that my mental state became quite suddenly maladjusted, so as to unfit me for the leadership of this or any vessel. It is quite clearly a hereditary predisposition.'

'Sir. Mr Bynoe says it is merely the effect of a want of bodily health, and of exhaustion following a period of onerous application to duty.'

'My dear friends.' FitzRoy reached across the table, placing five rake-thin digits across the back of Wickham's hand, and the remaining five across Sulivan's. 'That simply will not do. I must invalid, and appoint Mr Wickham to the command of the *Beagle.* My brains' – he permitted himself a wry smile – 'are even more confused than they used to be in London.'

'Sir – I will not accept it. I will not accept the promotion.'

'You have no option, Mr Wickham. I order you to assume command.'

Sulivan was almost in tears. 'Sir, look at the medical evidence. Any man would have been affected by the strain of being ordered to sell the *Adventure* – and at such a loss!'

'It is true, Mr Sulivan, that I am…involved in difficulties. My means have been severely taxed. This may even fix me out of England. And I grant you, it was a bitter disappointment to receive such orders. The mortification still preys deeply. But more distressing still – much more distressing – is that all my cherished hopes of completing the survey of South America must now utterly fail. The Admiralty has made it quite impossible for me to fulfil the whole of my instructions. But fail I have, and I must pay the price for it. My feelings and my health no longer respond to my commands, gentlemen. A mutiny has been effected. I must give way to someone better fitted for this command.'

FitzRoy felt exhausted but relieved: relieved that it was all over, relieved to be able to speak freely about his condition at last.

'But sir – what would be gained by your resignation? Absolutely nothing. The survey would not be completed. The orders in the event of a captain invaliding his command are most explicit.'

'Remind me.'

Wickham unfolded the Admiralty instruction sheet. '"The officer on whom the command of the vessel may in consequence devolve is hereby required and directed not to proceed to a new step in the voyage; as, for instance, if carrying on the coast survey on the western side of South America, he is not to cross the Pacific, but to return to England by Rio de Janeiro and the Atlantic."'

'It seems the author was almost prescient.'

'It means there can be no chain of measurements about the globe. The survey would go unfinished. The stigma of failure would attach not just to yourself but to the *Beagle* and all her officers. But were you to remain in command, there would still be time enough this summer to finish surveying the Chilean coast back down to Tres Montes, before heading home.'

'And what of northern Chili and Peru?'

Wickham offered a consoling smile. 'There shall be others after us, who shall survey the north. But our achievement to date – *your* achievement – shall accrue to the benefit of all those on board.'

'And what if I were to succumb to another attack of the blue devils – what then?'

'Then you have my word I should accept your invitation to assume command.'

'Please sir,' entreated Sulivan, 'you have been harassed and oppressed by troubles and difficulties of the most unexpected, the most unfortunate kind. It was undoubtedly these that caused you to fall ill for a brief period. But those troubles and difficulties are behind us – by which I do not mean to belittle the drain on your means, merely to say that the worst has now been thrown at you, and here you are, sir, in full command of your faculties, the finest leader and sailor that I, or any of us, have ever sailed under. The best man, the only man, to skipper the *Beagle*.'

FitzRoy looked from Wickham's round, honest, open, troubled face to Sulivan's dark imploring gaze. 'It seems, gentlemen, that the Admiralty has me between Scylla and Charybdis. Either the survey is to be abandoned at once, or it is to be left uncompleted. For the sake of those mariners who come after us, then, and only for their sake, we shall spend one more summer surveying the coast down to Tres Montes.'

Lit up with relief and delight, Wickham and Sulivan rose to shake his hand, but he cut them short with an upraised palm. 'But I also bear responsibilities to the officers and crew of the *Beagle*. Any sign whatsoever – *any* sign – that I am losing control of my wits once more, then you are to confine me in my cabin, by force if necessary. Is that understood?'

'Yes, sir – it is understood.'

The three men shook hands, and it was hard to say which of them prayed most fervently that the latest attack would prove to be FitzRoy's last.

'I thank the good Lord that you are back with us,' said Sulivan, pumping his captain's hand as if his life depended upon it.

FitzRoy felt himself bathed in the warmth and generosity of their love; but it was not enough to wash away the layers of shame and embarrassment that seemed to him to adhere to his immortal soul.

CHAPTER TEN

Concepción, Chili, 20 February 1835

Darwin lay flat on his back in a sunlit apple-orchard, reading a letter from his sisters, their convivial words waving in and out of the dappled light. Fanny Owen had become the proud mother of a baby daughter. 'We look forward to visiting you and *your* little wife in *your* little parsonage' – yes, yes. Catherine had included a pamphlet from the Society for the Diffusion of Useful Knowledge: *Poor Laws and Paupers Illustrated*, by Harriet Martineau. Oh, yes – she was that dreadful fierce bluestocking who tried to popularize Liberal policy by dressing it up in cheap romantic novellas. Ridiculous. What was this one about? A new theory devised by the recently deceased Reverend Thomas Malthus, an economist who had worked for the East India Company. Hmm.

Bereft of anything better to occupy his mind while his dinner chugged through his digestive system, Darwin began to read. Malthus's theory was pretty bleak. Apparently the population of Great Britain had doubled from twelve million to twenty-four million in just thirty years. Good grief. With the population rising faster than the food supply, struggle and starvation must inevitably result. Charity only aggravated the problem. Poor-relief hand-outs made paupers comfortable, and only encouraged them to breed. It was a vicious circle. The only answer was enshrined in a new Liberal Act of Parliament, the Poor Law Amendment Act, which established a national network of segregated workhouses. By making poor relief available only to new workhouses, pauper husbands and wives could be kept apart from each other and prevented from breeding. This would benefit the poor in the long run by making them self-reliant, and according dignity to their labours. It all made perfect sense. It certainly improved upon years of masterly Tory inactivity. The Tories had sat on their complacent aristocratic backsides for years, expecting the same little fields and allotments to produce sufficient food for ever-increasing hordes of starving, destitute peasants. The governments of Lord Liverpool and the Duke of Wellington had created a situation where the weakest went to the wall, and only the strongest survived. It was inhuman.

A faint rumbling interrupted Darwin's philosophizing, followed by a creak from the branches above, and a plump apple fell soundlessly on to his forehead. The moment, however unpleasant, served as a reminder that the problems of an overcrowded island were thousands of miles away, and of no immediate relevance to the greater concerns that currently occupied his mind. But no sooner had he filed the Reverend Thomas Malthus away in the further recesses of his brain than the ground was gripped by another low rumble – much louder this time, like the roaring of a bull in distant underground caverns – and a score of ripe apples plummeted from the trees above. The bombardment felt like being punched by several small boys at once. He noticed, as he attempted to compose himself following the assault, that his flagon of cider had glugged its contents wastefully on to the grass.

Darwin looked across to where Covington was attempting to untether Corfield's horse, but the manservant was fighting to keep his balance like a novice ice-skater. The solid earth of the orchard seemed to have lost all physical substance, as louder and louder bass rumbles shivered through the tree-roots. Covington had grabbed the animal's bridle for support, but the frightened beast's legs had simply given way, splaying out in opposite directions as it neighed in terror. Darwin felt himself being rolled from side to side, a helpless sausage in a pan. He tried to stand, but it was no use: waves were rolling in from the east, and he felt as sick as he ever had aboard the *Beagle* in a heaving sea. He sat down again with a bump. The tree trunks were swaying, the lighter branches thrashing madly about, the ground undulating as if all the laws of physics had been suspended for the duration. It was absolutely fascinating. It was an earthquake all right. But not one of the inconsequential daily tremors that plagued Valparayso. This was a really, really big one.

'A large star on the horizon to starboard, sir.'

FitzRoy glanced at his watch. It was after midnight. A star on the horizon should not have been entirely unexpected. Had the watch taken up astronomy?

'Correction sir. A large signal light on the horizon to starboard. A red signal light, sir.'

Again, it was not entirely unexpected that another ship should be ploughing the same furrow as the *Beagle*, hugging the Chilean coast rather than standing out into the Pacific. They were running north-west through the Chacao Narrows, which separated the mainland from Chiloé Island – a huge, wet, forested bulk that acted as a handy windbreak for Valparayso-bound merchantmen and packet-ships. The mainland was Araucanian territory, but in all their surveying operations they had seen hardly a sign of those redoubtable warriors, so feared on the Patagonian plains to the east. The Araucanians remained hidden in their hills, dim shadows in a veil of perpetual mist marking the western boundary of their proud, unconquered nation. Chiloé Island by contrast had been settled by the Spanish, but the settlers had merged with the native population to produce a desperately poor race of forgotten *mestizo* farmers, whose hand-pushed ploughs would have been considered primitive in medieval Europe. They used charcoal for money; pigs and potatoes were their only produce. With its endless rain-soaked bogs, woods and dank fields, Chiloé reminded FitzRoy uncomfortably of Ireland. The main town, Castro, was forlorn and deserted, with grass growing in its streets. At the big old church, built from shipwreck planks and iron, an elderly man rang the hour on the bell by guesswork, for there were no clocks or watches on the island. Travel was by *piragua*, a type of native canoe that – FitzRoy was excited to discover – exactly matched the *maseulah* canoes of south-east India. Had early man settled South America by ship from across the Pacific? No ships stopped at Castro now, that was for sure. Civilization seemed to have brought few benefits in its wake.

'Sorry sir.' The lookout changed tack again. 'I don't think it is a signal light, sir. Leastways, I don't think it's another ship. It's uncommon bright, sir.'

All hands were crowded at the starboard rail now. The red pinpoint scintillated in the darkness, an impossibly sharp ruby glowing fiercely in a black velvet sky.

'It's b-beautiful, whatever it is,' said Hamond.

'It's like the star as what the three wise men followed to Bethlehem,' breathed a reverential Chadwick, one of the maintopmen.

'It's not a star,' concluded FitzRoy. 'There are no other stars in the sky, so I think we may safely assume high clouds. And it is not another vessel, for I can observe no sign of motion. It is on the land, it is prodigious far off, and I should guess it is several thousand feet up.'

As if on cue, the mysterious light chose to reveal its identity. With a searing crimson flare and an ear-splitting explosion of rock, a column of light funnelled vertically upwards from the cone of the volcano. Torrents of lava spewed from splits in the mountain's nozzle, pouring in gorgeous, glowing rivulets down its slopes. Brilliant jets of flame lit up the night sky, bursting like the royal fireworks before scattering their abrupt reflections across the surface of the intervening sea. The silhouettes of vast boulders, each bigger than a house, were tossed effortlessly into the air by unseen forces lurking deep within the earth.

'It is Volcan Osorno!' said FitzRoy. 'Great God – this is incredible!'

While the crew stood transfixed by the light show, Stebbing fetched the captain's theodolite, and together they calculated the height of the eruption at 7550 feet.

'Look sir! To the north!'

Bennet was gesticulating at the prow. In the distance, beyond his outstretched finger, a further scarlet pinpoint had appeared in the dark; and beyond that, another, fainter spark.

'All the other volcanoes are erupting!'

'The whole of the Andes is going off tonight!'

'It's a regular knock-down!'

It was indeed an unbelievable sight.

The first shock hit the *Beagle* early the next morning, by which time the night's pyrotechnics had faded in the light of dawn, reduced to mere columns of smoke issuing sootily from the pristine file of snowy cones.

A shudder ran through the ship's timbers, juddering from one end of the deck to the other, turning her crew's knees instantly to india-rubber. It was not the sickening crunch that follows an encounter with a submerged rock; rather, a sudden, convulsing check to her momentum, as if she had collided with a whale.

'What the deuce was that?'

'Something in the water?'

'An earthquake!' said FitzRoy. 'By God, an earthquake! It is connected to the volcanic eruptions! It's not just a passing tremor – it is an absolutely *massive* earthquake!'

Just how massive an earthquake became apparent a few days later, as they neared the little town of Concepción, which lay concealed on a gentle slope behind the peninsular port of Talcahuano. With a clatter, the *Beagle* ran through a shoal of seaborne timber: odd beams and planks at first, then huge joists and entire pieces of furniture, as if a thousand ships had been shattered in a gale. Eventually the master had to take evasive action, as whole chairs, tables, shelves, even an entire wooden cottage-roof shouldered their way through the jumble of flotsam. A whole file of bobbing church pews followed, and a seventy-strong congregation of dead cows, swept in a moment of bewilderment from some exposed headland. Then came the human corpses: white-faced, open-mouthed rag dolls, many of them incomplete, wallowing helplessly on the undulating sea, their arms thrown wide in various attitudes of supplication. FitzRoy slowed the *Beagle*'s speed, to minimize the risk of a serious collision. The sheer volume of debris had the effect of quietening the swell, so they glided gently forward, the funereal silence broken only by the dead and all the accoutrements of their former lives, knocking sightlessly at the hull as if in search of readmission to the land of the living. The crew's excitement at experiencing both a volcanic eruption and a full-scale earthquake had slowly subsided, to be replaced by a horror that escalated in leaps and bounds.

Ahead in the sea, they saw movement: a small child, pale as a sheet, sitting bolt upright in the prow of a skiff. The boy's hand tightly clasped that of an Indian woman, who lay face down in the bottom of the boat, her other arm thrown across the top of her head as if in self-protection. A few feet beyond this point of fervent union, both the woman and the skiff came to an abrupt end. Her body had been sheared off at the waist, along with the stern of the little craft, both sliced away in parallel as if by an enormous rough-edged scythe. Somehow the skiff remained afloat, the boy's weight shifting the centre of balance and raising the shattered edge clear of the water.

'Lower the dinghy, fast as you can!'

'Aye aye sir!'

A few short minutes later, the small boy's reluctant fingers had been prised from the hand of his dead guardian, and he stood wide-eyed at attention on the *Beagle*'s maindeck, swathed in a woollen blanket. FitzRoy knelt down and spoke to him, in the gentlest tones he knew. '*¿Cómo se llama?*'

'I'm sorry, sir, but I do not speak Spanish.'

'Well, well. You are an English boy. What is your name, young man?'

'Hodges, sir.'

'Well, Hodges, I think you have been a remarkably brave boy. My name is Captain FitzRoy. Do you live in Concepción?'

'In Talcahuano, sir.'

'And your mother and father? Do they live in Talcahuano with you?'

'My mother and father are dead, sir. The roof fell on them, sir. There was an earthquake.'

'I am very sorry, Hodges,' said FitzRoy, gravely, 'but let us thank God that you are alive. You have had a most remarkable escape. Where were you, when the roof fell in?'

'My governess Isabela took my hand and ran into the street when she heard the rumbling noise, sir.'

'Was that Isabela in the boat with you?'

'Yes sir. But my dog knew there was going to be an earthquake, sir. He ran away.'

'Your dog?'

'My dog Davy. All the dogs in town ran away before the earthquake, sir, into the hills. And all the birds flew away too, sir. Hundreds of them. Will Davy be all right, sir?'

'I should think so. Davy sounds like a very clever dog. I am sure he will have found a safe place to hide. But tell me, Hodges, how did you get into the boat?'

'After the earthquake Isabela said there would be a big wave, sir. A giant wave. She said we would be drowned if we stayed in Talcahuano with the Europeans. She said we had to take a boat into the bay. She said if boats are out far enough, they rise over the wave and it doesn't break on them, sir.'

'Is that what you did?'

'Yes sir, but all the water in the bay was gone, and all the fish were dead. There was no sea, sir. We had to run through the mud. Then we found a boat, and we started to row out, but then the first wave came sir.'

'The first wave?'

'There were three waves sir. They landed in the town, sir. Then the water came back with lots of tables and chairs and dead people in it. The first one landed on our heads. There was a big fishing-boat in the wave, sir, and the wave picked it up and it landed on Isabela.'

The little boy stiffened perceptibly at the memory, and FitzRoy reached out to place a comforting arm round his shoulders.

'I didn't let go of Isabela's hand, sir, because she told me not to. I did what Isabela said, sir. Nobody will be cross with me, will they, sir?'

'No, Hodges. You did the right thing, so you must not despond. You are a very brave boy.'

FitzRoy bit his lip. He simply could not find any adequate words. A clammy little hand gripped his, the tiny white fingers digging into his skin with astonishing intensity. His rosy flesh turned pale as death where the boy's grasp held him tight.

'Please sir, I don't want to be left alone again.'

'Don't worry, Hodges, I promise I shall not leave you alone. You are aboard a Royal Navy vessel, called the *Beagle*, and we have come to rescue whoever we can. We shall find Davy too, and rescue him. Should you like to help me captain the *Beagle*? You can show me where to go. We can captain the vessel together. Should you like that?'

'Yes sir. I should like that very much.'

FitzRoy hoisted Hodges on to his shoulders, and placed his peaked cap atop the boy's head.

'Now, Mr Hodges – I shall have to call you Mr Hodges, seeing that you're a ship's officer – the first order we need to give is to make all sail for Talcahuano. Do you think you can manage that? Then we shall go below and find you some food and water.'

'Yes sir.'

'Loud as you can.'

'Make all sail for Talcahuano,' said Hodges, in a tiny voice.

'Aye aye captain,' snapped the bos'n, and the men moved smartly to their stations as the order was relayed. Hodges clasped his arms around FitzRoy's neck and, finding warmth and life within his grasp, hung on for all he was worth.

They rounded the headland, to find that Talcahuano had simply been obliterated. Only a few bricks and remnants of wall remained: the rest had been sucked out to sea. Every living being in the little fishing-port had disappeared. Further up the hill, beyond the reach of the devouring waves, a ghostly pall of smoke still hung over the remains of Concepción, two whole days after the initial shock had destroyed the town. Even at this distance, they could see that not a building was left standing. The damage to Concepción was more picturesque than the surgical eradication of Talcahuano, but evidently it had been hardly any less deadly. FitzRoy, with the help of his new co-captain, gave the order to let go the anchors, stow the sails and hoist all the ship's boats into the water.

'Mr King.'

'Sir?'

The young midshipman who had once stood shivering, a frightened child, on watch all Christmas night at Barnet Pool, was now a strapping lad of nineteen, well capable of knocking down any surly mutineer.

'You are in charge of the *Beagle*. The forenoon watch shall be under your command. I want every scrap of food in the ship, and I mean every last canister, unloaded ashore at the double. Mr Sulivan, Mr Wickham, the rest of the ship's company shall make haste to Concepción, with every blanket, every spare scrap of clothing and every water bottle we can muster. Tell May to bring every tool he has in his possession.'

'Aye aye sir.'

King wore a bothered expression. '*All* our supplies, sir?'

'That is correct.'

'But what of our own requirements on the homeward journey, sir?'

'We shall sail back to Valparayso, Mr King, and I shall purchase further supplies. Now, look lively, all of you.'

'You heard the skipper!' barked Bos'n Sorrell. 'Get the lead out, all of you!'

Within the half-hour, a large party of officers and sailors splashed into the shallows at Talcahuano beach. FitzRoy, the tiny figure of Hodges astride his shoulders, marched determinedly out in front. Two fishing vessels, the *Paulina* and the *Orion*, lay crushed and broken on their sides halfway up the shore: amazingly, they were still anchored, but their anchor-chains were tightly wound about each other, in spiral testimony to their last whirling dance. Two hundred yards further up the hill sat a fat white schooner, upside down and mastless, broken open like a raw egg dropped from a height. Of Talcahuano's former existence there was absolutely no sign: just a few cold pools of salt water lay amid the ruins, glinting here and there with the body of a lifeless fish. The path up to Concepción felt slimy and rotten underfoot.

From a distance, Concepción put FitzRoy in mind of a romantic engraving of Tintern Abbey. The side walls of the cathedral were fractured but still standing, their arched windows devoutly intact; but the vast anchoring buttresses had been chopped away systematically as if by a chisel. In fact, all the walls that ran from north-east to south-west had survived; but those that ran at right angles had been utterly flattened. The cathedral's fortress-like front, which had been ten feet thick at the base, had subsided into an incoherent pile of masonry and beams. Huge stones had rolled out from the rubble and come to rest half-way across the plaza. Streets radiated from the square in a neat grid according to the conventional Latin American pattern, streets which had once been lined with smart low houses: now, ranks of heaped ruins and hillocks of brick had taken their place. The ground was fissured with crevasses, as if some invisible hand had grabbed the edges of the town like a laden tablecloth and yanked it tighter than its fabric could stand. Smoke-drifts rose from a score of small pyres where damp thatched roofs had collapsed on to smouldering housefires. Amid the rubble, the dazed survivors wandered aimlessly, or sat warming their hands before these sporadic blazes, a pale, bewildered, dust-covered host, weeping or calling helplessly for friends and relatives. It was the most awful spectacle that any of the *Beagle*'s crew had ever beheld.

FitzRoy split his men into four groups. 'Mr Hamond. Salvage what timber you can and have the carpenter's crew build temporary shelters in the centre of the plaza – away from the rubble, in case of aftershocks. Mr Bynoe. You will see to the wounded. Mr Sulivan. You and your men shall search through the rubble for survivors. Mr Wickham. See to it that everyone here receives food, clean water and at least one blanket. And try to keep them quiet – we shall not hear any tapping from beneath the rubble if there is a commotion.'

As the four officers moved smoothly to complete their appointed tasks, a shout rang out in English: 'Lord be praised! Young Hodges! You're alive!' A short, rotund gentleman emerged gasping into the plaza: the top hat on his head had been concertina'd almost flat, and his suit was coated from head to foot with white dust, as if he had come hot-foot from a scrap in a flour-mill.

'Who is that, Mr Hodges?' asked FitzRoy.

'That is Mr Rouse, sir,' answered Hodges, from beneath the comforting shadow of FitzRoy's peaked cap.

FitzRoy extended a hand as Rouse panted towards them. 'Captain FitzRoy of HMS *Beagle*, at your service.'

'You are Englishmen – thank God! How do? I am Rouse, the British consul.'

FitzRoy passed his water bottle to the consul, who took a healthy swig.

'Keep it – it's yours.'

'Most generous of you, sir. And I cannot tell you how mighty glad I am to see *you*, young Hodges!'

'Mr Hodges here has been a sound good fellow ever since we plucked him from the water.'

'Excellent! Sterling work, Hodges.' Rouse wiped his wet lips with the back of his hand, leaving a clown's pink smear bordering his mouth. 'And the, um...parents?' he mumbled, in the direction of his own floury feet.

FitzRoy shook his head wordlessly.

At that moment a low bass rumble echoed from the direction of the sea, and the ground seesawed gently beneath their feet. Hodges tightened his panicky grip.

'Aftershocks,' explained the consul. 'Nothing to worry about, young shaver. We've had several hundred in the last two days. But the tides have gone to the very d—...the tides have gone all over the place. They don't know when to come in and out. Everything is topsy-turvy.'

'It appears you have had an abominable time of it.'

'You can say that again. The whole town was flattened inside six seconds. I've lived here since a good few years, so I ran into the courtyard at the first rumble. I had just reached the middle when the wall behind me came thundering down, just where I had run from. I couldn't stand up for the shaking, so I crawled to the top of the pile, thinking that if I once got on top of that part which had already fallen, I would be safe. A moment later the opposite wall collapsed – a great big beam swept this close in front of my head! I could barely see a thing for dust. I managed to clamber over the rubble and out into the street. From there I could see Talcahuano and the bay – and then, Captain FitzRoy, I saw the damnedest thing. Forgive me, the most deuced thing. The sea was boiling!'

'Boiling?'

'It had turned quite black, and columns of sulphurous vapour were belching forth. There were explosions in the sea, like cannon-fire. All the water in the bay had receded, as if someone had pulled out a gigantic plug. Then I saw the first wave, many miles out to sea, racing in. When it reached the shore it tore up cottages and trees. At the head of the bay it broke into a fearful white breaker, at least thirty feet in height. It was a monstrous awful sight. And there were three waves in all, each more enormous than the last!'

FitzRoy, who had felt Hodges's little hands tighten like thumbscrews as the consul's account unfolded, attempted to indicate with his eyes that perhaps the subject was best saved for later. He was excused from having to explain himself verbally by a tremendous outbreak of yapping, as Coxswain Bennet marched into the plaza holding aloft a slab of tinned beef, pursued by an enormous pack of hungry dogs.

'Mr Bennet, what ever...'

'Forgive me absenting myself from duty for a few moments, sir,' apologized Bennet, poker-faced but for the hint of a grin, 'but I felt it important that we should find the absent Davy. It is my notion he shall be here somewhere.'

Sure enough, with a squeal of recognition, Hodges had located his errant pet. FitzRoy restored him gently to the ground, whereupon he charged headlong into the pack and flung his arms round a large black mongrel. FitzRoy recovered his cap from the dust, brushed it down and replaced it on his head. 'Mr Rouse, it is your business, I believe, to see to the welfare of British subjects on this coast.'

'Indeed, sir, but what—'

'If you would oblige me by seeing to the welfare of Mr Hodges here, I do believe I have some digging to do.'

FitzRoy removed the beef from Bennet's hand and transferred it to that of the consul. In an instant, Rouse was surrounded by the pack of yapping dogs. Propelling his coxswain forward with a friendly hand, FitzRoy took his leave of the helpless diplomat. 'I bid you good day, sir.'

Rouse attempted to return the greeting but his mouth simply gaped instead. The two men marched off in step to join in the rescue effort, leaving the consul a beleaguered island in a frothing canine sea.

Three days on, and the *Beagle*'s crew had succeeded in feeding, clothing and housing upwards of a hundred survivors. Innumerable broken bones had been splinted, and bruises treated with vinegar and brown paper. A further six people had been pulled alive from the rubble, including two members of a work gang who had been restoring the ceiling of the cathedral when it had collapsed upon them in an explosion of masonry. A further eight bodies had been found crushed in the wreckage of the building: the other seven members of the work gang, and an old man who had rashly tried to take refuge beneath the sculpted arch of the great door. FitzRoy had ordered a huge pit dug for the burial of the dead, and had done the best he could to approximate a Catholic service, although one old half-caste lady had wailed that a Christian burial was of no account, for the Christian God had proved Himself weaker than the volcano-god who had sent the earthquake.

Now the men of the *Beagle* lay exhausted, sprawled on their tarpaulins in the plaza, having done everything in their power to help. Only Wickham – who had been deputized to act as emergency ship's artist – was still hard at work, producing a highly polished line-drawing of the ravaged cathedral. A figure trotted into the plaza from the Talcahuano side: it was Rensfrey, one of the foretopmen.

'Begging your pardon, sir, but the compliments of Mr King. He says to tell you there's a schooner in the bay, sir. He believes it to be the philosopher, sir.'

'Mr Darwin?'

'Mr King says to say so, sir.'

FitzRoy grabbed his cap and sprang to his feet. 'Excellent news indeed! Thank you, Rensfrey, for your trouble.'

With the foretopman in tow, FitzRoy strode anxiously down to the shore, where he encountered Darwin stepping out of a dinghy, accompanied by a short, dapper man in an expensive hat. In the bay behind, a small but elegant private vessel of some thirty-five tons lay at anchor. Overwhelmed with delight and riven with guilt, the two friends embraced on the strand.

'Captain FitzRoy, may I have the honour of presenting to your acquaintance Mr Richard Corfield, merchant, of Valparayso?'

'How do, Captain FitzRoy?' said the swell.

'The honour is entirely mine, Mr Corfield. Forgive me, but I cannot help but admire your schooner, if indeed she is yours.'

'The *Constitución*? Oh, she's not a bad old girl. She's my boat after a fashion – that is to say, as of today she is yours.'

'Mine? Forgive me, but…'

'I am making you a present of her, old man, for as long as you require her.'

'I informed Corfield of your having to sell the *Adventure*,' Darwin chipped in. 'How you have insufficient boats to complete the South American survey.'

'Mr Corfield, I beg you will not do such a thing. Your generosity is too great – I cannot trespass upon your kind offices in this manner.'

'Nonsense, old boy,' said Corfield, jamming his hands in his coat pockets like a gleeful schoolboy. 'I never use her anyway. I'm always so monstrous busy. Make what you will of her.'

'Mr Corfield, I…I am speechless with gratitude…'

'Tish!' Corfield waved away FitzRoy's awestruck thanks.

'But my dear friend,' said Darwin, 'how marvellous to find you quite yourself again!'

'And as anxious to reach dear old England as you are.'

'But we have news for you, FitzRoy. A missive from Commodore Mason in Valparayso. Good news.' A grinning Corfield extracted the folded letter from an inside pocket. 'Forgive the intrusion into your privacy, old man, but the commodore made us sensible of the contents when he appointed us his messengers.'

FitzRoy broke the seal and unfolded the paper. After six years as a commander – an acting captain – he had finally been made post. He was a full captain at last. He should have been pleased as punch. Instead he felt strangely empty. He perused the rest of the letter. There remained only an order to report to Mason in Valparayso at his earliest convenience.

'Were there any news of further promotions – for Wickham or Stokes?'

'I do not believe so.'

'I had made representations…I had hoped that their exertions might have obtained satisfactory notice at headquarters…'

'But are you not pleased?' asked Darwin, concerned. 'I apprehend that all goes by seniority from this point on – that this will like as not make you an admiral in due course.'

'That is so. Forgive me for seeming so ungrateful. I just wish that I could get one or two of my hard-working shipmates promoted. That would have gratified me much more than my own advance, which has been too tardy to be much valued. Six years – some stay a commander for only a year. Plenty have gone over my head. I deserve it, of course, for having burned my fingers with politics.'

His star, he realized, which had once burned so brightly, had dimmed with time. To be given his own vessel at twenty-three – that had been special. Captain of a little brig at thirty, or nearly thirty – that was no great accolade. The promotion was no more than a poultice applied by Beaufort, or some other interested friend in high places, to cover the gaping sore of his recent run-in with their lordships. The true test would come when he returned to England, and received his next commission. Then he would discover whether or not he was still considered a high-flier. Perhaps a change of administration, from Liberal back to Tory once more, would make life easier for him and his crew.

'Are there any news yet of who holds sway in Parliament? Is there a successor to Grey?'

'My dear fellow, have you not heard?' blurted out Corfield. 'Parliament is no more. It has burned down!'

'Burned down! When?'

'Last October. The whole Palace of Westminster is gone – St Stephen's Chapel, the cloisters, the Painted Chamber, all of it. Only Westminster Hall has survived. Concepción is not the only place to have suffered a conflagration. Everything is in chaos.'

'*¿Quien sabe*, my friend?' said Darwin, clapping FitzRoy encouragingly on the back. 'Perhaps it is a bonfire that will instigate much-needed change.'

Let us hope so, thought FitzRoy.

The trio strolled uphill, to give Corfield and Darwin their first sight of the ruins of Concepción. All conversation ceased as the newcomers took in the scale of the devastation, the serried lines of silent debris where once people had lived, shopped and prayed.

'It is a bitter and humiliating thing to see,' said Darwin at last. 'Works that cost man so much time and labour, overthrown in one minute. Such is the insignificance of man's boasted power. It is most wonderful to witness.'

'I say, steady on, old man,' said Corfield under his breath.

'Forgive me – I do not mean to forget my compassion – but from a scientific aspect this is absolutely fascinating.'

'Have you noticed how all the walls running north-west to south-east have been flattened,' said FitzRoy, 'but those running the other way have by and large survived?'

'By God, you are absolutely right.'

'It is like a ship in a heavy sea. Lined up with the waves, she will ride the shocks, but bring her broadside-on, and she will be put over on her beam-ends. Proof that the shocks of an earthquake arrive by a kind of wave motion, flowing in a single direction.'

Both men were charged with excitement now. They were passing the ruins of a spacious merchant's house, when Darwin dived in suddenly, reappearing with a torn rug and a scattering of books extricated from the rubble. Swiftly, he laid the rug in the street and stood the books upon it spine uppermost, half of them aligned with the rug, the others at right-angles.

'Observe,' he commanded.

Kneeling at one end of the rug, he proceeded to tug it gently back and forth. At once, those books standing at right-angles to the direction of movement toppled over, but those aligned with it stayed upright.

'As I said, Darwin old man,' exclaimed Corfield, balling his hands deep into his pockets, 'you're a confounded marvel!'

Dusk found FitzRoy and Darwin many miles along the Pacific shore, kicking their heels on what remained of the outer wall of Penco Castle, a seventeenth-century Spanish sea-fort. The building had been devastated even before the recent earthquake; it now wore a battered, defeated aspect entirely in keeping with the imperial ambitions of its mother country. The tide was in, and dark magenta waves lapped at the old Spanish battlements, gradually teasing the ancient stones from their crumbling bed of mortar. As the sun had sunk towards the blue wall of the horizon, Darwin had breathlessly expounded his discoveries in the mountains, and the startling conclusions he had reached – all except one. He had withheld his disturbing ideas about the divergence of the wildlife on either side of the Andean *cordillera*: those deductions were of such devastating import that he would – he knew – have to choose his moment carefully. But his evidence for the intermittent and continuing uplift of the mountains seemed overwhelming.

'So you see,' he concluded, 'the uplift is not caused by the earthquakes. *The uplift is the cause of the earthquakes.*'

'From what you say I must do you justice,' conceded FitzRoy graciously. 'I shall write to Lyell confirming that it is so.'

'You oblige me by your understanding. But…does this new evidence not bring the story of the Biblical flood into question?'

'Not in the least. The one does not preclude the other. Earthquake and flood may exist side by side – indeed, the two may have occurred in tandem.'

'But surely all the evidence of land having been under water is caused by the earth's crust being in a continual state of change. Places now far above the sea were once beneath it. Districts may have been inundated in one quarter – but a universal deluge could never have happened!'

'My friend,' said FitzRoy gently, 'everything might not be as clear-cut as you think. You say the land has been rising regularly for thousands of years, and continues to do so?'

'Yes.'

'Then why is this two-hundred-year-old Spanish fort, built by the water's edge, *still* by the water's edge?'

Darwin looked about him. FitzRoy was right.

Why *had* Penco Castle not been uplifted from the water, preferring to crumble where it stood? He had no answer. It had all seemed so simple, up in the mountains, in his delight at finding what appeared to be a universal solution. It would take a lifetime of study, he realized, merely to chip away at a few of the lesser complexities of God's universe. He laughed out loud at the sheer size of the task, and how easily he had underestimated it.

'I am sure you are correct in your observations,' said a placatory FitzRoy, as the pair wound their way home, 'but I am afraid I cannot bring myself to question the written word of God. I am sure there is room in the scheme of things for both eventualities.'

As he spoke, a deep roar echoed from the unseen caverns of the underworld, and the earth shook as if a huge subterranean beast were rattling its cage. It was the biggest aftershock so far. FitzRoy and Darwin found themselves hurled to the ground, like two statues in the cathedrals of old Byzantium thrown down by the armies of the Saracens. Thus forcibly prostrated, both men spread their arms and legs wide to avoid being rolled over and over in the grass. A few seconds later, when the assault had finished, they raised their heads warily. There was something odd, something different about their surroundings. Darwin was first to his feet and first to realize what had happened, scrambling eagerly down the slope towards the shore.

'Look!' he said, literally hopping from one foot to the other with excitement. 'FitzRoy, look! Look at this!'

There, behind the frantic naturalist, a glistening mussel bed adhered to the rock. But the shellfish did not lie beneath the lapping water, as they had a few moments previously: they lay with rivulets of clear salt water streaming between them, several feet clear of the high-water mark.

CHAPTER ELEVEN

Valparayso, Chili, 16 June 1835

'Captain FitzRoy! Captain FitzRoy, sir!'

FitzRoy wheeled round. He had just stepped out of a dockside masthoop merchant's on to the cobbled main street of Valparayso. Perhaps fifty yards distant, on their way up from the wharf and standing out like a sore thumb among the respectable Chilean gentlefolk, were three filthy, emaciated Englishmen. Their hair was matted, their clothing ripped, and two of them wore what looked suspiciously like the remains of British naval officers' uniforms. Really, FitzRoy was not in the best of moods. He had brought the *Beagle* back to Valparayso to replenish her hold for the journey home, and to report to Commodore Mason as requested; but when he had rowed out to HMS *Blonde*, the commodore's flagship, her crew had been surly and diffident. The commodore was no longer in residence aboard, the lieutenant in charge had wearily explained. No, he did not know when, or indeed if, the commodore would be back. No, he could not be of any further help. The *Blonde*, FitzRoy knew, had once been the proud frigate of Admiral Byron himself. What on earth would the admiral have made of the state of the modern-day *Blonde*? Her unkempt decks and mildewed sails indicated a ship in decline, ill-disciplined and rudderless. Such neglect of a fine old vessel invariably roused his ire.

'It's Captain FitzRoy, isn't it, sir? Of the *Beagle*?' The three scarecrows had run all the way up the main street. Their leader introduced himself.

'Lieutenant Collins, sir, of the *Challenger*. This is Assistant Surgeon Lane, and this is Jagoe, ship's clerk.'

'The *Challenger*? Seymour's brig?'

'That's right, sir. You came aboard off Port Louis in the Falklands, sir.

But the *Challenger* is lost, sir!'

'Lost? Lost where?' The blood ran cold through FitzRoy's veins.

'South of the river Leubu, sir. We were making eight knots an hour under treble-reefed topsails, courses and jib. By all fair calculations we should have been well out to sea – but something had happened to play merry hell with the tides and currents. Next thing we knew, sir, the officer of the watch noticed lines of foam in the water in the darkness. He ordered helm down and about ship, and Captain Seymour was fetched. The captain gave the order to haul the mainsail. The after-yards swung round, sir, but while we were bracing them up she struck. The rudder was destroyed, and the stern-post, the gunroom beams, the cabin-deck – all her timbers and planking were shivered to atomies, sir.'

'My God. Did she go down at once?'

'Not for a couple of hours, sir. The mate managed to get a line ashore in the jolly-boat. We cut the mizzen-mast down and made a raft, and got most of the supplies off. Just two men were lost in all, but the jolly-boat was the only one of the ship's boats to survive the impact. Captain Seymour ordered the three of us to sail her to Valparayso, to fetch assistance from the commodore, sir.'

'Thank God you have arrived safely. When did you get here?'

'Three weeks ago, sir.'

'Three *weeks*? What the deuce—'

'Commodore Mason, sir – he refused to send the *Blonde* south. He said it was too late in the season to land on a lee shore. And the Leubu river is Araucanian Indian territory, sir. He said it was too risky, sir. He didn't want to peril another ship. But we heard that the *Beagle* was due in port soon, so we waited—'

FitzRoy's jaw set hard. 'Then there is not another moment to lose.'

'Captain Seymour set up camp on high ground overlooking the river, sir. He had a ditch dug, and erected a defensive barricade from barrels and timbers that were thrown ashore. But there is only so much ammunition available, sir. Of course we couldn't get any of the cannon off the ship. We were hoping you might be able to use your influence to persuade the commodore to change his mind sir.'

'Oh, I shall make him change his mind, Lieutenant, I promise you of that,' said FitzRoy grimly. 'Where may I find this Commodore Mason?'

The three men from the *Challenger* led FitzRoy to a pretty ginger-breaded cottage in the suburbs. They held back at the end of the lane, while FitzRoy walked up and knocked smartly at the door. It swung open to the touch. Marching past a startled Chilean maid with no word of introduction, he found Mason slumbering in a cane chair on raised decking at the back of the house, under the shade of a canvas awning. The commodore looked as if he might once have been handsome: certainly, he sported the breeches and hairstyle of another era. But he was running to fat now, pink jowls inflating with each breath. His sandy hair had turned all but grey. The tracery of broken veins on his cheeks and nose, and the half-empty geneva bottle on the table, suggested even at this early hour that the commodore had been drinking.

'Captain FitzRoy, sir, of HMS *Beagle*, reporting as commanded,' said FitzRoy, doing his best to disguise his impatience. He was, at least, going to give the man a chance to explain himself.

'Is it your normal practice to enter the houses of superior officers without introduction, Captain?'

'The door was on the jar and unattended, sir.'

A harrumph from Mason. 'Well, I have been expecting you for some weeks. You have new orders. A pearl-oyster-fishing vessel, the *Truro*, has been plundered in one of the islands of Tahiti. The Admiralty is demanding compensation of two thousand eight hundred dollars on behalf of the owner. You are to make yourself known to Queen Pomare of those islands and extract the required sum of the Tahitians, using force if necessary. You are heading home via Tahiti, I take it?'

'In due course, sir. But in the meantime there is a more pressing matter. The crew of the *Challenger*, sir—'

'I know all about the *Challenger*, Captain.'

'Then may I take it you will be mounting a rescue effort without further ado, sir?'

'What you may take, Captain FitzRoy, is what you are given. Have I made myself clear?'

'Sir, the men of the *Challenger* have been encamped on an exposed and dangerous shore for some four weeks now—'

'The men of the *Challenger* will have to fend for themselves. Those are my orders. You have your own orders. The fate of the *Challenger* is none of your damned business.'

'Captain Seymour is an old friend of mine, sir.'

'Then you are allowing personal friendships to cloud your judgement, Mr FitzRoy. It would be foolhardy in the extreme to put more men on to that coast in the middle of winter. The Spanish have failed to defeat the Araucanians since three hundred years – I hardly see that one frigate's-worth of men will succeed where an entire nation has been found wanting.'

'There may be other means than military action, sir. Let me go, sir – I have only recently surveyed that very coastline.'

'Are you deaf, Captain?' Mason's tone was icy. 'I would remind you that you were only made post a few weeks since. You would do well to hold your tongue and go about your duty without further ado.'

'My duty, sir, is to go to the aid of my fellow officers and their men.'

'Your duty, Captain, is to do as you are commanded!'

'If you will not go to the aid of the *Challenger*, sir, then I shall have no option but to go myself.'

Mason's face turned puce as he levered himself from his chair. 'I will see you court-martialled if you do not get out of here this instant and do exactly what I tell you to do!'

'If you are too scared, sir—' began FitzRoy scornfully.

'Damn you for a scoundrel, sir! How dare you? You may be satisfied that you will pay for your impertinence!'

'On the contrary, sir,' said FitzRoy coolly, 'it is you who shall pay. I shall see to it on my return to England that you are court-martialled for cowardice.'

'By the devil!' spat Mason. 'If I was twenty years younger I would knock you down, you young puppy.'

FitzRoy's eyes gleamed. 'If you were twenty years younger you would not be standing now, you blackguard. That is, if I could bring myself to soil my hands upon a despicable coward – *sir*.' FitzRoy turned on his heel and stalked out of the house, leaving Mason speechless with rage.

He met the three ragged emissaries from the *Challenger* at the corner of the lane, their faces optimistic as puppies'.

'How was it, sir? Did the commodore change his mind?'

FitzRoy smiled grimly. 'Yes, Lieutenant. I found the commodore exactly of my opinion. He has ordered me to mount a full-scale rescue of the *Challenger*'s people. Follow me, if you please.'

The ship's company of the *Beagle*, mustered on the maindeck, waited expectantly for FitzRoy to speak. Something was up, they knew. Lieutenant Collins and his colleagues had been cleaned up and fed, and dispatched to wait on the wharf, safely out of earshot. FitzRoy was sure that he could trust each and every one of his own crew, but that was as far as it went. Poker-faced, he stepped up to the azimuth compass and gambled his entire career on a single eventuality.

'You will no doubt remember HMS *Challenger* from the Falkland Islands. I have grave news to impart. The *Challenger* is lost. Her crew are stranded three hundred miles south of here, in Araucanian Indian territory. To go to their aid would be a most dangerous venture. So dangerous, in fact, that the British officer commanding here in Valparayso, Commodore Mason, has refused to sanction any such rescue mission.'

A murmur of consternation rolled around the ship's company.

'I have decided to disobey that order.'

The murmur became an aftershock, a thunderstruck wave surging through the throng.

'It is my intention to commandeer HMS *Blonde*, the commodore's frigate. I am doing so in the contention that Commodore Mason is in serious dereliction of his duty. I am telling you this because I fear that the crew of the *Blonde* shall be almost no use as seamen. Were I to take a small contingent of men from the *Beagle* to lick them into shape, my task should be that much easier. So, in a moment, I shall call for volunteers. But I must warn you: our only hope of escaping the most serious repercussions, and it is a faint hope, will be to effect a successful rescue. I sustain myself with no flattering delusion otherwise. To be proved not only resolute and brave, but absolutely correct in taking authority into our own hands, will be the only possible defence of our actions. For all that I am aware, the men of the *Challenger* may already be dead. If our bid fails, I need not tell you of the consequences. Whoever volunteers risks not only their livelihood and their career, but also their neck. To be blunt, you might yet find yourself swinging at the end of a rope. But if nobody goes to their rescue, then the men of the *Challenger* will certainly die. Examine your consciences. I give you my absolute assurance, here and now, that there shall be no shame in failing to volunteer. No blame, no censure, shall attach to any man who prefers to leave this business to others. I am looking for fifteen men, and two officers. Think carefully before making your decision. Now – who is in for it?'

FitzRoy looked out across the mass of sailors and marines, and then behind him at the line of uniformed officers, their dark coats providing a neat and sombre backdrop to the raised stage of the poop deck. In front, a sea of hands had shot up, with not a dissenter among them. Behind, every single officer had taken a decisive step forward.

'Thank you, gentlemen. I am proud of each and every one of you. It seems I must choose among you. I shall inform you of my decision within a few minutes. You may return to your duties.'

As the milling crowd slowly dissipated, Darwin, who had observed proceedings from the rail of the companionway, gave FitzRoy a sympathetic smile.

'Whatever became of the officer who would follow any order given to him, however immoral, however illogical?'

FitzRoy grimaced. 'He grew up.'

John Biddlecombe, master of the *Blonde* and officer in charge of the afternoon watch, observed the *Beagle*'s packed cutter slice purposefully through the waters of Valparayso Bay with an inexplicable feeling of apprehension. Such was the determination etched into the approaching sailors' faces that, had they not been British tars, he would have said they wore the aspect of a boarding party. He recognized the captain, the highty-tighty sort who had been sniffing around that very morning, and had been sent away with a flea in his ear. His return, mob-handed, looked worryingly like some sort of retribution. *Let's hope he hasn't been stirring up trouble with the old man*, thought the master.

FitzRoy hauled himself aboard, followed by Coxswain Bennet, Bos'n Sorrell, Midshipman Hamond and fifteen hard-faced members of the *Beagle*'s company. He had deliberately opted, much to the bitter disappointment of Sulivan, Wickham and the others, to take with him his most junior officers: the higher up the tree his co-mutineers, the more they stood to lose. The only exception was Midshipman King. He dared not have looked the boy's father in the face, had he involved the younger King in an insurrection that had turned to catastrophe.

'Mr Biddlecombe, is it not?'

'Sir.'

'I have orders from the commodore to take command of the *Blonde*, and to proceed without delay to the mouth of the Leubu river where we are to effect the immediate rescue of the crew of HMS *Challenger*.'

'Orders from the commodore, sir?' Biddlecombe fairly goggled.

'As I said.'

'But where is the commodore, sir? Is he not to take command of the expedition himself?'

'The commodore is indisposed...He felt that his state of health was such that his presence would merely incommode our passage.'

That sounds like the cowardly old bustard, thought Biddlecombe.

'Tell me, is your bos'n aboard?'

'No sir, he is ashore. A number of the officers – Lieutenant Tait, Midshipman McKenna—'

'It matters not. I have brought sufficient matlows with me to cover any want of men. Mr Sorrell? The maindeck is yours. Let's have this ship ready for sea. The sooner we are under way the better.'

'You heard the officer,' growled Sorrell, advancing like a pugilist upon the *Blonde*'s startled crew. There was an air of confidence about the little Bristolian now: he seemed far removed from the nervous spinning-top of a man who had lashed out right and left with his rattan on FitzRoy's first day as captain. Today he did not use his rattan. He did not need to.

He was imbued with purpose, and the afternoon watch could feel the force of his intent.

'Those topsail gaskets are slack! Those horses want mousing – a man could fall from the yard if they're not tied properly! Where's the captain of the foretop?'

'Come on, look lively!' bellowed a furious Bennet. 'This is one of the King's frigates, not Almack's Assembly!'

The master's jaw, FitzRoy observed, had fallen slack.

'Let us see, Mr Biddlecombe, whether we cannot open the eyes of everyone, fore and aft, in this ship. Now, do you not have a course to plot?'

'Yes sir,' said the defeated Biddlecombe, and tottered off in search of his charts.

* * *

The country of Araucania, FitzRoy knew, was a beautiful, well-wooded land riven with steep, muddy ravines usually swelled to bursting with heavy rain. That, at least, was the theory. But embarrassingly, even with his newly drawn-up charts, he could not find the Leubu river for two days, so poor was the visibility. So thick were the wind and the rain, in fact, that he could scarcely discern the line of the surf, heavily as it beat upon the shore. The *Blonde* made sally after sally in towards the coast, the sea sucking at her hull as if to pull her on to the rocks, but, try as he might, he could find no sign of the missing crew. Finally, on the afternoon of the second day, Hamond caught sight of the *Challenger*'s flag through the spyglass, a faint rippling square on the distant heights, glimpsed for a scudding moment through rushing drifts of white. There was no way in for the big frigate, not on this coast, not in any weather. Her guns – which FitzRoy had hoped to have available as a bargaining tool – would be utterly useless in these conditions. He had no option but to haul off.

'Mr Bos'n!' he yelled, water sheeting from his oilskin. 'Hoist out the cutter!'

'Aye aye sir.'

'But – but you're mad, sir!' Biddlecombe protested. 'She'll be swamped by the waves. You'll never make it!'

'You have obviously never been surveying in Tierra del Fuego, Mr Biddlecombe,' FitzRoy shouted into the master's ear.

Biddlecombe had proved a thorough liability on the voyage down; luckily Davis, the assistant master, had shown himself to be a capable sort. It was to both men that FitzRoy now gave the order for the *Blonde* to remain under way until he returned, making short tacks all night if necessary. With Bennet piloting the cutter, FitzRoy, Hamond and his fifteen handpicked sailors bounced crazily towards the shore through the drenching surf, searching in the gloom for the estuary opening.

'We're sh-shipping 'em green, sir,' said Hamond, as icy water creamed over their thighs for the hundredth time.

'When are we ever *not*, Mr Hamond?' said a smiling FitzRoy, who was bailing like a Trojan. He was doing good, he knew, simple, uncomplicated good; so he was, for the time being, a happy man. All the dangers, the risks to his career, were as nothing compared to the fact that here, with his men at his side, he felt that he *belonged*.

Finally, after two weary hours in the ocean's maw, they were regurgitated on to the sodden shore amid a network of mud-laced channels and boggy islands inhabited only by a few foul-smelling seals. They dragged the heavy cutter across the shoals, caked to the waist in thick, miry treacle, before flopping down in the wet grass of the river's southern flank. FitzRoy allowed them five minutes' rest and no more, then they ploughed on. Bennet was left on guard by the cutter, with a gun and a supply of ammunition; the others followed the course of the riverbank uphill through a cleft in the wooded slopes, peering through silhouetted trees and swirling mists for another glimpse of the *Challenger*'s elusive ensign. After a mile, the forest opened out once more, and they marched knee-deep, up a soaking, sloping meadow; but even as the woods parted, the clouds descended about them in a billowing curtain, leaving them alone and stranded in a ghostly world of green and white. FitzRoy began to realize, uncomfortably, that he had no idea where in this disorienting wilderness Seymour and his men might be holding out – assuming, that is, that they were still holding out. The only direction he could safely follow was up.

'Wh-what was that?' Hamond froze. There had been a clinking sound, faint but unmistakable, in the mists ahead.

'Quiet!'

There it was again. Nobody moved. Had it been dead ahead, or slightly to the side? Wherever it had emanated from, the sound had been borne away on the wind before it could be safely located. FitzRoy's finger tightened about the trigger of his pistol. As he watched, a ragged hole was blown in the mists ahead; and through it rode a horseman, astride a raven mount. He was tall and muscular, with bronzed skin and cheekbones like the shoulder-plates of Darwin's Megatherium. His long, lush black hair was parted in the centre and gathered by scarlet fillets. His countenance was grave, almost regal. He would have put FitzRoy in mind of Van Dyck's studies of Charles I, were it not for the striped poncho and the wicked-looking *chuzo*, his bamboo lance, which tapered to an iron-tipped point some twelve feet forward of his body.

Seaman MacCurdy began to raise his pistol, but FitzRoy gestured urgently for him to lower it again, for it was clear now that the horseman was not alone. The mists were scurrying away apprehensively, chasing one another hurriedly into the woods, to reveal that the wide clearing was no longer fringed with trees. Rather, a ring of horsemen surrounded the little party, upwards of three hundred in number. They had stumbled right into the Araucanian battle-lines.

'D-dear God,' said Hamond.

'Nobody is to fire a shot, or we shall be cut to pieces,' whispered FitzRoy. 'Place your weapons slowly and carefully on the ground.'

His men complied. Deliberately, FitzRoy stepped out in front of the group, towards the lead horseman, and laid his pistol before the horse's forelegs. The Araucanian raised his *chuzo*, handling it as deftly as a lancet despite its immense length, and placed the point under FitzRoy's heart. FitzRoy felt the iron tip gently pierce his uniform: a trickle of warm blood mingled with the icy rain running down the spearshaft, hot and cold pooling together against his undershirt.

'*Us'hae ihlca*,' FitzRoy said, in Alikhoolip. Put down your spear.

An amused ripple ran through the ranks of Araucanian warriors. A lieutenant trotted over and consulted briefly with his leader.

'Who are you, Spaniard, that you speak the language of the *Sapallios*?'

'I am not a Spaniard.'

'You look like a Spaniard.'

Desperately, FitzRoy fought to remember some of the entries in the Patagonian glossary he had compiled at Gregory Bay six years previously: unfortunately, it lay gathering dust somewhere in the British Museum, waiting to be catalogued, along with the other specimens from the first voyage.

'*Catiam comps español. Catiam* English. *Auros chuzo*.'

The horse-captain narrowed his eyes at this novelty. A Spanish officer who refused to fight and die like a man, but who insisted, in different languages, despite all evidence to the contrary, that he was not a Spaniard. His curiosity pricked, the warrior gestured for the other white men to remain where they were, and for FitzRoy to go ahead of him at spear-point. The ranks of horsemen parted silently to let them through. FitzRoy walked uphill, his heart thumping in his chest; only the clanking of their spurs signalled that the Araucanian captain and his lieutenant were still behind.

Presently, they arrived at a rain-soaked encampment of smoke-shrouded tents. In the centre, rising above the others, was the dwelling of the *cacique*, or chief, guarded by a brace of fierce-looking warriors. The escort dismounted and, without further ado, prostrated themselves on the ground. FitzRoy was not quick enough following suit, and found himself hastened on his way by a heavy blow across the middle of his back. One of the guards placed a foot on his neck, pushing his face down into the mud. He could hear whispered consultations, all but drowned out by the spattering of the rain, which flicked off the mud into his eyes. Finally two feet, tightly clad in hand-stitched seal-fur riding-boots and surmounted by extravagant iron spurs cut in a sunburst design, made their elegant way out of the tent and stopped just before FitzRoy's nose.

He waited.

Surely these people possessed too much dignity, too much honour, to kill him here, now, in cold blood?

A commanding voice addressed him, in rough Spanish: 'I am the *cacique* of these people. These are my lands. Who are you, Spaniard, that you dare to enter my lands?'

'I am not Spanish, but English. I am a ship's captain. My name is Robert FitzRoy.'

'I am Lorenzo Colipí.'

FitzRoy craned his neck, and looked up at the chief in amazement. He found himself staring into the scarred, pitted and painted face of a fifty-year-old white man.

'You wish to know why I have white skin, like you.'

It was more of a statement than a question. His wrists bound, head hanging, FitzRoy knelt before Colipí in his tent. The Araucanian leader sat on a pile of skins, surrounded like a Turkish pasha by a flock of wives. The women were draped with beads and brass ornaments, their mantles secured by large, flat-headed ornamental pins. One was breast-feeding a boy who must have been all of ten years old. A guard stood with a sort of halberd pressed to the back of FitzRoy's neck, the cold iron blade pushing his head downwards at a suitably respectful angle.

'My mother was taken, when she was twelve, from an *estancia* on the other side of the mountains. My father's people drove the farmers from our lands and burned their farms. She was the only survivor – fortunate to be spared, and fortunate to be taken from her people. She was given to my father as one of his wives. My father was Hueichao, who once had land in that place. Lorenzo was the name of her youngest brother, who was two when he died. She named me for him, and taught me the language of the enemy. You see, white man, among our people the leadership does not pass to the oldest son of the chief, for this has always made the Spanish weak. Our people choose the strongest man, the bravest man, to be their leader. They chose me. With my face, with my blood, I had no choice but to be the strongest and the bravest. It is my task now to lead my people to victory, to kill every Spaniard who sets foot in our country.'

'I apprehend that the Spanish are gone now, Great Chief. There are only the Chileans, and on the other side of the mountains, the Buenos

Ayreans.'

'They are the same people. They have the same forefathers. Forefathers who agreed, three hundred years ago, that they would keep to the north of the Bío-Bío river. But again and again they have broken their forefathers' word. What kind of people are these, who do not respect the word of their ancestors? Their farmers take our land. Their soldiers kill our people. In the old days, their priests burned our people alive. Now there is a new butcher on the other side of the mountains, this Rosas, who sends the black-faced men to murder our families. He has big guns, which can kill many warriors with one shot. But he cannot drag his guns into the mountains. When he and his men try to take these mountains, they shall dig their own graves – you may be satisfied of it.'

'I am no friend to Rosas, Great Chief. One of his ships fired a cannon at my ship.'

'Then why do you trespass in my nation, like one of his spies? My men would have killed you, otherwise that you spoke in the language of the southern people. What is your business? Tell me why I should not have you put to death right here.'

'I make charts – maps of the ocean – so that other English ships will not be wrecked in the rough seas to the south. I have come to rescue the men in the camp on the hill.'

'Ah, the Spaniards in the little fort. They have guns, but they are in want of food and they are becoming sick. Their days are few.'

'They are not Spaniards. They are English, like me. They intended only to sail past your land. But the earthquake – when the ground shook – changed the currents, and their ship was wrecked upon your shore.'

'Ha, the shaking of the ground.' Colipí laughed bitterly, his greying topknot quivering with indignation. 'When we see the Spanish dig deep foundations for their buildings, we see them constructing their own sepulchres. They go in and pray to their God, then the building falls on their heads! He cannot protect them. Only the volcano-god can command the bulls below ground that cause the ground to shake. Always knowing this, at every full moon we sacrifice a bull to him so that he will protect us from the great bulls in their tunnels.'

It is exactly like ancient Crete, FitzRoy realized. *They share almost the same beliefs.*

'How many gods do the Araucanians have, Great Chief?' he ventured.

'We are not Araucanians,' spat Lorenzo Colipí angrily. 'That is the Spanish word. We are Mapuche. We have resisted the Spanish for three hundred years, and before them we resisted the great Inca. That is because the most powerful of all Gods, the God of Gods, El Chaltén, the God of Smoke, is our protector.'

'Where does El Chaltén live, O Chief?'

'Where does he live? *He* is a mountain, far to the south of here. A great mountain, which cannot be climbed. No white man has ever seen El Chaltén, and no white man ever shall. He is tall, and he reaches in pain to the sky itself, with two smaller pinnacles, one to each side.'

Like Jesus on the cross, thought FitzRoy.

'He has protected my people for thousands of years, since we came to these lands from the west.'

'Your people came across the sea from the west?' Excitement speared through FitzRoy. 'I knew it. I have seen the *piragua* canoes. They have exactly the same canoes in the lands to the west.'

'Once we lived in the land of the setting sun. Our forefathers had red hair and blue eyes. Then the gods sent a great flood to punish the world, a flood that covered the land. The great ancestor, Chem, built a boat, which came to rest on the mountain of Theghin. The volcano-god signalled to him with spark and fire to come to the mountaintop, for it protruded safely from the waters. Then he sent Chem far to the east, to live here, in these lands. But every time a *cacique* dies, his spirit follows the setting sun west, back to the mountains of his ancestors. One day my spirit will make that journey.'

FitzRoy's mind reeled. *The flood. Shem, Noah's son. The ark on the mountaintop. The story is the same.*

'Is this what your father told you, Great Chief, or your mother?'

'It has been known to my people for thousands of years, for this is how the world was begun. You know it to be true, white man, for you have seen the boats of the west.'

It was incredible. *Proof, surely, that early man had spread over the earth after the deluge, that all men had shared a common ancestor not once, but twice. Proof of the universality of the deluge.* He had to get out of here alive, if only to tell this remarkable tale.

'And now, white man, you have come with fifteen warriors to rescue your friends. Fifteen warriors to throw down the Mapuche, who could not be thrown down by the Spanish or by the Inca? You are very brave, or very foolish, or both.'

'It was not my wish to throw down the Mapuche. Quite the reverse. I have given aid to the men of the south. I wished only to find my friends and leave your lands as soon as possible. I adjure you to show mercy.'

Colipí smiled. 'Your bravery as a warrior has come in aid of your cause. Because I believe that you are no Spaniard, you and your friends shall have until sunset tomorrow to leave our lands. Anyone remaining after that will be killed. Tell your friends in the land of the English that anyone who comes here to take our land will also be killed.'

'You are most merciful, Great Chief.'

The watching small boy detached himself from his mother's breast, and gazed at the Englishman with undisguised contempt.

Breathing hard, FitzRoy was led to the edge of the encampment, where his bonds were cut and he was pushed down the slope. A winter's dusk was settling upon the sombre, silent woods. Squelching downhill as fast as he could in the gloom, he located the meadow where they had been surrounded, but there was no sign of anyone from the *Beagle*, or of any tribesmen. It was almost dark now, and his options were few. He chose to gamble once more, and plunged into the impenetrable blackness of the fringing forest, heading upwards in a southerly direction. Even if he could not locate Seymour's hilltop position, he might at least find some vantage-point from which to view the surrounding country when it became light again. Time was short, but he had to move with caution, for he could see nothing at all. Again and again he stumbled over tree-roots, slipped into streams or crashed into low branches, until he was transformed into a terrible ogre of the forest, his body caked from head to foot in mud, his uniform ripped and flapping behind him. At long last, after several hours of patient struggle, he saw a solitary pinpoint of light flicker briefly between the trees. He called out, at the top of his voice, 'Challengers ahoy!'

A faint answering shout of 'Hallo!' came back from the pinnacle above, and a more welcome sound he had never heard. Blazing torches appeared at the walls of the British encampment, and within a few minutes, the muddy apparition that had emerged blinking like some stone-age tribesman from the forest was being hauled to safety over the makeshift barricades.

'Our tried friend Captain FitzRoy!' exulted a voice. It was Michael Seymour, a great beaming smile on his face, missing a stone in weight and with several weeks' growth of beard clinging to his face. A huge cheer arose from the defenders, and Seymour embraced FitzRoy so tightly that when he finally withdrew the two were almost as muddy as each other.

'Mr Hamond has told us all about your efforts in our behalf.'

'Hamond is here?'

'They are all here.'

FitzRoy breathed a sigh of relief. 'The Araucanians have given us safe passage until nightfall tomorrow.'

'Thank the Lord. God bless you, FitzRoy – some food, here, for the captain!'

A plum-dough was brought out, which Seymour had been saving for the event of their rescue, and the lion's share was forced on an embarrassed FitzRoy. The massed ranks of Araucanians – wherever they were in the maze of trees – would no doubt have been bewildered, later that night, to hear an outbreak of spontaneous singing, comic songs and shanties overlapping, spilling over the little palisade and out into the night.

Daybreak found FitzRoy and Seymour still deep in conversation, laughing and joking about what they would say at each other's court-martials. The camp was abandoned soon after, with the mixture of relief and nostalgia that attends the end of any shared difficulty successfully overcome. Only the essentials were carried down to the cutter: it would take at least four trips to get the *Challenger*'s company off the beach. They found Bennet blue-nosed with cold, but otherwise hale and hearty, and immensely cheered to see his fellows again. Seymour, it was decided, would be the last man off; FitzRoy and Hamond would command the first run, and take charge of the wounded and the sick. The elements were still squally and tetchy, but in nothing so terrible a mood as they had been the previous day. They could see the *Blonde* clearly across a mile of broken grey water. FitzRoy had been concerned that Biddlecombe's short tacks might have taken her ever further from the coast, but the stern figure of Bos'n Sorrell, arms folded behind the wheel, had obviously attended to that difficulty. It was a rough crossing: the cutter was tossed about, her head turned this way and that by waves slugging at her from the opposite direction, and all aboard had to endure repeated facefuls of spray. A quarter-mile out from the beach, Hamond knelt over the side and, with what looked curiously like gratitude, voided the contents of his stomach into the sea.

'Lost your sea-legs, Mr Hamond?' enquired FitzRoy cheerfully.

'It's not s-seasickness, sir,' admitted Hamond, looking fleetingly guilty. 'It's sheer relief at g-getting away from there alive.'

FitzRoy had thought about not taking Hamond on the expedition but the man had volunteered, after all. In fact, Hamond had been as brave as any of them, in his way, and FitzRoy had appreciated a quiet, intelligent voice amid all the bravura aggression.

'I-I'm not sure I can t-take any more of this, sir.'

'Not long to go now, Mr Hamond. Another twenty minutes and we shall be in the *Blonde*.'

'Th-that's not what I m-meant, sir.'

FitzRoy looked into Hamond's eyes, two saucers in a pallid face, and at his hands, which were literally shaking with released tension. The young midshipman's nerves, he realized, were completely shot to pieces.

'I m-meant, sir, that I c-can't go on serving in the Navy. I just c-can't go on. I'm too f-frightened, sir.'

'I have come to report the successful rescue of the crew of HMS *Challenger*, sir, with no further casualties.'

Once again, FitzRoy found himself before Commodore Mason in the well-manicured setting of that officer's rented garden. The open geneva bottle stood to attention on the table.

Mason grunted. 'Do not think for one second that you have saved your skin, FitzRoy. I shall make damned sure you are court-martialled as a mutineer.'

'An accusation of the kind you describe could hardly fail to be damaging,' conceded FitzRoy expressionlessly, 'as, indeed, would a counter-accusation of cowardice in the face of the enemy and dereliction of duty. In fact, it is hard to see any benefit accruing to either of us from this sorry affair. But I should say, sir, that I have already composed a…rough draft of my report of the expedition.'

'To the devil with you and your report.'

'It is not a very detailed report, sir. It merely credits the successful rescue of the *Challenger* to the bravery of the officers and men of HMS *Blonde*, and by implication to her commanding officer, sir. No names are mentioned in this rough draft of what would – under normal circumstances – be regarded by the Admiralty as a most heroic action, sir.'

FitzRoy paused, to let this sink in. He could see the light dawning, gradually sweeping the shadows from Mason's furrowed brow.

'No names?'

'No sir. Just a straightforward rescue.'

Mason considered further.

'You have important business in Tahiti, do you not?'

'I believe so.'

'Then you had better get on with it, had you not? And this time you will obey your orders to the very letter. Is that clear?'

'That is clear, sir.' Mason, it appeared, had accepted FitzRoy's face-saving proposal.

'One further thing, sir.'

'Don't push your luck, Mr FitzRoy.'

'I have reluctantly agreed to terminate the commission of one of my officers. Mr Hamond is to leave the *Beagle* forthwith. I should like, with permission, to take Mr Davis from the *Blonde*, sir.'

'Who?'

'Your assistant master, sir. I should like him to remain behind and skipper the *Constitución*, a surveying schooner I have borrowed, on an expedition to northern Chili and Peru.'

'Should you indeed? Very well. If you say so,' acquiesced Mason gruffly. 'What's the matter with this Hamond fellow?'

'He is too frightened to continue in the Service, sir.'

'Cowardice, eh?'

'No sir. Mr Hamond is very far from being a coward. He appears to be suffering from a sort of extended shock. I think him an immensely brave man to admit to it, and to face up to it, sir.' FitzRoy touched the peak of his cap insouciantly and, without waiting to be dismissed, took his leave of the commodore. Only upon reaching the safety of the street did he allow himself a smile of relief.

CHAPTER TWELVE

Chatham Island, Galapagos, 16 September 1835

'It is indisputable evidence!'

'My dear FitzRoy, one piece of evidence can rarely be said to be indisputable.'

'"Chem" is clearly Shem. "Mount Theghin" is indisputably Mount Ararat. The legends of the Araucanians testify to the global nature of the deluge. My dear Philos, what more proof could you desire?'

'But the story could have been introduced into the Araucanian tradition at any point – by the *conquistadors* perhaps – or even earlier, by a lone Christian travelling across the Pacific. Without a weight of evidence to back them up, the tales of this chief of yours – half a Spaniard, by his own admission – would scarcely hold up as scientific evidence.'

'But the word of God is not a matter of scientific conjecture! Even if there were not a huge weight of evidence for the flood, God's word is absolute!'

'You will allow me to observe, I hope, that there is also direct evidence *against* the flood.'

'Direct evidence against the flood? What evidence?'

'Evidence I have witnessed with my own eyes.' There was no other way forward now. His enthusiasm for argument heated under the broiling, oppressive, leaden Galapagos skies, Darwin blurted out the most controversial of his conclusions. 'I did not wish to say this before, FitzRoy, for fear of offending you, but the natural life that I witnessed on the Patagonian side of the Andes was entirely different from that on the Chilean side.'

'What of it?'

'The Andes are newly uplifted land, which means that the differing species on either side of the *cordillera* came into being *after* the mountains were created. Those species were not created on the sixth day. They have – they have—'

'Transmuted?' FitzRoy uttered the word calmly but grimly.

'Yes, damn it, they have *transmuted* into existence, in relatively recent geological times. You will find an entirely different species of mouse on either side of the *cordillera*. If God created mice at the beginning of time, then why do not identical mice swarm over the western and eastern slopes today?'

'What you speak of is adaptation. Variation within a species. Species themselves are immutable.'

'I tell you they were different species of mouse.'

'Come, Philos, if transmutation between species is possible, then show me *your* direct evidence. The fossil record does not convincingly document a single transmutation from one species to another. Where are the countless fossils of intermediate species, embedded in the crust of the earth? If wings grew from forelegs, where are the half-winged animals, and how could they have half-flown? If lungs grew from gills, where are the half-lunged fish, and how could they have half-breathed? If giraffes grew from antelopes, where are the fossils of all the short-necked giraffes?'

'The fossil record is less than perfect, I grant you, but geology is a new science. In future ages, perhaps the fossil links you speak of will be discovered. Discontinuities in nature do not by themselves speak against transmutation, because these intermediate forms are now extinct, and may have become so very quickly. Did we ourselves not find the remains of an aquatic rodent the size of an elephant? Who knows what two orders of animals that creature might have bridged?'

'Are you suggesting that your Chilean mice transmuted from aquatic elephants, or vice versa?'

'No, of course I am not. I have simply come to realize that creation is far more fluid a business than our Church allows. How different are the fat little Fuegians from their lean, tall Araucanian neighbours? Yet all are supposedly descended from Noah and his wife. Where are the intermediate fossils there? And both species shall become extinct, I fear, when

General Rosas has his way.'

'Both species? The Fuegians and the Araucanians are men – one species – equal before the Lord, who one hopes in His mercy will save them from the depredations of your friend the general.'

'You believe God will save those heathen savages from the Christian armies? From white men?'

FitzRoy reacted with anger.

'Those "heathen savages" are heathens because they have yet to receive the word of God, and savages because they have yet to receive the blessings of civilization that attend it. Your friend Rosas may profess Christianity, but he is little more than a tyrant and a murderer who takes God's name in vain.'

'Perhaps the Fuegians are not men as we are, created indivisibly by God. Perhaps they are a separate species of man, more akin to the higher apes. I do not know. *I do not know*, FitzRoy. But I do know that to believe in every word of the scriptures, the ark, the creation of all life in a matter of days, is to believe in the impossible and the unintelligible.'

'If what you say is true, then the stars of heaven, the showers and the dew, the mountains and the hills may no longer be called to exalt the Lord with us by praise.'

'No. I merely question the word of God *as it is written by man* in the scriptures.'

'This won't do, Philos. The scriptures themselves say, "If any man shall take away the words of the book of this prophecy, God shall take away his part out of the book of life and out of the holy city." You are risking damnation in the hereafter!'

'Hang it, FitzRoy, such threats are themselves a damnable doctrine. The Old Testament is a manifestly false history of the origin of the world, and I do not believe that the true story of the creation of life by God is to be found there.'

'But look what you seek to put in its place!' Both men were fairly screeching at one another now. 'What are the chances of species somehow transmuting out of nothingness in the first instance? Something as beautiful and complex as a flower cannot result from a random process! An earthquake destroys a cathedral – it does not construct one! The grain that man makes into bread, the cattle that provide his meat and milk, the dogs that aid him in his work – did all these transmute by some accident of nature? A spider's web? A beautiful butterfly? An electric eel? Did all these transmute by accident as well?'

FitzRoy pulled a book from the shelf above. 'Listen to Paley: "The marks of design are too strong to be gotten over. Design must have had a designer. That designer must have been a person. That person is God." '

'I do not deny that the Lord God has designed all living things! I just…I just…' Darwin faltered, his sails sagging as the initial blast of his enthusiasm began to subside. 'I just believe that once an animal has been divinely created, it is free to transmute itself gradually, by some unexplained mechanism, into another related species.'

'Tell me, Philos, on your expedition, were there ants to be found on either side of the Andes?'

'Of course.'

'Different species of ant?'

'I dare say – I do not recall.'

'And the sterile worker ants – how precisely had they transmuted gradually from one species into another when they cannot breed?'

'I do not know.'

'You do not know. There is no mechanism to explain it – that is why you do not know. I repeat, what you have witnessed is *variation*. An adaptation from one mouse to another mouse through the vagaries of climate, which has been presupposed by God as part of His divine plan. A secondary consequence of a primary act of creation. There is a moral aspect to nature as well as a material aspect, and it is the task of science to link the material to the moral. Any man who denies this is deep in the mire of folly.'

Darwin attempted one last throw. 'If there is no such thing as transmutation, then why do the most closely allied species occur in the same countries? Why did the Lord place many species of penguin towards the South Pole, but none towards the North Pole?'

'You have yet to visit Australia, Philos. When you get there, you will find a swan identical in every respect to its British counterpart – except that where the British swan is white with a yellow beak, the Australian version is jet-black with a scarlet beak. The two birds were created many thousands of miles apart, in perfect isolation. Why? As objects of beauty, and no more.' FitzRoy folded his arms with cold satisfaction and sat back.

Darwin looked down at his shabby, sweat-stained shirt. All his shirts and waistcoats were showing their age now, patched and repatched as they had been during the preceding five years. He wanted to wear clean, new clothes again. He wanted to relax in his favourite armchair at the Mount. He was fed up with quarrelling. He was fed up with this wretched little cabin. He was fed up with ceaselessly feeling seasick. He was fed up with the dyspepsia and constipation and piles that had pursued him here from Valparayso. He seriously doubted whether any schoolboy had ever longed for the holidays as much as he craved his home and his family. The day when the lookout hailed the Lizard lights ahead would be a momentous one indeed. He no longer had the strength or the inclination to argue.

A few days later, Darwin, Covington and Midshipman King were landed in high surf on the north-east coast of Chatham Island, with armfuls of collecting-boxes. The water was goosepimple-cold on account of the polar current – Stebbing had fetched up a bucketful, which had measured 58 degrees Fahrenheit – but the air, roasting slowly in the glare of a high, burnished sun, had registered closer to 90. Darwin jammed his thermometer into the black sand, whereupon the mercury promptly shot off the scale, meaning that the ground temperature exceeded 137 degrees Fahrenheit. Within seconds, the glimmering heat had dried out their clothes, then resoaked the trio once more in their own sweat.

Before them lay a buckled, rippling, jagged country, black as anthracite, except that it resembled sea more than land, a churning nocturnal sea that had been paralysed in an instant. Everywhere they looked in this tortured, twisted wasteland were volcanic craters: craters bursting like sores from other craters, little craters concealed within bigger craters, craters with solidified lava spilling over their rims like boiling pitch caught at the moment of tipping from a cauldron. Here and there were fumaroles, smoking vents and steaming fissures that ran in angular, contrary splits against the flow of the rock. It was, reflected Darwin, reminiscent of the iron-foundry country around Wolverhampton. The south side of each crater was the lower, he noticed, and in some cases it had been destroyed altogether. *These cones have been formed under water*, he realized. *The wind and the waves here arrive from the south. They have battered at these rocks while they lay in the sea, before they ever were raised out of the water.*

By rights, such a furnace should have supported little in the way of life. The pitiless vertical sun, the stifling climate and the rocks that glowed like a cast-iron stove should have been no more hospitable than the infernal regions of Pandemonium itself. But it was not so: every square foot of land was dotted with shuffling, scaly, primordial creatures, while the surf teemed with darting, flashing shapes. The sea creatures were, for the most part, those of the polar regions – penguins, sealions and the like – whereas the cacti and lizards ashore were similar to those of the arid lands near the equator. Huge, crimson-chested frigate birds sailed overhead, puffed up with self-importance, arrowing down towards the surface of the sea where they would deftly pluck out a fish without even getting their feet wet. Little mockingbirds ran up and pecked at the explorers' boots. Bright vermilion Sally Lightfoot crabs swarmed across the glossy ebony rocks of the shore, shuttling backwards and forwards with aimless determination. It was an extraordinary panorama, the like of which none of them had ever seen.

The most commonplace denizen of Chatham Island was a fat, sluggish, sooty-coloured iguana, some three feet in length, clumsy of movement, with a horny mane, long webbed claws and a slack pouch hanging beneath its slack mouth. These imps of darkness lined the beaches, basking in the infernal heat, yet never straying more than ten yards from the sea. Occasionally one would lumber into the water, where it would be transformed into a sleek obsidian dart, its normally splayed legs tucked out of sight, its tail propelling it deftly through the water like a miniature crocodile. In common with the other land creatures of the Galapagos, these reptiles were extraordinarily tame, and utterly receptive to being poked and prodded. By way of an experiment, Darwin grasped one of the beasts by the tail, whirled it about his head and flung it into a tidal pool.

'What larks!' shouted Midshipman King, while Covington stared at his master with what looked like disapproval.

Really, it was good to be romping about the country with King once more; he was not much use as a naturalist's assistant, it was true, but he was much jollier than the servant. Covington, to be fair, was fast making himself indispensable – the horse-butcher's son was learning so quickly, he had even started his own limited sub-collection – but he remained curiously unapproachable. He was not, after all, a gentleman. King was putting the fun back into collecting.

'Look, Philos, it's coming back.'

The iguana had indeed crawled laboriously back to its former spot at Darwin's feet. As it arrived, he picked it up by the tail once more, and flung it back into the pool. Again, the beast attained the shore, and again disdainfully marched back to its place. A third time it was returned to the water, and a third time, pompously, patiently, it regained its former situation.

'Hereditary instinct is telling it that the shore is a place of safety,' concluded Darwin. 'I could kill it in an instant, yet it does not fear me.'

'Not very bright, is it, Philos?' said King cheerily.

'Lizards in Europe know to fear man,' Darwin mused aloud. 'It is a knowledge they possess from birth. Yet reptiles do not rear their young – indeed, they may never encounter them. They cannot teach their young anything. The knowledge is inherited. Were these iguanas to learn to fear man, how would that knowledge pass to their descendants?'

'Well…I suppose it wouldn't,' said King, by now somewhat baffled.

'He's talking about transmutation,' jabbed Covington, catching Darwin's eye and holding it for a telling second.

'Transmutation…That's a load of Godless gammon, isn't it?' said King, unhappily aware that he was not party to some shared knowledge.

'Yes. Yes it is,' said Darwin bluntly, and moved purposefully away across the corrugated ground.

*

They ascended the island's central cone by way of a series of paths through the undergrowth that seemed to be converging on some unknown central point. The mystery of who or what had made these tracks was solved when they came upon two huge tortoises, each as high as a man's chest, snuffling up the hill in front of them. The latter beast had the numerals '1806' carved into its shell. As the collecting party marched up behind, the animals took no notice; but when Darwin moved into the eyeline of the rear tortoise, it hissed at him, sat down, and withdrew its head and legs into its carapace.

'It seems they are quite deaf,' he deduced.

King took a run at the lead tortoise and leaped aboard. Even with the weight of a sturdy youth on its back, the vast reptile seemed unaware that anyone was behind or even upon it. Darwin jumped aboard too, but still the animal did not slacken its pace, keeping to a speed that – he calculated with the aid of his pocket-watch – would amount to about four miles per day.

'Giddy up!' yelled King, and thrashed the animal's hind-quarters with a switch. 'What about a race? We could be at the summit by the end of the week!'

Both men laughed, while Covington brought up the rear in respectful and possibly reproachful silence.

They lunched soon afterwards, watched by a large hawk that perched upon a low branch. Darwin approached the bird with his gun, and placed the barrel squarely in the centre of its face. The hawk remaining entirely unmoved, he nudged the nozzle against its beak, before finally shoving the bird to the ground. With an indignant flap of its feathers, it dusted itself down and climbed back to its perch as before.

'Extraordinary,' he murmured.

Covington, he noticed, was writing something in a small notebook. 'What is that, Covington?'

'It is nothing, sir,' mumbled the manservant.

'What is it?'

'It is my journal.'

'You keep a *journal*?'

'Yes sir.'

'Give it here.'

Covington complied, slowly and reluctantly. Darwin flicked through the pages. In a large, rounded, deliberate hand were entries – some of exceeding brevity – going back to the start of the voyage. Capital letters and underlined words mingled freely with those in lower case; on occasion, Spanish happily cohabited with English. Darwin stopped at the entry detailing their expedition northwards from the Rio Negro, in the company of Esteban and his gauchos.

> In the camp or country there are lions, tigers, deer, cavys, ostriches both large and small. Aperea here has a much finer fur THAN ELSEWHERE. THERE ARE armadillos. Partridges ARE both large and small (the former has a tuft or crest on its head). C. D. Caminando por tierra, desde Rio Negro a Buenos Ayres.

Darwin shut the journal and handed it back to its owner. 'Upon my soul, Covington, I never had you down as an author.'

'No sir,' muttered the big youth.

'Just so long as you remember that you are my servant, and that all important observations are to be shared. I am, if you recall, to be the author of the official natural history of the voyage.'

'Aye aye sir. Shall I do well not to write any more, sir?'

'As you will. It is up to you. Just so long as you remember.'

'Aye aye sir.'

After lunch, they pushed on to the principal crater, the floor of which was taken up by a grand assembly of blue-footed boobies. These preposterously earnest birds, white-bodied, black-winged, with bright turquoise beaks and feet, seemed to treat the business of guarding their nests rather casually. Darwin lobbed a few experimental stones at the nesting females, which bounced off their backs harmlessly, the victims looking no more than confused. King walked up and broke one's neck with his hat. The other birds around merely stared up at him with expectant faces.

'I suppose we had better shoot one to take with us,' said Darwin, loading his rifle with the mustard shot which would make a cleaner job than King's hat-brim. He levelled the barrel at the nearest booby. It gazed back at him, curious and uncomprehending. He tensed his finger on the trigger, and paused.

'Everything all right, Philos?'

'Yes, everything's fine. Do you know, King – I'm not sure I can actually do this.'

'How do you mean?'

'I mean, I am all for the chase, but this – this is ridiculous.' *And what is a love of the chase but a relic of an instinctive passion? It is like the pleasure of living with the sky for a roof – it is no more than the pleasure of a savage returning to his wild and native habits.*

The bird continued to gaze stupidly up at him.

He handed the gun to Covington.

'Covington, shoot this bird, would you?'

'Aye aye sir.'

Covington brought the gun up to his shoulder, took aim and fired. There was a deafening explosion, and he fell back with a scream, blood pouring from his shattered ear. The flame from the flash-pan had escaped into the magazine and detonated the loose powder within: one side of the weapon lay ripped open, where the explosion had torn the gunmetal apart from the inside.

'Covington? Are you all right, man?'

Darwin and King, their ears ringing, knelt on either side of the writhing manservant, who appeared not to hear their urgent entreaties.

'Covington! Are you all right?'

One hand pressed to the side of his head, fresh, bright blood streaming between his fingers, Covington rolled on to his back, his frightened eyes attempting to focus on his would-be rescuers.

'Are – you – all – right?'

'I cannot hear you,' he whimpered. 'Whatever it is you are saying, sirs, I cannot hear you.'

The drizzle having cleared, the party took their dinner out of doors, at a table set up on the governor's lawn.

'More turpin?' said Lawson. 'It is the breast meat – the most capital cut.' He indicated the bowl of fatty, primrose-coloured meat that occupied pride of place in the centre of the table. 'The rest of the animal is of indifferent flavour, except when employed in soup. The calipash is thrown away altogether.'

'This is a local tortoise, I presume?' asked FitzRoy, taking an elegant bite.

'Oh no – we have them brought across from James, or Hood, or Albemarle,' said the governor cheerfully. 'Here on Charles Island, they have been hunted to extinction.'

The discovery of Lawson's existence had been both a stroke of luck and a surprise, in that FitzRoy and his officers had been unaware that the Galapagos Islands – previously the province of buccaneers and whalers – even possessed a governor. Stopping at the postbox on Charles Island, they had come across Nicholas Lawson astride his horse, collecting his mail. Lawson was able to inform them that the islands had recently been annexed by the newly established Republic of the Equator, and that the Ecuadorians had not only constructed a prison for some three hundred black convicts on Charles Island, but had appointed him – as an Englishman of standing – their governor. The penal settlement was situated one thousand feet up and four and a half miles inland, where sodden, hanging clouds buffeted the highlands each year between June and November, creating a temperate zone of ferns, grasses and woodlands. There the prisoners cultivated plantain, banana, sugar cane, Indian corn and sweet potato, and hunted the pigs and goats that were permitted to run wild between the trees. Lawson had promised FitzRoy and the officers of his service, and had invited them to visit his domain later that day to enjoy, a dinner of succulent roast tortoise with home-grown vegetables.

'It would appear that there was once a prodigious number of tortoises here,' said FitzRoy, gesturing across Lawson's precisely manicured lawn. Arranged at geometric intervals around the neat green rectangle, upturned tortoise carapaces served as pots for a colourful assortment of woodland flowers.

'Ah, the flowerpots,' said Lawson, smoothing the angles of his clipped, triangular beard. 'We live something of a Robinson Crusoe existence here, Captain FitzRoy: happily self-sufficient in our necessities, but absolutely devoid of the merest luxury, and therefore forced to improvise. In answer to your question, there were indeed a great many turpin here, not ten years back. Some of the bigger frigates were taking away seven hundred at a time, to consume while crossing the Pacific. I myself once saw two hundred loaded in a day. Those that were too big to lift had the date engraved upon their carapaces: 1786 is the oldest I have yet witnessed. We killed those larger beasts ourselves where they stood, and carried the meat here, until every turpin on the island was gone. The other islands' populations are headed the same way. During the dry months they are killed for the water reserves in their bladders. The species shall be extinct, I believe, in another twenty years. Now our turpin must be brought from a variety of different islands, in an attempt to preserve the supply for as long as possible. Once they are gone, I dare say we shall consume the sea turtles.'

'It is an uncommon pity to see one of the Lord's creatures made extinct in this fashion,' offered a troubled Sulivan.

'But did the Lord not place the turpin here for man's benefit in the first instance?' said Lawson, carefully adjusting his wire-rimmed spectacles. 'One might reasonably propose it, Lieutenant.'

'Indeed one might.' Sulivan smiled politely.

'Forgive me,' said FitzRoy, who had been casting a scientific eye at the upturned tortoise-shells, 'but are there not some considerable differences between these several carapaces? Did you not say they originated in different islands?'

'You are most observant, Captain FitzRoy. The turpin of each island do not assort with each other at all. Those from Hood Island have a thick ridge of shell in front, turned up in the manner of a Spanish saddle, like that one there. The one to the left is from James Island – do you see? It is rounder and blacker, and its meat is incidentally more flavoursome.' He held up his loaded fork and smiled. 'Generally, the turpin of the lower islands have longer necks, whereas those of the high country are dome-shaped with shorter necks. You will find such variations in all the wildlife hereabouts, safe enough.'

'I am very much interested about this. Do tell us more.'

'You have seen the marine iguanas? The *Amblyrhynchus cristatus*? They are not strictly iguanas, I should say, but of the genus *Amblyrhynchus*. Well, they are larger on Albemarle Island. And there is also a land *Amblyrhynchus*, a burrowing animal, terracotta in colour, to be found only on Albemarle, James, Barrington and Indefatigable.'

'I apprehend that you are something of a naturalist, Mr Lawson.'

Lawson straightened his starched but threadbare waistcoat with a hint of pride. 'One does one's best to peg away at the subject, Captain FitzRoy. When one is a Robinson Crusoe, there is little else to occupy one's time.'

'The *Beagle* has its own naturalist, in Mr Darwin here.'

Darwin, who had been miles away, reliving the flaming explosion of his gun into Covington's ear over and over again in his mind, came to with a start. 'What? I'm sorry…I do beg your pardon…'

'Mr Lawson here was telling us of the varieties by which the wildlife of each island may be distinguished, and of his Robinson Crusoe existence.'

'Ah, but you will be interested to hear, Mr Darwin, that these islands had their own Robinson Crusoe,' related Lawson, pressing on to spare his inattentive guest any further embarrassment. 'His name was Patrick Watkins, an Irishman who was shipwrecked here at the turn of the century. He built a hut, and planted some potatoes he retrieved from his ship, and made a healthy living of it. By the time a vessel arrived to rescue him, he had become a ragged muffin, with wild, matted red hair and a beard down to his knees, and was sufficiently content that he quite refused to leave. He even abducted a Negro from a passing whaler to serve as his Man Friday, but the fellow escaped.'

A chuckle rippled round the table.

'You say that you are a naturalist, Mr Darwin.'

'Indeed.'

'Then you will be aware that the islands are volcanic, and of comparatively recent origin?'

'One could hardly fail to notice it.'

'It is my belief that we are not the only Robinson Crusoes here, Mr Darwin. The animal population of these islands finds its echo on the South American mainland. The south-easterlies wash driftwood from the mainland against our shores, as well as bamboo, cane-stalks and palm-nuts. One can see them strewn across the beaches at low tide. I believe that the animals of these islands floated across the Pacific on these natural rafts, and adapted to their surroundings once they had arrived. It is why there are no frogs or toads here.'

'Of course!' said Darwin. 'Because such reptiles cannot abide salt water.'

'Then the Galapagos are not an original centre of creation, but have been colonized since from other lands,' said FitzRoy. 'How fascinating.'

The debate was interrupted by the arrival of Bynoe, on a borrowed horse.

'Ah, the good doctor,' said Lawson, gesturing for Bynoe to dismount and take a chair at the feast. 'How is your patient? Recovering from his most tragic accident, I trust?'

Darwin cast a faintly guilty look in Bynoe's direction.

The young surgeon looked grave. 'Covington will live, I am glad to say. He begins to amend. But I do not think he will ever hear again. I am afraid he is become quite deaf.'

'These finches are not the same.'

'I beg your pardon, sir?'

'These finches are not the same as those of Charles Island. Nor, for that matter, do they even resemble each other.'

FitzRoy put down his collecting-cage and seated himself on a rock to watch. Bynoe came over and sat alongside.

'The ones we took on Charles had short beaks, thick at the base like a bullfinch. They were using them to squeeze berries and break seeds. But these birds have fine beaks, like a warbler. Look – that one there is piercing the fibre of the tree, in search of moisture I suppose.'

The two men observed the finches' miniature endeavours in absorbed silence for a few minutes, before Bynoe spoke: 'My God, sir, look. That little fellow there is using a twig like a tool. He appears to be trying to extricate something from the crevice in the trunk – an insect, or a grub.'

'Is it not extraordinary, Mr Bynoe? It is one of those admirable provisions of infinite wisdom by which each created thing is adapted to the place for which it was intended. One single species has been taken by the Lord and modified into a number of different varieties, for a number of different ends.'

Bynoe agreed that it was indeed extraordinary.

The *Beagle* lay anchored off the north-west coast of James Island, her decks groaning following a full victualling with thirty live tortoises, several piglets, and twenty sackfuls of convict-grown pumpkins and potatoes purchased from Mr Lawson for the journey home. The piglets, Lieutenant Wickham had noted with wry amusement, had been fetched aboard two by two. Now, the officers' collecting party was making a final sweep through the lowland thickets of Buccaneer Cove, just behind the rocky shore: it was to be the last halt of their visit to the islands.

Darwin, feeling debilitated and irritable and curiously bereft without the ministrations of his servant, had marched ahead: he now found himself suddenly at the centre of a clandestine meeting of several rust-red, swishing-tailed *Amblyrhynchus*. As the beasts adjourned their furtive business and lumbered away across the black lava, he was struck by the primeval nature of the scene: the reptiles had been first to colonize this virgin land, ahead of the higher mammals who were now driving them to extinction, the same process as had occurred throughout the rest of the earth during an earlier epoch. These land lizards, presumably, had transmuted from the marine lizards that had swum out to the newborn territory, just as the land tortoises would have transmuted from the sea turtles that were still to be seen making their laborious circuits of the islands. What was the creative force behind this explosion of life? Was it all controlled by the good Lord Himself? Or was it out of His hands, a process set in motion at the beginning of time that had been allowed to run riot of its own volition? One conclusion seemed reasonably certain: any species that moved into a new territory was reshaped by its altered environment to an extraordinary degree. Quite how, he did not know. There were clues here, he was sure, to that mystery of mysteries, the first appearance of new beings on the face of the earth; clues that might help to undermine the very stability of species itself. But they felt frustratingly and elusively out of reach. Here was a bare, naked rock that had been clothed for the first time in the not-too-distant past; here should have been everything he needed to crack the mystery. But in the absence of shade, with no escape from the beating sun, his head aching, his boils chafing and his guts rumbling, his brain simply refused to apply itself. He hated these islands, he realized. It was hard to imagine a location so entirely useless to civilized man, or even to the larger mammals.

Bynoe pushed through the leafless brush, mopping the sweat from his brow.

'Presents for you, Philos. For your collection. I found them in a fissure in the rock.'

Darwin forced himself to remember his manners. 'That is extremely decent of you, Bynoe. You oblige me.'

The young surgeon held out a boxful of giant tortoise eggs, perfect white spheres some eight inches in diameter. In his other hand he brandished a wooden cage. 'There are some interesting finches, too, that the skipper thought you should take a look at.'

'That is very kind...but I already have a pair.'

Darwin held up his own collecting-cage in which a sooty-coloured male finch and its tobacco-coloured mate twittered with annoyance.

'I think these are different, Philos. For one thing, the female of this pair is black.'

'Did you see the nest?'

'It was roofed, with a clutch of pink-spotted eggs. I have collected a few of those too.'

'Then it is almost certainly the same species. I dare say the female plumage darkens with age. But please inform the captain that I am most indebted to him for the thought.'

'I will, Philos, I promise.'

Bynoe moved away again, and Darwin was left to his thoughts once more.

If men and their dogs were now bringing destruction to the tortoise population of the Galapagos, because the huge reptiles were utterly ill-equipped to deal with their new predators, then surely there was no more wonder in the extinction of an entire species than in that of an individual? Was this the explanation for the jumps in the fossil record? Darwin's mind positively ached with the effort. He felt close, so tantalizingly close, to comprehending the scheme of things – to knowing the Lord's mind on this most momentous of issues. So close, but still not there.

CHAPTER THIRTEEN

Point Venus, Tahiti, 16 November 1835

Razor-sharp spires of rock, jagged like the shards of a broken window, the glens between them hiding quietly from the light of day; luxuriant groves of coconut palms crowding at their base, interspersed with stands of glossy breadfruit trees and cheerful clusters of bananas; below them, a glassy lagoon whispering softly at the sides of its fringing reef; and beyond that, breaker after breaker of dazzling white foam, beating optimistically against sturdy walls of coral, built up across the centuries by the herculean efforts of myriad tiny sea creatures. It was a picture all of them had seen a hundred times in engravings and watercolours, and daubed upon the canvas of their imaginations; but flushed with the brilliant light of the Pacific sky, it took on a welcoming glow to melt the weariest heart.

'Otaheite,' intoned FitzRoy reverentially.

'I apprehend that we are now to call it Tahiti,' objected Darwin.

'Indeed we are,' said FitzRoy, 'but Cook called it Otaheite by mistake, and I have too much respect for the great man to call it by any other name.'

It had been a glorious crossing, the *Beagle* swept across the Pacific on the warm trade winds, her studding-sails set, eating up the miles at a rate of one hundred and forty a day. The maindeck was thick with tortoises, an array of domes to match St Mark's Basilica in Venice, all sadly destined for the cooking-pot – save one fortunate individual by the name of Harry, which had been earmarked by Darwin as a domestic pet. Quite how his father would react to the sight of a giant Galapagos tortoise ploughing through his flower-beds was a question he intended to address at a later date.

The depth-sounding was called out as ten fathoms, and with it came the news that the tallow at the end of the leadline was no longer picking up dead coral and sand but impressions of the living reef. FitzRoy gave orders for the yards to be trimmed round, the anchor cables to be ranged and anchor buoy ropes to be made ready. As the *Beagle* swerved impeccably into Matavai Bay, her foretopsail was backed, the rest of the sails were furled, and the anchor was released into the turquoise water. This was the exact spot, he reflected, from which Cook and Banks had observed the transit of Venus in 1769, and the knowledge gave him a thrill of association. Point Venus was one of the key points in Beaufort's chain of meridian distances around the globe, so FitzRoy, too, had celestial observations to make; after which there remained the research into the formation of coral islands that the hydrographer had asked him to undertake, and the unpleasant business of extracting a fine from the Tahitians at the behest of Commodore Mason. Much as he disliked doing that gentleman's dirty work, he had sailed so close to the wind in the matter of the *Challenger* that he dared not rock the boat any further.

As the *Beagle* slowed to a stop, natives in canoes carved from hollowed-out trees swarmed into the water, laughing, chattering and calling out to the ship. 'Hey, *manua*! *Manua!*' they shouted, as their little vessels crowded about the *Beagle*, their outriggers clattering against each other and frequently becoming entangled, such was their enthusiasm.

'It means man-o'-war,' said Stokes, realizing. '*Manua* means man-o'-war.'

'It's a regular crush!' said King.

'I understood the Tahitians to have become a Christian people,' said Darwin. 'I cannot say much for their observance of the Sabbath.'

'My dear Philos, we have crossed the international date line,' pointed out FitzRoy. 'Yesterday was Saturday, and today is Monday – one less Sabbath for you to worry about, my friend.'

'That's a puzzle and a half,' said Sulivan. 'How to observe the Sabbath when there isn't one. "Verily, thou art a God that hidest thyself"!'

The Tahitians poured aboard without waiting for an invitation, gleefully brandishing items for sale: fresh fruit, live piglets, sea-shells, and old coins that had once belonged to Cook's men on the *Endeavour* or Bligh's crew aboard the *Bounty*. The Tahitian males were broad-shouldered, athletic and muscular; the females were smooth-skinned and seductive, with white or scarlet flowers worn as earrings or pinned into their hair, which they wore with a curious monastic tonsure shorn from the crown. Both sexes were heavily tattooed, wore garlands of coconut leaves about their foreheads, and were quite naked to the waist; a combination that lent them a bacchanalian aspect, as well as contributing to the sailors' keenness in welcoming the younger women aboard.

'The shape of their…heads is most attractive, phrenologically speaking,' said Darwin, a faint flush of embarrassment colouring his cheeks.

'Indeed – it would seem to indicate good humour, a tractable disposition, and other civilized characteristics,' agreed FitzRoy, as scientifically as possible.

'They are quite ridiculously naked, of course,' grumbled his friend. 'Really, they are in want of some becoming costume.'

'Absolutely,' said FitzRoy, averting his gaze from the display of flower-bedecked nudity. 'The absence of any decorous attire imports a certain gracelessness, would you not say? Or are my ideas unduly fastidious?'

At this moment a jolly-faced, grinning Tahitian ran up to present them with a pineapple, and both men gratefully seized the opportunity to change the subject. Such exotic fruit – luxurious greenhouse rarities in England – were being distributed freely all round the deck.

'Pineapples here are so abundant that the people eat them in the same wasteful manner as we would eat turnips,' marvelled FitzRoy.

Darwin sank his teeth into the fruit's soft flesh, and gave his verdict. 'Mmm – this is better even than those cultivated in England, which I believe is the highest compliment that can be paid to any fruit.'

In an effort to restore order to the deck, Lieutenant Wickham had called for tables and benches to be fetched, and for some semblance of an English-style market to be established, which was not at all easy, given the presence of a herd of giant tortoises in the midst of proceedings. The shells of the great beasts would, of course, have made excellent surfaces for the display of goods, were it not for their habit of lumbering away mid-sale. Unlike the natives of South America, the Tahitians knew the value of money, especially paper money, and were not to be fobbed off with cloth or spare buttons: anything, it seemed, could be purchased for one *dala*, as they liked to pronounce the word 'dollar'. After some negotiation, Darwin employed the services of two roasted-banana salesmen as guides, to lead him on an expedition up the island's peak the following day.

Once the clamour of the impromptu market had ebbed somewhat, FitzRoy and Darwin were rowed ashore, to be taken in hand by a host of giggling children, who led them along a cool, winding path through the palms. Native huts were dotted between the trees, light, elegant constructions thatched with leaves, elliptical in shape, with bamboo frames and little cane fences. Cloth screens hung in the doorways, affording occasional glimpses of stools and baskets and calabashes of fresh water. One householder sat before his domain reading the New Testament, while his wife cleared away the broad leaves that had served them as breakfast plates, and two gurgling children played contentedly in the grass. It seemed to FitzRoy a beautiful miniature of a nation emerging from heathen ignorance, and modestly setting forth its claim to be considered civilized and Christian.

'*Ia-orana!*' called a voice. The phrase was a traditional Tahitian salutation, but the accent was unmistakably that of Limehouse Reach. Coming up the path to meet them, flanked by a bevy of soberly dressed native junior deacons, was a missionary priest, his hand extended in greeting. 'Welcome to Tahiti, gents. May I take the liberty of introducing myself? Charlie Wilson, chief missionary here at Matavai.'

The newcomer was short and solid, with massive brawny forearms, furred like a chimpanzee's: quite literally, a muscular Christian. His manner was entirely respectful and generous, if lacking in the refinements of etiquette, and his smile was warmly deferential; but here was a man who could look after himself, thought FitzRoy, a man who exuded physical confidence. How very different from their own Mr Matthews, no more than a peripheral figure when he had been most needed in Tierra del Fuego, who had all but become a recluse in the months since. Matthews had vanished into the bowels of the ship in shame, reduced to a pale-faced wraith visible only at mealtimes.

The introductions seen to, Wilson led them to his immaculate little wooden church in the forest, painted all in white, a neat and simple one-roomed cottage adjoining. But for the palm trees and the sultry heat, they might have been in rural Shropshire. Not for the first time that day, FitzRoy thought bleakly of the failure of the Woollya mission, and of the whereabouts of Jemmy Button. Would he ever see Jemmy again, he wondered, that poor lost soul whom he had elevated to Christianity, then abandoned to his fate in the Godforsaken wilds of the south? The contrast between this idyllic setting and his own doomed attempts to create something similar could not have been sharper. Humbly, he congratulated Wilson on the condition of his flock. 'A more orderly, quiet, inoffensive community I have not seen in any other part of the world,' he said. Darwin nodded vigorously in agreement.

'Where, may I ask, did you train as a priest, Mr Wilson?'

'Oh, I didn't train, sir – I have no formal training. The London Missionary Society, sir, it's congregationalist – a knowledge of the Lord's works and a willing heart is all as what's required. I was a coal-whipper, sir, at the Port of London, unloading the big coal ships from the north-east into barges and lighters. Black as a Negro I was at the end of every working day. Then I found God, sir – I was born again, as they say – and I decided to devote my life to His works. I was sent here to assist Mr Henry Nott, and when that good gentleman retired these five years past, I took over the mission. I say "retired", but Mr Nott needed the time to complete his great work, sir.'

'His great work? What great work would that be?'

'Why, none other than the translation of the Old and New Testaments into Tahitian – a work worthy of the very fathers of our church, sir, which has taken up no fewer than forty years of his life. Utaame, fetch Mr Nott here directly, if you please.'

One of the junior deacons was thus dispatched, and quickly returned with an elderly, shrivelled gentleman, the last few wispy strands of whose hair spiralled about his liver-spotted pate as if attempting to ascend to heaven by themselves. Nott's handshake was firm, though, and his blue eyes unclouded.

'It would appear, Mr Nott, that we may credit you before all others for the changes that have overcome this place since Cook's day,' said FitzRoy.

'Oh, I will take none of the credit, for that is the Lord's doing and I merely His willing instrument, and others like me.'

'You were the first missionary here?' asked Darwin.

'That I was.'

'Then may I propose that you are become too modest? Was this not the most savage of lands when you arrived?'

'Oh, it was an uncommon savage land, all right, and an ignorant one. There were human sacrifices, bloody wars where the conquerors spared neither women nor children, the wanton destruction of the aged, infirm or sick, and, of course, an idolatrous priesthood. It is not twenty years since I saw the Tahitians with my own eyes flee in terror at the sight of a horse – a "man-carrying pig", they called it.' A little wheezy chuckle escaped from Nott's turkey throat.

'It is not sixty years since Cook himself could see no prospect of a change in these parts,' added Wilson, in tribute to his senior.

'But God's love was within these people, gentlemen. By His light we have freed that love from its former cloak of savagery, intemperance and licentiousness. In Cook's time, it was the custom of the Tahitians to practise fornication as a matter of routine.'

The four gentlemen tut-tutted at this, but before he could stop it, a sudden, momentary image of a blob of molten candlewax, cooling white against Maria O'Brien's skin, flashed into FitzRoy's mind. He hurriedly filed the image out of sight. He was the captain of a surveying-brig, here to do his duty.

'The natives will persist in going about semi-naked, in their shame,' said Wilson, a disapproving look scudding across his countenance too, 'but the younger generation what pass through the mission schools are learning the virtue of covering their modesty. Though you will have noticed that the women shave their heads, and decorate their skin with needles, and draw attention to themselves by placing flowers in their hair and other means.'

Nott grunted. 'Oh, we have tried to persuade the ladies of the need to change their sartorial habits, but it is the fashion, and that is answer enough at Tahiti as well as Paris.' The old man stood up. 'But here, Captain FitzRoy, let me make you a present, in honour of your visit.' So saying, he reached up to a shelf and, with surprising strength, heaved down a large leatherbound volume that lay there. 'It is the Good Book, as translated into Tahitian. One of the first copies.'

'You are too generous, Mr Nott. I was not aware that your great work had been printed.'

'Printed? This is the Pacific, Captain FitzRoy. There are no printing-works on Tahiti. Every copy is transcribed by hand.'

'By *hand*?'

Amazed, FitzRoy opened the cover. Sure enough, thousands of pages were filled with serried rows of neat and apparently flawless script. 'But, Mr Nott, I cannot possibly accept the fruits of this – this *immense* labour.'

'Nonsense. It gives the Tahitians something to do, and diverts them from their formerly licentious ways.'

After dinner of roasted breadfruit, wild plantain and coconut milk, with pipes and snuff to follow, FitzRoy and Darwin were taken on a tour of the Matavai mission school. In a simple white-painted schoolroom, a young, smiling Tahitian deacon had charge of a class of perfectly drilled juniors, who rose to attention wearing identical shapeless smocks. Once again, FitzRoy regretfully called to mind the infants' school at Walthamstow, where the brooding figure of York had lurked amid the children, mulling over his grand plan. Once again, he felt humbled by the industry and dedication of the men from the London Missionary Society. He and Darwin bade a formal greeting to the class.

'The captain wishes you happiness,' the deacon made clear to his beaming pupils.

'And we wish happiness to the captain,' responded a small boy in the front row, seemingly unbidden.

'Should the captain and Mr Darwin like to see the children perform for their benefit?' the deacon asked respectfully.

'Why, yes, that would be most agreeable. Perhaps a little Tahitian dance?'

A confused hush fell upon the class.

'I am sorry, sir,' chimed the boy at the front with a polite smile, 'but dancing is forbidden in Tahiti, along with all other frivolous entertainments. Anyone caught dancing is to be reported to the watchman, who will take them to the district governor to be punished *most* severely.'

The following day the *Beagle*'s cutter was hoisted out, and FitzRoy and his officers were rowed along a twisting seven-mile channel in the coral to Papiete, the capital, where they attended morning service at the English church. The building was an eyesore, a high, box-shaped structure resembling a Thames brewery, its ugly gabled roof dwarfing the elegant thatching of the surrounding huts. The service, conducted by a Mr Pritchard in both English and Tahitian, was an interminable affair that taxed the patience even of Sulivan. The congregation of some six hundred souls – although kept in order by a beadle with a white wand – began to shuffle and whisper long before the end. Many of the worshippers wore European clothes, sent from London and distributed apparently at random: big, burly Tahitian men had forced themselves into coats so small the seams had split, their arms protruding from their shoulders like the sails of a windmill; while small children sat marooned in enormous benjamins, their hands unable to reach their cuffs, thereby giving the impression that they had been chopped off.

When the service had finished and the congregation had filed out, FitzRoy sat alone in the front pew and waited, while his officers formed a guard of honour outside the main door; for it was here, in the English church following the service, that Queen Pomare had decreed that he might have his audience. He did not have long to wait. After some fifteen minutes spent in contemplation of the task Commodore Mason had given him, he heard the clack of the heavy iron latch lifting from its slot, and the creak of the door as it swung slowly open. The Queen of Tahiti entered, followed by a phalanx of her tribal chiefs, grey-haired but muscular, tattooed and stripped to the waist. FitzRoy rose.

Queen Pomare was a vast woman, almost spherical in shape, loosely dressed in a long, dark, simple gown, fastened at the throat like a priest's cassock. Her hair was divided into two simple braids. She held no regalia, and wore no crown. Nor, in fact, was she wearing anything at all upon her head, hands or feet, nor any kind of girdle or sash to confine her dress. No ceremony attended her arrival. She walked alone up the aisle to meet him, wistfully but gracefully, an air of melancholy pervading her expression. It was clear that her undoubted piety derived from the teachings of the missionaries, but FitzRoy could not help lamenting, for her sake, that her sense of ceremony appeared to have been discarded in the process. Almost embarrassed at finding himself alone with the monarch, he bowed low before her.

'Your Majesty. I am Captain FitzRoy, of His Majesty's brig *Beagle*. I come to you on official business, as a representative of His Majesty King William IV of Great Britain, and most humbly request an audience.'

'Come, Fitirai. Sit with me.'

So saying, the Queen wedged herself into an adjoining pew – not even one of the principal pews by the pulpit, but a rough-hewn public bench. Unable to sit behind or in front of her, for that would have entailed one of them having to twist in their seat, FitzRoy slid in alongside the ample monarch.

'Your Majesty, a British vessel, the *Truro*, was fishing for pearl oysters in the Low Islands, that you call the Paamotu Islands, and was plundered of her catch by the islanders. The government of His Majesty King William has set the compensation for the plunder at two thousand eight hundred dollars, to be paid by Your Majesty's government at once.'

'I know about this ship *Truro*, Fitirai. The islanders of Paamotu live by their pearls. Then the *Truro* came, a big ship, to take away all their pearl oysters. The chief was not asked. No money was given.'

FitzRoy coloured. Really, he had been given an abominable task. 'Unfortunately, Your Majesty, under our law one cannot own the sea, or the creatures that live therein. In law, the men of the *Truro* had every right to fish there.'

'If the men of Paamotu came to the shores of Britain in a big ship and took all the oysters from one place, would the government of King William give its blessing?'

FitzRoy did not reply. Both of them knew the answer perfectly well.

The Queen continued: 'The men of Paamotu are warlike, Fitirai. I cannot make them do my bidding. When my husband the King was alive, it was different. His word was law. But the men of Paamotu will not do the bidding of a woman. Pomare is my husband's family name. My name was once Aimatta. I took my husband's name when he died, but I am not strong like the true Pomare. If I command the men of Paamotu to pay, they will fight rather than obey me.'

'You understand, Your Majesty, what will happen if payment is not made? There will be many ships, big ships with cannon. A harsh punishment will be exacted. I wish it were not so but—'

'I can see that it is not your wish, Fitarai. I know the money must be paid. We have no choice. My people are but weak children. We often expect to see our island taken from us, and ourselves driven off.'

'Your Majesty...I assure you – Great Britain has an extent of territory far greater than is sufficient for her wishes. Conquest is not her object. I come here only in search of justice.' The word 'justice' tasted like ash on his tongue.

'We wish to do our duty, Fitarai. But I do not possess two thousand eight hundred dollars. This is a huge sum of money. Pray excuse me while I speak with my chiefs.'

FitzRoy withdrew, and a small deputation of the Queen's advisers was summoned from the back of the church. A period of hushed consultation followed, before he was called back.

'I have decided, Fitirai. You shall have all the money in the royal coffer. The people of Papiete shall pay the rest.'

FitzRoy was aghast.

'But Your Majesty, the innocent natives of Otaheite ought not to suffer for the misdeeds of the Low Islanders. This is not justice.'

One of the chiefs answered on her behalf. 'The honour of the Queen is our honour. We will share her difficulties. We have determined to unite in her cause, and pay the fine demanded by the *manua*.'

The Queen fixed her sad gaze upon FitzRoy. 'My name, Aimatta. In our language, it means "the eater of eyes". There was a time when my people ate the flesh of other people. The men of Great Britain have brought the word of God to these islands, and have replaced the old ways with God's law, which must be obeyed. The law of Great Britain, they tell me, is God's law. So if it is written in God's law that we must pay, then we must pay.'

'Your Majesty…I thank you profoundly, in the name of King William and all my countrymen, for your wisdom and generosity. I hope Your Majesty and all the chiefs of Tahiti will do me the great honour of visiting the *Beagle*, and allowing my officers and crew to entertain you before we go off to England.'

'Thank you, Fitirai. You are a kind man. I accept your invitation.'

The Queen smiled and inclined her head, and the various chiefs followed suit. FitzRoy felt only a burning sense of shame.

The following day a trestle table, knocked together quickly by May, was set up in the lee of the church, just by the main door, where the big square bastion of Anglicanism blocked out the light of the rising sun. A strongbox sat on the tablecloth in front of Lieutenant Sulivan, and a ledger lay before Lieutenant Wickham. An armed marine stood guard to either side, while FitzRoy paced about in an agitated frame of mind. A line of Tahitians queued to make their contributions, male and female, young and old, some virtually naked, some in their ill-fitting European clothes. There were elderly, stooped men clutching clay pots containing their life savings. There were small children, single coins clasped sweatily in their palms. Many of the islanders who had sold livestock and historical artefacts at the impromptu market on the *Beagle*'s maindeck were present, returning the coins they had accumulated so assiduously that day.

'Dash it, sir, this is rotten,' said Sulivan bitterly. 'Absolutely rotten.'

'It's a confounded filthy matter,' Wickham agreed, his jaw set tight. 'I didn't join the Service to go about the world stripping good Christian nations bare in this pinchbeck manner.'

'You do not need to tell me, gentlemen,' said FitzRoy with a scowl. Anger and embarrassment fought to overwhelm his customary good manners. Savagely, he kicked a stone into the grass.

'I feel like one of the moneylenders in the temple,' complained Sulivan.

I was brought up to obey orders, FitzRoy told himself. *To do my duty. But increasingly I am being given orders that do not tally with natural justice – with God's justice. Orders that I cannot in all conscience accord with. These people should be helped to found a decent, God-fearing society – not plundered, as if the Royal Navy were little better than pirates. Little better, even, than General Rosas.*

After four hours' march, the width of the ravine scarcely exceeded that of the bed of the stream, and near-vertical walls of volcanic lava a thousand feet high hemmed in the party on either side. Yet in the soft, porous rock, splashed by innumerable waterfalls and warmed by the steaming, humid climate, ferns, small trees, wild bananas and trailing plants sprang from every ledge or crevice. Using dead tree trunks as ladders, clambering up rock chimneys and knife-edge ridges, and employing ropes where necessary, they inched their way up the gorge. Darwin had scaled mightier mountains than this, but none so precarious or precipitous. Finally, after several hours of sweat-drenched effort, they hauled themselves out on to a cool, windswept plateau at the head of a waterfall. The view was spectacular.

'Good Lord, Covington – what I would forfeit for a cold beer!' he gasped, forgetting for the hundredth time that his remarks were falling literally upon deaf ears; not, he mused, that the response would have been very different in former days.

'Beer, very good!' giggled Hitote, one of the Tahitian guides. 'But no tell missionary!' He put one finger to his lips.

It was hard to see, up here, what they would do for food or shelter. The Tahitians had been insistent about the futility of lugging supplies up to the heights, particularly with regard to the delicately mooted suggestion of bringing an entire bed. Surely, now, they would have to furnish a miracle?

Furnish a miracle they did, however – constructing an entire house in a matter of minutes from bamboo-stems and banana-leaves, bound together with strips of bamboo-bark. Then, producing a small net from his loincloth, Hitote dived into the stream above the waterfall, flashing back and forth through the water like an otter, before emerging with a wriggling netful of tiny fish and freshwater prawns. A wild lily-root, sweet as treacle, would serve as pudding. A fire was lit, the dinner was cooked, grace was said, and finally the party fell upon their feast.

Shading the banks of the stream were the dark, knotted stems of a plant Darwin had not seen before, each leaf a sultry green ace of spades. 'What is that plant, Hitote?'

The Tahitian grinned conspiratorially. '*Ava.* Very good. Chew *ava*, see many strange things, feel good. When missionaries find *ava*, they burn it. Missionaries say is devil's plant. *Ava* only left now in mountains. You want try?'

Purely in the spirit of scientific enquiry, Darwin accepted a slice after dinner. He found it acrid and unpleasant on the tongue, but before long a sense of well-being crept over him. He and Hitote sat out on the grass before the cliff-edge, gazing down upon the lavish sweep of the landscape, watching the play and interplay of colour, outline and shape as the sun's slanting rays and the gentle mountain breezes set the leaves dancing with each other, not just seeing but *feeling* the radiance of God's universe as its beauty swept over them. Darwin's eyes followed the course of the stream down the valley to Point Venus: there, opposite the stream's outflow, was a break in the encircling reef, where the *Beagle* lay at anchor, her officers no doubt carrying out depth-sounding experiments on the coral. Tiny men on a tiny boat, lost in a vista that he alone could see in its entirety, that he alone had the vision to encompass.

For years, men had thought that coral reefs grew up thousands of feet from the sea bed. Then Lyell, not unreasonably pointing out that coral cannot live below ten fathoms, had postulated that it grew instead from the rims of submerged volcanoes that were themselves rising from the seabed. His was the very latest theory on coral atolls. Lyell, however, had no answer to the reefs that fringed the Pacific's tropical coasts. Why was there a line of coral along the shore, then a further wall of it, half a mile off the beach? Lyell did not know. None of them knew. For Darwin, floating high above them all, the pieces of the universe suddenly seemed to fit together, as if part of a gigantic jigsaw. For if there was dead coral below the ten-fathom mark, then it must once have grown in the light zone nearer the surface. The coral was not *rising*, or it would have been pushed clean out of the water, like the sea beaches he had seen high in the Andes. The coral was *falling*. As it fell below ten fathoms each little creature died, while its fellows above struggled to grow back towards the surface. Coral atolls were the rims of volcanoes that had *sunk* below the surface. The fringing reef? Why, the fringing reef marked the line of an old beach, thrust suddenly below the surface – that was why there was a break in it, opposite the mouth of the stream, and opposite every stream, because the freshwater torrent would have cut through it in the days when it lined the shore. Coral was a shore creature. The coral out on the reef had suddenly found itself marooned in open water following the descent of the land, the Pacific falling as the Andes rose into the clouds.

Darwin lay back in the grass, a sense of profound relaxation stealing over him, while his mind floated away, high above their little eyrie, high above the limpid shallows of the lagoon and the dark, heaving waters of the ocean beyond.

'I have to hand it to you, Philos – you're a deuced marvel! You really do take the palm for deduction.'

'Well, I must confess, I did have a little…help.'

FitzRoy and Darwin had squeezed into the latter's cabin, the library shelves crammed not just with books these days, but with snakes and insects in jars, armadillo shells, stuffed birds and lizards, all the accoutrements of a natural-history museum in miniature. Darwin, who had outlined his theory of reef formation to FitzRoy, sat at the chart table, examining a section of live coral beneath his microscope.

'I could not swear to it,' he pronounced, 'but it appears to reproduce – asexually. There are similar creatures by the shore at Edinburgh. I used to wade through the shallows of Leith harbour with Professor Grant. "Zoophytes", he called them, plants that reproduce by releasing free-swimming eggs.'

'If it released an egg, how could it be a plant?'

'Well, like the coral, it is a creature so close to both categories that one could happily place it in either. They are animals *arranged* as plants.'

Both men sensed where the conversation might be headed. Professor Grant, scourge of the late unlamented McCormick, was a follower of Lamarck. Tiny sea creatures arranged as plants afforded perhaps the only real ammunition for the transmutationists as to the origins of animal life.

'It is a fine evening. Shall we take a stroll upon the deck?'

Darwin readily agreed to FitzRoy's diversion, and folded away his microscope. The pair walked out on to the maindeck, sidestepping a huddle of giant tortoises conspiratorially mulching a mound of green leaves, and headed for the starboard rail, where they stood in silence and drank in the view. The coconut palms lining the shore cut jet-black silhouettes into the purple evening sky. A loose-limbed youth was shinning with no apparent difficulty up one of the featureless tree trunks. Along the beach, a line of little cooking-fires blazed, putting FitzRoy in mind of the bonfires of Tierra del Fuego. Was it only a year and a half since they had braved the thundering seas and lashing rain of South America's wild tip, and gained admittance to that isolated, mysterious world, primitive man's last true kingdom on earth? It seemed like a lifetime ago. There the dogs had barked, the drums had beaten out their primal tattoo, and the surf had curled unchecked against the rocky shore. Here, the flames were reflected in the mirror of the lagoon, glittering like gems, and in their glow little children played, or sat in companionable circles singing sweet-voiced hymns, melodious and clear.

'What an opportunity for writing love-letters,' mused Darwin. 'Oh, that I had a sweet Virginia to send an inspired epistle to!'

The next evening, every one of the ship's boats was hoisted out and dispatched, under the reliable command of Mr Stokes, to ferry Queen Pomare and her retinue to the *Beagle*. May had rigged up a jury-cradle, so that Her gracious but undeniably weighty Majesty could be lifted aboard with all due dignity. A salute could not be fired, of course, for fear of disturbing the chronometers, but the ship was dressed with flags, and the crew sent into the yards to stand to attention and give Her Majesty a rousing three cheers as she rose slowly from the cutter. The poop deck had been cleared of tortoises, and a long table had been laid with linen, silverware and candles. So many years into the voyage, the fare was of necessity extremely simple, and FitzRoy thought it no meal to put before a queen; he was conscious throughout of trying his damnedest to compensate for the shabby way in which she had been treated. But there were fireworks after the meal: every rocket, blue light and false-fire to be found on the ship was lit. All were received rapturously by the royal party, as well as prompting a chorus of ooohs from the Tahitians lining the bay. There were presents for each guest, followed by the entertainment: chairs were drawn up, and the best singers and musicians among the crew brought out to perform before the assembled dignitaries.

'I should like to present Harper, our sailmaker, singing "Rule Britannia",' announced Coxswain Bennet, to commence the concert.

'Peace be with you and your King William,' replied the Queen, smiling at him.

Harper's mellifluous baritone having been well received, Bennet stepped up once again to introduce Wills, the armourer, accompanied by Billet, the gunroom boy, performing 'Three Jolly Postboys'. It was a jaunty number, and the watching crew began to tap their feet and clap along. It soon became apparent, however, that something was wrong. The Tahitians were whispering and muttering among themselves in worried tones, and Queen Pomare's customary expression of placid melancholy had been replaced by one of genuine distress. FitzRoy waved the two performers to a halt. 'Pray forgive me, Your Majesty, but is something the matter?'

'This is not a hymn, Fitirai?' asked Pomare in dismay.

'No, Your Majesty. This is a...a sea song, not a hymn.'

'But, Fitirai – the singing of songs is forbidden in Tahiti, except hymns. Singing is one of the illicit pleasures, forbidden by God's law. We have followed God's commands, as told to us by your British missionaries. This is God's way. It is the British way. What is going on? I do not understand.'

CHAPTER FOURTEEN

The Bay of Islands, New Zealand, 21 December 1835

Viewed through the spyglass, the little village of Kororareka seemed quiet enough, a drab and undistinguished huddle beneath a range of low, drizzly hills. Three whaling ships sprawled lazily at anchor, and the occasional solitary canoe could be seen pottering across the bay, but there was no boisterous welcome like the one that had greeted the *Beagle* in Tahiti. New Zealand's only English settlement presented a tidy, reticent aspect to the sea, as if its back were turned. Any closer inspection would have to wait, for the ship lay becalmed at the entrance of the Bay of Islands. Darwin, who had been feeling seasick for a week, used the respite to pace the poop deck irritably.

'Another wretched island. There is nothing I so much long for, as to see *any* spot or object which I have seen before, or *any* which I am likely to see again! To think this will be our *fifth* Christmas away from home!'

'We are all of us homesick, Philos,' muttered FitzRoy, as Darwin stalked past.

'I feel sure that the scenery of England is ten times more beautiful than anywhere else we have seen on our travels. What reasonable person can wish for great ill-proportioned mountains, two and three miles high? Give me the Brythen, or some such compact little hill!'

Wickham and Stokes exchanged the faintest of grins.

'As for your boundless plains and impenetrable forests, who would compare them with the green fields and oak woods of England? People are pleased to talk of the ever-smiling sky of the tropics – what precious nonsense! Who admires a lady's face who is always smiling? England is not one of your insipid beauties. She can cry, and frown, and smile, all by turns.'

'Actually, when I went to Shropshire it looked rather like this,' offered

King, helpfully. 'Imagine that those ferns behind the shore are meadows, and you will see the similarity at once...'

The young midshipman tailed off, as Darwin glared at him.

'Come on, Philos,' put in Sulivan cheerily. 'Let's not growl. What is five years around the world, compared to the soldiers' and sailors' lives in India?'

'I did not sign up to be a sailor! Not for five years, at least. And I am convinced that it is a most ridiculous thing to go round the world. Stay at home quietly, and the world will go round with you.'

With that, he stomped off to his cabin.

A light breeze picked up after dinner and gently ballooned the *Beagle*'s sails, enabling them to reach anchorage by early afternoon. FitzRoy, Sulivan and Bennet went ashore in the cutter. When they arrived at the main thoroughfare of Kororareka, they discovered that appearances had indeed been deceptive. The place was a pit.

A mucous coating of mud and faeces lined the main street, splattered by passing footsteps up the rough wooden walls of the adjoining buildings. Every second dwelling was either a spirit-shop, a musket-seller's or a public house. It seemed that the entire population – to judge from the evidence of those on view – was blind drunk. Two men were fighting at the end of the village. A whore, crawling on all fours, was retching up a thin stream of vomit, consoled by a scarcely less sober companion. A man with a Newcastle accent shouted meaningless obscenities at anyone who would listen. Everyone, worryingly, appeared to be armed. A heavily tattooed native, pasted with filth and wrapped in a grubby blanket, lurched towards them shouting angrily. 'You English captain! You help me!'

FitzRoy halted – he had little option, as the man had blocked his path – while Bennet moved protectively to the front in case the skipper needed rescuing.

'I am Captain FitzRoy. How may I help?'

'Englishman steal my wife! Take on whale-ship! You get my wife back!'

'Then you must call out the watch. The authorities.'

The man's face was a mask of furious incomprehension.

'Who is in charge here? Who is boss?' asked FitzRoy firmly.

'You English captain! You boss!'

Another native, long-haired and raw-boned, as well built and ferocious as the first, his face a whorl of angry black tattoo-cuts, bore down upon them. 'You help me!' he shouted. 'I work on whale-ship one year. Promise me big money. Leave ship, no money! White man steal my money!'

A drunken white woman cackled at them from a puddle of her own urine.

'Gentlemen – please!' FitzRoy managed briefly to silence the furious complainants. 'Who is the chief here?'

'No chief. This is white-man town!'

'Who is the British chief? The British resident?'

The second native jabbed a finger accusingly towards the far end of the street, whereupon the two supplicants fell to arguing with each other.

'Is it not mystifying?' pondered a troubled Sulivan, as the trio picked their way through the clinging mud. 'In a pleasant climate, surrounded by beautiful countryside, can one account for human nature degrading itself so much as to live in such a den?'

Bennet, who remembered his excursion into the rookeries behind Oxford Street with the three Fuegians, kept his thoughts to himself.

The main thoroughfare petered out at the foot of a small hill, atop which two flags fluttered gracefully from a white pole: the Union Jack, and another they did not recognize, a red cross on a blue background. The cottage of Bushby, the British resident, was the last house in the street. After they had pounded upon the front door for some minutes, a metal hatch was finally opened, and two frightened eyes peered out from behind a pair of cracked spectacles. Seeing their naval uniforms, the resident drew back a platoon of bolts and let them in, casting a furtive glance up and down the street before rebolting the door behind them. He beckoned them to follow him down a little corridor, scuttling ahead like a pursued mole, into a dark and shuttered parlour. Mr Bushby's left arm, they noticed, hung uselessly in a sling.

'Are you wounded, sir?' enquired Sulivan solicitously, once the introductions had been made.

'I was shot,' explained Bushby bluntly, 'during the course of a robbery upon this very house. The swine would have murdered me, but I escaped through the back door. Barely a day goes by, gentlemen, without another murder being added to the charge-sheet of villainy that shames this settlement.'

'Can you not take action against the miscreants?' asked FitzRoy. 'In a place this size, surely it must be possible to identify them?'

The resident laughed sardonically, a high-pitched little bark that escaped from his throat in a rush, his hands pawing nervously at his side-whiskers. 'I am a resident, gentlemen. I reside here. That is my sole occupation. I am not granted even the power of a magistrate. I am here to observe. There are no laws, no police and no judges to prevent the vicious, worthless inhabitants of this vile hole practising whatever excesses they wish – be it drunkenness, adultery or murder. They are escaped convicts, for the most part, from New South Wales – although the whalers are no better. They are the very dregs of the earth, all of them – a fact which, had I been apprised of it in London, would have militated against my taking the position.' Bushby shuddered at the full realization of what he had got himself into.

'But what of the New Zealanders themselves – the natives?' asked Sulivan. 'Do they posses no authority?'

'None in Kororareka, to be sure,' said Bushby bitterly. 'The chiefs only stopped fighting each other long enough to declare New Zealand a sovereign nation seven weeks ago. That is the new flag up on the hill. But this is a nation in name only. It is the New Zealanders themselves who require protection from the abuses of the worst of our citizenry. I tell you, gentlemen, these islands are gone to the very devil.' The resident drew his coat about him and quivered with silent outrage.

'Pray excuse my asking, but what do you actually do here, given that you are denied the opportunity to exercise authority?' enquired FitzRoy.

'I grow vines. In my garden. Prior to taking up this position, I journeyed through France and Spain, solely for the purpose of collecting vines to grow in my adopted country. The climate here is most admirable for the production of wine. You shall see, gentlemen – at a future day not only the citizens of New Zealand but of Australia, too, will have cause to thank me, and to acknowledge my foresight.'

'I do not doubt it,' said FitzRoy hurriedly, for a fervent gleam of enthusiasm had appeared in Bushby's eyes. 'And what of the missionaries? We seek a clergyman by the name of Matthews.'

Bushby's own missionary glow faded as quickly as it had ignited. 'Matthews? Matthews is at Waimate. Would that I were at Waimate, and not stationed here at the pointless behest of His Majesty.'

'Waimate? Is it far?'

'It is but fifteen miles' walk. I shall take you there.'

The following day, augmented by Darwin and the *Beagle*'s own Reverend Mr Matthews, the party set out for Waimate, along a well-worn path cut through tall, waving ferns. At intervals they passed mean clusters of native houses, flea-ridden, smoky, windowless ovens in Bushby's derisive estimation. At one point they encountered a funeral ceremony, if that was indeed the correct word: the deceased, a woman, had been shaved, painted bright scarlet and staked out upright, flanked by two canoes driven vertically into the soil and surrounded by a ring of little wooden idols. As her macabre, rotting face looked on, her relatives beat themselves and tore at their own flesh until they were covered with clotted blood, in a communal howl of grief.

'By all that's holy,' said a shivering Matthews, who wondered if he had not merely exchanged the frying-pan for the fire.

'When Cook first discovered the island,' said Bushby, 'the New Zealanders threw stones at his ship and shouted, "Come ashore and we shall eat you all."'

'Phrenologically speaking, these are people of the most savage kind,' said Darwin.

They pressed on quickly.

Presently they came to a small creek, which had to be forded. Bushby kept a skiff tied up in the reeds, and as he untethered it a fiercely tattooed old chief, wreathed in a stinking blanket, appeared through the undergrowth and stepped into the boat, muttering a cursory word or two in his own language.

'They like to ride in the skiff. Sort of a pleasure cruise,' explained Bushby, as the chief took a seat unbidden opposite the Englishmen.

'I don't think I have ever seen a more horrid and ferocious expression,' whispered Darwin. 'It reminds me of one of the characters in Retzsch's outlines to Schiller's "Ballad of Fridolin".'

'It is not an expression,' said Bushby. 'The tattoo incisions destroy the play of the superficial muscles, giving an air of permanent aggression. The designs are actually heraldic ornaments.'

'Fascinating,' said FitzRoy. 'So all those cuts and whorls are the armorial bearings of a knightly warrior.'

'He can speak English, by the bye,' said Bushby.

'Good morning to you sir,' said Sulivan politely. The old chief bestowed a look upon him, which could have been anything from a friendly smile to a glare of demonic rage.

Matthews shuddered.

As they stepped out of the skiff at the end of their short trip up the creek, the New Zealander spoke. 'Do not you stay long. I shall be tired of waiting here,' he commanded Bushby, who ignored him.

'Good day sir,' said Sulivan.

'The hoary old villain,' muttered Darwin, when they were safely out of earshot.

Matthews, who had found it difficult since Tierra del Fuego even to say good morning to the captain without feeling guilty, remained silent, lost in his own thoughts and fears. But he need not have worried: after three hours' further walk through the ferns, the most extraordinary vista opened before them.

'Waimate, gentlemen,' said Bushby, with a wave of the hand.

There, placed as if by an enchanter's wand, was a fragment of old England. A church set amid golden cornfields; thatched cottages clustered around a stream, with a waterwheel to drive a little flour mill; orchards, groaning with every kind of ripe fruit; pigs and poultry running about, squealing and clucking; a barn, for threshing and winnowing, and a blacksmith's forge. To cap it all, a game of cricket was taking place on an adjoining meadow, the shouts of the white-clad players mingling with the thrum of insects carried past on the summer breeze.

'By the Lord Harry!' exclaimed Darwin.

The others stood open-mouthed; Matthews looked as if he would weep with relief.

'All of it constructed within these past ten years,' said Bushby.

'It certainly inspires high hopes for the future progress of this fine island,' marvelled FitzRoy.

A native miller came to the door of the mill, and waved a polite good-day. His face was powdered white with flour.

'How very admirable,' said Darwin.

'Yours is the most extraordinary achievement, and we salute you for it,' said FitzRoy. 'Following our experiences of Kororareka, your mission was the very last thing we expected to see on these benighted shores.'

'Kororareka is known as "the Pacific Hell" for good reason, Captain,' replied the Reverend Clarke, earnest and long-nosed. 'Satan maintains his dominion there without molestation.'

'Sad to say, in nearly all the affrays there, it is the white man who is the aggressor,' said the older, graver Reverend Davies alongside him. 'Ignorance of the local language, customs or taboo marks has not caused so many quarrels as have deliberate insult, deceit or intoxication. As a nation we have cause to be ashamed.'

Four reverend missionaries sat around the farmhouse table: Messrs Clarke, Davies, Williams and Matthews. The elder Matthews, married to Davies's daughter, was an altogether more confident and inspiring character than his younger brother, whom he had not seen since the latter was a small boy. His delight at being reunited so unexpectedly with his sibling was genuinely affecting. The younger Matthews, for his part, had recovered some of the unctuous self-possession that had characterized his arrival aboard the *Beagle*, and was now basking vicariously in the glow of his brother's achievements. Together, the missionaries exuded a pious eagerness and generosity of spirit, undercut by that slight air of anxiety common to all pioneers in potentially hostile lands. The final member of the welcoming party, though, was an interesting exception: an elderly New

Zealander, tall and spindly as a church steeple, attired in a shabby, long-tailed coat and threadbare pantaloons, his heavily tattooed face surmounted by a battered top hat. The old gentleman sat grinning and sipping tea from a cracked china cup, saying nothing but seeming thoroughly to relish the occasion.

'We are fighting a war,' said the elder Matthews, fist clenched, a flame in his youthful eyes. 'A war against ignorance and savagery, not just among the native population, where God's blessings have yet to percolate, but among those of our own kind who have relapsed from the state of grace that our civilization affords them.'

'My own feelings exactly,' said the younger Matthews, drawing confidence from his brother's stout piety. 'When the ranks of savages attacked the mission at Woollya, with their spears and their stones, I felt myself to be God's warrior, at war with the sins of ignorance and covetousness. I fought as bravely as I could, of course – had I a real army at my back I could have achieved something that day – but, being alone, my efforts were doomed to failure, and I was overwhelmed.'

Those who had been present when the drenched and beardless Matthews, gibbering with fear, had hurtled yelling into the lead whaleboat at Woollya, immediately formed a mental image somewhat at odds with the picture painted by the missionary; but for his fellows, his words seemed as hot coals upon the fire of their enthusiasm.

'Your efforts in Tierra del Fuego do *not* constitute a failure, gentlemen,' said the pale, whippet-like Mr Clarke. 'They are a most promising first step. You have lit a spark in that country, which, by God's grace, will never go out. Why, your experiences sound similar to our own first steps in this country. We too failed at first, but by God's blessing upon our exertions, we have at last succeeded far beyond our expectations.'

FitzRoy felt himself encouraged, consoled and strangely touched by their optimistic concern.

'When we first came here,' said Mr Williams, a stout, jovial Welshman with the air of a medieval archer, 'the New Zealanders' warlike tendencies had to be seen to be believed. One tribe went to war, I remember, because they possessed a barrel of gunpowder that would have gone to waste were it not used up!' He gurgled with laughter at the memory. 'Such attitudes can take a long time to change, is that not so, Chief Waripoaka?'

The old man at the end of the table continued to grin silently, but his steady gaze gleamed briefly at the mention of his name.

'Chief Waripoaka here was once a cannibal. But he was the first chief to be converted to God's word, and it was by his personal intervention, back in 1814, that our erstwhile colleagues King and Kendal were saved from being killed and eaten.'

At last, the wrinkled old fellow spoke, intoning his words like the tolling of a bell: 'Wonderful white men! Fire, water, earth and air are made to work for them by their wisdom, while we New Zealanders can only command the labour of our own bodies.'

'Now the chief drinks tea, instead of…' Williams paused, and opted to change tack rather than complete the sentence. 'We will not hear of your calling the Woollya mission a failure.'

'Jemmy is a spark all right, he's a bright spark,' said Sulivan, 'but he's a tiny spark in an almighty darkness.'

'We will send word to London,' said Williams. 'We in the Church Missionary Society have the whole organization of the Anglican Church at our backs. We do not operate independently of authority and of each other, like the London Missionary Society. We are no catechists, plucked untrained from ordinary life. We are professional men, trained in holy orders, a veritable army of God. We will have London send missionaries to Tierra del Fuego – a host of missionaries – to make contact with this Jemmy Button of yours, and kindle your spark into a blazing fire.'

Was it possible? Was it too much to hope for? A properly organized and equipped missionary effort, sent to the relief of Jemmy Button? FitzRoy could only dare to believe.

Mr Davies, apparently the *de facto* leader of the group, spread his hands in a gesture of restraint. 'I should stress that we are normally constrained to act only within a diocese of the Anglican Church. New Zealand falls within the diocese of New South Wales. But given that Tierra del Fuego is virgin territory, under no formal ecclesiastical control, I see no reason why Lambeth Palace might not be persuaded to make an exception. Be assured that we will do everything in our power to assist you, Captain FitzRoy.' The creases about Davies's eyes tightened imperceptibly. 'But we, too, should be most grateful were you to lend your reputation in assisting us.'

'How may I help you, gentlemen? You have only to ask.'

'A book has been published – a most regrettable book – which is gaining some notoriety but which paints an entirely false picture of the work we do here. You and your colleagues, as men of repute, can testify upon your return to England that this volume does not speak the truth, before any more damage can be done.'

'What is this book?'

Davies produced a slim, leatherbound volume: *Narrative of a Nine Months' Residence in New Zealand*, by Augustus Earle.

'Earle,' said FitzRoy, his eyes wide.

'By the Lord Harry!'

Sulivan, beside him, and Bennet, respectfully standing guard by the door, were instantly alert.

'You know him?'

'He was briefly our ship's artist,' confessed FitzRoy. 'But I had no knowledge…'

'Your former colleague was our guest here in 1827. Now he damns us for foisting Christianity upon a people "ill-adapted" to receive God's word. He claims that our "narrow outlook" has killed the "innocent gaiety" of the New Zealanders. I quote: "Any man of common sense must agree with me that a savage can receive but little benefit from having the abstruse points of the Gospel preached to him, if his mind is not prepared to receive them." I can see no logic to his reasoning. For how can any human mind not be ready to receive the word of God?'

'The man lived openly in sin – fornicated, no less – with a native woman,' huffed Mr Williams, all trace of his former jollity gone. 'If he had an interest about the "innocent gaiety" of the New Zealanders, it was with a view to plundering it for the benefit of his openly licentious habits!'

'Mr Williams is criticized by name in Mr Earle's volume,' said the elder Matthews, quietly. 'He is openly accused of lacking hospitality. Yet I know that my colleague here always treated Mr Earle with far more civility than his open licentiousness could have given reason to expect. Perhaps Mr Earle was disappointed at not finding the field of licentiousness here in New Zealand quite as formerly, on account of our efforts.'

'You see, it is our mission here not just to spread the word of God,' said Mr Clarke, his fingers enmeshed, 'but to suppress licentious habits and ardent spirits. To teach the virtue of covering naked flesh. To help the natives to understand that there is a state of future punishment awaiting those who do not follow the path laid out for them by the Church of England. Some of their customs are most barbarous: for instance, did you know that when a New Zealander falls ill, or meets some calamity, the other members of his tribe – even his family and friends – descend like locusts and rob him of all his belongings? Thus do the strong survive and the weak go to the wall. What kind of Godless system is that, for Earle or any other to advocate?'

'It is disgraceful,' said Darwin.

'You have my word, gentlemen,' vowed FitzRoy, a guilty pink flush about his cheeks. 'I shall use my every and utmost endeavour, upon returning to England, to promote your efforts to civilize the people of New Zealand and to counter Mr Earle's propaganda.'

'Wonderful white men!' intoned the chief.

'More tea, Chief Waripoaka?' said Davies, keen to present a little tableau of civilization.

'Good sweet tea,' said the chief, ladling spoonful after spoonful of sugar into his cup. 'Englishman meat taste too salty. Not taste sweet, like New Zealander. I eat a Captain Boyd once. Whaling captain. Too salty. Now Chief Waripoaka good Christian – no eat human meat. Drink sweet tea instead!'

The old man grinned conspiratorially, and took a big wet slurp from his teacup.

FitzRoy spent the next few days completing tests upon an ocean thermometer he had devised to detect and trace currents in the water. Darwin kept to the library, magnifying-glass fastened to his forehead by an elastic garter, microscope unfolded upon the table. Nobody went ashore: even the crew, it seemed, had little inclination to risk the dangerous fleshpots of Kororareka. New Zealand, it appeared to FitzRoy, was at a crossroads. The settlements of Kororareka and Waimate offered two alternative visions of its future. British intervention was surely now essential, to rein in the excesses of his countrymen and to steer the fledgling nation down the Christian path. A British governor was required, backed up by a considerable force of troops, to restore order and to protect the native population. He would do his utmost, upon returning to England, to press for such a policy to be imposed.

He decided to weigh anchor and head home for England following Christmas dinner. As this could hardly be taken ashore, a small, uninhabited island out in the bay was selected, and Mr Stokes charged with organizing the day's festivities. With preparations well under way, FitzRoy, Bynoe, and King were rowed ashore to see Christmas taking shape. A large area of flat ground had been cleared, and planted with chairs and tables festooned with decorations. A Galapagos turtle was turning slowly on a large spit. At one end of the clearing they found a beaten-down circular area, with the remains of a cooking fire at its centre.

'It was still warm when we got here, although the island is deserted now,' related Stokes. 'Looks like somebody else had their Christmas dinner here before us.'

'Those are mighty big bones,' remarked FitzRoy. 'What are they? Beef? Lamb?'

Bynoe knelt down to have a look.

'Neither, I'm afraid. This is a human femur.'

There was a long silence. Eventually King spoke.

'The deuced filthy black savages.'

FitzRoy looked at him.

'And what makes you so sure, Mr King, that this was not the act of deuced filthy *white* savages?'

CHAPTER FIFTEEN

The English Channel, 1 October 1836

It took the *Beagle* just over nine months to arrive at that glorious morning when, defying the swell, the crew could clamber as one into the yards – not just the deck watch, but the idlers and the off-duty men as well – each hopeful of being the first to see a low, dirty blemish break the distant line of the horizon. Every man aboard had 'Channel fever', as they called it, a desperate, yearning desire to gaze upon the undistinguished blue-grey hills of England's south-western tip. For Charles Darwin, the sea had become a heaving desert, and the previous nine months just so much existence obliterated from the page of his life.

'I loathe, I abhor the sea, and all the ships which sail on it,' he muttered to himself, as his stomach surged and his gorge rose for the thousandth time that week. A blustery autumn gale was driving the *Beagle* up through the western approaches with close-reefed topsails set, the wind at her back, her progress rapid but not rapid enough for her reluctant passenger.

It seemed like an age since they had sailed beneath the revolving red beacon of the lighthouse in Sydney Cove, there to discover not – as expected – a grubby, scratchy little settlement akin to Kororareka, but a glorious gilded boomtown of windmills and white stone mansions shimmering in the heat. The liveried servants standing to attention on the coaches that clattered through the cobbled streets may have been ex-convicts; there may have been precious few gentlewomen in evidence; there may have been no sign of theatres, bookshops, galleries or any other outward manifestation of intellectual life; but there was no denying the incredible vibrancy of Australia's youthful capital. Captain Phillip Parker King was there to meet them, having retired from England to an estate on the Bathurst Road, and keen to reclaim his son. FitzRoy generously consented to Midshipman King's discharge from the Service, and there followed many an anguished farewell, Darwin's parting from his boisterous young friend being one of the saddest. They found Conrad Martens, too, in Sydney, the little Austrian's path having preceded their own footsteps across the Pacific: this was quite a stroke of luck, as it transpired that he had painted many of the locations subsequently visited by the *Beagle*, canvases that FitzRoy and Darwin were able to purchase from their creator at three guineas apiece. Darwin had felt himself obliged to draw a further hundred pounds on his father's account, complaining of Sydney's 'villainously dear' prices.

They had gone on to Hobart, where Darwin had withdrawn a further fifty pounds, and then to King George's Sound in south-western Australia, where they had witnessed an aboriginal *corrobery*: a meet of several hundred painted warriors drawn from two tribes, gathered to dance in contest against each other. The two battle-lines of performers had thrown themselves enthusiastically into terpsichorean imitations of emus and kangaroos, gleaming with sweat in the firelight, to be rewarded for their efforts with a mass handout of rice pudding doled up by the *Beagle*'s crew. Darwin, armed with a ladle, had been the principal server, and had assumed the gracious air of a nanny feeding her charges; although he professed the aboriginal warriors, whose nobility of bearing had been much admired by FitzRoy, to be among the very lowest of barbarians. The following day they had encountered real emus and kangaroos, bizarre strains of animal life so utterly different from any to be found elsewhere that Darwin had seriously begun to wonder whether there might not be two Creators.

May had seen the *Beagle* dock at Cape Town, where FitzRoy and Darwin had dined with the celebrated astronomer Sir John Herschel, who had travelled to southern Africa to witness the passage of Halley's comet. A shy, diffident, highly intelligent man with soil-rimmed fingernails, Sir John had listened with interest to their stories of Augustus Earle, and the missionaries of Waimate. He had subsequently put them in touch with the editor of the *South African Christian Recorder*, who had commissioned a piece – authored jointly by FitzRoy and Darwin – in praise of the missionaries' efforts in the South Pacific. Sir John had also given Darwin his newly published copy of *Volume 4* of Lyell, which promised to rid the voyage home of its threatened *ennui*: Darwin told himself he would eke out each and every one of its precious pages.

Cape Town brought further good news in the shape of letters from home, the first they had encountered in fifteen months. It was new mail: all the intervening correspondence seemed to have vanished into the ether, the sadly probable cause being that a mail packet, perhaps even two, had been lost at sea. There were a couple of letters for FitzRoy, one for Lieutenant Sulivan from Miss Young and, most thrilling of all, a brace of letters for Darwin from his sisters Catherine and Susan. Catherine reported that Professor Henslow had edited a number of Darwin's letters together, to form a paper on the link between earthquakes and the uplift of the Andes, which he had read to the Cambridge Philosophical Society in November: it had, by all accounts, caused a sensation. Public demand had seen the paper printed as a booklet, and Darwin was the name on everyone's tongue in polite society. Dr Darwin had been so proud that he had purchased a huge stack of copies, to be given away to friends and family. Although horrified at the thought of his dashed-off, misspelt prose being published without revision, the doctor's son could hardly fail to be delighted at the news.

Susan reported, meanwhile, that further extracts from his letters had been published in the *Entomological Magazine* at the instigation of Professor Sedgwick, who had given a lecture to the Geological Society of London on the subject of Darwin's findings in South America. No less a figure than Lyell himself had been in the chair, and had apparently been heard to remark: 'How I long for the return of Darwin.' Sedgwick had predicted that his former student would take a place among the leading scientific men should he return safely, while Samuel Butler had forecast that Darwin would surely have a great name among the naturalists of Europe. Darwin had read the letter with shaking hands. 'Papa and we often cogitate over the fire what you will do when you return,' his sister had written, 'as I fear there are but small hopes of your still going into the Church – I think you must turn Professor at Cambridge. We are fond of reading your exploits aloud to Papa. He enjoys it extremely, except when the dangers you run make him shudder.' Emboldened by the extraordinary vision of his father beaming with paternal pride, he had drawn a further thirty pounds on the doctor's account, and had given his pet tortoise Harry an unusually huge meal by way of celebration.

Cape Town should have been the *Beagle*'s last stop, but FitzRoy had infuriated his impatient, ambitious young charge by recrossing the Atlantic, to recheck his longitudinal observations off the Brazilian coast. The diversion had at least afforded Darwin the chance of one final walk in the rainforest: it was a sentimental affair, as he knew in his heart that he would never – could never – leave Britain's shores again. Each of the brilliant and luxuriant sights that swam now before his sated eyes would fade, he knew, like a tale heard in childhood, the living flesh falling from his memories until only the skeleton of bald scientific fact remained, all those morsels of vibrant beauty reduced to a cold, inexorable agglomeration of statistics with which he would build a career. Ultimately, it was not something he regretted, for his career promised to be the most beautiful creation of all. And, as he reminded himself, his first glimpse of home would surely be better than the united kingdoms of all the glorious tropics.

The undulating months that passed, slow and tiresome, on the rising and falling Atlantic, were spent ordering and organizing the fruits of the voyage. Darwin discovered that he possessed no fewer than 1529 specimens preserved in spirits, and 3907 labelled skins, bones and other dried specimens. Covington was put to cataloguing each one by class, in his large, round, painstaking hand. The other officers had their collections to organize too, even though all had generously donated their most impressive specimens to the philosopher. Then there were the live animals on board: a Brazilian coatimundi, several Patagonian wild dogs, a Falklands fox and, of course, Darwin's giant tortoise. FitzRoy was tied up with the main business of the voyage, the editing and production of charts and sailing directions. He had dispatched more than a hundred maps to the Admiralty already: by the time he finished the men of the *Beagle* would have produced a staggering 202 charts and plans, a task that would require a minimum of two years' hard toil in London for him to complete.

There remained, of course, the matter of the book that FitzRoy and Darwin were due to write. The two men had been getting on extremely well of late, persuaded by their labours away from confrontation and into their private corners, but both knew that a deal had to be struck regarding the more contentious areas of the exercise. What would it say about the flood? What would it say about the creation and the extinction of species? About the very origins of life itself? By unspoken consent, they left the discussion until the last possible moment. Finally, on the day of their projected arrival, FitzRoy approached the subject over dinner, via a circuitous route. 'I fear I have been too busy to look at Lyell. Is there anything in his new volume that I should be aware of?'

'He is most interesting concerning the origins of life. He feels that life itself – its boundaries, its rules if you like – are all enshrined in natural laws laid down by God, laws which God Himself is bound to observe.'

'God might *feel* bound to observe His own laws, but He could hardly be *required* to do so. It sounds as if our friend Lyell is fudging the distinction between the laws of nature and the laws of God.'

'Is there a distinction?'

'I should think so. The laws of God, as laid down in the scriptures, are commands – rules composed by the divine legislator, which man disregards at his peril. The laws of nature, like the laws of physics, are not strictly laws. They are unwavering natural occurrences observed by man.'

'Whether they are true laws or not, the laws of nature are nonetheless immutable – for instance, the law of gravity cannot be altered.'

'Indeed. They are observations of fact that cannot be obeyed or disobeyed or altered by those subject to them. In my book, however, a law is a rule, which we as rational beings have the choice to obey or to disobey. It is the God-given power of rational thought that makes all the difference, that makes our relationship to God in His heaven superior to our relationship with nature's earthly power.'

'But, FitzRoy, is it truly logical to suggest that the universe is subject to the laws of nature, whereas mankind alone is subject to the higher law of God? Is thought, which in biological terms is a physical function of the organ of the brain, truly more wonderful than gravity, which is a physical property of matter?'

'Of course it is. It is the very property by which God distinguishes us from the animal kingdom.'

'But animals can think.'

'Not rationally. That is why I take such issue with transmutation and its propagandists. It is a damnable reduction of beauty and intelligence, of strength and purpose, of honour and aspiration. It reduces mankind to a casual aggregation of inert matter. Furthermore, I do not believe such a process can exist, for it is surely impossible, by virtue of those immutable laws of nature you speak about.'

'And yet you believe that men can transmute into angels.'

Both men smiled at this.

'Here, my dear Philos, you have gone beyond the boundaries of nature and into God's heavenly realm. The legislator need hardly legislate in His own kingdom.'

'But, FitzRoy, is it not possible that some kind of transmutation can exist *within* God's law, and *within* the laws of nature? Does the idea of transmutation not frighten you merely becuase it would seem on the face of it to remove the need for God – when in fact that need not be a condition of its existence?'

'I am not frightened by transmutation – I am intellectually, morally and aesthetically repelled by it. Nature is not a progression. No creature is any more or less perfect than its fellows in the eyes of the Lord. Every creature is adapted to the condition and locality for which it is designed. You saw that in the Galapagos. If there has indeed been progress in nature for countless aeons, as you suggest, explain then the persistence of supposedly lower organisms, the primitive, the immobile, the microscopic creatures, all of which have remained completely unchanged since the dawn of time. Furthermore, why are fossilized sharks, crocodiles, tortoises, snakes, bats, frogs and so forth identical to their living brethren? Why have *they* not progressed?'

'If every species has a fixed lifespan, like an individual, then perhaps a transmuted species is the offspring of another, the Lord's way of giving birth to a new family of living creatures?'

'You still believe that entire species vanished from the globe by commonly expiring all at once? That there was no catastrophe? No flood?'

'The geological record, FitzRoy…I mean, where did all that water come *from*?'

'Perhaps the ice at the poles melted and the sea level rose? Who is to say that the earth's temperature has always been constant? Or perhaps there were immense tidal waves? Who is to say that the movement of heavenly bodies has always been constant?'

'But the science of geology now calls the Old Testament story into question. The earth is hundreds of millions of years old, not merely a few thousand!'

'Geology is a young branch of science, which has yet to undergo the trial of experience. I am convinced that in due course it will contribute its share of nourishment and vigour to that tree which springs from an immortal root. If the earth is indeed several hundred million years old, tell me, where has all the excess sodium chloride gone?'

'I beg your pardon?'

'Every year salts pour into the ocean. Yet apparently they have been doing so for hundreds of millions of years without altering its salinity. By now the sea should be a saturated solution, all life within it choked. Yet the fish in the ocean, and the fossil fish that once thrived within it, are identical.'

'I do not know about the salt, but the sea creatures uplifted high into the Andes did not get there in six thousand years, I assure you. The geological record is unequivocal.'

'Every major geologist believes in the flood. Buckland, Conybeare, Silliman in the United States—'

'They are all clergymen. Of course they believe in the flood.'

'So are you. Or, at least, a clergyman in training.'

'Not any more. I shall be a geologist, perhaps, or a naturalist, or both. But I cannot take up holy orders, FitzRoy. I cannot do it.'

'I am saddened to hear so. Why ever not?'

'I simply can no longer believe in the miracles of the scriptures. No sane man could believe in miracles! The more I know of the fixed laws of nature that pertain on this earth, the more incredible do such miracles become.'

'And the miracle of creation?'

'I believe God created all things – but I do not know how. Maybe some random principle applies…'

'Consider a butterfly, Philos. It grows from a caterpillar via an amorphous soup, a mere liquid that fills its chrysalis. The organizing principle of that transformation is external to the material substances involved. Do you not see? There is a pattern to the universe, an order. It is the same with the weather: weather patterns are not random, although they appear so to the untrained eye. We should be trying to deduce the patterns of God's ordered universe, not attempting to decry their very existence!'

Both men sat perfectly still, facing each other, not saying a word. It was a grim silence at first, then their expressions melted into wry smiles. The moment had arrived.

'And now, my friend,' said FitzRoy, 'I must prepare to have the disposal and arranging of your journal, to mingle it with my own, without offending you.'

'I am perfectly willing, of course,' replied Darwin carefully, 'but my conclusions must remain my own.'

'Of course. If you wish discreetly to dispute the flood, then you must do so, even if I should find it regrettable. You would not be the first. The same goes for the age of the earth, the extinction of species and other such matters. And I believe that your work on the subject of geological uplift, and the formation of coral atolls, constitutes a major contribution to our nation's scientific knowledge.'

'You are most kind.'

'Not at all, my dear friend. But as I am sure you are aware, to espouse transmutation is to risk everything. Social ostracism, ridicule, even hatred must follow, as your own grandfather regrettably experienced. It is, effectively, to abandon Christianity – and to abandon Christianity is to turn one's back on society. This book is to be the official journal of the voyage, sanctioned by the Admiralty. You are aware, I hope, that this voyage, and this volume, cannot be sullied by any suggestion of a transmutationist argument.'

'I am well aware of it.'

'My dear Philos, I must ask for your word as a gentleman that you will keep any such thoughts to yourself, to be aired only in private discussions such as these. That you will never make public your more…controversial conclusions. You are, it seems, to be for ever fixed in the public mind as the naturalist of the *Beagle*.'

'Of course. I understand completely, for I am well aware of the possible consequences of any such action. You have no cause for concern – I give you my word, FitzRoy.'

'Thank you, my friend. Thank you for your invaluable contribution to this voyage, for your insights and for your companionship, which I am sure has saved me personally from the most melancholy of fates. I am personally proud to have sailed with you.'

'On the contrary, FitzRoy, it is I who should thank you. You have given me a unique opportunity – an extraordinary opportunity – the like of which, I think, has been given formerly to very few naturalists, and certainly to no geologists. I shall remain eternally in your debt.'

The two men stood up and shook hands.

'And now, Philos, I have a surprise for you. At least, I hope it shall be a surprise.'

'I am agog.'

'My dear friend – I am to be married.'

'Married?'

Darwin was too stunned to offer his congratulations. He simply reeled. 'Married? But…to whom?'

'To Miss Mary Henrietta O'Brien, the daughter of Major General Edward O'Brien. I asked her father for her hand five years ago, before we sailed from Devonport.'

Darwin felt as if he had been shot. Five years confined in a tiny cabin with this man, all the confidences he had shared, and all the while…! Objections and queries fought each other in his mind, competing to get to the front of a very long queue. 'But, FitzRoy, you do not write letters home,' he offered weakly, and sat down, his mental confusion apparently sapping his physical strength. 'You have not *written* to her.'

'My first and absolute duty on board is always to my men. I told her that it would be so. Of course, there was a risk that she might not wish to wait for me – a risk I had no option but to take into account. I am a serving naval officer. But Miss O'Brien wrote to Cape Town to confirm the arrangement. So you see, Philos, I am a very happy man.'

'But you never mentioned her! Not once. I told you everything. About Fanny Owen's betrothal. About Fanny Wedgwood's death. About my feelings for Emma Wedgwood. I confided my most private thoughts on the subject of marriage. And you – all the while, you concealed this most enormous of secrets from me – from everybody.' Darwin's stare was openly hostile and accusing now.

'My friend, forgive me, but that is simply the way I preferred it.'

FitzRoy looked him directly in the eye. *Why should I share my innermost confidences with you, or with anyone? My command of the* Beagle *is a matter for public record – but my emotions, my most private feelings and fears? They are a matter for myself and my God alone, and not for your prying ears. I cannot and will not share such confidences.*

Darwin stood up again, as FitzRoy sat down. 'You have my congratulations,' he finally managed to say, and walked stiffly and silently from the cabin.

Barrelling before the south-westerly blow, the *Beagle* sighted land, to cheers and hugs, on the first day of October. She made Plymouth dockyard on the second, in softly falling autumn rain. FitzRoy put on his dress uniform, and composed himself before his looking-glass. He was rake-thin, he knew, his skin a weatherbeaten copper, a pale, wiry exhausted shadow of the handsome young man who had put to sea five years previously. He was thirty-one. In all, he had spent nearly a quarter of his life aboard the *Beagle*. It was the same for the philosopher, he reflected, who had spent five of his twenty-seven years folded into his tiny quarters. Darwin, a once-burly six-footer, was no more than eleven stone in weight now, his prematurely thinning hair and thickening eyebrows combining with his long arms to lend him even more of a simian aspect than before.

But whereas Darwin was champing at the bit to get off the ship, FitzRoy realized with a pang that this would be one of the most painful partings of his life. This ship was his body, its men his lifeblood. His relationship to the little vessel felt organic, indivisible and well-nigh impossible to break.

A surprisingly large crowd was gathering on the quay as they approached, augmented all the time by dark, running figures heading from the town. A small brass band had assembled in the drizzle, and had started to play a popular song apparently entitled 'Railways Now Are All The Go, Steam, Steam, Steam'.

'Is there a man-of-war due?' asked Wickham, glancing round worriedly as if the *Beagle* were about to be run down.

'I think it's all for us,' said Sulivan at last.

'For *us*? Whatever for?'

The crew were crowded at the rail or clinging to the rigging, desperate for a glimpse of their loved ones; but most of those on the dockside appeared to be strangers.

'Who the deuce are they all?' asked Wickham, with furrowed brow.

'My dear Wickham – you must excuse me! Oh, my God!'

With this most uncharacteristic exclamation, Sulivan tore himself away and threw himself excitedly at the rail. For there, hurtling down the white, marble-chipped avenue from the dockyard gates, her skirt flying, her bonnet-ribbons streaming behind her, her companion lagging breathless in her wake, all pretence of dignity thrown to the winds, was the overjoyed figure of Sophia Young.

The accommodation-ladder was put down, and the result was pandemonium, with as many people trying to get on to the ship as off. FitzRoy came forward to try to make some sense of the chaos. A press of aggressively ill-mannered men made a rush forward, all shouting at once.

'George Dance, *Morning Post*. I believe you have the celebrated Mr Darwin on board?'

'Where is Mr Darwin?'

'Arthur Hodgson, *Hampshire Telegraph*. May I speak to Mr Darwin?'

'Gentlemen, I beg you, order, please. I am Captain FitzRoy. I would kindly request that you speak one at a time.'

'You are the captain of the *Beagle*, sir? What was it like sailing with the world-famous Mr Darwin?'

'James Burling, *Times*. Could you describe Mr Darwin to us, sir?'

'May we speak to the great man?'

'Would you say it was an honour, sir, to have sailed with Mr Darwin?'

'What does Mr Darwin eat for his breakfast?'

'Is there a Mrs Darwin, sir?'

On the quayside, two young girls had unfurled a home-made banner reading 'Welcome home Mr Darwin'. FitzRoy wished he had been man enough to feel no wound to his vanity, for he considered the sin of pride one of his more regrettable weaknesses, but on this occasion he had no option but to concede defeat. He retreated, and left the maindeck to the stentorian tones of Lieutenant Wickham. Marine sentries were posted at the bottom of the accommodation-ladder, with orders to admit only respectable-looking persons aboard. The crowd continued to gather, meanwhile, as sightseers came down to view the *Beagle*, to lay a hand on her well-travelled hull, perhaps even to catch a glimpse of the celebrated Mr Darwin.

After a few minutes, FitzRoy was astonished to witness the elegant bonnet of a stylishly dressed woman appear at the rail, before the bonnet's owner somehow clambered up the battens and over the gunwale. Her rather more plainly dressed husband followed, and introduced himself to the bemused FitzRoy as George Airy, the newly appointed Astronomer-Royal.

'I'm afraid the sentry at the accommodation-ladder would not permit...'

'My dear sir, my dear madam, I am most terribly sorry. Please accept my most profound apologies – this is inexcusable. I shall speak to the miscreant most severely. I am afraid that this press of people has created confusion among my crew – it seems that half the country has taken up occupation as a journalist!'

'You can thank the steam-press for that,' smiled Airy. 'As the editor of the *Athenaeum* said, "It takes four men to make a pin, and two to describe it in a book for the working classes." '

Stokes was quickly deputized to show the dignitaries below, while an irritable FitzRoy took issue with the marine sentry.

'Damn it, Burgess, I have just had the Astronomer-Royal and his wife, no less, hauling themselves up the manropes because *you* would not admit them aboard!'

'I'm sorry, sir,' stammered Burgess, colouring. 'Mr Wickham said respectable, sir, and the gentleman did *not* look respectable. It's all these reporters, sir, as want to speak to Mr Darwin.'

'Where the devil is the philosopher, anyway?' FitzRoy caught sight of his steward crossing the deck. 'Fuller! Have you seen Mr Darwin?'

'He's gone, sir.'

'*Gone?*'

'Yes sir.'

'You mean, he has left the ship?'

'Yes sir.' Fuller looked unhappy.

'Gone without saying goodbye?'

'Yes sir. He, er—'

'Yes, Fuller?'

'He took Covington with him, sir.'

CHAPTER SIXTEEN

31 Chester Street, London, 8 October 1837

The FitzRoys travelled the short distance to Sunday service by barouche, partly because Mrs FitzRoy was six months pregnant, and partly because – even in such a well-to-do district as Belgravia – Sunday morning was not the best time to be out on the streets. Eleven in the morning was 'chucking-out time', when the bars and gin-palaces finally disgorged the drunken revellers of the night before, and it was not uncommon for churchgoers to have to negotiate brawling prostitutes, quarrelling labourers and any number of helpless or unconscious devotees of that other great spirit. FitzRoy liked to worship at the vast, Romanesque, pale-brick edifice of St Peter's, Eaton Square, for its ceiling caught the light from its great window and flung it down upon the congregation from high above, an important consideration for one who had spent the previous five years in the middle of the vaulting ocean. With its massive portico and six Ionic columns of honey-coloured stone the church resembled a temple of Ancient Rome, but he did not subscribe to the current and censorious school of thought that decried such architecture as pagan.

He liked to watch his wife at prayer, for the serenity of her devotions always reminded him of the night they'd met, and the calm, almost beatific manner in which she had seemed to float across the dance-floor. They had married at the end of December, Sulivan acting as groomsman just a couple of weeks before his own wedding to Miss Young, the *Beagle*'s officers reunited joyfully twice in a fortnight. FitzRoy had barely known his bride, of course – they were only just getting to know each other even now – but right from the first her wisdom, her confidence and her sheer certainty that theirs was a union made in heaven had banished any doubts he might have felt. Their wedding night had been, quite simply, a revelation. There, in the dark, holding her in his arms for the first time, he had experienced feelings of happiness so profound and so unexpected that he could not have believed such an experience possible. He had fallen in love with his wife, utterly and without reservation, from that moment. It was, he felt, as if God had touched them both at the same instant.

They had taken the house in Chester Street while he laboured six days a week at the Admiralty, often late into the night, upon his charts and sailing directions, and upon the story of the voyage. They had holidayed just once – a visit to his sister's family at Bromham, near Bedford – but he had found the enforced lay-off frustrating. The compulsory rest day of the Sabbath was, of course, a weekly hindrance, but he was aware, too, of the benefits that such a respite afforded his physical, mental and spiritual health; and, of course, he wished to spend as much time with his new wife as possible before he returned to sea. After church they would join the traditional promenade of the great and good through Hyde Park and Kensington Gardens, and around Shrewsbury Clock. Despite her condition, Mary FitzRoy always insisted that a little light walk along the banks of the Serpentine river would do her good. On this particular Sunday, however, the crowds were thin: it was not just the hunting season that was taking its toll but the first of the winter smogs, a thin, yellow, insinuating, vinegary mist that dampened their clothing and caused their lungs to ache. He suggested that they cut short their constitutional, but she would not hear of it; indeed, she insisted on walking as far as the Uxbridge Road, which bordered the north side of the park.

There, outside the railings, a different world stared in, like spectators at the zoo. Drunken vagrants and starving agricultural labourers up from the countryside jostled for space with gaunt Irishmen.

'Spare a penny for a poor Johnny-raw, sir,' yelled a voice, but whose voice amid the forest of hands it was impossible to tell.

The high price of corn, the doctrines of the Reverend Thomas Malthus and the terrifying new spectre of the workhouse had turned even more people out on to the streets during the *Beagle*'s absence, swelling the army of the hungry and dispossessed. As if to taunt them, Sunday was the principal day for the city to suck in and chew up its livestock supplies: great droves of oxen, sheep and pigs, cart- and waggon-trains full of struggling calves, goaded and propelled forward by crowds of graziers, cattle-jobbers, pig-fatteners and calf-crammers, a squealing, bleating, lowing, shouting mêlée, surged up the Uxbridge Road towards the holding pound at Paddington. A knacker's drag jogged through the crowd of unheeding animals, laden with the obscenely mangled carcasses of dead and used-up horses, their torn-out bowels dangling over the side. Rabble-rousers moved among the mud and blood-spattered multitude distributing pamphlets and protest sheets, keen to provoke the dispossessed to anger; others sold Bible tracts, popular journals and Sunday scandal-sheets. No day, it seemed, was quite as boisterous, quite as hungry and desperate, quite as starkly bloody as the Lord's day. Mary FitzRoy momentarily detached her gloved hand from her husband's, went to the railing and shared the contents of her purse among the reaching hands.

'Take care, my dear,' murmured FitzRoy, his hand gripping his cane more tightly, but she moved among the beseeching supplicants like a yacht upon the sea, her donations a mere shining drop or two swallowed up by the hungry ocean.

Darwin trotted down the front steps of number thirty-six Great Marlborough Street to find his jobbed cabriolet the only one unattended, all the others at the little stand tenanted by loafing teenage drivers with hats and pipes at the most rakish angles their owners could affect. 'Have any of you fellows seen my devil?' he asked peevishly.

'Yer honour, he's just gorn a little way round of the corner for summat short. Why, here he comes, sir, right as a trivet. Jump up, sir.'

A small, gin-stunted coach-boy in frock-coat and top-boots took his place at the reins. Darwin settled in under the hood. 'Thirty-one Chester Street. And take care, if you've been gilding your liver.'

Cheerfully ignoring the gibe, the boy swung the buggy round through Argyll Place and joined the traffic stream heading south along Regent Street. From there they bore west down Conduit Street, linking up with Piccadilly via Old Bond Street, until finally they found themselves clattering down Grosvenor Place, keeping the wall of the still unnamed royal palace to their left. It was a whole year since he had seen FitzRoy; they had corresponded about their co-authored book entirely by letter, even though they lived less than two miles apart. Nor had he any particular wish to set eyes upon him now. What had occurred that morning, however, had altered matters. Gould's letter had thrown him into a panic of excitement. Unfortunately, he would have to negotiate a boatload of tiresome courtesies before he could get down to business, but that could not be helped. It was five o'clock in the afternoon, rather late to go visiting, but he knew FitzRoy well enough for such informality.

Grand, multi-storeyed mansions in white stucco stacked up along Grosvenor Place; Chester Street proved to be one of the narrow thoroughfares linking it to the equally grandiose terraces of Belgrave Place. It was a prosperous area, reflected Darwin; trust FitzRoy to pitch up on the aristocratic side of Regent Street. So much for his former cabin-mate's supposed shortage of cash. Obviously he was enjoying the benefits of full pay while he prepared the charts from the voyage.

A flight of white marble steps led up to a wide, stucco-fronted ground floor divided by a trio of arched windows; thereafter the house was a plain brick, its upper windows more prosaically rectangular. He handed his card to the housemaid and enquired if the FitzRoys were 'at home'. The reply came back in the affirmative, although the matter was hardly in doubt as the lamps had already been lit to fend off the gloom of the afternoon. He was shown past a panelled dining room, up a spiral staircase at the rear of the house – the building was only one room deep, he noted, more imposing from the front than inside – and into a bright, pleasant drawing room on the first floor where the FitzRoys dwelt amid dark mahogany furniture.

'My dear Darwin,' said FitzRoy, rising, but his manner was cold, and Darwin knew immediately that something was wrong. It did not matter: his business here was more important than whatever was bothering the inflexible old curmudgeon today.

'Mrs FitzRoy, may I have the honour of presenting to your acquaintance Mr Charles Darwin.'

'The honour is all mine, Mrs FitzRoy, believe me. And if you will forgive so forward an observation, I see that congratulations are shortly to be in order.'

'I am delighted to meet you at last, Mr Darwin.' Mary FitzRoy extended a hand. 'And, yes, it would appear that we are to be blessed, as I believe Lieutenant Sulivan and his wife have been earlier this week.'

'I pity the poor lady, then, for I apprehend that her husband has a new commission, which will snatch him away at what must be an inopportune moment.'

'Mr Sulivan has command of the *Pincher*, my dear, an anti-slaving schooner due to sail for West Africa,' FitzRoy explained.

'Then we must be happy on Mr Sulivan's behalf. No one who enters into marriage with a naval officer can fail to be aware of the separations involved.'

Don't patronize me, thought Darwin. *I am only here on sufferance*. Mrs FitzRoy was astonishingly beautiful, he decided, but he could not work out whether her solemn, direct manner betokened gracious piety or insufferable self-satisfaction. Certainly, she did not seem the sort of empty-headed woman to dote on the romantic heroines of Byron and Scott. There was something intimidating about her, something almost evangelical.

'But I understand that we must congratulate *you*, Mr Darwin,' said the object of his study, as the housemaid served tea. 'My husband tells me that you are to be made a fellow of the Royal Society, and secretary of the Geological Society.'

'Indeed so. The offers came about through the good offices of Mr Lyell. I often dine at his club, or he at mine – did I tell you that I had been elected to the Athenaeum, along with Mr Dickens, the novelist?'

'What elevated circles you do move in, Mr Darwin.'

Again, Darwin had the faintest sense that he was being patronized, but he refused to be ashamed of his achievements.

'Oh, I have made a good many interesting new friends of late. I am a frequent guest at Mr Babbage's *soirées*, along with Herbert Spencer, Mr Brown the botanist, Sydney Smith, Thomas and Jane Carlyle – he writes all the articles on German literature in the *French Quarterly* – and Miss

Martineau, of course, who is a friend of my brother.' *All fascinating and influential people*, he thought, *not tuppenny-ha'penny aristocrats.* 'The company cannot be faulted – sadly, it is my own digestion that usually lets me down.'

'You continue to remain unwell? We are sorry to hear it.'

His ill-health was evident. Darwin was even thinner and more sickly than he had been at the end of the voyage, a condition that lent his overhanging brow an air of perpetually furious concentration. He could not have weighed more than ten and a half stone.

'Yes, I appear to be suffering some sort of chronic complaint, brought on no doubt by many years of constant seasickness.' He grinned humourlessly at FitzRoy. 'I have tried all sorts of physic, from calomel to quinine to arsenic – even Indian ale – but nothing seems to work.' *Damn it, this was like confessing to a Catholic priest.* 'I dare say that London's murky atmosphere does my constitution no help.'

'Then perhaps you would be well advised to spend more time with your family in Shropshire.'

And less time collecting influential friends like trophies, thought FitzRoy. *He is here because he wants something, that much is clear. He would not come for any other reason.*

'I was back home only last week, in fact – I travelled by train as far as Birmingham. I cannot say that I was much impressed. One has to pay for one's own candles to read, and one must hire a footwarmer to stave off the cold. It was tremendously fast, though – just five hours, once the locomotive had been pulled up to Camden by the winding-cables.'

'And what intelligence is there of your family, Mr Darwin?'

'Oh, we have cause for great celebration. My sister Caroline is married now, to my cousin Josiah Wedgwood – the eldest son of my uncle Jos – who has recently returned from travelling in Europe.'

'And what of yourself? Is it your intention to take a wife?'

Mary FitzRoy posed the question with disarming directness, but Darwin deflected it. Negotiations with Emma Wedgwood were at too delicate a stage to make the matter public.

'I fear I am too busy cataloguing the specimens from the voyage to consider capturing such a rare specimen as a wife.'

'It would appear that both you and my husband will spend more years organizing your discoveries than you spent actually circumnavigating the world.'

'What with the book and the charts, I feel like an ass caught between two bundles of hay,' put in FitzRoy, who had barely spoken, and only did so now for his wife's benefit. 'Both hail me, and tell me they require my undivided attention to do them full justice.'

What's biting the old goose? thought Darwin, but he ploughed on nonetheless. 'I have been fortunate enough to enlist the most excellent help, FitzRoy. Lyell has introduced me to Richard Owen, the Hunterian professor at the Royal College of Surgeons. Do you know Owen? He is the man who first coined the term "dinosaur". My fossils from Punta Alta are entirely new to science. He has christened the giant aquatic rodent a *Toxodon*, the giant armadillo is to be called a *Scelidotherium*, there is a giant sloth called a *Glyptodon*, and a giant guanaco that he has named *Machrauchenia*. Owen says, and this is the remarkable thing, that all the South American fossils are related to the animals still living on the same continent – it is as if there is a continuous process of change. Do forgive me, Mrs FitzRoy. All this scientific talk must be rather dull for you.'

'Not in the least, Mr Darwin – I am fascinated. Indeed, I am intrigued to know what you make of the recent discoveries in Trafalgar Square. I apprehend that workmen laying the foundations for the column have found the bones of enormous elephants, rhinoceroses and sabre-toothed tigers.'

Touché, thought FitzRoy, with a glow of pride.

'A fascinating discovery indeed,' replied Darwin evasively. 'And there are now live elephants and rhinoceroses – or should one say rhinoceri? – at the Zoological Society, and a giraffe too. They are the most astonishing creatures. You really must go, when your condition permits it. I was there yesterday – the Society is opened privately to members at weekends – did I tell you that I had been elected a member of the Zoological Society? – and I saw a chimpanzee named Tommy, who had been dressed up in human clothing and allocated a human nurse. I assure you, you would find his antics most amusing. During my visit, the nurse showed him an apple but would not give it him, whereupon Tommy threw himself on his back, and kicked and cried precisely like a human child. He then looked very sulky, and after two or three fits of passion the nurse said, "Tommy, if you stop bawling and be a good boy, I will give you the apple." The ape certainly understood every word of this – and though, like a child, he had great work to stop whining, he at last succeeded and got the apple, jumped into an armchair and began eating it with the most contented countenance imaginable!'

'And is your own interest in Tommy the chimpanzee a scientific one, Mr Darwin, or purely a matter of entertainment?'

'Well, I was at the Zoological Society principally to see Mr John Gould, the taxonomist. Did I say? He has agreed to classify all the birds that I collected on the voyage. Waterhouse is attending to the insects, Bell the reptiles, and my friend Leonard Jenyns the fish. In fact, it is upon a matter of Mr Gould's classification that I am here to see Captain FitzRoy. I wonder, Mrs FitzRoy, if you would be so kind as to permit us a few moments in private? It is a technical discussion – most tiresome, I assure you.'

'Of course, Mr Darwin. That would be no trouble at all.'

'Then, if you have no objection, my dear, we can repair to my study, upstairs,' said FitzRoy. 'Mr Darwin might like to inspect the work in progress.'

'And may I venture to hope, dear lady, that your confinement proceeds in as smooth and untroubled a manner as possible, God willing.'

The preamble completed, FitzRoy led Darwin up the winding staircase, noticing as he did so that the philosopher pulled a silver snuffbox from his coat pocket and took a furtive pinch, before loping on after him. They went into FitzRoy's study, as neat and tidy a workplace as his cabin in the ship had been, and shut the door.

'It is opportune indeed that you have chosen today to pay your visit,' remarked FitzRoy icily, 'for there is an urgent matter I must discuss with you. But you indicated that you also have business with me.'

'It is Gould,' said Darwin, simply. 'He has been working on the Galapagos finches. He says there are no fewer than four sub-groups, and that one, *Geospiza*, contains no fewer than six species with insensibly graduated beaks. *Separate species*, FitzRoy. The variants have become *separate species*.'

'I find that hard to credit.'

'All three mockingbirds are different species, too, from three different islands! All of them are unknown to zoological science. And Bell says that each of the lizards from each of the different islands are different species as well. I tell you, FitzRoy, these are not variants but *species*! Would that I had paid more attention to Lawson's lecture about the differing tortoise carapaces.'

'How came you by several different types of finch? Bynoe told me that you refused my offer of a cage of finches on James Island.'

'My assistant – Covington.' Darwin looked shamefaced. 'It was he who collected the birds. I failed to observe any distinction at the time. I am convinced that Covington's birds differ from island to island, but I cannot be absolutely sure of the labelling. I fear I have mingled together the collections that he made at the different locations. I never dreamed that islands just fifty or sixty miles apart, most of them in sight of each other, formed of precisely the same rocks, under the same climate, rising to a nearly equal height, would be differently tenanted. That is why I have come to you, FitzRoy. You and Bynoe...I know that you both made properly labelled and differentiated collections. I need your permission for Gould to access the collections made by yourself and Bynoe in the British Museum. I need your help, FitzRoy.'

'You ask for *my* help to try to prove your transmutationist theories?'

'I merely ask for access to the specimens.'

'You and this ornithologist of yours – this Gould – you claim that they are different species of finch, but I still fail to see by what *mechanism* any creature can cross the barrier between species. They are all finches. Surely by definition they are variants?'

'But, FitzRoy, I have the mechanism now. *I have the mechanism.* I read Malthus's *Essay on the Principle of Population*, and it came to me, as clear as day. Why is the world not overrun with rabbits, or flies, when they can breed at such an incredible rate? Why is the world not overrun with poor people? Answer: the weakest die off. Death, disease, famine, all take their toll. Only the best-adapted survive. It is why the lower races, such as the Fuegians and the Araucanians, will be eliminated, and why the higher, civilized white races will vanquish their territory. It is why Christianity conquers heathenism, because Christianity better meets the demands of life. Death is a creative entity! It preserves the most useful adaptations in animals, and plants, and people, and weeds out the least useful ones. So the favourable adaptations become fixed. That is how a species adapts.'

'All this does not explain how one species could possibly transmute into another.'

'Suppose six puppies are born. Two have longer legs, and can run faster. They are the only two of the litter that survive. The next generation – their children – shall *all* have longer legs. Species adapt by throwing up random variants – a process of trial and error – which persist if they are advantageous. They are selected, if you like, by nature herself, into winners and losers!'

'You are assuming that nature acts but externally on every creature. Yet the two are indivisible. Do not creatures define their own environment just as it defines them? Does not mankind, for instance, cut down the forests?'

'But this is where Malthus, God bless him, has given me so much! Mankind works *against* nature! We civilized men do our utmost to check the natural process of elimination. We build asylums for the imbecile, we treat the sick, we institute poor laws. Vaccination has preserved thousands who would formerly have succumbed to smallpox. Thus the weak members of civilized societies propagate their kind. What we are doing is highly injurious to the race of man!'

'You speak of Christian mercy as if it were somehow reprehensible. Malthus saw the expanding numbers of mankind as symptomatic of man's fall, not his rise through some brutal competition! He saw such a competition as one that must be halted, not celebrated!'

'But do you not see, FitzRoy? *Every single* organic being is in competition, striving to the utmost to increase in numbers! The birds that sing around us live on insects, or seeds, and are thus constantly destroying life. They in turn, and their eggs, are constantly destroyed by beasts of prey. Nature is not the creation of a benevolent God! The only order in God's universe is a coincidental side-product of the struggle among organisms for reproductive success.'

'What of co-operation in nature? Beetles that feed on dung? Birds that live on the backs of hippopotamuses?'

'Mere parasites.'

'What of beauty? What of the origin of life itself? What of something as beautiful and complicated as the human eye, which can adjust itself a million times faster than any spyglass? How did such a mechanism come into being through accidental modification? Only the Creator Himself could have designed such a thing.'

'Maybe the eye developed gradually, as man gradually designed the spyglass.'

'The gradual design of the spyglass was the product of God-given reason.'

'Must a contrivance have a contriver?'

'Yes, by definition! I cannot believe I am hearing you speak in this blasphemous fashion!'

'Come, FitzRoy, the design of a man is far from perfect. We must rest for eight hours a day. We must feed ourselves three times a day. We eat and we breathe through the same orifice. We fall prey to every illness. We are not so wonderfully designed.'

'Tell me, then, about consciousness. How do your long-legged puppies account for the creation of consciousness? How is it that we are even having this conversation, are even aware of our own existence, if God has not given us the power of rational thought? How does your all-embracing theory explain generosity, kindness to strangers, self-sacrifice – qualities that I shall admit you seem to possess in short supply – unless man is created by God in His own image?'

Darwin, effervescing, sidestepped the insult. 'Man is arrogant indeed to think himself created by God in His image. Our image of God is merely human egotism made flesh. Whoever or whatever God is, He is more than merely mankind writ large. Humility leads me to the inescapable conclusion that we are merely animals.'

'Humility? You?' FitzRoy could barely splutter out the words. '"Shall the clay say to him that fashioneth it, what makest thou?"'

'Think about it – human and animal consciousness are not so dissimilar. Is our smile not our snarl? Are we so far from Tommy the chimpanzee? Is the black man, whose reasoning powers are only partly developed, not closer to the higher apes than the white man? Black and brown children look less like human beings than I could have fancied any degradation might have produced. Charles White has postulated an intermediate but taxonomically separate sub-group of dark-skinned people. Your Fuegians are living proof that Christian civilization is ephemeral, a mere gloss on the biologic facts – see how quickly they reverted to savagery! I tell you, FitzRoy, our Christian society is no more than an arm of nature – a Malthusian struggle for existence. Hobbes's *bellum omnium contra omnes*. We are riding a wave of chaos!'

'I will not have this – this *nonsense* in my house! The civilized universe is fashioned by divine wisdom. It is a machine, and God is the mechanic!'

'If the universe is a machine, then life exploits only its stutters.'

'But this theory of yours, this *perversion* of Malthus, is a mathematical absurdity. Any single variation in any creature would be blended back into the species through breeding, being halved and halved again in successive generations until it disappeared. A marooned white sailor on an African shore could never blanch a nation of negroes!'

'Oh come, FitzRoy, it is patently obvious that there is much inherited variation. Successful characteristics are somehow dominant, otherwise every generation would be more uniform than the previous one. And those characteristics are passed down to both sexes by inheritance. Man would be as superior in mental endowment to a woman as the peacock is in ornamental plumage to the peahen, if the beneficial characteristics of the male sex were not equally transmitted between both sexes at the point of conception. That, my friend, is how one species of finch arrived at the Galapagos Islands, and transmuted itself gradually into a number of entirely separate species. Not variations, but *separate species*.'

'It is ironic – is it not? – that you make so much of the absolute barriers between species being supposedly thus vaulted, yet by your own argument, one species gradually transmutes into another without any impediment or barrier whatsoever.'

'You must help me, FitzRoy. You must give permission for Mr Gould to access those specimens.'

'You gave me your word that you would not publish any transmutationist argument! Your manuscript is complete – do you intend to rewrite it?'

'No – of course not. I shall adhere to my word. But I have to know. I *must* know the truth.'

'Why then should I help you? Why should I help you when you have delivered *this* to my house and to the publisher?'

FitzRoy angrily lifted the proof sheets of Darwin's manuscript from his desk and brandished them in the air.

'Aha! Now we are getting to the nub!' shouted Darwin. 'I could tell by your very demeanour upon my entrance that you were harbouring some ridiculous grievance at my work.'

FitzRoy began to read quotes scornfully from his blotter. ' "No possible action of any flood could thus have modelled the land." "Geologists formerly would have brought into play the violent action of some overwhelming débâcle, but in this case such a submission would have been quite inadmissible." '

'I tell you, FitzRoy, no reputable geologist believes in the flood any more! Buckland has disavowed it! Sedgwick has disavowed it! Lyell's new volume entirely discredits the idea that there has ever been a major catastrophe on this earth! Lyell's volume, incidentally, which laments the delay to *my* book on account of *your* tardiness. Mr Lyell agrees with me that some part of your brain wants mending, for nothing else will account for your manner of viewing things!' Darwin was purple-faced with rage now, and FitzRoy not much better. Their argument could be heard all round the house.

'How dare you discuss me in such terms, or any terms, with Mr Lyell? Have you told your *new friend* of your transmutationist theories? I doubt it! For I, too, have read his latest volume, which makes it abundantly clear that although varieties may change a great deal, they can *never deviate far enough to be called separate species*.'

'Of course I have not discussed such matters with Mr Lyell! I have discussed my most private thoughts with you and you alone, because I was confined in a cabin with you for five years, and because I trusted you as my companion and as a gentleman to keep such confidences to yourself! Although, God knows I regret those confidences now. You gave me your word *as a gentleman* that you would have no objection to my casting doubt upon the Biblical flood in my account of the voyage, although now it seems that you have reneged upon that understanding.'

'On the contrary. You are quite entitled to print whatever nonsense you wish concerning the flood, although I believe our understanding was that you should do so discreetly. My objection to this volume is of an entirely different nature, and concerns the disgraceful remarks, or lack of them, on the title page.'

'On the title page? Remarks? What are you talking about?'

'Your page of acknowledgements, or lack of them, in which you ascribe your place on the voyage to the *wish* of Captain FitzRoy, and to the *kindness* of Captain Beaufort.'

'What of it?'

'I am further astonished at the total omission of any notice of the ship's officers, either particular or general. What of Sulivan? What of Stokes? What of Bynoe? Officers who assisted you in the furtherance of your views, and who gave you preference in the collection of specimens. A plain acknowledgement, never mind a word of flattery or fulsome praise, would have been slight return due from you to those who held the ladder by which you mounted to your current position. Or were you not aware that the ship which carried *you* safely round the world was first employed in exploring and surveying, and that her officers were not ordered or obliged to collect anything for you at all? To their honour, they gave you the preference. To your dishonour, you make no mention of them.'

'I shall write to them.'

'It is not enough. This page must be altered at the publisher's. I do not trust you to write to them.'

'You have the most consummate skill in looking at everything and everybody in a perverted manner! All this is about a simple oversight! You would do better to concentrate your energies upon finishing your part of the manuscript – which I would remind you was due for publication at the end of this month – than upon such petty matters. What in God's name is taking you so long? This delay is holding up my efforts to prosecute a successful scientific career.'

'You forget that I have two volumes to contend with,' said FitzRoy, coldly. 'My own and the editing of Captain King's. A total of more than half a million words—'

'Half a million words? I read some of King's journal on the *Beagle*. No pudding for schoolboys was ever so heavy. It abounds with natural history of the most trashy nature. I trust that your own volume will present an improvement. Half a million words! No wonder the three volumes are to cost two pounds eighteen shillings!'

'The publisher Mr Colburn tells me that the high price derives from a shortage of rags to make paper. And, of course, your friends in the Liberal government continue to tax paper at a penny-halfpenny a pound.'

'Henry Colburn is a villain of the worst sort! I have had to pay him no less than twenty-one pounds ten shillings – in advance – for the copies I intend to distribute to my friends and family. That is more than I am receiving for my contribution! I am writing this book at a considerable loss. You, on the other hand, are on a full surveyor's salary.'

'On the contrary. As I am able to dedicate only part of my time to the surveying work, I have written to Sir Francis Beaufort offering to return half of my salary. And if the work continues beyond the end of 1838, I shall complete it unpaid.'

'Unpaid? Return half your salary? When you have found yourself in financial difficulties? You are quite mad!'

'No – I am not mad. I simply have ideas of money, and ideas of duty, which are different from persons such as yourself. A gentleman should always place duty and public service ahead of all other things. I am sure that it is a gesture that Sir Francis will properly appreciate, as being undertaken from the best of motives.'

Darwin sneered across the study. 'A gesture that has precipitated such universal admiration that you have not been reappointed to command the *Beagle*'s next voyage.'

'What?'

FitzRoy's blood had turned to ice.

'What did you say?' he repeated.

'It is nothing…just a rumour…Beaufort…' Darwin realized, uncomfortably, that he had gone too far.

FitzRoy was pressing him, desperate to know more: 'What do you know of the *Beagle* sailing again? What do you mean, "Beaufort"? You have met him?'

'He is a frequent guest at Mr Babbage's *soirées*,' confessed Darwin, weakly. 'He has lately become a considerable friend of mine. He has read my manuscript and given it his unqualified approval. He mentioned that the *Beagle* was sailing again, under Wickham, to survey the coast of Australia. I supposed that you knew…'

FitzRoy's expression revealed that, without a shadow of doubt, he had not known of Wickham's appointment.

Darwin barged on into the ensuing silence: 'Sir Francis has arranged for me to receive a government grant of a thousand pounds to edit five large illustrated volumes on the zoology of the *Beagle*, to be authored by Owen, Waterhouse, Gould, Jenyns and Bell. They are to be published by Smith and Elder – a *reputable* scientific publisher.'

FitzRoy was stunned. 'You are to produce an official guide to the zoology of the *Beagle* – with no reference to myself?'

'It was my understanding that you had been informed.'

'I think that you had better leave.'

Darwin rose without a word. Both men knew that their friendship was finally and irrevocably at an end. *The weakest go to the wall*, thought Darwin, angrily. *Your kind shall be swept aside like the great beasts of old. Scientists, industrialists, enterprisers, inventors, businessmen, these are the ones who shall inherit the earth. Your species has reached the end of its natural lifespan.*

*

FitzRoy's carriage deposited him outside the imposing stone portico of Montagu House, home of the British Museum. He stepped down as deftly as ever, but anyone who knew him well, seeing him alight, would have noticed that something was missing, a certain spring, an optimism in his step. Still ramrod straight, however, he rustled through the meagre crowds that pushed, head down, along Great Russell Street, his sober black frock-coat cut high at the neck and drawn tightly about him to keep out the cloying yellow mist that streamed in his wake. His bearing wore the dignity of habit; inside he felt like an empty shell, more like the ghost of Captain FitzRoy than his living, breathing spirit.

He was made to wait for what seemed an eternity in a narrow corridor behind the vestibule. Eventually an adenoidal clerk appeared, and announced that Mr Butters would see him now. The curator of Natural History was finally revealed to be a short, round, irritable man of middle age, attired in a sober and shapeless suit of comparable vintage, although the cinched-in waist hinted that its owner had once fancied himself as something of a swell about town. Even if that had indeed been the case, there was nothing swell whatsoever about Mr Butters's present-day incarnation. He looked his uninvited guest up and down with barely concealed headmasterly annoyance.

'And to what, Captain Fitzwilliam, do we owe the pleasure of your visit?'

'I am – that is, I was – the captain of HMS *Beagle*, a surveying-brig, from 1828 until the present day. If you will be kind enough to suffer the imposition, I am here on the matter of some specimens gathered by myself and Mr Bynoe, our surgeon, at the Galapagos Islands.'

'And how may I assist you with regard to these specimens?'

'A Mr John Gould, a taxonomist of the Zoological Society, wishes to examine the specimens in question further. I am here to make it clear to you that I have no objections whatsoever to Mr Gould's work – unless, of course, it should conflict with the researches being carried out by your own experts.'

'The Zoological Society, you say?' Butters pronounced the name of that new-fangled institution with the kind of lofty disdain he might have reserved for a gang of Thames mudlarks. 'We are very busy here, Captain Fitzwilliam.'

'FitzRoy.'

'I do beg your pardon, Captain FitzRoy. Do the officers of the Zoological Society not have sufficient animals of their own to experiment upon, without interrupting our own most industrious endeavours? They have a chimpanzee, I gather, dressed in a morning-coat for the entertainment of the public.'

If the museum was indeed the site of any industrious endeavours, then those labours were certainly not making their presence felt. The building was utterly silent, and the motes of dust that had risen politely at FitzRoy's entrance were now settling drowsily once more upon the aged books and charts that slept on Butters's desk. FitzRoy felt as if he had stepped back into the last century.

'These particular specimens – they are finches, of various types – are the subject of some considerable scientific controversy. Although I cannot say I agree with Mr Gould's diagnosis, I felt it only fair to give him the chance to examine the birds properly and at his leisure.'

'No good ever came of scientific controversy, no good at all. If you will take my advice, Captain FitzRoy, you will advise this Mr Gould to stick to dressing up chimpanzees.'

'Be that as it may, sir, I fear I must impose upon your kindness. It has become a matter of honour, sir.'

'Has it, by Jove?' Butters winced in disapproval. 'Well, we have a great many specimens here at the museum. Yours may not be easy to locate. They may not yet have been examined or catalogued. When did you say you returned?'

'One year ago. The twenty-sixth of October 1836.'

Butters burrowed into the teetering piles of books that cluttered the corner of his office, before emerging with a dust-coated ledger. 'HMS *Adventure*...HMS *Agamemnon*...HMS *Arethusa*...Here we are, HMS *Beagle*. FitzRoy and – who was it?'

'Bynoe. Benjamin Bynoe.'

'Ah, yes. Specimens collected by Robert FitzRoy, Benjamin Bynoe, John Lort Stokes, Phillip Parker King…not catalogued yet, I'm afraid. The cases haven't even been opened.'

'After a whole *year*?'

'As I believe I mentioned, Captain FitzRoy, ours is a busy department of a busy museum. We do not have the time to fling ourselves upon every crate or packing-case that every passing sailor chooses to deposit on our doorstep.'

'The collection of these specimens was not undertaken lightly, Mr Butters. Indeed, it was often undertaken at considerable personal risk to the officers involved. And for the record, your ledger is incorrect. Our midshipman's name was Philip Gidley King, not Phillip Parker King.'

'I very much doubt it, sir. We are not prone to such errors. Besides, Phillip Parker King is not a midshipman. According to the ledger, he was the expedition's commander.'

'Captain Phillip Parker King was the commander of the *first* expedition, which returned to these shores in October 1830. He has been retired these last seven years.'

'As I said. Not catalogued yet. The cases have not been opened.'

'The cases delivered here *in 1830* have not been opened?'

'As I believe I have made abundantly clear, Captain FitzRoy, ours is a busy department in a busy museum. No doubt they will be dealt with in due course. Now, if you will excuse me, I, too, am an extremely busy man. If your Mr Gould wishes to make himself known to me, I undertake to refer him to my clerical staff. I bid you good day, sir.'

FitzRoy crossed town, a prizefighter winded by blow after blow to the solar plexus who yet refused to buckle under. As he walked up the Admiralty steps, he realized that he had absolutely no memory of the journey he had just undertaken. He was a man in a daze. He scarcely had time to pull himself together before it was announced that the hydrographer would see him at once, even though he had taken the liberty of calling without an appointment.

At least Beaufort is being generous to me, he thought. *Which might yet be a good sign*. If it was true that he had lost the *Beagle*, then – at best – it might mean a promotion. Alternatively, at worst, he might find himself relegated to a coastal guardship, and the relative ignominy of anti-smuggling patrols or fisheries protection. At least it would mean he could visit his wife more often. Whatever hand the good Lord and the Admiralty were about to deal him, it would surely be for the best, he reassured himself.

The door opened. Beaufort hobbled round his desk and limped across the turkey-carpet to pump his hand. FitzRoy's stomach knotted itself tightly into a ball. *Pull yourself together*, he told himself.

He smiled, and returned Beaufort's enthusiastic greeting. Was that sympathy or congratulation flickering in the Irishman's grizzled smile?

'Well, FitzRoy, I must congratulate you. Seymour has passed his court-martial with flying colours, no small thanks to you.'

It took FitzRoy a moment to realize what Beaufort was talking about.

'Your letter explaining that the ocean currents had been altered by the earthquake was entirely accepted by the tribunal. Seymour was completely exonerated of blame for the loss of the *Challenger*. Indeed, he was praised most highly for his subsequent conduct in protecting his men from the hostile Araucanian tribesmen. He has been honourably discharged, and given another brig.'

'Thank God. I am profoundly relieved to hear it, sir.'

'There was praise, too, for Commodore Mason, for the alacrity and bravery with which he came to Seymour's rescue.' Beaufort stared hard at FitzRoy, a glint in his eye. FitzRoy remained blank-faced. 'You don't have to tell me about it if you would prefer not to, FitzRoy,' he said, 'but there is precious little goes on in the Service that escapes my knowledge.'

'So I have heard, sir.'

Beaufort maintained his gaze for a moment or two more, after which his expression indicated that the matter had been dropped. 'Now. Your Lieutenant Sulivan – Commander Sulivan, as we must now call him. What sort of a man is he?'

'He is as thorough a seaman, for his age, as I know. He is used to the smallest craft as well as to the largest ships. He is an excellent observer, calculator and surveyor. I may truly say that his abilities are better than those of any man who has served with me. Besides these advantages, he has the solid foundation of the highest principles and an honest, warm heart. Nothing on earth would induce Sulivan to swerve from his duty, even in the smallest degree.'

'Good. I was hoping you would say something of the sort. And I gather he has a soft spot for the Falkland Islands, is that not so?'

'He refers to them as God's own country.'

'The Admiralty has decided to appoint a naval officer to command the waters around the Falkland Islands, by way of a protection vessel. He shall also have responsibility for any isolated British communities on the South American coast.'

'I supposed that Sulivan was to have the *Pincher*, sir, on slaving duty.'

'Indeed so – he has already spent a fortune modifying her, I hear, according to the FitzRoy model.' Beaufort smiled. 'But this is a bigger job. A much bigger job. Not, mark you, that we should have any more trouble with the Buenos Ayreans. Government policy is to extend the hand of friendship to President Rosas, and to the new nation of Argentina.'

'And dare I say it, sir, we gave Rivero and his men a bloody nose at Port Louis.'

'Ah. I was coming to that.' Beaufort grimaced. 'The Argentines have made a complaint. Two complaints.'

'Two complaints, sir?'

'The first was that Captain Rivero's treatment – being manacled in your hold – infringed his rights as a citizen of the new Argentine Republic. The second was that, on a separate occasion, you insulted the commander of a Buenos Ayres guardship, and collectively abused the people of that city.'

FitzRoy could barely believe what he was hearing.

'But Rivero was a murderer, sir – a cold-blooded murderer. And their guardship attacked *us*. If I recall, I described its conduct as "rotten" and "uncivilized", sir.'

'I am sure your memory is exact, FitzRoy. Nevertheless, the government has decided to apologize to the Argentines, and has ordered Rivero and his men to be released without charge. The government are keen to have President Rosas on our side. Argentina could become a considerable trading market, especially for the sale of arms, what with their continuous wars in the south. I'm afraid you have to look at the wider political picture.'

'Indeed sir,' replied FitzRoy bleakly.

'And, of course, if friendly relations are maintained, then your friend Sulivan will be in no danger, sitting on his little rock in the South Atlantic. So let us hope for the best.'

'I am very glad for him, sir. Very glad indeed. But I came here, if you will forgive my boldness, to discuss my own situation. I heard from Mr Darwin that the *Beagle*—'

'Ah, yes. I owe you an apology for that. Mr Darwin should not have spoken out of turn as he did. It was an overheard remark – no more than a rumour at the time – but it has since become a matter of fact. The *Beagle* is to survey the coast of Australia, completing the task begun by King in the 'twenties. Captain Wickham is to have the command, with Lieutenant Stokes as his deputy. It will be a six-year voyage. You should not have found out in the way that you did, and for that you have my profound apologies.'

'I accept your apology unreservedly, sir.'

'But you have a family to consider now, FitzRoy. Would you have wished to be absent for six years?'

'I suppose not…but where does that leave me, sir? Am I to have an anti-slaving vessel?'

'Anti-slaving vessels are much sought after.'

'Or perhaps…They say there is to be a war against the Chinese. Perhaps a fighting commission, sir?'

'Well, of course, if there is war against the Chinese, then I am sure everything will change.'

With a terrible sense of foreboding, FitzRoy began to realize that whatever the news was, it was not good.

'There have been other complaints,' reported Beaufort, bluntly.

'Other complaints?'

'Surgeon McCormick, who left the *Beagle* at Rio de Janeiro. He presented an official complaint on the grounds that he had effectively been dismissed.'

'But that's—'

'Mr McCormick is not without influence. You are not the only man with friends in high places, FitzRoy. Except that your friends appear to be thinner on the ground than before. Ever since His Majesty died in the summer, the Liberals are keeping a velvet grip on the new Queen. There can be no help from that quarter. And the Tories, of course, seem quite incapable of winning an election. McCormick's complaints would have amounted to nothing much on their own, but these things add up, you know.'

'Evidently so.'

'Then, of course, there were those in the Admiralty who were not best pleased by your forcing their hand in the first place, and who were even less pleased by your decision to purchase no fewer than three supplementary schooners.'

'Three schooners without which I could never have accomplished my commission, sir – you know that. The chain of meridian distances…'

'I am grateful to you. But it was a commission of your own making – you know that.'

The two men faced each other across the desk in silence. Finally, FitzRoy spoke. 'So what am I to get, sir?'

'Damn it, FitzRoy, don't be obtuse. I am trying to be as clear as I can without rubbing it in.'

'I don't understand. I—'

'Yes, you do. There isn't going to be another boat.'

'There isn't going to *be* another boat?' FitzRoy fought for balance in his chair, as the room whirled round and round. 'For how long?'

'There isn't going to be another boat, ever again. Ever. It's over. I'm sorry, Robert. I did the best I could.'

FitzRoy shut his eyes, hung on to his chair arms and fought hard not to throw up.

Acknowledgments

I should like to thank my father, Gordon Thompson, for his tireless and invaluable assistance, both in the researching and the plotting of this book; the indefatigable Pippa Brown, for coming to the rescue of an abysmal index-finger typist, and typing out the entire manuscript; Martin Fletcher and Bill Hamilton, for all their helpful suggestions, and the wonderful Lisa Whadcock for the benefit of her wisdom and insight; Peter Ackroyd, for pointing me in the direction of George Scharf; the staff of the London Library, for their assistance in locating long-forgotten electoral results and ancient guides to Durham; Robert and Faanya Rose, for graciously inviting me into FitzRoy's old home in Chester Street; the Norwood Historical Society, for its help in locating FitzRoy's latterday whereabouts; John Morrish, for allowing me access to his unpublished manuscript about living with manic depression; Tom Russell and Paul Daniels (no, not that one) for slogging up to the fort in Montevideo Bay with me; Patrick Watts (he won't remember, it was so long ago) for giving me a guided tour of Stanley harbour; the staff of the Fazenda Bananal Engenho de Murycana in Brazil, for showing me round their property; and the penguins of Dungeness Point in Patagonia, for taking care of me when I was the only human being for miles and miles around.

Bibliography

I am, of course, indebted to the various biographers of Robert FitzRoy: H. E. L. Mellersh (*FitzRoy of the Beagle*, Rupert Hart-Davis, 1968), Paul Moon (*FitzRoy, Governor in Crisis 1843–1845*, David Ling Publishing, Auckland, 2000), Peter Nichols (*Evolution's Captain*, Profile, 2003) and those exceptional scholars John and Mary Gribbin (*FitzRoy*, Review Books, 2003). These last two works were suddenly published in the middle of my writing this novel, and afforded me considerable assistance. There are, of course, Darwin biographies by the score, but it would be difficult to better Janet Browne's *Charles Darwin* (2 vols, Jonathan Cape, 1995), Adrian Desmond and James Moore's *Darwin* (Michael Joseph, 1991), Randal Keynes's *Annie's Box: Charles Darwin, His Daughter and Human Evolution* (Fourth Estate, 2001), Ronald W. Clark's *The Survival of Charles Darwin* (Random House, 1984), and covering this area alone, Richard Keynes' exceptional and infallible *Fossils, Finches and Fuegians* (Harper-Collins, 2002). Keynes was also responsible for *The Beagle Record* (Cambridge University Press, 1979). From a pictorial point of view, Alan Moorehead's *Darwin and the Beagle* (Hamish Hamilton 1969) and John Chancellor's *Charles Darwin* (Weidenfeld & Nicolson 1973) were especially valuable.

Jemmy Button has been the subject of one excellent biography, Nick Hazlewood's *Savage* (Hodder & Stoughton, 2000), as indeed has the *Beagle* herself (*HMS Beagle*, Keith S. Thomson, W. W. Norton & Co., New York, 1995). Then, of course, there are FitzRoy and Darwin's own works. Darwin's *The Voyage of the Beagle* and *The Origin of Species* are available in many editions. By contrast, FitzRoy's *Weather Book*, *Remarks on New Zealand* and *Narrative of the Voyage of HMS Beagle* are hard to find outside the Bodleian (the library's copy of the latter volume still had its pages uncut – nobody had bothered to read it in 165 years); extracts from his

Narrative were, however, published by the Folio Society of London in 1977. Charles Darwin's correspondence has been edited for publication over many disparate volumes by his granddaughter Nora Barlow. Bartholomew Sulivan's letters were edited by his son, Henry Norton Sulivan (published by Murray, 1896), although they too are long out of print; as is Augustus Earle's *A Narrative of Nine Months' Residence in New Zealand*, which was published by Longman & Co. in 1832. *The Journal of Syms Covington* has only been published on the Internet, by the Australian Science Archives Project, on ASAPWeb, 23 August 1995. Among other contemporary documents, the report of the 1860 British Association meeting in Oxford was published in the *Athenaeum* magazine. The British Government Select Committee reports on New Zealand are also available for scrutiny, at the House of Lords Record Office, London.

For technical maritime information, I used the book that FitzRoy himself always recommended to his subordinates: *The Young Sea Officer's Sheet Anchor* by Darcy Lever (John Richardson, 1819, miraculously reprinted by Dover Maritime Books, Toronto, 1998). But I am also indebted to Christopher Lloyd (*The British Seaman 1200–1860*, Collins, 1968), Michael Lewis (*England's Sea-Officers*, Allen & Unwin, 1939), Henry Baynham (*Before the Mast*, Hutchinson & Co., 1971), Stan Hugill (*Shanties and Sailors' Songs*, Barrie & Jenkins, 1969), Lew Lind (*Sea Jargon*, Kangaroo Press, 1982), Nicholas Blake and Richard Lawrence (*The Illustrated Companion to Nelson's Navy*, Chatham Publishing, 2000), Peter Kemp (*The Oxford Companion to Ships and the Sea*, Oxford University Press, 1976), Tristan Jones (*Yarns*, Adlard Coles Nautical, 1983), W. E. May (*The Boats of Men of War*, National Maritime Museum/Chatham Publishing, 1974 and 1979), the long-deceased Captain Charles Chapman (*All About Ships*, Ward Lock, 1866), Frederick Wilkinson (*Antique Guns and Gun Collecting*, Hamlyn, 1974), and Colonel H. C. B. Rogers (*Weapons of the British Soldier*, Seeley, Service & Co., 1960); and, of course, I must not forget the contemporary works of Captain Marryat, Sir Francis Beaufort and Sir Home Popham, and the considerable later writings of C. S. Forester, Patrick O'Brian and Dudley Pope.

For help with the descriptions of London, I should like to thank Peter

Ackroyd (*London – the Biography*, Chatto & Windus, 2000), Peter Jackson (*George Scharf's London 1820–50*, John Murray, 1987), Eric de Maré (*London 1851*, The Folio Society, 1972), and Felix Barker and Peter Jackson once more for *London* (Cassell, 1974). The parliamentary scenes came courtesy of *The Houses of Parliament – History, Art and Architecture* (ed. Christine and Jacqueline Ridley, Merrell, 2000) and *The London Journal of Flora Tristan* (first published in France, 1842; modern edition trans. Jean Hawkes, Virago, 1982). Another contemporary perspective came from George Cruikshank (*Sunday in London*, Effingham Wilson, 1833). More general historical information came courtesy of comtemporary issues of *The Ladies' Magazine*, as well as Elizabeth Burton's *The Early Victorians at Home* (Longman, 1972), A. N. Wilson's *The Victorians* (Hutchinson, 2002), J. F. C. Harrison's *Early Victorian Britain* (Fontana, 1988), G. M. Trevelyan's *English Social History* (Longman, 1944), Christopher Hibbert's *Social History of Victorian Britain* (Illustrated London News, 1975), Leith McGrandle's *The Cost of Living in Britain* (Wayland, 1973), D. J. Smith's *Horse Drawn Carriages* (Shire Publications, 1974), Henny Harald Hansen's *Costume Cavalcade* (Eyre Methuen, 1972), and Daniel Pool's *What Jane Austen Ate and Charles Dickens Knew* (Simon & Schuster Inc., USA, 1994). Dickens himself was shamelessly plundered for much of the vocabulary, as were Thackeray, Hughes and Captain Marryat.

For the Durham scenes, I consulted *A Historical, Topographical and Descriptive View of the County Palatine of Durham* by E. Mackenzie and M. Ross (Mackenzie & Dent, 1834), *The History & Antiquities of the County Palatine of Durham* by William Fordyce (Thomas Fordyce, 1855), *Cathedral City* by Thomas Sharp (The Architectural Press, 1945), *In and Around Durham* by Frank H. Rushford (Durham County Press, 1946) and *Durham* by Sir Timothy Eden (Robert Hale, 1952).

Among the various scientific books and articles consulted during the preparation of this novel, I should like to mention *Bones of Contention* by Paul Chambers (John Murray, 2003), *Return to the Wilberforce-Huxley Debate* by J. Vernon Jensen (British Journal for the History of Science, 21, pp. 161–79, 1988), *A Journey to a Birth – William Smith at the birth of Stratigraphy* by L. R. Cox (International Geological Congress, 1948),

The Pony Fish's Glow, and Other Clues to Plan and Purpose in Nature by George C. Williams (Basic Books, 1997), *Darwinism – A Crumbling Theory and Evidence for Creation by Outside Intervention* by Lloyd Pye (*Nexus Magazine*, volume 10, number 1, December 2002–January 2003 and volume 9, number 4, June–July 2002), *FitzRoy's Foxes and Darwin's Finches* by W. R. P. Bourne (Archives of Natural History, 1992, 19 (1)), *Noah's Flood – the Genesis Story in Western Thought* by Norman Cohn (Yale University Press, 1996), *The Weather Prophets: Science and Reputation in Victorian Meteorology* by Katharine Anderson (*History of Science*, 37, June 1999), *Matthew Fontaine Maury – Scientist of the Sea* by Francis Leigh Williams (Rutgers University Press, New Brunswick, NJ, 1963), *From Wind Stars to Weather Forecasts: The Last Voyage of Admiral Robert FitzRoy* by Derek Barlow (Weather London, 1994, volume 49, number 4), *Not in our Genes* by Steven Rose, Leon J. Kamin and Richard C. Lewontin (Penguin, 1984), *The Biblical Flood – A Case Study of the Church's Response to Extra-biblical Evidence* by Davis A. Young (Paternoster Press, 1995), and of course many, many fine articles by the inimitable Stephen Jay Gould. For their insights into the processes of manic depression, I am utterly indebted to the work of Andrew Solomon, Dr Irene Whitehill, Sally Brampton and John Morrish.

As to the geographical descriptions, the vast majority were obtained by personal visits to the actual locations. FitzRoy and Darwin themselves provided plenty of supplementary assistance, as did *A Journey in Brazil* by Louis Agassiz (1868, modern ed. by Praeger, Westport, CT, 1970), *Giants of Patagonia* by Captain Bourne (Ingram, Cooke & Co., 1853), and *The Narrative of the Honourable John Byron* (Baker & Leitch, 1778). John Campbell's *In Darwin's Wake* (Waterline, 1997) provided specific information regarding the *Beagle's* South American anchorages.